THE
DRAGONWARD
The Godsfall Trilogy: One

MICHAEL
MEYERHOFER

Unlocking New Worlds

The Dragonward
The Godsfall Trilogy:™ *Book 1*
Copyright © 2016 by Michael Meyerhofer All rights reserved.
First Print Edition: July 2016

Print ISBN-13: 978-1-940215-76-1
Print ISBN-10: 1-940215-76-5

Red Adept Publishing, LLC
104 Bugenfield Court
Garner, NC 27529
http://RedAdeptPublishing.com/

Cover and Formatting: Streetlight Graphics

For my readers,
whether they're returning to Ruun or discovering it for the first time

PROLOGUE

THE BLIND MAN STEPPED OFF the barge and faced Saikaido Temple. A morning breeze blew the smell of salt off the Burnished Way, punctuated by the cry of seagulls behind him. Before him, the Shao temple covered most of the island. A splendid, ancient-looking structure of stone and painted bamboo, it had been built at the summit of a high, rocky hill and crowned with azure flags, with only one approach, which consisted of one thousand meticulously carved steps. Despite the early hour, the temple bustled with activity. Squires descended and ascended the stairs as part of their training, overseen by bored Isle Knights. A few priests moved about as well. One, who looked to be in his early thirties, spotted the blind man and touched his arm.

"My child, if you wish, I can help you up the steps."

The blind man erased his smile at being called *my child* by someone who was hardly older than he was. "I didn't come for the temple, sir. I was told I could reach New Atheion from here."

"Ah, of course." The priest looked disappointed. He started to point, blushed, and stopped. "On the far side of the island, another boat can take you there. I'll show you the way."

"No need." The blind man smothered a grin.

He started off on his own, swaying a staff before him as squires and priests politely moved out of the way. He passed a small town that was little more than fishing huts and a few temples, surrounded by children playing. There, everything reeked of fish.

The blind man hurried by, forcing himself to appear polite as he refused additional offers of help. He resisted the impulse to look up at the splendid temple as he circled around the rocky hill, toward the far end of the tiny island.

After the better part of an hour, he came upon a harbor at least thrice the size of the one he'd arrived at earlier. Instead of squires, Knights, and priests, that one was crowded with tradesmen. Carts were being loaded and unloaded. The smells of straw, sweat, and animal dung overwhelmed the more pleasant brine of the sea air. He winced. Then, he looked beyond the harbor and saw New Atheion.

For a moment, he could hardly believe it. He'd heard stories of the famed City-on-the-Sea for years, including how it had been sailed in its entirety from Nosh to the Lotus Isles, but seeing the impressive city for himself was quite another matter. It looked as though a brilliant, bustling city were simply rising out of the water. As he neared the edge of the harbor, he spotted countless skiffs, upon which New Atheion's temples, homes, and shops sat like plates floating down a calm river. The buildings themselves looked to be made either from white marble or clean, white adobe. Bridges and walkways joined the various skiffs, somehow floating with the motion of the sea without shattering.

Thanks to the ancient magic of the Dragonkin...

The blind man pushed the bygone sorcerers from his mind and looked instead for a way to get across. He spotted a ferry soon enough. He hesitated when he saw it already crowded with drovers and a herd of cattle. Though he had no desire to submerse himself in such a chaotic reek, he did not want to wait until a more appealing and sparsely inhabited ferry became available. He had hardly started onto the ferry when a young man grabbed him.

"Five cranáfi for passage, if you please."

Feigning surprise, the blind man reached into the pocket of his tattered robe and withdrew five coins, each one stamped with the sigil of a crane balancing on one foot. He pressed them into the ferryman's hand.

The ferryman frowned. "One of these is an iron crown, sir. I'll need three more if that's how you're paying."

The blind man considered killing the ferryman for the lie. He reached back into his robe, withdrew three more cranáfi, and gave them to the ferryman. "Will this suffice?"

2

The ferryman grinned. "Barely." He tucked the coins into his apron and took the blind man's arm. "Here, I'll help you sit down."

"You're too kind." The blind man pretended to stumble. When the ferryman moved to catch him, the blind man said, "Thank you, brother. The gods saw fit to curse me at birth." With one hand, the blind man lifted the worn strip of cloth tied around his eyes, revealing dark, empty eye sockets.

The ferryman blanched.

While the ferryman was busy staring, the blind man reached into the ferryman's apron with snake-like speed and took back a handful of coins. "You're too kind," he repeated as he sat down.

The ferryman, unaware that he'd just been robbed, returned to the front of the boat to welcome and collect his fee from a few more passengers. Then, when the ferry was full, he nodded to two other men at the other end of the ferry, and they pushed off. The blind man glanced back, watching as the Shao temple shrank smaller and smaller. He wondered if the Grand Marshal was inside.

Then, he turned to face New Atheion. The City-on-the-Sea was farther than he'd suspected. As a testament to its size, it grew and grew until the blind man felt as though he were staring at a sprawling metropolis like Lyos—or even Syros, before it had been destroyed. He stood up as the ferry docked. The blind man forced himself to wait with a banal smile as the drovers and their herd disembarked, followed by the rest of the passengers. The ferrymen offered to assist him, but the blind man shook his head and started out on his own, swaying his staff and nearly falling on purpose before setting foot in the city.

A fresh wash of sounds and smells nearly overwhelmed him. Shrill street vendors were selling crisp slabs of fish and spiced vegetables. Flesh-peddlers moved through the crowds as well, smiling and barely dressed. The blind man realized he had enjoyed neither women nor food in ages but pressed on. He spied a few pickpockets, as well, but none paid him any mind. He doubted that was due to their conscience so much as the fact that he was dressed in rags.

The blind man considered asking directions then remembered that the Scrollhouse was known as the greatest structure in New Atheion and decided to simply follow the crowds. He passed from one skiff to another, making his way over bustling walkways. Though he had never heard the Scrollhouse described, he recognized it by its size alone—even though a great portion of it had been ravaged by fire. Carpenters and stonemasons still labored to restore it.

The blind man passed between twin columns of statues depicting the gods and goddesses then paused when he reached the stairs leading into the famed library. Clerics in sea-blue robes milled on the steps, along with similarly dressed guards. Both wore the sigil of the goddess Armahg: a swirl of tiny stars.

One guard came forward. "I beg your pardon, but Armahg's Scrollhouse is not open to general admittance this day."

The blind man glanced up. While the roof of the Scrollhouse indeed bore the flag of Armahg, he also saw the balancing crane of the Isle Knights, flying just above it. He glanced past the guard and, for the first time, saw two smartly armored Isle Knights standing in the distance, taciturn and formidable in their gleaming kingsteel. He smothered a grin.

"I have heard as much," the blind man said, "but I'm afraid I can't wait. I must see the High Father at once."

The guard's unimpressed expression indicated that he'd heard such pleas before. "I'm sorry, brother, but none but the ordained may enter today. If it's food and sleep you're after, there's a temple just a little ways south of here—"

"I'm not a beggar, sir. I'm here by invitation." He reached into his tattered robe, withdrew a scroll, and passed it to the guard. He leaned on his staff, smiling faintly, as the guard read it.

The guard's eyes widened. "Of course. Apologies, brother!" He snapped his fingers and gestured. Two more guards hurried forward. "Show this one inside. Take him straight to Father Matua." He handed one of them the scroll, stepped aside, and touched the blind man's shoulder. "If you'll go with these men, brother, they'll show you the way."

"Thank you." The blind man allowed himself to be led by the arm.

The temple was crowded within and smelled of mulled wine and lamp oil. He spotted row upon row of books and scrolls, along with endless rows of tables at which clerics of Armahg sat, either reading or debating. The guards led him up a narrow, winding stairwell then down a hallway to an open door. One walked in ahead of him to announce his arrival.

Moments later, the blind man found himself in a modest office, surrounded by books, facing a plainly dressed, middle-aged cleric who sat at his desk. Father Matua had the faintly bronze skin of a Queshi. He was missing an arm, and more than half his face had been badly burned. Nevertheless, he smiled as he stood.

"Welcome. Please be seated," Father Matua said.

He gestured, and the guards helped the blind man to an empty chair across from that of the High Father. The cleric sat back down, appeared to ponder his next move for a moment, then dismissed the guards. At his command, one closed the door to the office behind him.

When the cleric was alone with the blind man, he used his remaining arm to lift the scroll and read it again. "You did a remarkable forgery of my name."

The blind man nodded. "Thank you. I practiced many times."

"Where did you find a copy?"

"In an old letter you sent to a priest in Syros."

Father Matua grunted. "I'd ask what happened to the priest, but if he was in Syros, I'm guessing he's been dead for years." He sighed. "Too bad I had to learn to write with my other hand after the Nightmare burned my good arm off. To be honest, my new signature resembles that of an addled child. But that's beside the point. Who are you, and why are you here?"

"I'm not here to hurt you, if that's what you're asking." The blind man flexed his fingers around his staff and leaned forward in his chair. "I'm only here for information."

The cleric scowled. "The Scrollhouse has no secrets. I've seen to that. Come here on the right day, and you can read anything you want. Or I could have a priest read it to you... though I'm guessing reading isn't a problem for you."

The blind man smiled in grudging admiration. He leaned his staff against Father Matua's desk, lifted his hands, and removed the strip of cloth tied around his head. His admiration increased when the priest did not even flinch at the sight of his hollow eye sockets.

"There," the blind man said. "Does this help reassure you that I'm not an assassin?"

"Not really," the High Father said. "I noticed that your ears are rounded, but the tops are scarred... almost like someone cut them to *make* them look rounded."

The blind man nodded. "My parents carved out my eyes when I was a child... either for my benefit or theirs—I couldn't tell you. The ears I did myself, much later." As he spoke, he allowed tiny embers of violet flame to ignite within his eye sockets.

He expected the sight to unsettle the priest, if anything would, but Father Matua nodded slowly. He reached out with his remaining arm, picked up a glass goblet, and took a sip of dark-red wine. "I've seen Shel'ai before... but never one like you."

"Oh, I doubt there are any quite like me." The blind man paused. "My name is Algol. Do you know what that means?" When Matua shook his head, Algol smiled. "Too bad. I'd tell you, but jokes and threats are similar in that both lose something when they're explained."

Matua was quiet for a moment. "I saw the Nightmare once, during the War of the Lotus, when he came to New Atheion. You remind me of him."

Algol laughed, allowing his wytchfire eyes to enlarge until they nearly spilled out of the hollow sockets. "I don't know whether I should feel complimented or insulted."

The High Father touched the scarred half of his face and shuddered. "Were he still alive, I suppose I should thank him. The other clerics were so impressed that I survived that they thought Armahg herself wanted me in charge of the Scrollhouse. It didn't hurt that the four or five clerics ahead of me in line all got turned to ash."

He's stalling. He's wondering if he made the right decision, sending the guards away. "I told you, I'm not going to hurt you. I just came here for information."

"And I told you, you can have it. You didn't have to sneak in here. And you don't have to threaten me or anyone else. Times are different. Even Shel'ai are welcome here now."

"Not where I want to go." Algol paused again. "There's a secret room at the bottom of the Scrollhouse. Most of it was burned when the Nightmare threw his tantrums, but some of it survived. That's where you keep certain scrolls that you and Rowen Locke deemed too... sensitive for common viewing."

Father Matua winced. "I trust you've already paid a visit to the Sword Marshal."

"Not yet. But Locke and I will meet in time. For now, he's the least of my concerns. Are you going to take me where I need to go"—Algol gripped his staff again—"or not?" Tendrils of ghostly violet flame blossomed from one hand, scouring the wood. Then the flames vanished, though the wood continued to smolder for a moment.

To Algol's surprise, the High Father chuckled. "This isn't the first time I've seen wytchfire. I've even known a Shel'ai who can summon flaming hands to replace the ones that got chopped off at the wrist. You'll have to do better than that if you want to intimidate me."

"How about this? Either you help me, or I'll kill every priest *and* burn every scroll I possibly can. Yes, your guards will kill me eventually, but not before I turn even more of your precious Scrollhouse into a smoldering ruin."

Father Matua raised his remaining eyebrow. "I imagine it takes a great deal of magic to see without the use of your eyes. That must be very tiring."

Algol caught his meaning. "I've spent years practicing this, priest. I may not be a Dragonkin, but I assure you I am the most dangerous Shel'ai you'll ever meet, and I have strength enough to make good on my threat. Now, do we have a deal or not?"

Father Matua was quiet for a moment, then he stood up and circled around the desk. Algol stood, too, clutching his darkened staff.

The High Father pointed at a suit of ancient-looking armor propped up against the far wall. "Can you move that yourself, or should I summon the guards?"

"Summoning the guards will get them killed... but you already knew that."

Algol eyed the tiny dagger hidden in the cleric's robes. He waved his hand, and the dagger sailed free of the cleric's robes and clattered to the floor. Before Father Matua could speak, Algol waved his hand again, this time directing his attention at the far wall. The suit of armor rose in the air and floated forward, just a few inches off the ground. He waved again, and it settled with just a faint metallic rattle.

The High Father hesitated then started forward, Algol right behind him. The High Father faced a smooth wall of blank stones for a moment then pressed on one. The wall rumbled open, revealing a passage into darkness.

The High Father glanced back and scowled. "Shall I bring a lantern?"

"No need." Algol prodded him forward with his staff. Then he raised one hand, igniting a bright, silent sphere of wytchfire. He followed the High Father down a stairwell so narrow they had to turn sideways. At the bottom, they faced an iron door. The High Father removed a key from a chain around his neck and unlocked the door.

Algol squelched a rush of exhilaration as he prodded the cleric into the secret chamber. The room was barely half the size of the High Father's office, with a low ceiling and just three small shelves crowded with books and scrolls. The room contained no tables or chairs, though Algol spotted a luminstone on one of the shelves. He leaned his staff against the wall and waved his hand, and the luminstone sailed into his grasp. It ignited at once, filling the room with a soft blue glow.

He dismissed his wytchfire and gave Father Matua a shove. "Kneel and face the wall, cleric. Keep quiet and you'll live. I swear it before the gods."

The scarred cleric obeyed. Algol went to the bookshelves. He did not take long to find what he sought. Though the small, simple scroll bore no dust and did not even appear weathered, as though it had been written only the day before, the writing itself was in ancient Dragonkin. Algol read it once then read it again.

Finally, he glanced up. "You should have destroyed this."

"We tried," Father Matua said, half turning. "The Sword Marshal even tried using that damned flaming sword, Knightswrath. Not even wytchfire will burn it. So we hid it down here."

"You should have hidden it in Cadavash."

"It's a scroll. If we can't destroy it, it belongs here." Father Matua paused. "Throughout the entire War of the Lotus, as bad as things got, even Chorlga refused to use that scroll. That should tell you something."

"Chorlga didn't use it because he wanted Ruun for himself." Algol closed the scroll and tucked it into his tattered robes. "I don't."

Then he reached out and tapped the luminstone, extinguishing its magical light. The small chamber plummeted into darkness, and the cleric's breathing quickened.

Algol smirked. "No need for fear, priest—at least, not yet. I told you, I'm not going to kill you. In fact, I want you alive so that you can tell everyone that I was here. Locke, Zeia, the Knights… everyone." He paused. "Do you believe me?"

Father Matua shuddered in the darkness. "I have a hard time believing a word you say."

Algol grinned and stepped forward. "Like I said, I promised I wouldn't kill you. But I never promised I wouldn't *hurt* you."

Father Matua stood. His good hand formed a fist. "Actually, you did."

"So I did." Algol reached out and seized Matua's good arm. "I lied." Wytchfire blossomed from his grasp.

Matua screamed.

CHAPTER ONE

ROWEN LOCKE PAUSED TO WIPE the sweat from his brow then swore as his opponent's sword angled for his throat. Rowen moved to block, but his enemy's sword changed direction midswing and rattled off his armored thigh. Rowen backed up and swung, hoping to keep his adversary at bay. Instead, his opponent drove forward. One armored twist knocked Rowen's sword aside while the other hand stabbed toward Rowen's face.

Rowen managed to parry the blow, but a second stab gouged his azure tabard and rang off the kingsteel cuirass underneath. His frustration turning to anger, Rowen swung as quickly as he could, but his opponent had already danced away as though his armored body were made of smoke.

Onlookers applauded, and Rowen blushed.

I deserve that.

He gripped his sword with both hands. Rather than attacking, he waited, eyeing his enemy—a younger man with a stoic, handsome face and a dark braid trailing behind him. The young man circled cautiously, half a dancer. After a moment, Rowen realized his opponent did not mean to attack at all but to wait until Rowen's frustration got the best of him.

Rowen did not have to turn to feel all the onlookers eyeing him with impatience, and he realized he couldn't blame them. Rowen had been taking the worst of the duel, which meant it was up to him to either turn the tide or concede. He had no intention of doing the latter, but his arms already felt leaden. He rotated steadily, to keep his adversary from getting around him. Then he shrugged one shoulder and winced, feigning a muscle cramp. As he'd hoped, his opponent tensed, about to spring forward.

Rowen answered by throwing his sword.

He had the pleasure of seeing his opponent's eyes widen a split second before a deft swing knocked Rowen's sword out of the air. But Rowen was already charging. He grabbed the young man's sword and tried to twist it out of his hands. Though Rowen was stronger, his opponent held on with an iron grip. Then iron turned to water, and somehow, Rowen found himself pitching toward the ground.

He landed in a roll and came up as quickly as he could, but it was too late. Rowen felt a sword bash his shoulder, his cuirass, and then his other shoulder. Then the sword stopped, the tip poised at Rowen's face.

"Do you yield, sir?"

Rowen bit back a curse and nodded. "I'd damn well better."

His sparring partner withdrew his sword, reversed it, and tucked the wooden blade under his arm. He bowed, then held out his hand. "Apologies, sir."

Rowen let the younger man pull him onto his feet just as the onlookers applauded. "Dammit, Sang Wei, you're not supposed to apologize when you beat me. And when I lose... which the gods know I always do... I'm supposed to bow first."

"Apologies," Sang Wei repeated. He picked up Rowen's wooden sword and handed it back to him with a second bow. "Fine move at the end, sir. I've never seen someone throw their sword like that before."

"Desperate men will do almost anything." Rowen took Sang Wei's arm and raised it aloft.

The onlookers applauded again. That time, it was Sang Wei who blushed. Rowen sensed that the younger Knight was as uncomfortable receiving praise as Rowen was being bested by his subordinate.

"Consider this payback, you quicksilver bastard," Rowen muttered, still smiling.

He kept turning, forcing Sang Wei to turn with him then stopped. In the distance, among Knights and squires, one of the onlookers was a young man with angular features, tapered ears, and brilliantly purple eyes. The Shel'ai was applauding.

11

"You have an admirer," Rowen whispered.

Sang Wei turned an even darker shade of red.

Rowen let go of his arm, suddenly feeling guilty. He'd seen the young Shel'ai and Sang Wei exchange more than a few glances over the past few months, though something told him the young Knight was more than a little reluctant to pursue anything. Rowen wondered why. While some kingdoms frowned on romantic relationships between people of the same gender, that was perfectly acceptable among the Shao.

Then again, Maddoc isn't just a man. He's a Shel'ai.

"Enough," Rowen called loudly, catching everyone's attention. "As Sword Marshal of Cadavash Temple, I declare Sang Wei, Knight of the Stag, to be the fastest bastard who ever lived!" As the onlookers cheered again, Rowen added, "If anyone can prove me wrong, I'll exempt him from an evening meditation and give him enough wine to keep him sodden for a week."

As the onlookers cheered yet again, Rowen clapped Sang Wei on the shoulder then stepped out of the practice ring, tossing his sword to the nearest Knight rushing to take his place. He forced himself to smile as he made his way toward a woman at the far end of the practice ring. Unlike the others, who wore armor or loose-fitting fighting garb, Igrid wore a short fighting skirt, high boots, and a barely adequate fighting top, the sight of which quickened his blood.

She offered a lopsided grin at his approach, brushing one hand through long red curls that hung well past her waist. "How much pain are you in right now?"

"Sweet gods, you have no idea." Rowen smiled with clenched teeth, tapping his chest through his armor.

Igrid's green eyes flashed with mirth and a touch of worry. "Did he break anything?"

"Maybe a rib or three. I'll have Maddoc take a look later."

"Are you sure you don't want him now?"

Rowen shook his head. "My pride stings enough as it is. I can wait a while."

"If you say so. I don't think he ever looked my way, but I was hoping to distract him so you'd win for once." Igrid winked.

For a moment, Rowen thought she meant Maddoc but then realized she was referring to Sang Wei. "No offense, my love, but you might be the wrong gender for that."

Rowen saw no need to point out that he knew Igrid was lying. She wore her eye-catching attire because she intended to join in the sparring matches—she was still an Iron Sister, after all—and part of her fighting style involved using her appearance to distract men into making a mistake.

Igrid said, "If I beat him, do I get that wine you promised?"

Rowen turned. Sang Wei was busy fighting off a man his own age—a powerful, newly minted Knight of the Crane named Berric, whose barrel chest and thick arms barely fit inside his armor. The man bellowed each time he swung. His swings were powerful but quick. Two drove Sang Wei backward. The third shattered Sang Wei's wooden sword. The crowd applauded. Sir Berric held his arms aloft, cheering.

"He shouldn't do that," Rowen muttered with disapproval.

Maddoc stepped forward, a new wooden sword in hand, and handed it to Sang Wei. When the Knight of the Stag took it, the Shel'ai leaned forward and whispered something. Sang Wei blushed, and Maddoc backed away, smiling. When the duel resumed, Sir Berric came at Sang Wei in a bellowing blur of speed and steel. That time, though, Sang Wei dodged every swing and thrust and rained blows on his opponent's legs then one on his backside that nearly knocked Sir Berric off his feet.

"He's not holding back this time." Rowen wondered how much the young Knight had been holding back when he'd fought him and decided he'd rather not know.

Sir Berric bellowed again—in frustration that time—and doubled his attack. But Sang Wei moved even faster, as though his speed were limitless. Seconds later, the burly Knight found himself disarmed and forced to one knee, with Sang Wei's sword held in a reverse grip against his throat.

For a moment, Rowen feared that Sir Berric would answer with rage. Instead, he laughed. "I yield! Gods, I yield! Now somebody get me a tub of ice to sit in." He stood up, laughed again, and hugged Sang Wei as if they were brothers.

The onlookers cheered. Sir Berric tried to get others to take his place, but Sang Wei bowed and refused to fight any more. The Knights and squires paired off to practice with each other instead. Sang Wei wandered off toward the temple in the distance, still holding his wooden sword. After a moment, Maddoc followed.

Rowen was about to ask Igrid to help him back inside when another familiar Knight ran toward them. Rowen noted that he was coming from the direction of the gates and wore a serious expression on his face.

"Trouble," Rowen whispered to Igrid and went to meet the Knight halfway. "What is it, Issa?"

Sir Issa bowed, out of breath. "Visitors, Sword Marshal."

"Dragon-worshippers?"

Sir Issa shook his head. "Not this time, sir. Looks like Sons of Maelmohr this time."

Gods, is that better or worse? Rowen glanced past Sir Issa and made sure the gates of Cadavash were still closed. He noted as well that the few Knights standing watch along the walls were standing straight as lances, looking out over the battlements.

Meanwhile, Igrid moved to a nearby weapons rack, snatched up a sheathed adamune with a sword belt, and brought it back. She handed it to Rowen. "Want me to get Sang Wei and Maddoc?"

Rowen faced Issa instead. "How many?"

"Just five, Sword Marshal."

"Don't bother," Rowen told Igrid. "I'll just go out and insult them until they go away."

Igrid raised one eyebrow. "No diplomatic pleasantries this time?"

Rowen shook his head. "If Gaulgodd is going to keep threatening the people under my protection, I think it's safe to say we're not ever going to be the best of friends."

Igrid's lopsided grin returned. "I should ask Sang Wei to trounce you more often."

Rowen winced as he girded his sword. When he started toward the gates, Igrid followed. Rowen considered ordering her to keep back. After all, the Sons of Maelmohr disapproved of many things—including women who wore swords and dressed like Igrid. But he reminded himself that he was in no shape for a fight, and he could think of no one he wanted by his side more than her.

Sir Issa jogged ahead and ordered the gates to be opened. By the time Rowen arrived, a squad of Knights stood ready to escort him. He glanced over his shoulder and saw still more Knights turning from the practice yard to see what was the matter. Rather than wait for a larger audience to gather, he ignored the pain from his ribs and strode through the gates to greet their guests.

Outside, five figures on horseback scowled. They had gray skin and unusually dark eyes. Though short, all were muscular and clad in armor made of scales so deeply red that they appeared almost black. He saw no sigil until the Dwarrs rode closer and he noticed the armbands tied around their bulging biceps: black armbands depicting black dragons surrounded by what was either red flames or a cloud of blood.

One of the figures dismounted. He appeared younger than most of his comrades, though his eyes shone with unrivaled malice. Almost as an afterthought, he unslung a long axe from his back and handed it to the rider next to him. He approached Rowen on foot, one hand on the hilt of a wide-bladed shortsword.

Rowen rested one hand on his own sword hilt but forced a smile. "Welcome to Cadavash, m'lord. I don't think we've—"

"A message from the Scion." The young Dwarr thrust forward a rolled-up piece of paper as though it were a weapon.

Rowen took it but didn't unroll it. He considered passing it to Igrid then handed it over his shoulder to Sir Issa. After all, if a fight broke out, he valued Igrid's sword arm more than anyone else's.

The unnamed Dwarr stood on the plains for a moment, arms crossed, then said, "The Scion deserves an answer."

"And I am happy to provide one," Rowen said. "Tell the Scion that on behalf of the Knights and Shel'ai at Cadavash, we accept his apology."

The young Dwarr narrowed his eyes.

"That *is* what this message is about, is it not?" Rowen reached back and took the scroll from Sir Issa but still did not open it "Forgive me, I assumed the Scion wanted to apologize for that last message he sent, presumably while drunk or throwing a tantrum." He glanced at Igrid. "What did it say, my love? Something about children with purple eyes being damned to Fohl's hells…"

"And us, too." Igrid fixed the Dwarr in a murderous stare. "I was partial to the bit about us drowning in our own blood unless we agreed to turn the Shel'ai over."

The Dwarr ignored Igrid, fixing his gaze on Rowen. "Magic is an abomination. Magic is responsible for the destruction of Stillhammer and the near annihilation of my people, not to mention countless deaths among the Free Cities. Do you deny this?"

"Since I saw most of this firsthand… not in the least."

The Dwarr blinked, clearly surprised by the answer.

Rowen continued. "But here's what you're forgetting: magic is also responsible for the destruction of Chorlga and his Dragonjol. Magic is why you're still alive. As for the Shel'ai, they had nothing to do with what happened at Stillhammer—especially those Shel'ai children who are under my protection."

The Dwarr answered quickly, as though he'd already been waiting to give his carefully prepared answer. "All magic's the same. That's how it's been since the days of the Dragonkin. It is a corruption of the natural order of things. The Scion requests that you repent your sins and join him so that this land may be cleansed. Do so, and you will be forgiven."

Despite the pain in his ribs, Rowen took a step forward. Though he stood half a head taller than the Dwarr, the latter met his gaze without blinking.

Rowen said, "I've seen women and children butchered by steel, yet still you wear a sword."

The Dwarr frowned. "Is that your best answer?"

"No, *this* is my answer." Rowen stepped back and drew his sword.

The Dwarr recoiled, but Rowen already had the tip of his adamune resting against the Dwarr's throat. The riders behind him tensed as though about to charge but changed their minds when Igrid and the other Knights drew their own blades and stepped forward.

Rowen waited until the commotion died down. "I'm told I have a temper. I don't like that, so I'm willing to repeat myself from time to time. But this is the last time I intend to say this. These children are under my protection. If your so-called Scion has a problem with that, tell him he can ride to Cadavash to discuss it with me in person. I'll be waiting."

Rowen sheathed his sword. His Knights followed suit though Rowen noted that Igrid kept her shortswords drawn and a derisive gaze locked on the Dwarr, as though daring him to strike.

Instead, the Dwarr shook his head and backed away. "We came in peace, Knight. You had no cause to act this way. But still, forgiveness is possible. We serve the gods. Repent—or next time, we'll come with fire and steel."

Rowen watched as the Dwarr mounted his horse, wheeled about, and led the others away in a haughty gallop. Then Rowen unrolled the scroll. He'd hardly begun to read it when he stopped, tore it in half, and let it fall from his hands.

Igrid snickered. "Not an apology, I take it?"

"No, but they're getting more open with their threats."

Rowen waved the Knights back inside, noticing as he passed through the open gates that nearly the entire population of Cadavash—Knights, squires, and Shel'ai—had gathered in the courtyard. A handful of violet-eyed children stared up at him with worry. Murmuring filled the courtyard, but all fell silent as Rowen stood before them.

Rowen scooped up one of the Shel'ai children and held her. Though painfully aware of the many eyes on him, he forced himself to speak anyway. "Humans, Sylvs, Shel'ai… all are welcome here. If any fool insists on testing that… well, I wouldn't say much for his chances."

Someone laughed. Someone else cheered. His Knights picked up the cheer, and a few clapped him on the back. Rowen winced with pain but forced himself to smile. He set the child down and watched her run away. A few Shel'ai in the distance stared at him with indecipherable expressions before they turned and walked away as well.

He turned to Igrid. "Help me back inside."

Igrid slipped one hand around his waist. "As you say, m'lord." She winked again.

While the Knights and squires cheered, she led him toward his house. The house itself had once been the manse of some high-ranking dragonpriest, next to what was currently the barracks. All trace of the manse's previous occupant had been erased, and the once-ghastly place looked rather plain, save for the banners of the Lotus Isles flying over it.

Two Knights of the Crane stood at attention at their approach. Rowen stiffened and nodded back, forcing himself to move slowly, as though unhurt. But the moment Igrid got him inside, he nearly collapsed. Waving off the servants, Igrid helped him down the hall to the bedchamber, helped him lie down, and set to work unbuckling his armor. She stripped off first his kingsteel cuirass then the padding he wore underneath. When she saw his bare chest, her smile vanished. An ugly bruise covered his side—purple in places, almost blood red in others.

"I'd better get Maddoc," she said.

Rowen caught her wrist. "If you fetch him now, people will think it's about the Sons of Maelmohr, that I'm worried and need advice. Better they think I couldn't care less. Just get me some wine."

Igrid snaked out of his grasp but stayed where she was. "I know as much about fighting as you do, dunce. Something's jagged in there. Move wrong, and you'll slice up a lung. And I have enough trouble sleeping without you lying next to me, coughing up blood." She hesitated. "If you don't want me to get Maddoc, let me take you down to the vault."

Rowen considered making the dizzying descent into the chasm of Cadavash, level after level, down to the heavily guarded vault where Knightswrath lay in darkness. Months had passed since he'd worn the sword, and more than a year since he'd last invoked its magic. His pulse quickened at the thought of sheer, unimaginable power flowing through him, electrifying his senses, until he would lose himself in its intoxicating embrace.

He shook his head. "No, leave the sword where it is. But go get Maddoc if you must."

Something in his voice made Igrid wince, but she left without a word. When she was gone, Rowen considered closing his eyes and resting but stood up. He crossed the room and was pouring a glass of wine when he heard the sound of a crying child. The sound grew closer. Rowen downed his glass then turned.

A Human girl, no older than twelve or thirteen summers, stood in the doorway to his bedchamber. She rolled her eyes, face flushed with anger, and she was holding the hand of a crying toddler. Tapered ears peeked through the toddler's wispy golden hair, and her violet eyes ran wet with tears. One hand—the one not holding that of the Human girl—was curled into a tight, tiny fist. Violet plumes of fire crept out between her fingers.

"Thessa, what's wrong?" he asked the older girl.

"She had another nightmare while she was napping." Thessa half led, half shoved the toddler toward Rowen.

Despite the pain in his side, Rowen forced himself to kneel and open his arms. The toddler ran toward him. Rowen fought the impulse to recoil, though the wytchfire vanished from the toddler's hands a moment before she wrapped her arms around his neck.

"She burned three of my toys!" Thessa complained. She looked around. "Where's Igrid?"

"Outside. Go find her." Rowen held the toddler close. "Easy, Sariel. You're safe. It was just a dream."

"She burned *three* of my toys!" Thessa repeated.

"Thessa, go," Rowen snapped, adding "please" when Thessa winced.

The girl turned and ran out of the room. Her footfalls echoed like a miniature thunderstorm as she sprinted down the hall. He braced himself and stood, lifting Sariel with him. She weighed so little that his ribs hurt only a bit more than they had when he'd knelt, though he felt a sting against his flesh where she was gripping the back of his neck, as though she were burning him. Her touch seemed to reignite the pain he sometimes felt in his left shoulder and arm, where his final battle against Chorlga had left him burned more deeply than even Knightswrath could heal. The pain intensified. Rowen's eyes watered, but he resisted the impulse to cast Sariel away.

"Just a dream," he repeated through his teeth.

"Moshi," Sariel sniffled.

Rowen recognized the Sylvan word for *mother* and wondered who had taught it to her. "Igrid will be right back," he whispered. He started to ask himself how Igrid would feel about a Shel'ai child thinking of her as her mother but reminded himself that Sariel might inadvertently be reading his mind. He cleared his thoughts, carried Sariel to a chair, and held her close as he sat down. "Just a dream," he said again.

"Moshi," Sariel repeated.

To Rowen's relief, the burning faded from his shoulder and arm, replaced only by a dull ache. A moment later, he heard footsteps. Thessa raced back into the room, followed by Igrid and Maddoc. Both were smiling as though sharing some secret joke. Their smiles vanished when they saw the look on Rowen's face.

Maddoc raced forward and scooped up Sariel, smiling and singing to her in Sylvan. Sariel laughed. Meanwhile, Igrid helped Rowen stand.

She eased behind him and inspected the back of his neck. Rowen winced, biting back a curse.

Igrid whispered, "Gods," and turned to Thessa. "Step outside, sweet roll. Go down to the practice yard and play. I'll find you later."

Thessa's eyes went wide, but for once, she did not argue. When she was gone, Maddoc closed the door with his heel, still holding Sariel. He cradled the child a moment longer then carried her to Rowen and Igrid's bed and laid her down. She spoke in Sylvan, requesting a story. Maddoc laughed. Then he gently pressed one hand to Sariel's forehead. A soft violet glow emanated from his fingertips, and Sariel instantly fell asleep.

Maddoc stood, facing Igrid. "How bad is it?"

"Bad enough," Rowen answered for her.

Maddoc came forward to see for himself. He whistled. "I can heal this, though."

"And his ribs," Igrid said. "I'll have you know your lover did a fair bit of damage to *my* lover's insides."

Rowen cast her a scathing look, but Maddoc laughed, eyeing Rowen's horribly bruised chest. "So he did. If you want him to feel guilty for the rest of his life, I'll tell him."

"I'd rather you didn't," Rowen said through clenched teeth.

Maddoc nodded as his smile vanished. "First things first. Kneel, please, sir."

Igrid helped Rowen kneel as Maddoc stood behind him, pressing one cool hand to the back of his neck, the other to his shoulder. The Shel'ai's touch grew hotter and hotter. Just when it was about to become searing, the heat faded.

Maddoc asked, "Better?"

Rowen cautiously moved one arm then turned his neck. He nodded and stood, and Maddoc repeated the process with his ribcage. That hurt less and healed more quickly than the burn given him by Sariel.

Maddoc said, "It seems your old wounds make it easier for her to burn you. I don't know why. I would have thought the opposite would be true."

Igrid scowled. "Would that still be true if he wore Knightswrath?"

Maddoc considered that. "I don't think so. In fact, you'd probably be safe from anything less than a Dragonkin."

"I'm not going to start wearing the sword again." Rowen glared at Igrid as he picked up a cloak and threw it over his bare shoulders. "And if memory serves, the two of you didn't like me wearing it any more than I did, so stop suggesting it."

"No, I didn't like it," Igrid said, "but did you catch what I said earlier about not liking it when you cough up blood? Besides, it would have been nice to see you draw it and scare off those Sons of Maelmohr."

"No need," Rowen said. "Every Dwarr with half a brain has already left Stillhammer. This Scion has only a couple hundred boys and old men with him. He can make all the threats he wants, but if he attacks Cadavash, he won't stand a chance."

"What about their armor?"

"Red and scaly. What of it?"

"Just that most lunatics don't have the patience to make uniforms. Once they do, maybe they should be taken seriously."

"And killed," Maddoc added.

The casual animosity in the Shel'ai's voice surprised Rowen until he reminded himself that the relatively new cult known as the Sons of Maelmohr had made it their chief aim to eradicate magic from the continent.

"I won't wear the sword," he said, hoping to change the topic.

Igrid shrugged again. "Look, I'm not crazy about the notion of you wearing a sword infused with the spirit of your dead wytch, but I'm even less fond of watching you burned alive by your own daughter." She cast a quick glance at the sleeping figure of Sariel, lowering her voice midsentence.

"Sariel doesn't want to hurt me," Rowen said.

Maddoc cleared his throat. "She doesn't have to *want* to hurt you to hurt you, m'lord. I've seen this many times before. Shel'ai children need to be taught to contain their passions if they're ever going to control their powers. If they don't, a tantrum or a bad dream could get people killed. I've been trying, but—"

"Nobody's blaming you," Rowen said.

"I might be," Igrid muttered. "I don't see any of the *other* children acting like this!"

Maddoc smiled thinly. "Sariel is… particularly strong-willed. Some of that might come from knowing she's adopted." He added, "The truth is, she'd listen better if the lessons came from *you*."

"She likes you," Rowen said. "We all make mistakes."

Igrid gave Rowen a look so hurt that his anger melted into guilt.

Before he could speak, she stepped away. "I don't hate the poor child. Don't treat me like I do. I just don't want her turning my lover into a pillar of ash. Or *me*, for that matter." After a moment, she faced Maddoc. "Apologies."

Maddoc bowed, but Igrid was already walking out, closing the door behind her.

Rowen shook his head. He started toward the chair but changed his mind and returned to the bed, sitting beside Sariel. He smoothed back her hair. "Can you do anything about the nightmares?"

"No more than I can do for yours."

So nothing, then. Rowen reflected on the nightmares he'd had ever since the War of the Lotus. Some of them incorporated the death of his brother or other grisly memories of the battlefield. Other times, they featured a frightening sight he'd never actually beheld in real life: a massive dragon frozen under the ice of the Wintersea, its dark eyes staring up at him—half murderous, half pleading. "Why does she keep having them?"

Maddoc shrugged. "Shel'ai children aren't like Humans. Their memories are better. Sometimes, that works against them."

Rowen touched the soft tips of the girl's tapered ears. "You told me she'd forget being abandoned by her parents."

"I told you she *might* forget, in time."

"Did *you* ever forget?"

Maddoc was quiet for a moment. "Do you know what my name means? It's the Sylvan word for—"

"Unwanted," Rowen finished. He thought back to El'rash'lin, the tragic Shel'ai who had imparted a great many of his own memories into Rowen, in an attempt to make him understand the plight of the Shel'ai. "I'm sorry, I shouldn't have asked."

"If it helps, she's better off here," Maddoc said. "If she'd stayed in Sylvos, no matter what the new laws are, they would have killed her. Besides, it'll get better as she gets older."

You don't sound so sure. "What about the other children?"

"Lady Igrid is half right. There are still problems from time to time, but not as many… mainly because they're being raised by Shel'ai."

Rowen caught Maddoc's meaning and shook his head. "I promised I'd raise Sariel, and I will. I have to."

"To prove a point?"

That the Shel'ai are safe with Humans? Maybe… "No." Rowen touched the tips of Sariel's ears again. "She's my daughter… by choice if not by blood." He stood, picked up a blanket, and covered her. "I'm sorry I asked, Maddoc."

"About what?"

"About your life… before this. It's none of my business."

"You have a right to ask, m'lord. I only guarded the little ones at Coldhaven. I never fought with Fadarah and the Throng, if that's what you're worried about."

"You know it isn't—nor would you be unwelcome here even if you had."

Maddoc smiled faintly. "You are exceptionally merciful, m'lord—some would say to a fault. But I doubt my story is very different from that of most any other Shel'ai. I was cast out of Sylvos as a baby. Shade found me. Another Shel'ai raised me, but the Olgrym killed him. They said I was too young to fight, or else you and I might have been enemies. I'm glad we weren't."

Rowen's thoughts had darkened at the mention of Shade, but he reminded himself that in the end, his brother's tormenter had died heroically. If Shade had not made amends for the many sins of his life, he had come as close as possible in the time he'd had. Rowen glanced at Maddoc. "Do you ever wonder if there are other Shel'ai out there? I mean ones none of us ever found. Not me, not Fadarah, not even Chorlga or the mobs."

Maddoc was quiet for a moment. "I don't wonder," he said finally. "I'm sure of it."

Gods save us… "So much for my grand experiment."

"M'lord?"

Rowen shook his head. "For a while, I had everybody here. Shel'ai, Knights, Sylvs, Dwarrs, all together, all helping me to guard Namundvar's

Well. Then, one by one, they all went away. Now, the Dwarrs are talking about how magic is an abomination… even though it was bloody magic that saved what's left of them!"

"And magic that all but destroyed them in the first place."

Rowen glanced at Maddoc. "I wouldn't have expected a Shel'ai to admit that."

Maddoc smirked. "Believe it or not, Knight, we're not all one unified people sharing a single brain. If we were, history would have gone quite differently." He paused. "Keswen is still here. So are the children. So are the Shel'ai."

Rowen tensed at the mention of Keswen. Three years before, a small band of Sylvan women had taken refuge at Cadavash. They had been forcefully impregnated in a devilish attempt by Chorlga to breed an army of Shel'ai and had nowhere else to go. But after delivering their babies and half entrusting, half abandoning them into the care of the Shel'ai, all had returned to the Wytchforest. Only a young Wyldkin woman named Keswen had stayed even though her own child had been stillborn.

"One Sylv stayed. The rest turned this place into a godsdamned orphanage." Rowen stroked Sariel's hair. "How many died in the war, Maddoc? By the Light, we didn't learn a single thing."

Maddoc smiled again. "Apologies, m'lord, but if you thought you were going to erase over a thousand years of hatred and mistrust just by having former enemies share guard duty…"

"Then maybe I'm as naïve as Igrid says." Rowen nodded, fighting back a rush of irritation. "Yeah, I know."

"I wouldn't say that," Maddoc countered. "You still have Humans and Shel'ai here, living together. We may not be friends, exactly, but we're not trying to kill each other. When was the last time that happened?"

Rowen thought of the scroll he'd stolen from the Scrollhouse at New Atheion, with Silwren's help, which held the early, lost history of the Knighthood.

Maddoc continued. "This place is a haven for my kind, m'lord. Because of you, half a dozen Shel'ai *won't* grow up hating everyone, and the rest don't have to live in constant fear for their lives." He bowed. "As one of them, I appreciate it."

Sariel stirred, opened her eyes, and regarded Rowen with ghost-white pupils. Rowen smiled and smoothed back her hair again. He feared she would cry, but the child closed her eyes and slept again. "It's all right, Maddoc. You can go."

"Are you sure? I can stay a while, in case..."

Rowen wondered if Maddoc had been about to say, *in case she has another nightmare* or *in case you want to talk to Igrid*. He chose to believe the former. "Go," he repeated.

When a new sound reached his ears, he stood. Someone was running down the hall. Unlike Thessa's footfalls, though, they were the heavier ones of a grown man in armor.

Rowen wondered if the Sons of Maelmohr had returned. He instinctively reached for a weapon. Sariel's eyelids flew open, and she started crying as though sensing his change in emotion. Maddoc rose just as quickly and stepped in front of him. Wytchfire ignited from his fingertips, racing back and forth along his forearms.

The door flew open, and Sang Wei rushed in. Igrid followed a step behind.

Rowen saw the look on Sang Wei's face and asked, "What's wrong?"

Barely pausing to catch his breath, Sang Wei said, "A message from Aeko Shingawa." He held out a tiny roll of parchment. "It just arrived by wytch-raven."

Gods, what else is going to happen this day? Rowen took the parchment, looked at Sariel, then glanced at Maddoc. The Shel'ai caught his meaning. He scooped up Sariel, whose tiny fists were flaring with wytchfire, and comforted her. Rowen forced himself to step away as he unrolled the parchment and read the message. When he had finished, he read it again. Then he turned to Sang Wei. "Have you read this yet?"

Sang Wei blushed. "Yes, m'lord. There was no seal—"

"That's fine. I was going to have you read it anyway." *Not like Aeko to forget to seal something this important, though...*

Igrid stepped forward, green eyes flashing. "Are you going to tell me what's the matter, or do I have to wring it out of you?"

Rowen read the message aloud. "Someone named Algol attacked Father Matua in the Scrollhouse. Come to Saikaido Temple at once. We must talk." He frowned. "*Algol* is a Sylvan word. It means 'vengeance.'"

"More like 'divine judgment,'" Maddoc corrected.

"Either way, I doubt that's his real name." Rowen handed the parchment to Igrid. "That's definitely Aeko's signature, but she calls me *Rowen*."

Igrid read it then glanced up. "So?"

"Aeko usually calls me *Squire*," Rowen said with a faint smile. "A private joke."

"So you think she didn't send it?"

Instead of answering Igrid's question, Rowen glanced past Sang Wei, at Maddoc. The Shel'ai had gotten Sariel to quiet down, but his clothes were singed, though he appeared unhurt. Maddoc mouthed the word *Go*.

Rowen nodded and gestured for the others to leave the room. In the hallway outside, a few Knights and squires glanced at him with curiosity, but Rowen led the others to his office and closed the door.

Igrid asked, "Who in the hells would attack Matua?" She handed the parchment back to Rowen.

"He *is* a High Father of Armahg," Sang Wei offered. "Perhaps someone from a rival temple?" He eyed Rowen. "I know you've met the priest a few times, but for how urgent she sounds—"

"I don't think this is about Matua." Rowen sat down and gestured for the others to do the same, but both remained standing. "It matters that he was attacked inside the Scrollhouse by someone with a Sylvan name. I'm guessing a Shel'ai was responsible, but she didn't want to say it."

Igrid frowned. "Saikaido is *her* temple, isn't it?"

"Not anymore. That's where Crovis lives now." He paused. "The Grand Marshal took it to spite her, I think."

Sang Wei shifted uncomfortably. Rowen did not think the young Knight was any fonder of Crovis Ammerhel than he was—despite the fact that it was Crovis who had promoted Sang Wei as a political maneuver. Still, Sang Wei had always frowned on speaking ill of the Knighthood's new leader.

Igrid said, "Ammerhel's been quiet for months. Ever since he gave up trying to break into Shigella's Tomb."

Sang Wei's eyes widened. "He did *what?*"

Rowen faced the young Knight. "There's no proof, but a few years ago, Aeko thought that Crovis might be trying to break into the tomb of the Sylvan king." Before Sang Wei could interrupt, he said, "Don't ask me to explain why a Sylvan king was buried on the Lotus Isles. It's a long story. Anyway, Aeko thought that Crovis thought there might be another sword like Knightswrath buried inside."

The young Knight paled. "Is there, m'lord?"

"No," Rowen said quickly. "But there's something else in there besides dust and bones. Something we'd prefer to keep quiet."

Igrid asked, "Do you think Crovis knows?"

Rowen glanced at the parchment again. "I don't know, but *somebody* does. Maybe she's just warning me to be careful. Wei, do we have any wytch-ravens that know the way to Dhargoth?"

The Knight of the Stag looked puzzled. "That might be too far north. I'll have to ask Maddoc."

"Zeia," Igrid said in a low voice. "Do you think she'll come?"

"No," Rowen admitted. "Last I heard, she and Prince Saanji had the Red Emperor's forces trapped in the capital, but the siege had ground to a halt. I don't think she'll leave until it's done. Still, she has to know."

Sang Wei opened his mouth then closed it.

Rowen faced the young Knight with sympathy. *You want to know what I'm hiding, what Matua and Zeia and I found out... but that's only because you don't know any better.* He turned to Igrid. "I'll leave in the morning. I'll take Sang Wei and Maddoc with me. Cadavash will be under your command while I'm gone."

Igrid's face flushed red with anger.

Sang Wei cleared his throat. "I'll go and begin the preparations, m'lord."

Rowen stood. "Do that." He remembered the burly Knight who had nearly defeated Sang Wei in the practice yard. "And on second thought, we'll take Sir Berric, too."

Sang Wei bowed then hurried out of the room as though anxious to be gone before the inevitable fight started. He had hardly closed the door behind himself when Igrid seized an empty goblet off a nearby table and threw it at Rowen's head.

Rowen caught it. But the next object, a ceramic serving platter, shattered against the wall behind his head.

"Gods, woman... " Rowen sidestepped then ducked to avoid another goblet.

When he straightened, he expected to see Igrid livid. Instead, the

Iron Sister looked almost calm as she plucked a dagger from her belt and threw it at him. Luckily, she left the sheath on.

"Are you finished?"

"Nearly." Igrid kicked a chair out of the way, stepped forward, and slapped him. "I thought we were done with this."

"Done with what?" Rowen blushed at the thought of who might be listening outside.

"You playing the Knight, me the obedient maiden."

Rowen forced a smile. "*Obedient* is one word I've never used to describe you."

Igrid did not laugh. "You just got done telling everyone that you're going to protect them against these Sons of Maelmohr bastards, and now you're *leaving*?"

"The Sons of Maelmohr aren't a serious threat yet. But a Shel'ai learning about that scroll—"

"If it is a Shel'ai," Igrid cut in. "This could be anything. It could be a trap. So I'm going with you, Knight. That's how this works."

"That's how this *used* to work. There are children here now. Thessa, Sariel…"

"Neither of which is actually ours."

Rowen picked up the sheathed knife, set it on the table, and sat back down. "I'm going to forget you said that."

Igrid winced. Then she turned her back on him and paced. "I have a better idea. I'll go check on the Scrollhouse while *you* guard the children. Nobody will expect that."

"Aeko asked for me. Not you."

"She asked for Knightswrath, you mean." Igrid shook her head. "She didn't mention the sword, but we both know that's what she's thinking."

"I'm not taking Knightswrath."

Igrid turned, leaned over his desk, and regarded him as if he'd just gone insane. "It can chop through armor and burn up armies. If this *is* a trap, you should have it with you!" She paused. "Look, dunce, I might not like how you mutter that damn dead wytch's name in your sleep, but there's no way in Fohl's hells I'm letting you go without the sword."

Rowen shook his head. "If this *is* a trap of some kind, I don't want the sword anywhere near Ammerhel. I don't have to explain why." He paused and lowered his voice. "Besides... I don't *want* it."

Igrid's expression softened as she apparently caught his meaning. "I'd rather you at least wait for Zeia."

"I told you, she probably won't come. And even if she does, I might very well be back by then."

"Or dead," Igrid countered.

Rowen felt a lump in his throat. "This isn't up for discussion."

Igrid fumed for a moment then turned when they heard Sariel crying through the door. The child's screams were frantic and terrified. Rowen thought he smelled smoke. He stood up.

"No," Igrid said bitterly, "let me. Looks like I'll need the practice."

She left the office and slammed the door behind her. Before the door closed, though, Rowen caught a glimpse of Thessa standing in the hallway beyond, her eyes full of fear and confusion. Rowen glanced down at the parchment again. Then he held it in a candle until it burned away.

CHAPTER TWO

ROWEN PACED ALONG A RAILING of wood and stone as sunset descended upon Cadavash. Even though he knew he was in no danger, part of him was glad he had donned his armor and girded an adamune. As he walked, he resisted the impulse to look over the railing, down into the deep chasm. He disliked how darkness flooded the chasm once the sun went down, as though it had been filled with ghostly earth.

Still better than how it used to be, though.

He'd gone there the first time as a bodyguard for the Soroccan merchant, Hráthbam, and found the chasm crowded with fey dragon-worshippers. He shuddered, remembering how the worshippers had wept and wailed, many of them slashing their own bodies in some kind of crazed act of penance. He reminded himself that some good had come from that trip—he'd met and rescued Silwren in the depths of the chasm, after all—but his thoughts turned instead to the children he'd seen in Cadavash, forced to participate in the same mad religion as their parents. He wondered how many of them were still alive.

Probably none, he realized. During the culmination of the War of the Lotus, nearly all the dragon-worshippers had sided with the mad Dragonkin, Chorlga, who in turn sacrificed them to heighten his power. Rowen had seen the bodies afterward, burned and frozen in the snow. At his command, those corpses had been gathered with all possible reverence and stacked onto massive funeral pyres whose ghastly flames still haunted Rowen's dreams. His Knights had gathered the metallic remains of Chorlga's Jolym, as well. But while Jolym could be smelted down and put to good use, the dragon-worshippers left nothing behind but ashes and bad memories.

"I should have done more," Rowen said to himself. He imagined what his friend Jalist would say to that. But the knowledge that he could have done nothing did little to ease his guilt.

He glanced around for some form of distraction. He had already visited the stables but found that Berric and Sang Wei had readied the horses and supplies then retired early. Presumably, the latter was with Maddoc, since Rowen had not seen the Shel'ai since their meeting a few hours earlier. Most of the Knights and squires had retired to the barracks, except for a few who stood guard duty on the high wooden walls encircling all of Cadavash.

Nearby, a group of Shel'ai children played in the shadow of the temple. Rowen did not see Thessa among them and wondered if she was with Igrid. The children were overseen by two Shel'ai in cloaks and hoods, both of whom were facing him. Rowen nodded toward them. One nodded back. The other looked away. Rowen remembered Maddoc's gibe from earlier. *Perhaps I need to make the Shel'ai stand guard duty more often.* Then he turned toward the practice yard and saw Keswen.

The Sylvan woman had a longbow in her hands and was busy destroying a line of six straw dummies at the opposite end of the practice yard. Despite the distance and despite the fact that the setting sun caused her to squint, she placed arrow after arrow in the chests of her imaginary opponents. Unlike the Shel'ai, who usually wore cloaks, Keswen still dressed Wyldkin-style, in soft hunting leathers with feathers in her hair. She also wore a bracer and a finger tab to protect her hands while she fired, though something told him she would have been perfectly comfortable firing a bow without them. Matching Sylvan blades hung from her belt, along with a bulging quiver of arrows.

Keswen paused a moment, lowered her bow, and massaged a crick in her neck. Then, her sun-bronzed limbs blurred. As Rowen watched, Keswen fired faster and faster. Despite the draw weight of the longbow, she drew and fired a continuous stream of arrows in one smooth, steady motion, barely pausing to aim. She fired by placing each arrow on the right side of the bow, rather than the left. *Like the Shao.* He knew from experience that allowed one to fire arrows far more quickly but made aiming at distant targets harder.

Keswen did not seem to be having that problem, though. Halfway through the quiver, she began sidestepping right before she fired—sometimes one step, sometimes several. When just a few arrows remained in her quiver, she changed tactics once again and began nocking and firing two arrows at once. Still, every arrow struck home. Then, on her last shot, one arrow struck a straw dummy in the throat while the other skimmed its shoulder and thudded into the wooden barrier beyond.

Keswen swore. Then she stalked over to the targets and began ripping out arrows. He approached her.

Without turning, she said, "Good evening, Sword Marshal." After retrieving the projectiles, she resumed her former place, armed with so many arrows that she had to carry half a dozen in her draw hand because they would not fit in her quiver. Nevertheless, with lightning speed, she went to work. Before Rowen could count to ten, she had fired all six arrows, placing one in the chest of each target. Then she went to work on her quiver.

"Are you practicing for a war?"

Keswen fired, drew, and fired again. "My people have a saying. Practice—"

"Practice in peace to survive the war," Rowen finished. "I spent some time with the Wyldkin, you know."

Keswen glanced at him, her expression unreadable, then turned her attention back to the targets. After firing three more arrows, she said, "Strange saying, since my people are *never* at peace."

"They are now. That last message from Briel said the Olgrym are quiet."

"That won't last." Keswen paused a moment. Then, instead of one or two, she drew *three* arrows at one time. She fired. One arrow sank into a straw dummy's chest. The other struck its thigh. The third missed and struck the barrier beyond.

Keswen swore again. Then she drew three more arrows and tried a second time. That time, two arrows struck one target in the chest while the third struck the chest of the target next to it.

Rowen held up one hand to block the glare of the setting sun. "Gods, well done!"

Expressionless, Keswen answered with a faint nod then resumed firing one arrow at a time. After a moment, Rowen asked, "Do you think you'll go back to them?"

Keswen was quiet for so long that Rowen wondered if she hadn't heard him. Then she said, "Not my people anymore."

"The other Sylvs went back." *After they handed me their children,* Rowen almost said but stopped himself. "You could, too."

This time, Keswen twisted the bowstring before she fired. That gave the arrow a peculiar corkscrewing motion, though it still stuck in a target's throat. "Is this your way of replacing me?"

"Not just yet."

Rowen wondered if she was joking. Officially, Keswen had been made an ambassador of the Wytchforest—which saved them from having to send for someone else—but the stoic huntress served him mainly as a tracker. The War of the Lotus might have resulted in the deaths of nearly every dragon-worshipper in Cadavash, but those living elsewhere had survived, and many continued to flock to Cadavash. At any given time, dozens camped in the surrounding countryside just so they could get as close as possible to their precious chasm full of dragon bones. Sometimes, they caused trouble. When they did, Keswen's job was to help Rowen and the Knights track them down.

Keswen fired her last arrow and paused a moment to lean on her bow, her strong, lean arms slick with sweat. "Big day tomorrow."

Rowen nodded. "I thought about taking you, but I want you here, helping Igrid, while I'm gone."

For the first time, Keswen smirked. "I don't think the Iron Sister needs my help. But I'll be here if she does." She glanced at him. "Don't worry, Sword Marshal. We'll keep your children safe. And the sword." Before Rowen could answer, Keswen went to retrieve her arrows. As she walked, she turned and nodded behind him.

Rowen turned in the direction she had indicated and saw Thessa, watching from the open doorway of the manse. She darted to duck back inside, but Rowen motioned to her. She paused, leaning first on one foot then the other. Then she sprinted toward him. One of the Knights standing guard closed the door behind her.

Rowen thought she meant to hug him, but she stopped short and crossed her arms.

"I'm mad at you," she said.

"So I see. I don't blame you. I'm pretty reprehensible."

Thessa scowled. "Don't be funny."

"Sorry." Rowen sat down on a nearby bench.

Thessa also sat but turned away from him.

"Is Sariel asleep?"

"She was, then she woke up screaming. She set her bed on fire, but Maddoc put it out. Now she's sleeping again."

"I'm sorry you have to share a room with her. It seemed like a good idea at the time."

"Can I just sleep in the barracks with the Knights?"

"I don't think that's such a good idea."

Thessa turned and gave him a critical look. "I don't care if they swear or smell bad. I used to sleep in a sewer! I killed rats all the time, and sometimes the Dhargots came down to do things to kids, and we had to run."

"I remember." Rowen forced a smile. "The answer's still no." He took Thessa's hand and examined her wrist. "Maddoc did a good job healing this. The scar's almost gone. It doesn't still hurt, does it?"

Thessa pulled away. "No, but it'll hurt if it happens again!"

"It *won't* happen again. Sariel's gotten better with Maddoc around, hasn't she?"

"But Maddoc's leaving tomorrow. With *you!*"

"But the other Shel'ai will still be here. They'll help. And your mother knows—" Too late, he recognized his error, though that time, Thessa did not protest. "Igrid knows what to do. You have to be patient, Thessa. Sariel is... different than we are. Do you understand?"

Thessa crossed her arms again and said nothing. In the distance, the twang of a bowstring and the thud that followed told him Keswen had started practicing again.

Rowen asked, "Do you think Igrid's still mad at me?"

"Yes," Thessa said without turning.

"More or less mad than she was when I left to spend a week in Lyos?" Rowen turned for a moment, watching Keswen as she continued to shred the straw dummies with arrows.

Thessa scoffed. "A *lot* more!"

Rowen whistled. "I better bring her back some flowers."

"Igrid doesn't like flowers! Bring her a sword."

"We have plenty of swords."

"Like that curvy one that sets itself on fire?"

Rowen glanced toward the chasm as a sudden breeze made him shudder. "Yeah, that one. But Igrid can't touch it. Nobody but me can. You shouldn't, either."

Thessa rolled her eyes. "You don't have to keep telling me that. It's locked up, and none of us play down there. It's too dark. Even when one of the Shel'ai kids makes light come out of their hands, I don't like it down there."

"I don't either," Rowen admitted. He touched Thessa's braid then stood and kissed her forehead. "Let's go inside. I want to see if I can make Igrid stop hating me before I go."

He offered Thessa his hand. She stood but did not take it.

"What if Sariel starts crying again?" she asked.

"We'll douse her in water. Do you think that'll help?"

"No," Thessa said but smiled and ran ahead of him.

Crovis Ammerhel watched sunset spill through the boughs of trees and color the garden he viewed as his sanctuary. The others were all either eating or attending evening meditation. As far as he was concerned, they could stay there. He preferred to be alone. Situated just behind the massive, ancient structure that was Saikaido Temple, the garden had an otherworldly quality that he appreciated but could not identify.

His appreciation for the garden came not just from the white, fragrant dogblossom trees that had come to symbolize the Lotus Isles. Nor was it the admittedly beautiful wytchwood trees that, according to legend, had been taken there as saplings from the Wytchforest shortly after the Shattering War and had risen even higher than the temple roof. *It's in the air. This place is sacred, ancient. Fâyu Jinn once stood here. No wonder Aeko loved this place so much.*

Crovis shook his head, chiding himself. The Knights had no proof that Saikaido Temple had actually been home to the legendary Fâyu Jinn. In fact, dozens of temples throughout the Lotus Isles made that same claim, with more or less equal weight. And Masaka Temple, seat of the massive audience chamber where Knights gathered in time of crisis, was still considered the greatest temple on the Isles. But that temple had been built centuries after the Shattering War and half destroyed when Jolym invaded during the War of the Lotus.

No, Saikaido is the true heart of the Knighthood. Somehow, Aeko sensed that.

Kneeling in an empty clearing at the center of the garden, Crovis took a deep breath and let it go. That shared knowledge almost made him regret what he had done. But he knew he'd had no choice. The gods would understand. The Light would forgive.

But will they forgive what I must do next?

Crovis rose. He tightened the belt that bound his loose fighting robes around his waist, brushed his long, dark braid back over his shoulder, and drew his sword. Sundown made the brilliant kingsteel appear bloodstained. Lifting the sword, he began the sha'tala: the graceful but grueling martial dance practiced by the Isle Knights. His feet stepped and twisted as he swirled through the clearing, his adamune flashing in a steely blur.

Near the end of the sha'tala, he paused before an ancient stone pedestal. On the pedestal sat an empty goblet, a pitcher of cool water, and a bowl of grapes. He plucked one of the grapes. Instead of eating it, he closed his eyes and tossed it over his head. Then he twisted about with lightning speed, sword in motion. Then, bowing to an imaginary foe, he sheathed his sword. After a moment, he opened his eyes and regarded the neatly severed halves of the grape, lying at his feet.

"Impressive," a voice said.

Crovis turned, alarmed both that someone had dared interrupt him and that he had not heard the approach. Then he saw the newcomer's ragged attire and forced himself to relax—though it irked him that his guards had grown so lax that a wayward blind man could wander that far into Saikaido Temple. He would have to punish them for that. One or two forced marches up and down the thousand temple steps might be in order.

"I'm afraid this garden is off limits to all but the ordained," Crovis said. "If you're looking for a place to meditate... " He started forward, intending to take the blind man's arm and lead him away.

Before he had covered half of the distance between them, the blind man grinned and tugged away the strip of cloth tied around his eyes. Crovis blinked at the sight of scarred, empty eye sockets but did not slow. Then, eyes of violet flame formed in the sockets.

Crovis drew his sword and swung at the Shel'ai's neck.

The flaming eyes widened—either in surprise or amusement—and the Shel'ai stepped back. One hand waved, and Crovis staggered sideways as though struck by an invisible battering ram. Righting himself, he clenched his teeth and started forward again.

Still grinning, the Shel'ai waved again. A second bolt of force drove Crovis to his knees. He felt his bones shake and his muscles shudder as though he'd just been struck by a hundred fists all at the same time. He grunted but did not cry out. Somehow, he kept a hold of his sword.

The Shel'ai waved a third time, and the sword was wrenched from Crovis's grasp, sailing across the garden and clattering to the ground somewhere beyond the trees.

"Again, impressive," the Shel'ai said. "But if you move, the next thing you feel will be burned flesh dropping off your bones." Violet flames sparked to life, coursing along the Shel'ai's forearms to emphasize his point.

Blinking through his pain, Crovis forced himself to face his attacker. "Who are you?"

"My parents never bothered to name me, but my master calls me Algol." He added, "I can tell both by your expression and by plucking the thoughts from your brain that you know who I am. What puzzles me is why you still haven't called for help."

Crovis forced his thoughts to clear, imagining his mind as an empty, snowy field. "I'll not give you that satisfaction. The sooner you kill me, the sooner you'll send me to the Light." Despite the pain, he forced himself to rise.

Algol appraised him for a moment. "I think I was right about you. Oh, and don't bother hiding your thoughts from me. I've been in your mind before. For example, I know what you did to a she-Knight named Aeko. And I know you're trying to lure Rowen Locke here." His flaming eyes narrowed. "Only it's not to steal Knightswrath. You wanted the sword once but not anymore. Why?"

Crovis tried to keep pace with everything the Shel'ai had just said. He glanced around, half afraid that other Knights or monks might be close enough to overhear. "Magic is an abomination. I was wrong to crave Knightswrath. I have repented that sin and crave it no longer."

"Yet you tried to claw your way into Shigella's resting place. They say it was because you thought there was another sword like Knightswrath entombed within." Algol smirked. "But you and I know better, don't we?"

Crovis stared, speechless.

"I'm not here to kill you." Algol reached into his tattered robe and withdrew a tiny scroll. "This isn't the one I took from the Scrollhouse, but I think you'll find it just as interesting." He sidestepped to the pedestal and tucked the scroll into the bowl of grapes. "Don't worry about replying, Grand Marshal. My master and I already know your answer, even if you don't." He stepped back, into the shadows of the trees, and was gone.

For a long time, Crovis stood, unmoving. By then, the pain had faded from his body, but part of him wondered if what had just happened had only been a dream. He headed in the direction where the Shel'ai had cast his sword. He found it tangled in the undergrowth, gleaming dully. He picked it up and sheathed it. Then, he made his way back to the pedestal and picked up the scroll. For a moment, he considered tearing it up. Instead, he opened it and fixed his gaze on the elegant, forceful script.

"Impossible," he muttered. Still, he kept reading.

Morning light spread across the grassy hills, crawling up the high wooden walls surrounding Cadavash. Rowen blinked. Beyond the open gates, the others waited with the horses. Sang Wei quietly held the reins to Rowen's mare. Sir Berric wore a smile nearly as bright as his armor and seemed to view Maddoc's quiet demeanor as a personal challenge to make him laugh by telling dirty jokes. So far, the cloaked Shel'ai had answered with nothing more than a polite smile.

Igrid touched Rowen's arm. "I'm still mad at you."

"I know." Rowen pulled her close and kissed her forehead then her lips. "I'm sorry about that."

He turned. Thessa stood in the distance, holding Sariel by the hand. Both wore nightgowns and looked half asleep.

Rowen knelt before Sariel first. "I'll miss you, little firebrand. Be good. Don't burn anything while I'm gone. Understand?"

Sariel nodded, yawned, and rubbed her eyes.

Rowen kissed her forehead then turned and faced Thessa. "Do I need to remind you to stay away from the chasm?"

Thessa shook her head.

"Want me to bring you back something from the Isles? Or Lyos?"

"When you get back, you should teach me how to fight."

"Why wait? Ask Igrid. She's as good as I am."

"Lies." Igrid moved closer. "I'm better, and you know it."

Rowen moved to hug Thessa. She backed away, changed her mind, and embraced him, still holding Sariel's hand. Then, she turned and hurried away, dragging Sariel after her.

Igrid said, "She doesn't think you'll come back."

Rowen nodded. He thought of all the child had been through: seeing her parents killed by Dhargots, hiding in the sewers, risking not only starvation but torture and rape—the latter of which both Rowen and Igrid suspected had occurred more than once, though they had not pressed her to talk about it. "Teach her how to fight."

Igrid said, "I will. But I'm starting to think half of Sariel's nightmares are actually Thessa's. I heard her crying last night, right before Sariel started in."

Rowen blinked back unexpected tears. "Could be. If Sariel doesn't know how to control her powers, she might be reading Thessa's thoughts... her dreams... without meaning to. We could try putting them in different rooms."

"I don't think they'd like that." Igrid hugged him again. "I still think you should take Knightswrath."

Rowen let the comment go unanswered. "Be firm with the Knights, but tell a joke once in a while. Most don't have a problem with female commanders, but they'll chafe at taking orders from someone who isn't a Knight."

"You could always Knight me right now." Igrid winked. "Skip the first two Orders and go straight for the Lotus. I'd look good in kingsteel armor."

"You look good in anything." Rowen kissed her forehead then her red curls. "I'm going to stop in Lyos and talk to Jalist. I'll send word when we get there. Could be a week, though."

"Tell the Dwarr he owes me money." Igrid took hold of Rowen's cuirass and adjusted one of the straps. "But I'll forget it if he goes along and watches your back."

"I'll tell him." Rowen hesitated, tempted to embrace her again. Instead, he squeezed her hand. "See you soon." Then he forced himself to turn and walk through the open gates, toward the figures waiting beyond.

CHAPTER THREE

THEY HAD HARDLY RIDDEN OUT of sight of Cadavash when Sir Berric began regaling the group with tales of a prostitute he'd known in Lyos. Rowen could tell the burly Knight was just trying to lift their spirits, probably sensing Rowen's concern for Igrid and the children, but Berric's boisterous voice grated on his nerves. Rowen blocked him out as best he could and tried to enjoy their surroundings instead.

The Simurgh Plains rolled eastward, vanishing into a horizon washed by clear, pale sky. Early spring still reigned, so even the weight of his armor did not bother him. He hoped the world would seem that pleasant a week later, though he doubted it.

At least we're riding east. It could be worse. Less than a day's journey west of Cadavash lay Leander's Field, a dismal place still heaped with bones from the great host of Dwarrs and Queshi that had been burned alive by the Dragonjol. In the chaos afterward, as Rowen worked furiously to assemble another army to hunt down Chorlga, he had had no time to bury the dead. Since then, the bones had bleached in the sun, moldering amidst rusted mail and tattered cloth. Few visited that place, pronouncing it cursed.

"We'll steer clear of the Red Steppes," Rowen said, interrupting Sir Berric's attempts to draw a less-than-enthused Sang Wei into his discussion on proper lovemaking techniques. "I don't think the Sons of Maelmohr will be this far north, but…" He glanced at Maddoc.

The Shel'ai noticed the scrutiny and smiled slightly. "If we could avoid a cadre of strongmen who think my kind are responsible for all the evils in the world—yes, that would suit me fine."

Sir Berric scoffed. "If any of those gray-skinned bastards want to cause trouble, Sang Wei and me'll cut them to ribbons. Right, my friend?" He clapped Sang Wei on the shoulder with such force that the young Knight nearly tumbled from his saddle. Berric glanced at Rowen and added, "Meaning no offense to your friend, Sword Marshal."

Rowen thought of Jalist Hewn, supposedly still serving in Lyos as Captain of the Guard—and probably no more sober or consolable than he'd been the last time Rowen had visited him. "None taken. I doubt Jalist approves of what his people are saying, either. But remember, they've lost even more than we have. Men do crazy things when they're desperate." He glanced at Maddoc. "Not that I'm justifying—"

"No need for that, Sword Marshal." Maddoc laughed. "After that last war, I'm pretty sure there isn't a clan or kingdom in all of Ruun that doesn't have reason to apologize."

"Or a person," Rowen added.

By then, Sir Berric had talked himself into weariness, and the four rode in silence until sundown. Rowen spied a copse of trees in the distance and called a halt. Berric rode on ahead to scout the trees and make sure they were free of bandits. Despite the patrols Rowen sent out on a regular basis, the roads had been choked with highwaymen since the war, and he did not relish the idea of getting attacked in his sleep.

Sir Berric returned, out of breath and scowling. "There was somebody there. A mean-looking sellsword, looked like. But he took off. Want me to ride him down?"

"No, that won't be necessary." Rowen stifled a grin. His Isle Knights tended to have so low an opinion of sellswords that they often forgot Rowen himself used to be one, as had Fâyu Jinn, the legendary founder of their Order. Then again, Rowen had met plenty of sellswords in his day who deserved every inch of the Knights' ire.

I wonder if it was someone I knew from the old days. Rowen glanced down at his kingsteel armor and azure tabard. He imagined people who had last seen him filthy, unwashed, and in mismatched armor—or more likely, no armor at all—seeing him like this. Then, he realized with a

42

sinking feeling that they would probably ask what had ever become of his brother, Kayden.

When they reached the trees, they saw the sellsword had made his camp in a small clearing. He'd kicked dirt on his fire, though a few embers still smoldered beneath a pile of dry wood. All he'd left behind was a chewed-up leaf of sweetbitter, ashes that smelled of *fran-té*, and a shattered pitcher that smelled of wine.

Sang Wei kicked the refuse away then began tending the horses. Rowen tried to stand idle—he'd learned that his men not only expected but preferred that he not bother himself with menial duties—then gave up and went to help Sang Wei. As he did so, he kept an eye on Sir Berric as the big Knight busied himself with the fire.

First, Berric brushed as much dirt as he could from the fire pit. Then, he took the wood the sellsword had left behind and arranged it in what he informed Maddoc was a far superior configuration. Finally, he surrounded it with stones to keep the fire from spreading. He was just drawing out his flint and tinder when Maddoc said, "Allow me," and stretched out one hand.

A tongue of purple flame spurted from his fingertips, striking the wood with such force that one piece shattered and the rest scattered within the circle of stones. Nevertheless, the purple fire washed over everything, igniting it to a searing blaze. A moment later, the purple flames turned yellow orange and died down a bit. Sir Berric stood, staring, flint and tinder forgotten in his hands.

Sang Wei flashed Maddoc a disapproving look. Rowen also looked at Maddoc and noted the faint smile on the Shel'ai's face.

"Apologies if I startled you," Maddoc said to Berric.

Berric's face reddened. "Nice trick. We'll have to keep you handy in case it rains." The burly Knight took off his helmet and used it as a seat, though Rowen noted he chose a spot at the fire opposite from where Maddoc was standing.

Their evening meal consisted of dried rations and warm wine, but after months of eating food far more exotic than he was accustomed to—the result of all the quality provisions they were routinely sent as gifts from other cities throughout Ruun—Rowen did not mind the change. When he was finished eating, Rowen considered devising a watch schedule.

Maddoc said, "No need to set a watch, Sword Marshal. I can cast a spell around the perimeter of the camp that will wake me if anybody approaches."

Rowen half smiled, remembering a night seemingly a lifetime before when Silwren had made the same offer. "Fine," he said, "but don't sleep too deeply. I'd lay even odds that sellsword wanders back to take a look at us."

"I hope he does," Sir Berric said, drawing his sword and laying it in the dirt beside him.

Rowen rolled his eyes but said nothing. He took off his cloak and balled it into a pillow, removed his boots, and placed his weapons within easy reach. Already, he felt himself drifting off to sleep.

Rowen woke to cursing. He sat up, blinking in the early morning light, and scrambled for his weapons. Instead of an entire company of sellswords bearing down on them, he saw only his companions, all on their feet. Sir Berric dashed about, bare chested, swearing vehemently as he swung his sword at empty air. The campfire was just a heap of ashes within a circle of cold, darkened stones. Sang Wei stood statuesque, glowering at Maddoc, who in turn was the color of a ripe tomato.

Rowen looked around. "Maddoc, care to tell me where the horses are?"

Maddoc had to clear his throat before he could answer. "I… I cast the warding spell around the camp, but I didn't include the spot where we'd tied off the horses."

"They might have just wandered off," Sang Wei offered.

Sir Berric stopped cursing long enough to say, "Not likely! I've had that destrier for three years. We're close as brothers. He wouldn't go unless somebody up and *dragged* him off." He cast Maddoc a menacing look.

"The sellsword," Sang Wei said.

Maddoc faced Rowen. He cleared his throat again. "I… I'm sorry, Sword Marshal. I know that's not adequate, but… "

Rowen buckled on his sword belt. He glanced at the western sky, still smeared with the cloudy darkness of night. "Well, we could walk back to

Cadavash and get new horses, but that'll take at least two days." *And I don't particularly want to hear what Igrid will say when she sees me.*

Sir Berric said, "It'll take us at least twice as long to reach the Isles without our horses! To say nothing of all those lost supplies... "

"We still have some." Sang Wei pointed at a few knapsacks positioned by the fire, one of which he'd used as a pillow.

"Not enough." Rowen felt his coin purse. "I have enough to buy a pack horse, but not four palfreys, let alone four warhorses." He added, "Berric, stop swinging that damn blade and sheathe it before you cut your own head off."

Sang Wei placed a hand on Berric's shoulder, trying to calm him. Then he pointed at the ground, where the horses' tracks led eastward. Facing Rowen, he said, "He couldn't have done this long ago. It's a long shot, I know, but if we hurry... "

Rowen nodded his agreement. "Everybody, carry what you can. If we're lucky, the thief will stop to sell the horses at the closest village."

Sir Berric shook his head even as he grabbed two of the four knapsacks and swung them easily over one shoulder, followed by a full wineskin. "No way the villagers'll just *give* us our horses back! We'll either have to buy them or steal them." He added a belated, "Sir."

Rowen grabbed the final knapsack, which left Maddoc the cumbersome duty of carrying a wineskin and four canteens. The look of shame and embarrassment on the Shel'ai's face was so profound that Rowen's rage evaporated.

He squeezed the sorcerer's shoulder then turned eastward. "Let's go."

The next few hours were a blur of exhaustion and irritation. They'd had no time to eat and rested only when absolutely necessary. Soon enough, all four men were drenched in sweat, and even Rowen's kingsteel armor felt as though it had been carved out of lead. He was tempted to hide what remained of their supplies and come back for them later, but the thought of having to backtrack only further soured his mood.

By midafternoon, Rowen realized the horse thief had turned southward, angling toward the very area he'd hoped to avoid. Pausing to catch his breath, he glanced at Maddoc. "If we encounter any Dwarrs..."

Maddoc nodded. Out of breath, he answered by tugging meaningfully on the hood of his cloak. Then, all too soon, they were running again.

Sang Wei raced ahead of the others, seemingly inexhaustible, while Berric brought up the rear. The big Knight's face was slick with perspiration, and he muttered a curse with every other exhalation, but he kept readjusting the two knapsacks he was carrying and waved off all offers of assistance.

Rowen tried to ignore the cramping in his legs. For one wild moment, he considered forcing Maddoc to don Berric's armor, as punishment. Then, they crested a low hill, looked down, and saw their horses. The grubby sellsword who had stolen them was kneeling on the plain, hands on his head.

Surrounding him were at least two dozen Dwarrs, all Sons of Maelmohr on horseback.

Sir Berric stopped to catch his breath, letting the knapsacks slide off his shoulder and land in the grass. Rowen gestured, and the others did likewise. Sang Wei scowled down at the Dwarrs. "Maybe Maddoc should stay here while—"

Before he could finish, one of the Dwarrs shouted and pointed up at them. Half the Dwarrs encircled the sellsword while the rest formed a wide row and galloped up the hill.

Too late. Rowen cast Maddoc a quick glance. The Shel'ai had adopted the mannerisms of a humble priest, bowing his hooded head and folding his hands before him. Sir Berric stepped in front of him, all but obscuring the smaller Shel'ai with his armored bulk.

Rowen resisted the impulse to draw his sword and held up his empty hands instead. He stepped ahead of the others, smiling. He hoped none of the approaching Dwarrs were the same ones that had visited Cadavash earlier.

One rider held up his hand and gestured in two directions. The rest fanned out, encircling Rowen's companions but keeping their distance. Rowen studied the leader, a grizzled-looking Dwarr with close-cropped hair that might have been white had he grown it out. Unlike the others, who looked nervous and appeared either too young or too old for fighting, the leader rode with practiced ease.

The Dwarr reined in his horse so close that Rowen had to back up a step. Then he fixed Rowen with a long, quiet scowl. "Keidu," he said finally.

Guessing that was the leader's name, Rowen bowed. "My name is Rowen Locke."

Keidu's eyes widened. Then, somehow, his scowl deepened. "You're a long way from home, Sword Marshal."

"So are you. May I ask what you're doing this far north?"

"That depends. Can I ask what you're doing this far east?"

"We have business on the Isles," Rowen said.

Keidu's horse drew closer and snapped at him, though Rowen could not tell if Keidu intended that. He drew back another step.

Keidu's expression said he was hoping for more information. He continued to scowl for so long that Rowen wondered if the Dwarr ever blinked. Finally, without looking, the Dwarr gestured down the hill toward the still-kneeling sellsword. "I trust those are *your* horses?"

Rowen nodded. "They were stolen in the night." Thinking quickly, he added, "The fool I left on guard duty decided it was a good time to nod off."

Keidu scoffed. "My people have a particularly dissuasive punishment for that."

"I know. Tying a Knight to the ass-end of a galloping horse isn't quite what I had in mind, though I can see how that would be effective."

For the first time, Keidu smiled faintly. "I forget, they say one of your friends used to be one of us."

Used to be? "Jalist Hewn. He's the Captain of the Guard in Lyos now." Rowen added, "He's a brave man."

"He defied the will of Maelmohr and corrupted our prince. He's lucky the king banished him instead of tearing him to pieces." Keidu leaned forward in the saddle as though watching Rowen for his reaction.

Rowen could tell he was being baited. He bit back an angry retort and stared back, unblinking. "You have my thanks for intercepting our horses, Lord Keidu. I don't have much in the way of coin, but if you like, I'd be happy to—"

"I'm no lord," the Dwarr said. "And keep your money. We're not profiteers, nor thieves, for that matter." He gestured toward the bottom of the hill, and four more Dwarrs rode toward them, each leading one of the stolen horses.

Rowen maintained his smile despite the Dwarrs' suspicious looks.

"Again, you and your men have my thanks." He took the reins of the closest horse. The Dwarrs led the other horses to his companions, who mounted their horses. Rowen did likewise but held his breath as Maddoc climbed into the saddle. Thankfully, the sorcerer's hood remained in place, concealing his tapered ears and violet eyes in shadows.

Rowen faced Keidu. "As for the thief, we can deal with him if you like."

Keidu did not answer but nodded down the hill. There, a Dwarr had already dismounted and unslung his long axe and was standing before the kneeling sellsword, who cried out, pleading. The Dwarr swung. Then his long axe changed direction midair, striking the man's chest instead of his neck. The sellsword toppled, gurgling and writhing in agony, denied a quick death. Another Dwarr drew a knife, stepped forward with deliberate slowness, and finished him.

Rowen turned back to Keidu. "That wasn't necessary."

"And why is that, Knight? Do you think the world is enriched somehow by the presence of another cutthroat?" He glanced over Rowen's shoulder, and his dark eyes widened.

Rowen cursed. A slant of sunlight had broken through the clouds to illuminate the darkness of Maddoc's hood. He turned back to Keidu, easing his hand along his belt, toward his sword hilt.

Keidu scowled at Maddoc then at Rowen. By then, the other Dwarrs had pulled back and were riding down the hill to join the rest. For one moment, Rowen feared Keidu would call them back. But Keidu simply shook his head, spat on the grass, and wheeled his horse about.

"Times are changing, Knight," he called over his shoulder as he rode down the hill. "Best be careful!"

Rowen sat in the saddle for a moment. He watched the Dwarrs ride away then fixed his gaze on the corpse of the sellsword, wondering if they should bury him. Instead, suppressing a shudder, he turned north and flicked the reins.

CHAPTER FOUR

I GRID SAT IN ROWEN'S OFFICE and wondered which she was worse at: administration or motherhood. Since Rowen's departure, the Knights and Shel'ai had set to bickering. Each blamed the other for everything from interloping on the other's scheduled time in the practice yard to, most recently, anonymous and hateful messages scrawled on walls. With Rowen and Sang Wei gone, the most high-ranking Isle-man was a middle-aged Knight of the Stag named Jontin. Igrid had hardly ever spoken with him before, but she knew him as a quiet man with a mild reputation as a lickspittle.

After much debate, Sir Jontin suggested that any disorder he couldn't attribute to the Shel'ai must not be the fault of his Knights, either. Instead, it had probably been the work of a few immature, unruly squires. His advice for dealing with the problem vacillated from simply dismissing all the squires and sending them back to the Lotus Isles, to promoting them all to Knights of the Crane to improve their mood.

The Shel'ai were no better. With Maddoc gone, the rest had set to arguing with each other even more than they argued with the Knights. When they would not tell her the cause, Igrid bribed some of their children with sweets and discovered that the argument went deeper than the old distrust between Human and Shel'ai. Some of the grown Shel'ai wanted to abandon Cadavash and return to Coldhaven, their previous sanctuary on the frigid Wintersea. Still others wanted to abandon the continent of Ruun entirely and make for another Shel'ai sanctuary on an island somewhere to the north.

Enraged, Igrid had marched straight into the separate barracks where the Shel'ai lived, called for their attention, and said, "Locke has a fool's dream of holding this place together. I won't let it fall apart while he's gone!"

But the Shel'ai seemed unmoved by her words. After a lengthy conversation punctuated by moments in which Igrid was sure they were speaking telepathically with each other—probably mocking her—the Shel'ai finally swore not to leave Cadavash before Rowen's return.

Well, at least they aren't talking about bloodshed again, she'd thought. *At least, not yet.*

Back in the office, Igrid seized a goblet and took a long drink of wine. Then, she tried to focus on a mountain of tedious reports on supplies costs, repair schedules, and the various holidays of the Knighthood that required celebration. She also considered word she'd received from Keswen and the scouts that the Sons of Maelmohr were being seen on the Simurgh Plains more and more frequently. Keswen thought they were plying Human villages for potential allies.

Igrid considered Jalist's account of how the Jolym had wiped out much of the kingdom, slaughtering everyone they could. The remaining Dwarrs had banded together, joined with the famous riders of Quesh, and set out for revenge—only to be obliterated by Chorlga's final and most devastating weapon, the Dragonjol. The Dwarrs had been a judgmental people before, driving away men like Jalist simply because they loved other men. Igrid was not surprised they had taken this most recent dark turn—though she suspected this would be something they'd have to deal with, in time.

Maybe they'll try and make friends with the dragon-worshippers and wind up destroying each other!

She shoved the reports aside and considered the other vocation at which she had been faring poorly. Sariel's nightmares had gotten worse. Maddoc had a way with her that even Rowen could not rival. Igrid tried, but though the child often cried for her attention, screaming the Sylvan word for "mother," she would only grow angrier when Igrid tried to comfort her, as though she were doing it wrong. Finally, after a tantrum resulted in a fire that nearly burned down the manse, Igrid was forced to entrust Sariel to the Shel'ai women.

Three days had passed since then. Igrid was relieved at first and slept better, but then she found herself missing the child and coming up with excuses to go and see her. But that caused problems as well, for Sariel always cried when Igrid left.

As for Thessa, she had been consistently cold and distant, as though she blamed Igrid for Rowen's departure. She refused to help with Sariel, as well. But Igrid had finally curried the girl's favor by offering to teach her how to fight. Igrid smiled at the memory of how Thessa's eyes had widened at the offer, and Igrid had to run to keep pace with her as she sprinted toward the practice yard. Still, that had resulted in an additional problem: despite a bloodied nose and bruises that covered the scrawny girl's legs and arms, Thessa always wanted more training and stomped off—hurt and enraged—each time Igrid had to leave.

Igrid finished her wine, considered refilling her glass, then decided to tour Cadavash instead. Though she doubted the Knights respected her even a tenth as much as they respected Rowen, she'd found that letting herself be seen still helped soothe tensions. She stood and headed for the door, grabbing a cloak along the way. Lately, she'd been dressing more conservatively and had taken to wearing a matching pair of kingsteel shortswords called tashi instead of the straight Hesodi shortswords she preferred. She had even tied back her red curls in a tight, simple braid and donned a leather doublet embroidered both with the iconography of the Lotus Isles—a crane, a stag, and a nine-petaled lotus—and the burning hand of the Shel'ai.

She passed the practice yard, where a line of squires was training with wooden swords. She stopped to watch a moment, praised two of the squires for their footwork, and rebuked two others for dropping their guard. Then she remembered Rowen's advice and softened her criticism with a story of how she'd done the same thing once and her commanding officer struck her so hard that she'd been surly ever since. A few men laughed.

As she left the practice yard, Igrid nodded to Keswen, who answered with a curt nod of her own. The Sylvan woman was seated on a bench, quietly polishing her longbow. Two Shel'ai children sat cross-legged at her feet. The children had a ball made of rags and took turns levitating it back and forth. Igrid turned and saw a Shel'ai woman—she could not remember her name—nursing a Shel'ai child in the shadow of the great hall.

A child that's not hers...

Igrid turned, looking for Thessa or Sariel. She saw them playing on the temple steps with some other children. She noticed the children—all Shel'ai—seemed fine with Sariel's presence but tended to look away whenever Thessa spoke. Finally, the orphan girl shrugged and walked away. Sariel left the other Shel'ai and toddled after her.

Igrid considered going to them but decided against it. "Need is the god of invention," she muttered, remembering the old saying.

The more the two had to play together, or the more Thessa had to decide whether or not to confront the other children, the better it might be in the long run. Still, it stung her heart to turn her back and walk toward the chasm.

She strolled along the railing of stone and wood Rowen had ordered constructed to keep any of the children from falling. She glanced into the chasm itself and shuddered. It was a frightful sight, stark and lifeless, even in daylight. She looked away just as a figure stepped out of the shadow of a woodshed and started toward her. Igrid tensed, reaching for her swords, but instantly relaxed.

The woman had the long, tapered ears and violet eyes of a Shel'ai, but instead of a cloak, she wore ornate leather armor emblazoned with the sigil of a dragon clutching a spear in its talons. A pair of shortswords hung at her belt. She had a quiet fierceness about her that reminded Igrid of Keswen. Most striking of all, though, the woman had no hands. Each of her bare arms ended in a ghastly, puckered scar, despite the swords hung on her belt.

Igrid forced herself not to stare at Zeia's ruined wrists and met her fierce gaze instead. "Your hair's even shorter than I remember."

"Easier to keep the lice off."

"You're still in the field, then?"

"Saanji has his father trapped in U'dan. The Red Emperor's forces are outnumbered and half starved, but the walls are too damn high, and the gates might as well be thick as mountains."

"So it's a waiting game?"

Zeia nodded. "But every day, more of the Red Emperor's men desert to our cause. Soon enough, one of his own generals will kill him to curry our favor."

May the world be so lucky. Igrid hesitated. "I wasn't sure you'd come."

"I almost didn't. But Saanji can fend for himself for a while. Considering what's at stake… " Zeia glanced around. "I trust Locke's gone ahead?"

"He left a week ago. Last I heard, he'd reached Lyos. Given how long that message must have taken to get here, he's probably in the Lotus Isles by now."

Zeia's eyes narrowed. Then she turned and faced the chasm. "I trust he took Knightswrath."

"No, it's still down there in the vault."

Zeia faced Igrid with a look so angry that Igrid drew back a step and reached for one of her swords. "And the reason why the most powerful weapon on the continent, perhaps the world, has been left unguarded?"

"It's far from unguarded." Igrid gestured to the chasm. "I have as many men patrolling the wall along the far side of the chasm as there are on this side. As for the vault itself, Rowen had that secret stairwell blocked off. There's only one way in now, and two Knights and a Shel'ai guard it day and night. We change shifts at dawn and noon. You just missed them."

"And the key?"

"The guards have one. Rowen left me the other. I wear the damn thing like it's a gift from the gods." Igrid tugged the little silver key out of her bodice to show her, dangling on its gold chain. "Besides, nobody but Rowen can even draw the sword without turning into a plume of smoke."

"But anybody can carry it so long as they don't try to draw it."

"Maybe," Igrid conceded. "Maybe not. Truth is, we've never really tested that. But it doesn't matter. People here know what that sword represents, what it can do. They'd die before they let somebody carry it off."

Zeia relaxed a little. "He still should have taken it with him."

"You don't have to convince me. But he said he wanted to keep it away from Ammerhel."

"But Ammerhel can't use it."

"He could still use it as a symbol to gain more power." Igrid shrugged.

"Really, I think he just wanted to keep it from whoever attacked Matua." She turned around.

By then, other Knights, squires, and Shel'ai had stopped what they were doing and were looking in their direction. Some pointed.

"You should have announced yourself at the gates," Igrid said.

"Wanted to see if I could sneak in."

"Which you did," Igrid said with grudging admiration. "The Knights won't be happy about that."

"Let them fume. Truth is, you need better guards. Knights are fine in the field, but if you want to keep out Shel'ai, you need to use Shel'ai of your own."

"I didn't know we were at war with the Shel'ai again."

"At least one. Whoever burned Matua and stole the scroll."

"Any idea who that is?"

Zeia shook her head. "No one I can think of. Most of us died in the war. There might be some I've never met or heard of, but I don't know any who—" Zeia stopped as a fly buzzed past and landed on her cheek. She raised one wrist on instinct to brush the fly away as though she'd forgotten she had no hands. A bright plume of violet flame unfurled from Zeia's scarred wrist in the blink of an eye and formed a palm and five ghostly fingers. The fly vanished in a tiny wisp of smoke. Just as quickly, Zeia's flaming hand disappeared.

Igrid blinked at the awesome sight then tapped the symbol of the burning hand emblazoned on Igrid's armor, interwoven with the iconography of the Lotus Isles and the Iron Sisters. Then she pointed at Zeia's leather cuirass, which bore the new sigil of Prince Saanji and his Earless. "Why is it that I'm wearing your symbol and you aren't?"

Zeia's eyes narrowed again. "Not *my* symbol. The other Shel'ai... " She shook her head. "I'm not their leader, and I don't want to be."

"Is that why you ran off with Prince Saanji?"

For the first time, the faintest of smiles touched Zeia's lips. "Not exactly." Her face turned stern again. "I'll sleep here tonight and head for the Isles in the morning." She paused. "I'm tempted to take Knightswrath with me."

Igrid was about to say that was impossible when she remembered that during the final days of the War of the Lotus, Rowen had lost the sword in the sewers under Hesod, and Zeia had gone to retrieve it, trusting that her burning hands would allow her to carry the sword without suffering its fiery defense. She'd never had the opportunity to test that, though.

"I have half a mind to let you," Igrid said, "but Rowen would kill me. Besides, we don't know if your new hands would even let you use it."

"I wouldn't *use* it. I wouldn't *wear* it, either. I'd wrap the damn thing in a cloak and hide it away until I could put it back in Rowen's hands and call him a fool for leaving it behind."

Igrid smirked. "Tempting, but no."

Instead of arguing, Zeia simply nodded. "At least send more guards down there. There could always be a way into the chasm that we don't know about." Zeia looked around and swore under her breath. "This place is too big, too open. If a Shel'ai wanted to steal the sword—"

"He'd get himself killed," Igrid finished. "You sneaking through the gates is one thing. Someone getting all the way down to the vault and back out again is something else. Besides, even if a Shel'ai stole the sword, using it would kill him."

"I know." Zeia waved her wrist stump. "I'm tired of talking. It's been a long journey, and I've hardly even started. Let me sleep, then I'll chase after the Knight at dawn."

Igrid pointed. "The barracks the Shel'ai use are over there. Or I'll give you a room in our house—"

"I'll sleep in the temple. There's a quiet room in back. I'd appreciate it if you'd keep the Shel'ai from mobbing me with questions."

Igrid smirked again. "I'll do my best."

"Somebody kill me," Rowen muttered as the sound of trumpets pierced the air.

He had hardly stepped off the boat and onto the island of Saikaido, in the shadow of the huge and familiar temple, but already a great crowd barred his path. Smartly armored Knights arrayed themselves in two long columns and used their gleaming polearms to form an archway straight from the boat to the thousand steps leading up to the temple. Beyond them, crowds cheered and minstrels played.

Sang Wei said, "Begging your pardon, Sword Marshal, but all these people—"

"Are in my damn way," Rowen interrupted. "I knew we should have gone straight to New Atheion." He eyed the archway of drawn swords. "Imagine how disappointed they're going to be when I walk right by them."

Maddoc cleared his throat. "Perhaps we could stop for a moment—"

"It takes more than a moment to climb a thousand stairs. Trust me, I did it every morning for four years." Rowen looked around and frowned. "I don't see Aeko."

"Maybe she's waiting for us at New Atheion," Maddoc offered.

"Maybe." Rowen glanced over his shoulder. "Sir Berric, take the horses and the supplies to that stable over there. Wait for us. Stay sober if you can manage it."

Upon hearing that he would not be required to ascend the thousand steps to Saikaido Temple, Sir Berric spoke his thanks, only to be drowned out by another blare of trumpets. Rowen spotted a Knight on horseback riding toward them. White-haired and haughty, the man wore the armor of a Knight of the Lotus, polished almost to the point of being blinding.

Rowen bit back a rush of revulsion and forced himself to smile. "Well met, Sir Kai."

Wyn Kai bowed from the saddle. Without dismounting, he waved. Another Knight of the Lotus rode forward, dismounted, and offered Rowen the reins. "And you, Sword Marshal. Welcome back to the Isles. We heard you left Lyos but had no time to prepare a parading befitting your rank." Though the Knight spoke kindly, his eyes were dagger thin and glanced often at Rowen's belt.

No, I don't have Knightswrath. Aloud, Rowen said, "Thank you, Sir Kai, but parades are unnecessary. My companions and I have urgent business in New Atheion. I'm afraid we cannot delay. But I was hoping to find Aeko Shingawa here."

Wyn Kai nodded noncommittally. "The Grand Marshal is in the temple. He requests a word with you." He touched his sword hilt then turned his horse toward the archway of gleaming polearms. "If you will follow me…"

Rowen frowned. He realized he was being invited to *ride* up the thousand steps: something that, as a squire, he'd been taught was crass and expressly forbidden. He took the reins but did not mount the horse.

Glancing over his shoulder, he told Sang Wei and Maddoc to go with Sir Berric. Both looked as though they were about to protest, but Rowen turned away and mounted the horse.

"Sir Kai, forgive me for repeating myself, but where is Aeko Shingawa?"

Without answering, Wyn Kai rode ahead of him. Cursing, Rowen followed. As he rode beneath the archway of polearms, he resisted the impulse to glance at the other Knights' faces with the hopes of deducing whether or not they were about to kill him. Meanwhile, the cheering continued. Out of the corner of his eye, he saw Sang Wei and the others making for the town, all of them ignored by the crowds. He felt a pang of envy for them then wondered how the people would react when they saw Maddoc.

Officially, Shel'ai were welcome on the Lotus Isles, but Rowen was not foolish enough to think that sentiment was shared by everyone. After all, not long before, the Lotus Isles had been nearly annihilated by Jolym. Though those undead men of steel had been wrought and sent not by Shel'ai but by the Dragonkin, Chorlga, Rowen doubted everyone on the Lotus Isles grasped that distinction. *Watch yourselves*, he thought then urged his horse closer to Wyn Kai.

By then, they'd reached the thousand steps and started up. The steps were low and close enough that the horses climbed without much trouble, but Rowen winced when Wyn Kai's horse shat upon the steps. His escort took no notice, though, and Rowen felt sympathy for whichever Knight following them had to clean up the mess. Rowen waited until the noise of the crowds fell away, then he asked about Aeko Shingawa again.

That time, Wyn Kai answered without facing him. "You will have to ask the Grand Marshal about that."

Rowen reined in so sharply that his horse reared up, lost her step, and for a few fearful seconds, struggled to regain her footing. Rowen waited until Wyn Kai reined in and glanced back. "I beg your pardon, Sir Kai, but your Sword Marshal asked a question—asked the same damn question three times—and would appreciate an answer."

Wyn Kai raised one eyebrow, unfazed. "I beg your pardon, Sir Locke, but I am acting under the direct orders of the *Grand* Marshal. I have given you the only answer that I can." He faced Rowen, unblinking, as though wrought of stone.

Gods, what's happening here? "I remind you, Sir Kai, that Aeko Shingawa is a Knight of the Lotus, as we are. She deserves our respect. If I find that she has been mishandled in any way—"

"Lady Shingawa has not been mistreated… at least, not by us." Wyn Kai sighed, then urged his horse closer. He lowered his voice. "Lady Shingawa is missing. She disappeared shortly after sending you that message. Beyond that, I know nothing. But I have committed no offense against her, nor am I aware of any offense committed against her by anyone else, including the Grand Marshal. I swear this on the Light."

Rowen hesitated. He wondered if Crovis had learned what ghastly information was contained in the scroll that had been stolen and if Aeko had fled the Isles before he could seek revenge. That seemed possible, but if so, he would have expected her to ride to Cadavash or at least meet him in Lyos.

Unless Wyn Kai is lying… Rowen considered that notion for a moment then dismissed it. Wyn Kai was Crovis's man—everyone knew that—but he was still a Knight. Even in such cases, some vows could still be trusted.

"Proceed," he said finally.

CHAPTER FIVE

KEIDU REALIZED WITH DULL HORROR that he'd grown accustomed to the smell of bodies. He shook his head, trying to remember what Tarator had been like before the Jolym came. He hardly remembered. He found it hard to believe that only a few years had passed since he'd been reclining in the great mead halls near King Fedwyr, surrounded by laughter, lost in the smells of fires and spiced stew and perfumed serving girls.

All that was gone.

Every time he tried to remember, his thoughts turned instead to slaughter. He saw again how the Jolym had swept into Tarator from all sides, huge and metallic but impossibly quiet, nearly invulnerable. He thought again of how arrows and axes had simply slid off their bodies, how the mighty Housecarls fell before the Jolym's merciless blades, how even those thrusts that found the chinks in their armor struck nothing but hollow air.

A young warrior approached him at a run. Keidu turned, grateful for the distraction. "Yes, Haydn?"

The young warrior's eyes widened. "General, I didn't know you'd come back! I thought you were still out on patrol."

"Not much to patrol. Besides, I was called back." Keidu chafed at his new title. A year before, he'd been just another fighter. But at present, veterans were in short supply.

Haydn nodded. "I didn't even know you were back until he sent me to find you!"

"All right, Haydn. Take a deep breath. I'll go see what he wants." Keidu turned his back on the massive pit where other Dwarrs were still burying the bones of corpses that had been decomposing in the previously abandoned ruins of Tarator for years.

Haydn followed. "Do you think it's time?" His dark eyes shone with excitement.

"I don't know, lad. Maybe you could ask him."

Haydn stopped in his tracks. "I... I don't think so, General. I'm just a soldier. I shouldn't even be using his name unless—"

"Maelmohr's beard, lad, he's just a priest! He's not even a king, and he's certainly not a god."

Haydn said nothing, but disapproval shone in his expression. Keidu shook his head and kept walking. *These young warriors talk about the Scion as if he's some kind of god! Of course, it doesn't hurt that he has "god" in his name.*

Keidu passed the barracks then the stables—both empty—and edged around a gigantic statue that had fallen in the street and still not been removed. He reminded himself not to look at the remains of the crushed bodies still trapped beneath the stone. His gaze fell on the gates of Tarator, which lay closed and barred in the distance. The original gates had been centuries old and wrought of solid oak, covered end to end in detailed carvings of ancient battles, beautiful maidens, and handsome Dwarrish heroes.

The Jolym had smashed those. The new gates had the look of freshly cut wood, stout but undecorated. He spotted the Scion on the battlements over the gates, speaking with a small cluster of disciples. As he ascended the steps toward the battlements, Keidu felt as though he were heading into battle. He chided himself, wondering why he always felt that way when he approached his ruler, given that the Scion had shown him nothing but kindness.

Keidu slowed his pace, giving the Scion time to finish his conversation, as well as giving himself time to calm down. He stood behind the disciples and waited. He turned sideways so that they would have room to pass when the Scion's sermon had ended. Haydn did likewise. But while Keidu folded his hands and looked at his feet, he noted that Haydn stared at the Scion and listened, enraptured.

Keidu could not blame him. He had to admit the Scion was an impressive figure. While most of the survivors were gaunt and dirty, the Scion was built more like a Housecarl, with legs like tree trunks and biceps even thicker than Keidu's. The Scion was tall, too—a full head taller than most Dwarrs, tall as a Human. No one ever saw him eat or train, but he looked nothing like any priest Keidu had ever seen. In fact, he had the look of a man who spent half his time in the mess hall and the other half in the tilting yards, swinging doubly heavy training axes.

The only sign of his age was a streak of white in his long and otherwise dark hair, which he kept tied back with the help of a bone clip shaped like the fiery hand of Maelmohr. He wore the red garb of a cleric of that order but without sleeves, let alone a cloak. And unlike any other cleric Keidu had ever known, he carried a sword.

But not just any sword…

Keidu tried his best not to eye the familiar broadsword hanging from the Scion's belt, with its quillons shaped like flaming hands set with tiny rubies, rising to grip the extra-wide blade. When the other survivors suggested giving the Scion the sword of the late king, Keidu had not voiced any objections. After all, the Scion had been responsible for forcing the Dwarrish survivors to finally overcome their superstition and return to Tarator and bury the dead. Still, it bothered him to see Forgefang worn by anyone but the king himself.

"We live in strange and trying times," the Scion said to his followers. Despite his menacing physique, he spoke with astonishing gentleness. Each hand rested on the shoulder of a disciple. "For years, most of us lived in the wild, like animals. We have returned to find our homeland choked with death. There is no one here, myself included, who has not lost loved ones."

Tears stung Keidu's eyes. Images of his wife and children, his brothers and sisters and cousins, came unbidden to his mind. He squelched them like an insect beneath his boot, pressing his hands so tightly that his fingernails dug into his flesh.

"We have woken from a nightmare," the Scion continued. His gaunt disciples nodded, many of them streaming tears. "We must wash that nightmare from our bodies, just as we must wash it from our streets, our houses, our hallowed halls. Only then will we be strong enough to remake this world as the gods would have it." He stretched out his arms, palms open. "Be at peace, my brothers and sisters. Remember... first, we weep. Then, we rage."

His disciples bowed. A few shuffled away, giddy smiles on their faces. A few paused long enough to kiss the Scion's hands. When they were gone, the Scion stepped forward and squeezed Keidu's shoulder. The general winced.

"I heard you arrived an hour ago. Forgive me for making you wait. The need for comfort runs deep."

Keidu said, "As does the need for shovels, Father."

Haydn tensed, but the Scion nodded with a sad smile. "Well said. Idle sermons are less important than giving our dead a proper burial. Again, I ask your forgiveness."

Keidu noted that when the Scion bowed, they were almost the same height. "No need for apologies, Father Gaulgodd."

He fumbled as he said the name. It still stuck in his throat. Technically, the priest's new name simply meant "weeping rage" in an ancient, Dwarrish dialect, but Keidu suspected that was not a coincidence. After all, the Scion had chosen the name himself.

"Haydn said you wanted to speak with me," Keidu said.

Gaulgodd smiled. "So I did." He nodded toward Haydn. "Would you excuse us, young warrior?"

"Of course, Father." Haydn hesitated then fell to one knee and kissed the Scion's hand before hurrying off.

"I wish they wouldn't do that," Gaulgodd whispered when he was gone. "I was born on the floor of a kitchen in a tiny village in the Red Steppes. Even *this* is more than I deserve." He touched Forgefang's pommel of brass-banded oak. "Give me a plain staff and a simple shrine any day."

Keidu marveled that he'd just learned more about the Scion's past in that simple exchange than most had learned in an entire year. "Agreed... Father," he said, fumbling his words.

Gaulgodd placed one strong hand on Keidu's shoulder and left it there. "Walk with me, General."

Keidu resisted the urge to pull away. "Of course, Father."

"I saw the report you sent back. You met the Sword Marshal on the road and let him pass."

Keidu tensed. "I did, Father."

"I trust that when you did so, you were not aware of how he mistreated young Haydn at Cadavash."

"No, Father, I was not." Keidu opened his mouth to say more but stopped himself.

Gaulgodd turned with surprising quickness, blocking Keidu's path so abruptly that he barely stopped himself from colliding with the priest. Gaulgodd removed his hand from Keidu's shoulder and folded his hands in front of him. "Speak," he said. "Please, General. I value your honesty."

Keidu blushed. "Forgive me, Father, but the only mistreatment Haydn got was a verbal thrashing. Besides, you can't threaten someone then be surprised when they respond in kind."

"Then you agree with Locke's words?"

"Not at all. They just don't surprise me. Besides, this isn't the first time we've sent such sentiments. Locke wants supplies, not sermons. As ghastly as things are for us, our larders are still full. And Governor Rachus *did* make a promise to—"

"Governor Rachus died of fever. So did his replacement. I don't pretend to know the will of the gods, but it seems that Maelmohr has chosen me not only to help rebuild our ravaged kingdom, but also to avenge the fallen." Gaulgodd's voice took on a hard edge. "The sinners at Cadavash are *not* our allies. My predecessors were wrong to treat them as such. Our attempts to turn Sir Locke and his minions from their unholy ways are already more than they deserve. If it's Maelmohr's will, they will humbly accept our help... lest we turn to more drastic means of conversion."

Keidu hesitated. He had heard such sentiments voiced many times over the past few months but never so openly. "Begging your pardon, Father, but Stillhammer has been retaken. We're rebuilding Tarator and burying the dead. The demons that ravaged our kingdom have been destroyed." *By Sir Locke and his minions, no less!*

Gaulgodd looked down at Keidu, his gaze darkening. "My son, I am not referring to Chorlga or the Jolym or the Dragonjol. They may have ravaged our kingdom, but they are but symptoms of a larger disease."

Keidu's memory flashed back to the snowy field west of Cadavash, where the skeletal Dragonjol had descended from the sky, sweeping over Prince Leander's army over and over again, exhaling fat gouts of wytchfire that turned men and horses into screaming candlewicks. He pushed the cleric's hand off his shoulder. "You forget yourself, Father. I know something about these matters."

Gaulgodd blinked. "You are the last of King Fedwyr's Housecarls and the only one who survived the Dragonjol's attack. I cannot imagine the horrors you witnessed. I should not have spoken so callously. But it's precisely because of your experience that I speak to you so openly. I need you, Keidu. No one understands better than you the abomination that is magic. No one understands better than you do why it must be erased."

Keidu forced himself to meet Gaulgodd's fierce gaze. He held it as long as he could then looked away. "I'm no friend to magic, Father. But we have no army. Two-thirds of our people are women and crying infants. This is no time for a war, let alone a far-flung crusade."

Gaulgodd nodded. "On this, we agree. I am not proposing a crusade. As you said, we are not strong enough yet. Instead, I am simply considering an alliance."

Keidu frowned. "What alliance? The Queshi and the Noshans are scattered. We're out of friends."

Gaulgodd smiled. "True believers are *never* without friends, General." He placed his hand on Keidu's shoulder. "Much happened while you were gone. Come, let us talk. I have much to tell you."

The summit of Saikaido Hill rose quiet and serene, in stark contrast to the cheering, jostling crowds below. Though Rowen saw Knights, squires, and clerics milling in front of the temple, almost no one spoke. Many turned and bowed at his approach—some smiling, some not—but the only sound was the afternoon breeze rustling the branches of surrounding dogblossom trees, punctuated by the steely *clip-clop* of hooves on stone.

Rowen dismounted, patted his exhausted horse's neck, and passed the reins to an approaching squire. He turned to find Wyn Kai. To his surprise, the Knight of the Lotus had started on without him and was already halfway up the final few stairs leading into the temple. Rowen followed, passing twin columns of fierce statues depicting Fâyu Jinn and his first champions. Like the steps, the statues were carved from polished marble.

The temple itself was a humbler structure, though, wrought of bamboo that had been painted brown and burgundy. The roof, with red tiles and curved eaves extending far beyond the walls, lent an air of quiet elegance. Large but plain rectangular buildings served as adjoining barracks, stables, and smithy, beyond which he caught sight of tilting yards and small ponds surrounded by trees.

Rowen's pulse quickened. Though it felt a lifetime since he'd last seen this place, he realized with amazement that it had been less than five years. He half smiled, remembering how he'd left Saikaido Temple in disgrace: a failed squire slipping out in the middle of the night, hoping to escape unseen. Now, he was returning as a Sword Marshal and the second most powerful Knight of the Lotus in the whole Order.

Gods, how did that happen?

He glanced about and wondered how many pairs of eyes were watching him, probably more interested in Knightswrath, hoping to catch a glimpse of the famous sword of Fâyu Jinn. He considered the possibility that the only factor that made him noteworthy was the very thing he'd left behind.

Rowen passed through the open gates of Saikaido Temple, nodded to the bowing guards on either side, and he half-feared Crovis's men might attack him from the shadows before his eyes could adjust. A moment later, though, he saw that the vast, open chamber before him was nearly deserted. A few Knights sat reading, or kneeling in meditation, but most of the ornamental stone benches sat empty.

Rowen quickened his pace to catch up with Wyn Kai, who was already halfway through the great hall. They passed through another open doorway, down a long hallway, and up a narrow, winding staircase. Wyn Kai said nothing, as though he'd forgotten Rowen were following. At the top of the staircase, they passed down another hallway—that one lined with statues and lit braziers—and stopped at the last of a series of closed doors. Instead of sentries, two empty suits of ancient-looking armor stood vigil beside the door.

Wyn Kai knocked twice on the closed door, paused, then knocked again. Without waiting for an answer, he opened the door, entered, and immediately closed it behind him. Left standing in the hallway, Rowen scowled and touched his sword hilt. He wondered if he shouldn't have pressed for his companions to be allowed to accompany him, though he doubted he had anything to fear. Crovis Ammerhel might detest him, but the Grand Marshal still had a spark of something resembling honor. He would not knife a fellow Knight, if only to avoid risking the ire of all those who still viewed Rowen as a hero.

Nevertheless, Rowen glanced around to make sure nobody was about to spring from the shadows, and he loosened his sword in its scabbard. A moment later, the door opened again. Wyn Kai bowed, as though greeting him for the first time, and ushered him in.

The office of the Grand Marshal—which had once been Aeko's office—was dimly lit, crowded with tables and bookshelves. Weapons hung on the walls—not just the curved weapons of the Lotus Isles but others that Rowen guessed were trophies from vanquished enemies. So many suits of armor stood on display that Rowen wondered if half weren't actually assassins waiting for him to lower his guard.

The Grand Marshal himself sat at an ornate wooden chair behind a great desk covered in books and maps. The Grand Marshal wore simple meditation robes, accentuated by fine golden bracers around his wrists. He stood at Rowen's approach. Though he smiled, his eyes remained dagger thin. He made no move to circle around and shake Rowen's hand.

Rowen fell to one knee. "Greetings, Grand Marshal. I honor you." He bowed his head, almost touching the floor, then straightened. He waited for Crovis to bow in return. Crovis was still for a moment then offered a curt nod. Rowen stood.

"Indeed, you honor all of us," Crovis said, his voice so soft that Rowen had to strain to hear it. "I have not seen you since you attended Lady Shingawa's promotion at Masaka Temple last spring. I'd hoped to see you sooner. Tell me, how was your journey?"

"Mostly uneventful," Rowen said. "We did meet some Sons of Maelmohr on the Red Steppes, though. They didn't cause trouble, but the way they looked at my friend…"

"Ah, yes. The Shel'ai." Crovis smiled despite his narrowed gaze. "The Dwarrs seem to be choosing a different path lately. Their new leader, this so-called Scion, has made some surprisingly lucid arguments. There are even some on the Isles who agree with him."

Rowen tensed. "I did not realize things had gotten that far."

"Perhaps you would have realized that had you attended more councils."

Rowen forced himself to bow again, though not as deeply as before. "Apologies, Grand Marshal. Matters at Cadavash have demanded my full attention."

"Not a wife, though. From what I hear, you have not yet formally bound yourself to that Iron Sister I met some time ago."

Rowen blinked, caught off guard. "I was not referring to Lady Igrid. But in answer to that, we just haven't gotten around to it. But we *are* married, in all ways but ceremony."

With a cold smile, Crovis sat back down. Wyn Kai circled around the desk and quietly stood at Crovis's elbow, statue still. Empty chairs sat in front of Crovis's desk, but the Grand Marshal did not gesture for Rowen to sit. Rowen remained standing.

"Ceremony is important," Crovis said at last. "Some Knights may not agree, but the Codex Viticus teaches otherwise."

"I beg your pardon, Grand Marshal, but I don't think you brought me here to discuss my romantic relationships."

Crovis scowled then glanced back at Wyn Kai. "You have not been summoned. It was my understanding that *you* were coming here to visit *me*."

Rowen hesitated, realizing he'd spoken too sternly. "Sir, if anything has been misunderstood, the fault is mine. I intended no insult. I simply meant to visit Father Matua in New Atheion and see how he is recovering from his injuries."

"Ah." Crovis sat back in his chair, folding his hands before him. "Puzzling business, that. A sorcerer—one we've not had any previous dealings with—tricks his way into the Scrollhouse, burns the good cleric within an inch of his life, and steals... something. A scroll, I'm told, but no one seems able to tell me what it contains."

"I could not say, sir," Rowen lied. "I know little of such matters. But Matua is an old friend of mine. I'm sure he would be happy to answer—"

"I questioned the priest as he lay in his bed, writhing in pain," Crovis said. "I spoke with him again... *after* I learned that Lady Shingawa had gone to see him. Both times, the cleric feigned ignorance. But Lady Shingawa insisted on sending word to you. Now, she has vanished."

Rowen felt an awful tension creeping down his arm to his sword hand. "Sir, perhaps you could tell me where Lady Shingawa has gone, and—"

"I have no idea where she's gone. She abandoned her post without leave and disappeared over a week ago. I've sent men to search for her. They've been to Lyos, Phaegos, and every one of the Isles. They cannot find her. I am torn between concern and annoyance. As I said, she left her post without first obtaining my permission."

"Sir, Aeko is a dedicated Knight of the Lotus. I'm sure she wouldn't—"

Crovis waved his hand. "I'm not questioning her loyalty to the Order. I suspect that in some misguided way, she genuinely believes she's doing the right thing. She and I have had our differences, you know, but this goes beyond that." He leaned forward. "Allow me to speak frankly, Sir Locke. Based on what I've seen, I suspect that she and you are colluding with the clerics of New Atheion, and perhaps the Shel'ai, to supplant me as Grand Marshal."

With great effort, Rowen resisted the impulse to draw his sword. "You are mistaken, sir. I have no interest in your office. Neither does Aeko." *If I did, I could have taken it after the war.*

"Then you are prepared to divulge whatever dirty little secret you've been keeping?"

"There *is* no secret, Grand Marshal. I'm not a bookkeeper. I have no idea what scroll was stolen, nor can I imagine any that would be worthy of this kind of response."

Crovis settled back in his chair. He rested his hands on his chest and pressed his fingertips together. "You're lying. That's forbidden, you know."

Rowen bowed. "Forgive me, Grand Marshal. It seems I've displeased you. That was not my intention. With your leave, I'll be gone from here." He stepped back.

Crovis stood. "I have *not* given you my leave, Sir Locke."

Rowen glanced from Crovis to Wyn Kai. The latter stood expressionless, though Rowen noted that he had moved one hand onto his sword hilt.

"I didn't come here to fight," Rowen said. "I came to see my wounded friend and, if I can, help track down his assailant. That is all."

Crovis nodded. "Very well. You do not need to go to New Atheion for that. Father Matua is here, at Saikaido."

"Father Matua is *here*?"

"Here, in the temple. Sir Kai will take you to him. I did not wish to move him, as injured as he was, but I feared for his safety At least here, he can be protected." Crovis snapped his fingers, and Wyn Kai started forward. The white-haired Knight cast Rowen a cold look and passed him, heading for the door. But Rowen did not follow. Instead, he stepped forward and leaned toward Crovis, seething.

"Something tells me removing their High Father when he was near death did little to win New Atheion's favor."

"Probably not," Crovis answered lightly, "but New Atheion is not an independent city-state anymore. It's a protectorate of the Lotus Isles. So long as we are acting in their best interest, we will do as we like." He waved past him, at Wyn Kai. "Take him to see the cleric, then let him rejoin his friends." He faced Rowen again. "You may stay in the town, of course, but you are *not* welcome back in this temple, nor will you see the cleric without my permission. Is that understood?"

Rowen hesitated. Then, he nodded. "Understood, Grand Marshal." Instead of giving the final, traditional bow before departure, he backed out of the office.

Wyn Kai said nothing but led Rowen down the hallway to another closed door. He knocked. The door swung open almost at once, and Wyn Kai led Rowen inside.

The room was dim and smelled of death. Two Knights of the Lotus stood at attention, each holding a polearm that nearly brushed the ceiling. Amazingly, the room had no windows. Rowen had to cover his mouth to keep from gagging. When his eyes adjusted to the darkness, he discerned that the room contained nothing but a bed, two chairs, and a table. On the bed lay a corpse.

At least, he looks like a corpse, Rowen thought ruefully.

Father Matua lay uncovered, half naked. His body appeared gaunt and shrunken. One arm was already gone—lost to the Nightmare—and the surrounding tissue was wrinkled and scarred, as was half the cleric's face. Rowen thought of his own burn, suffered in his final battle against

Chorlga, and touched his left arm. Then he shook his head and knelt beside the cleric.

The cleric's eyes were closed, and he was sleeping so soundly that Rowen checked his breathing then his bandages. Matua's remaining arm was covered in gauze, through which blood and pus had seeped. Bandages had been wrapped around his chest, too, though those were clean. Rowen frowned. He doubted the Knights would have changed only half of the cleric's dressings and figured Matua's back had been injured, as well. He stood and faced Wyn Kai.

"He should be lying on his side. There should be half a dozen clerics tending him. And at the risk of stating the obvious, he should be in a godsdamned room with windows!"

Wyn Kai answered coolly, "This is the safest room in the temple. It's an honor that he's been placed here, so close that his screaming often keeps the Grand Marshal awake."

Rowen resisted the impulse to strike the man and faced the other two Knights of the Lotus, neither of which he recognized. "Have his wounds been cleaned, at least?"

One of the Knights nodded stiffly. "He's been given herbs for the pain, as well. A healer checks on him three times a day. No one enters without the Grand Marshal's approval. I assure you the cleric is safe here."

Rowen wondered if that was supposed to please him. He knelt beside Matua again. "I want to talk to him alone. All of you, get out."

Wyn Kai cleared his throat. "With respect, your request is declined."

"It wasn't a request."

"I don't care." Wyn Kai drew a dagger and stepped forward.

Rowen reached for his sword, but Wyn Kai held up his hand. "I'm not challenging you, Sir Locke. I just need to show you something. Grand Marshal's orders." He knelt at the opposite side of the bed. "Help me turn him over."

Rowen hesitated then joined him. He winced when the cleric moaned with pain. The smell of urine and feces filled Rowen's nostrils. The cleric did not wake, though, and Rowen wondered just how deeply he had been drugged. Then, his gaze fell on Father Matua's back.

"Gods…"

The bandages were soaked in red and yellow. The sheets smelled of rotten flesh. Now that Matua was lying on his stomach, Wyn Kai leaned in and, with two deft strokes, sliced off the cleric's bandages. He peeled them open. Then, saying nothing, he glared at Rowen as though bidding him to look.

For a moment, Rowen saw nothing but burned, ruined flesh. Gradually, he discerned a pattern in Matua's wound. With a cold chill, he realized that something—a word—had been painstakingly seared into Matua's flesh. Then, he realized what it was.

"Igrid…" He leapt up and started for the door.

Wyn Kai grabbed his arm. "There is no need for that, Sir Locke. We'll dispatch a raven. It'll arrive far sooner than you."

Rowen pulled free but stayed where he was. He closed his eyes for a moment, fighting to control his temper. When he opened his eyes, he faced the two Knights guarding the cleric. "I want his bandages changed. I'll return within the hour with a Shel'ai who can use magic to clean his wounds properly. If either of you have a problem with that, I suggest you go somewhere else." He faced Wyn Kai. "Either the Grand Marshal can grant permission for me to bring a Shel'ai into the temple, or I'm taking the cleric out of here by force. Decide now."

Wyn Kai smiled faintly, as though daring Rowen to try. "No need for threats, Sir Locke. As the Grand Marshal already stated, you are not welcome to return to this temple once you've left. However, since the High Father has already contaminated himself with magic, you may send in your sorcerer to tend him. I will personally guarantee his safety. When he's finished, the sorcerer must leave." He added, "The cleric stays."

Rowen nodded. "And I'm sure there's a good reason why you didn't let me bring Maddoc with me right away. Every second lost raises the chances that the High Father will die."

As though in response, Matua whimpered.

Wyn Kai did not answer.

Rowen swore. "Take me to your birder. I need to get a message to Cadavash as fast as feathers will carry it."

Wyn Kai nodded and stepped out into the hallway. Rowen started to follow then glanced back. The other two Knights had quietly gone to the bed and started to change Matua's bandages. As Rowen watched, one produced a wet cloth and gently traced it over Igrid's name.

Rowen shuddered. Then, he hurried out.

CHAPTER SIX

I GRID WOKE TO POUNDING ON her bedroom door. Instinctively, she rolled out of bed and crouched on the floor, snatching her dagger from under her pillow as she moved. Her other hand reached under the bed and grasped a sword. Then she stood and backed up until she was against the far wall—certain, at least, that she would not be stabbed in the back.

The room was still dark. Igrid took a deep breath and braced for battle. She realized the bedroom door was still closed. Someone knocked again. Cursing, she returned to the bed, tucked one blade under her arm, and touched the luminstone on the nightstand. A soft blue glow flooded the room as she headed for the door. She unlocked it and threw it open.

A young Knight of the Crane stood in the hallway. He blinked at the sight of her. "Begging your pardon, Lady Igrid. I'm sorry to wake you, but—"

"Is it Sariel?" Igrid inhaled, checking the air, but she did not smell smoke.

"No, Lady Igrid. A night patrol just came back. They said they spotted some dragon – worshippers on the plains, heading this way. About twenty of them."

Igrid raised one eyebrow. "You woke me up for *that*?"

Thessa appeared in the hallway behind the Knight, dressed in her nightgown. She covered her mouth and giggled. Then she pointed. Igrid followed her gesture and, for the first time, realized she was naked. She resisted the impulse to close the door in the blushing Knight's face.

Instead, she touched the Knight's chin and directed his gaze from her bosom to her eyes.

"Are they armed?"

The Knight blushed even further. "M'lady?"

"The dragon-worshippers, damn you. Are they armed?"

"Just knives and staves, looks like. But the way they're wailing—"

"Dragon-worshippers *always* wail." Igrid rubbed her eyes. "All right, I trust the gates are already closed and sealed?" When the Knight nodded, she said, "May as well wake the garrison, though they're probably awake already. I want a dozen Knights in full battle dress by the time I meet you out front." She started to close the door but then added, "And find me a Shel'ai. A grown one. Any will do. A little wytchfire might scare off those fey bastards without the need for bloodshed."

The Knight bowed and hurried off, seeming to walk strangely.

Igrid turned to Thessa, who was still standing in the hallway. "As for you, sewer rat, get back to bed or no practice tomorrow." She winked.

Thessa raced back to her bedroom.

Igrid closed the door, tossed her weapons on the bed, and dressed herself. Over her underclothes, she donned her leather doublet, boots, tight gloves, and a long fighting skirt made from strips of studded leather. Then she went to the weapons chest in the corner of the room, withdrew the matching kingsteel shortswords, and girded them. She was halfway toward the door when she stopped, glanced at Rowen's half of the bed, and muttered, "And here I finally got to sleep after hours of missing your godsdamned snoring." She rushed out of the room.

All the Knights in Cadavash seemed to have massed in the courtyard, along with an equal number of squires, except for a handful stationed along the walls. All turned at once to face Igrid. Drawn steel gleamed in the torchlight, mingling with the smell of smoke and sweat. She nodded at them.

Sir Jontin approached her at a brisk walk, joined at his elbow by the young Knight of the Crane who had awakened her. The latter was still blushing.

Gods, why does the sight of a naked woman always turn men into monsters or little boys?

"Bone-worshippers, m'lady," Jontin said. "I count twenty-three. They're outside the walls now, demanding entrance."

Igrid glanced at the large assembly of armed Knights and squires. "Pretty sure we have enough swords to rebuff a siege."

"No need for swordplay, m'lady. We can shred all twenty-three with arrows the moment they try to scale the walls. None will reach the top. I swear it." Sir Jontin's response told her that he had missed the joke.

"They've offered to pay," protested the Knight of the Crane, whose name Igrid could not remember.

Sir Jontin scoffed. "By the look of 'em, Sir Issa, I don't think they have two copper coins to rub together."

Keswen melted out of the shadows, a Sylvan longbow in hand. She leaned on the bow and said, "Nor would it matter if they did. Locke has declared that dragon cultists aren't welcome here anymore."

Sir Issa cleared his throat. He glanced at the Sylvan woman but directed his rebuttal at Igrid. "Cadavash was their most holy place for centuries. If they've only come to worship—"

Igrid asked, "Have you ever actually seen a dragon-worshipper before?"

The young Knight of the Crane blinked at the question. "No, m'lady."

"Well, I can promise you that they didn't come here to pray and burn incense. They might not attack us if we let them in, but I'm not keen on watching a bunch of wailing madmen slash themselves bloody."

"Agreed," Sir Jontin said quickly. "Shall we drive them off?"

Yes, Igrid was about to say, but she saw Thessa watching them through an arrow slit that served as a window. The orphan's eyes were wide. Igrid suspected she could hear them through the walls, because it took her a few seconds to duck down and hide after she realized Igrid was staring back at her.

Igrid glanced at Sir Jontin. "Are there any children with them?"

"Four or five little ones, I think, plus a baby."

Igrid swore. Already, she immediately regretted asking.

"Sir Locke's orders are clear," Keswen said in a low voice, as though guessing her intentions. "This is a stronghold, not an orphanage."

"That, from a man who takes in orphans the way old priests adopt stray kittens."

The Knights winced, and she realized that, as far as they were concerned, even her relationship with their commander did not give her leave to mock him.

"Fine, let's try scaring them off. Where's my Shel'ai?"

Sir Issa blushed again. "I went to the Shel'ai barracks, but none would come. They said this was a matter best left to steel and arrows."

"No, this is a matter best left to whatever gets it done the quickest," Igrid snapped. "My bet's on wytchfire… especially since most of these fey bastards worship magic." She glanced past the restless crowd of Knights, at the Shel'ai barracks in the distance. The structure's windows blazed with lantern light. She imagined the various Shel'ai watching her—either with their eyes or their minds—and snickering.

She was about to march up to the barracks herself when someone said, "No need to fume, Iron Sister. I'm here if you need me."

Igrid turned. Zeia emerged from the shadows, exchanged curt nods with Keswen, and came to stand before her. The Shel'ai wore a plain cloak. Knights drew away at the sight of her, though Igrid could not be sure whether they were more unnerved by the fact that she was a Shel'ai or that she had no hands.

Igrid glanced at Zeia's maimed wrists. "How can I say this delicately… ?"

"You're addressing a woman who survived a life of battle and torture, only to have her hands chopped off by a rapist sellsword." Zeia smirked. "I'm not sure phrasing is something you need to be concerned with."

Igrid fought back a smile. "I need a Shel'ai who can hurtle wytchfire. I know you surpass the rest of the Shel'ai in other areas, but the ability to flay minds might not be useful when these dragon-worshippers are already insane."

"Just open the gates. I'll take care of the rest." Zeia started toward the gates without waiting for a response then stopped and glanced back. "What do you want me to do about the children?"

Igrid scowled. "That depends what you're going to do to the adults. I told you, I don't want a bloodbath here."

"You won't have one." Zeia turned back to the gates and resumed walking.

With a sigh, Igrid waved for the Knights to open the gates. Then she hurried forward, drawing one of her swords. A chorus of steel and leather told her the others had followed suit.

"Sir Jontin, keep the men back unless I say otherwise," she called over her shoulder. She followed after Zeia but stopped a few yards behind her.

By then, the gates of Cadavash had been pushed open. Knights pulled back, weapons drawn. Zeia stood out in the open, calm and unmoving. Igrid looked past her and saw a cluster of wretched people—some of them naked, all of them half starved. Some carried crude staffs or had ceremonial knives stuck in their belts, but none looked especially intimidating. Then her gaze fell on the dark eyes and swollen belly of a little boy, being prodded along by parents whose own eyes widened to the point of insanity.

Gods, these people...

The ragtag band of dragon-worshippers started forward. One or two had already begun to wail when Zeia stopped them. She raised lean, bare arms, showing them her wrist-stumps. In a bright flash of wytchfire, hands of flame blossomed from the stumps. The dragon-worshippers froze in their tracks. Some backed up. Others fell to their knees.

"A wonder the sorcerers never recruited *these* crazy bastards for their army," Jontin muttered.

"Would *you* want these people armed and marching behind you?" Keswen countered. The Wyldkin woman came forward and stood beside Igrid, longbow in hand, two arrows resting on the string. Meanwhile, Zeia addressed the dragon-worshippers in a low, lethal voice that echoed through the air with such crispness that Igrid wondered if Zeia were using magic to enhance it.

"As you can see, I am a Shel'ai, descended from those who drank the life from dragons." She paused, and Igrid wondered if Zeia's statement would cause the worshippers to view her as an enemy. But they merely stared, wide-eyed. "Cadavash is no longer yours. As the gods turned us away, I now turn *you* away... but not empty-handed."

One burning hand reached into her cloak and withdrew something. Igrid thought for a moment that it was a weapon. Then, telltale red streaks told her it was a length of dragonbone, probably from a wing, about the length of a child's arm. Zeia held the bone aloft. Wytchfire spread from one burning hand, engulfing the bone for a moment then retreating.

The dragon-worshippers gasped in amazement. Those not already doing so fell to their knees. Several wept. An infant screamed, either hungry or terrified.

Zeia said, "This bone came from the corpse of Godsbane, the greatest of all dragons, who sleeps even now in the darkest depths of Cadavash. I give it to you, so that you may pray for his resurrection."

The dragon-worshippers gasped in awe. Zeia's arm bent back, as though she meant to throw them the dragonbone, but then stopped.

"But first," she said, "you must prove yourselves worthy. In return for this sacrifice, we demand your children."

One woman grasped her daughter—dirty, naked, barely old enough to walk—and shoved her forward. A moment later, the parents of the dark-eyed boy did likewise. Then a man came forward with a squalling infant, unwrapped it from its blanket, and laid it unceremoniously on the dark grass. He stepped back.

Igrid felt tears stinging her eyes. One by one, without the slightest sign of hesitation, the dragon-worshippers abandoned their children. For their own part, some of the children appeared frightened, but most simply looked blank and confused.

Zeia watched, stonelike. When the last child was huddled in front of her with the others, she threw the dragonbone high over the worshippers' heads, end over end, far out into the night. As one, the bone-worshippers wailed, turned, and raced after it. Watching, Igrid could not decide whether to laugh or cry. Meanwhile, Zeia gestured for the children to go inside the stronghold. They obeyed. Igrid and Keswen hurried out to help her, herding them along. When everyone was inside, Igrid gestured, and the gates slammed shut.

Zeia paused beside her, her flaming hands having vanished. In sharp contrast to the fierceness she'd shown a moment before, Zeia appeared exhausted.

Igrid said, "I thought Godsbane's bones were still on display in Hesod."

Zeia shrugged. "How should I know where they are?"

"Still, you went down into Cadavash."

"I wanted to check on the vault."

"You should have told me."

"Didn't know I needed to."

"Why did you bring back a dragonbone?"

"I wanted to make a weapon out of it. Something that won't smolder when I touch it. Guess I'll have to get another."

"Don't bother. I'll get one for you."

Zeia glanced at Cadavash's newest orphans. Igrid followed her gaze. Something about the mindless way they stood there reminded her of Jolym. The dark-eyed boy had picked up the infant but held her in a wooden, loveless manner, and the infant continued screaming and kicking. Igrid shuddered.

Zeia said, "If I were you, I'd search them for weapons," and walked away.

What have I done? Igrid faced Keswen. "All right, we'll take this a step at a time. Give them baths, food, clean clothes…"

Keswen raised one eyebrow as she tucked her arrows back into the quiver at her side. "I'm not a nursemaid, Iron Sister. Do it yourself." She walked away before Igrid could stop her.

Igrid glanced back at the manse, then she waved Sir Issa over. "Go get Thessa. Tell her I need her out here right away. You'll find her watching us through one of the arrow slits."

When the Knight of the Crane was gone, Igrid turned to the rest of the Knights and squires, many of whom still milled about, watching the dirty orphans with bemusement. "Sir Jontin, in the morning, I'll want to send a message to the king of Lyos, asking for supplies and clerics to help teach these wretches how to read. For now, pick four squires with kind faces and arm them with towels and soap. You, too. It seems we're going to play at being nursemaids for the next few hours."

Sir Jontin's grin vanished. He paled, opened his mouth as though he might protest, then nodded. "Yes, m'lady. Of course." He started to leave, but Igrid grabbed his arm.

"Have someone prepare food and baths, too. And tell one of the Shel'ai midwives that she's needed whether she likes it or not. But first… help me check them for weapons."

Algol stood on the dark plains and watched the dragon-worshippers fighting like dogs over a single span of dragonbone. When they moved, he followed, unseen. The fight drew them farther and farther away from the walls of the stronghold until its watch fires were just a faint orange sheen on the horizon. And still they fought.

Algol was tempted to laugh at their primal foolishness, but the revulsion he felt prevented him from doing so. As he watched, a young man—relatively strong, compared to the rest—managed to wrest the bone from the hands of the half-starved woman who had seized it last. He beat her with it. The others wept and prayed, though Algol could not tell exactly what they were praying for.

After a moment, raising the dragonbone like a scepter, the young man started to chant. He shifted his weight from side to side in strange ecstasy—a foul ecstasy made all the more apparent by his lack of clothing. He held out his hand, and someone passed him a ceremonial dagger. As the young man chanted, wide-eyed, he traced the blade over his bare chest over and over again. Blood ran past his waist and legs in dark rivulets. The others' prayers became louder, punctuated by occasional outbursts of exaggerated, theatrical sobbing.

Then, one of the dragon-worshippers drew away from the rest. An old man with arms and legs no thicker than those of a child, he appeared at first to be abandoning the others. However, the old man turned back, circled around, picked up a rock, and drove it into the back of the young man's skull. The old man struck the younger man three more times and took the dragonbone for himself.

The chanting and sobbing continued, unperturbed.

That time, Algol laughed. He stepped forward, throwing back his hood. No one acknowledged his presence. Then, he tugged the strip of cloth from his eye sockets. He allowed eyes of wytchfire to blaze to life, and the dragon-worshippers cried out.

The old man, still clutching the dragonbone, asked, "Are you Fohl's son?"

"Near enough." Algol cast a scalding wash of wytchfire from his hands.

Dawn was creeping into the stronghold by the time the last child had been washed, dressed, fed, and given a place to sleep. Not one protested or seemed the slightest bit perturbed to be tended by strange hands. Igrid wondered what horrors the children had suffered in the past.

"When will you give us to the Dragongod?" the dark-eyed boy had asked, pushing away the steaming bowl of porridge that Thessa kept offering him.

Igrid said, "Never."

The boy's eyes welled with tears. "You *must* give us to the Dragongod! You have to!"

"To Fohl's hells with your Dragongod," Igrid snapped.

She was just leaving when Thessa screamed a warning. Igrid whirled back—in time to see Sir Jontin vaulting over a washtub filled with filthy water. The Knight tackled the boy a moment before he would have plunged a knife into Igrid's back.

Recovering from her shock, Igrid stepped on the knife, pinning it to the ground as Sir Jontin grabbed the boy's wrists. Several squires rushed to help, but as soon as the boy was tackled and the knife wrested from his hands, he went slack. He closed his eyes, but his lips moved as though in feverish prayer. When Sir Jontin tried to pull him to his feet, the boy sank back down into a crouching position and rocked himself.

Igrid faced Sir Jontin. "I'm grateful."

The white-haired Knight shook his head. "Don't be. That's *my* knife he's holding." Jontin blushed and slid the knife back into the empty scabbard at his belt.

Afterward, Igrid had the boy taken down into the chasm and placed in one of the empty cells located there. The way the boy's eyes had widened, as though he were being taken to see the gods, filled her with pity and revulsion. The other children had not attempted any violence, all of them having fallen asleep almost as soon as they were given a place to lie down.

As for the infant, Igrid had finally convinced one of the Shel'ai midwives to care for her, but only after pointing out that, like the Shel'ai themselves, the infant had been cast aside. The infant had calmed somewhat, though Igrid still heard it crying sometimes from the other end of the stronghold, occasionally touching off a chain reaction that caused all the Shel'ai children to cry as well.

I bet Sariel's one of them.

Igrid's throat felt dry. She wished she had some wine. Instead, she walked back into the manse with Thessa. The sun continued to rise, driving the shadows from the courtyard. Thessa yawned and rubbed her eyes. On a sudden impulse, Igrid pulled her close and kissed her sweaty forehead.

"Thank you."

Thessa wriggled out of Igrid's grasp, stepped away, then stepped back. "I didn't think I had a choice."

"You didn't. We usually don't. Still, thank you." Igrid gently shoved the orphan girl on ahead. Hearing a sound, she turned to see Zeia walking toward her. "Come to help us tend the orphans?"

"We have to talk," Zeia whispered.

Something in Zeia's expression made Igrid refrain from further biting comments.

"Then talk." Igrid yawned. "If I fall asleep while you're talking, write down what I miss."

"I don't think you'll be sleeping any time soon, Iron Sister." Zeia lowered her voice still further. "There's a Shel'ai close by."

Igrid started to reach for her swords before she remembered that she'd taken them off. "I don't suppose you mean the ones sleeping in the barracks."

Zeia shook her head. "I sensed him after the dragonpriests left. It was faint, though. I thought I might be mistaken. But I felt it again a while after. Someone was using magic out on the plains." She added, "Someone who didn't bother hiding his presence."

Igrid rubbed her eyes again. "Gods, pretend I don't know a tenth as much about magic as Rowen does, because I probably don't."

"A Shel'ai can hide his presence if he wants to," Zeia said. "It's hard, but you can do it. Unless you're trying to hide from someone more powerful, that is."

"Do you think that's the case here?"

"No, I think whoever it was just got careless." Zeia glanced at the gates of the stronghold as though she could see through them. "Send someone out to search the plains, just over the hill, and you'll find a pile of charred bodies. I'm sure of it."

Igrid glanced at the chasm instead. "I'd rather check on the vault."

81

"I just came from there. The guards are alive and well. I warned them to be careful."

"So you think this Shel'ai sent the dragon-worshippers?"

Igrid considered this. "No, there would be no need. If he wants something, putting us on our guard is the last thing he'd want to do. I think he just happened to be nearby when the dragon-worshippers appeared... and for whatever reason, he killed them."

"A Shel'ai with a temper. How lovely."

Zeia said, "There are only two reasons for him to be here: Knightswrath and Namundvar's Well. But the Well doesn't seem to work anymore, thanks to Chorlga. So it *must* be Knightswrath."

Igrid glanced at the distant barracks of the Shel'ai and wondered if any of the other sorcerers had felt the presence of one of their own. She doubted it. The sorcerers might not regard her as a friend, but withholding that kind of information was another matter entirely. *Then again, maybe they're just not as powerful as Zeia. Gods know she's had reason to refine her skills.*

Igrid resisted the impulse to eye Zeia's wrist stumps and looked the Shel'ai in the eye instead. "I'll send a few more guards down there."

"I'd rather you station half the garrison down there," Zeia said, "and half the Shel'ai, too."

Igrid snickered. "You act like you just sensed Chorlga out there. Powerful or no, it's still just one Shel'ai."

Zeia said, "I'm staying down in the chasm until Locke comes back. Send word if you need me." She stalked off, her matching swords riding her hips.

Igrid watched her go. Then she turned back to the manse. A tired Knight stood on either side of the door. Both straightened at her approach. Igrid passed them then found Thessa standing inside the doorway, a kitchen knife in her hand. "Put that down before you scratch me."

"Are we in trouble?" Thessa asked worriedly.

Of course. "Not a bit." Igrid mussed Thessa's hair. "Just more talk of nonsense. Trust me, sewer rat, no one can trouble us in here."

CHAPTER SEVEN

"**I** THINK HE'LL LIVE," MADDOC SAID, "but it might be days before he can talk. The infection must have spread after they moved him. I can't imagine the pain he's suffered. I could have spared him a lot of it if I'd gotten to him sooner."

Rowen nodded wearily, staring into his full cup of ale. "I know. But the Grand Marshal had to make a show of not letting you into the temple too easily."

"I'm not talking about the Grand Marshal."

Rowen glanced up, faintly smiling. "I know. You want to know why Aeko didn't tell us everything… about his injuries. About Igrid. I know. I don't know why she didn't, either."

Sang Wei, the final occupant of their small table, cleared his throat. Though the tavern was crowded, he spoke in a low voice. "Sir Berric won't reach Cadavash for at least a week, but—"

"But the message may reach her as soon as tomorrow," Rowen finished. "That doesn't make me feel better about sitting here." After forcing himself to take a sip, he set his cup down.

Maddoc and Sang Wei exchanged looks.

Maddoc said, "I think what the young Knight means is that perhaps you shouldn't have sent away one of the only three bodyguards you had."

Rowen glanced around the tavern, whose name he could not recall, at the other patrons. Most were townspeople, plus a handful of Knights and squires. Though Rowen and Sang Wei had left their armor in their rooms and dressed in simple traveling clothes, and though Maddoc had drawn the hood of his cloak, they had still been recognized. The inn's patrons had greeted him with cheers, however, and might have given them no peace had not Maddoc in particular, as well as Sang Wei, cast them so many scowls that Rowen was left alone. Maddoc was still the recipient of the occasional mistrustful look, but Rowen sensed no malice.

Sang Wei suggested, "I could send word to Lyos. Perhaps Captain Jalist could—"

"Sober up long enough to read it?" Rowen immediately regretted saying it. "We couldn't have won the war without Jalist. But he lost more than any of us. Now, what's left of his people are spiraling into madness. Let him stay drunk if that's what he wants. He's earned it." He sighed. "And anyway, I don't need bodyguards. If Crovis wanted me dead, I'd be dead already."

"Maybe not." Maddoc said more, but a chorus of shouts and laughter from across the common room drowned him out. He leaned forward and repeated himself. "Could be he wants something. Could be he was thrown off by you not bringing Knightswrath. Either way, I wouldn't be so quick to trust the Grand Marshal."

Rowen took another sip of ale. "Maddoc, if I were any slower to trust the Grand Marshal, I'd die of old age before I let him open a door for me."

Maddoc snickered, but Sang Wei scowled in obvious disapproval. "Begging your pardon, sir, but this is still the Grand Marshal we're talking about."

Rowen set his cup down and pushed it away, along with an uneaten bowl of stew. "Whoever attacked Father Matua wanted to get me here as quickly as possible. That must be why he seared Igrid's name into his body. And maybe that's precisely why Aeko didn't tell me. She didn't want me rushing into a trap. Yet, here I am." He scratched the stubble on his chin. "Igrid's in a stronghold full of loyal Knights and Shel'ai. She's probably safer than we are. What's important right now is finding Aeko. If she's missing, if she ran, then she might know something that could help us."

Maddoc said, "But the Shel'ai who took the scroll—"

"Could be anywhere, any*one*," Rowen finished. "Whoever he is, the scroll is useless to him without Knightswrath. And Knightswrath is useless without me."

Maddoc considered that for a moment then nodded. "I do not think she could be in New Atheion, or Crovis would have found her."

"Do you think Crovis has her?"

"Even for my kind, it's hard to read minds. Zeia can do it fairly easily now, but she's better than I am." Maddoc smiled sheepishly. "I tried to find the Grand Marshal with my mind while I was tending the cleric, read his thoughts, see if he was hiding anything… but I failed." He added quickly, "I was able to read the thoughts of some of the other Knights in the temple, though. None knew anything about Lady Sh_ngawa. Still, if she's locked away somewhere on the Isles…"

"Find her," Rowen said. "Her or…" He swallowed hard. "Her body."

For a long time, no one spoke. Then Sang Wei cleared his throat again. "Forgive my curiosity, Sword Marshal, but—"

"You'd like to know what in the hells we're talking about." Rowen snickered. He glanced at Maddoc. "I'm impressed that you never told him."

"You made me swear not to discuss it with anyone."

"And if I had a cránaf for every vow I've broken… I'm sorry, Maddoc. I was right to trust you." Rowen turned to Sang Wei. "Are you sure you want to know? Besides myself and Maddoc, only four other people know this… and one is missing while another is lying in bed, writhing in agony."

Sang Wei blinked. Then he nodded.

Rowen glanced about to make sure none of the tavern's patrons were close enough to eavesdrop. Nevertheless, he lowered his voice so that Sang Wei had to lean forward to hear him. "We found the scroll after the War of the Lotus… That is, Matua found it when they were rebuilding the Scrollhouse. It was hidden in the wall of a secret room. Silwren took me there once." He stopped himself, shrugging off the memory of the platinum-haired wytch. "We don't know if Chorlga knew about the scroll, but we don't think Fadarah did. I'm sure El'rash'lin didn't. And I doubt Silwren did, either."

Rowen realized he was stalling. Even though he did not feel right drinking when he was consumed with worry over Igrid, he grabbed his cup of ale anyway. "The scroll says what's in Shigella's Tomb. But more than that, it contains… instructions. The kind you wouldn't ever want falling into the wrong hands… which appears to be what's happened now."

Rowen took a drink, set the cup down, and pushed it away. Sang Wei leaned forward, more urgent than ever, but still, Rowen hesitated. He glanced at Maddoc.

Gods, should I tell him? Does he really want to know?

He turned back to Sang Wei, took a deep breath, and let it go. Then, he said it. "The scroll tells how to demolish the one and only thing that keeps the Dragonkin from returning to Ruun." He paused. "It tells how to bring down the Dragonward."

For a long time, Algol sat cross-legged on a hill, deep in meditation. His new scepter of dragonbone lay on the grass before him, still smelling faintly of charred meat. But in his mind, Algol was beyond the hill, beyond the stronghold's wooden walls, flitting like a cloud of vapor through the home of his enemies.

He ghosted through the courtyard, carefully avoiding the barracks where Shel'ai slept. He felt their collective slumber like a sailor feeling the ocean beneath his raft. The vessel rocked but did not tip. Satisfied that none of the Shel'ai had sensed him, Algol moved on. He found a second barracks, but that one was filled with Humans, whose thoughts roiled with dreams of lust and conquest.

Beyond the two barracks, he found what must once have been the home of a powerful dragonpriest. His spirit flitted past the dozing guards, through walls and doors, over the body of a sleeping Human girl. He sensed that she was having nightmares. She woke, crying softly, and went to the room of a Human woman with striking red hair and a beautiful body left uncovered. The crying girl woke her. The woman pulled on a nightgown and went to comfort her.

Even in spirit form, Algol felt his passions roused by the sight of the woman. He realized who it must be and lingered a moment, drinking in the sight of her. Then, he saw a small silver key around her neck, hanging by a gold chain. While the key could have been to anything, something told him it was vitally important.

Knightswrath, perhaps? Maybe the Knight left it behind!

He drifted out of the manse, toward the chasm. It appeared to him a great, deliberate wound in the earth. He sensed more Humans down inside, dozing in the depths... and something else.

He did not think locating the sword would be that easy. Nor could he imagine that he was sensing Namundvar's Well since that ancient portal had no more life than the stone that shaped it. Dimly, he realized that what he was sensing was not a thing, but a person.

Another Shel'ai... attempting divination, as I am! Algol considered fleeing before he was discovered. Instead, he threw himself at his opponent. His spirit clawed the other.

His opponent recoiled, hurt and surprised, then fought back. As they grappled, Algol learned more about whom he was fighting. He sensed his opponent was female, and her memories tangled with his in a blur of strange, frightful images. Once, she had been no stronger than any other Shel'ai but had trained and pushed herself until her abilities far surpassed those of the others in the stronghold. She was like him, broken in some way.

For a long time, they fought. Algol thought she might defeat him or it would end in a stalemate, at best. Then, she buckled.

With great delight, Algol pinned her spirit beneath his then savaged her so badly that she had to surrender and leave the ethereal plane entirely, returning to her body—wherever that was. Exhilarated, Algol lingered in the chasm for another moment, drinking in his victory, then did likewise. But he had hardly reentered his body, like water poured into a cup, when he doubled over.

He coughed into his hand and saw blood. An awful sensation filled him—half exhaustion, half panic. He straightened his legs, tried to stand, and fell. His breath came in labored gasps. Exhaustion turned to stabbing pain then a frightful, dulling numbness.

Too far... I went too far...

Algol realized he was about to die. Desperate, he roused all the magic left within him, willing himself to be healed. Left with nothing to spare, he had to forsake even the small, constant expenditure of magic that granted him vision. The world blurred then went black. Panic returned.

"No," he said, choking on his own blood. "No, I won't die here. I *know* when I will die and how. And this is not it." Despite his weakness, he forced himself to stand. He turned until he felt the sun warming his hollow eye sockets. "I will die when I choose," he told the gods, the world.

Panic fell away. The numbness ebbed. Gradually, Algol felt his strength return. Still, he did not dare risk expending enough magic to restore his vision. He knelt, stumbled, and groped about the grass until he found his scepter. Then, using it as a cane, he stumbled blindly down the hill.

He remembered a cave, not far from there—a deep, dark place where he could sleep.

CHAPTER EIGHT

"**H**OLD IT HIGHER. THAT'S SUPPOSED to be a sword, not a stick!"

Sunlight gilded the lawn of the practice yard. True to her word, Igrid had taken Thessa there and continued their lessons. The child learned quickly, though Igrid could tell she was self-conscious sparring with so many Knights and squires watching. Then, Thessa caught sight of some of the Shel'ai children watching as well and threw herself at Igrid with renewed ferocity.

"Don't swing blindly," Igrid cautioned. She easily parried each of Thessa's swings but, for the child's sake, chose not to smack her across the backside with her wooden sword—something Igrid had done in the past each time Thessa forgot her lessons. Igrid even allowed Thessa to score a strike, which brought a bright grin to the orphan's face, before shoving her back. "Easy," she warned, smiling.

But Thessa glanced back at the Shel'ai barracks, saw she was still being observed, and launched herself at Igrid. That time, Igrid sidestepped, allowed Thessa to overextend, and pushed her off balance. Children laughed in the distance.

Igrid saw the look on Thessa's face as she rose and almost apologized. "Forget who's watching," she said instead. "Fighting isn't about looking good. It's about being smart enough to kill your opponent before they can kill you."

"Then why do you dress like that?" Thessa shot back.

Igrid glanced down at her own attire then barely looked up in time to parry a frantic stab at her chest. "Clever girl," she said with a grudging smirk then feigned a fast lunge of her own. When Thessa moved to block, wide-eyed, Igrid stepped in and swept Thessa's legs out from under her.

Thessa pushed herself back onto her feet, fuming.

"Distracting your enemy is one thing," Igrid countered. "Distracting yourself is something else." She noted a trickle of blood running from Thessa's elbow, though the child did not seem to have noticed.

"How do you distract different people?"

Igrid frowned. "You mean, like men? I've found looking pretty works on most, unless they prefer parts no woman is born with." She glanced around, noting for the first time that more Knights and squires were milling in the practice yard than usual.

"That's not what I mean!" Instead of saying more, Thessa glanced back at the Shel'ai children still snickering at her, raised her hand, and made a rude gesture.

Igrid stifled a laugh, stepped forward, and pushed Thessa's hand down. "Don't do that. You're the daughter of a Sword Marshal."

Thessa cast her a scathing look. "No, I'm not!"

"Sure you are. We took you in. We *want* you here. You said *you* wanted to be here. What do *you* think you are?"

Thessa thought for a moment. "A servant. Like, a servant you care about."

"Because we ask you to help with Sariel?"

"You should see her more. Every time I visit her, she keeps saying *moshi*. They told me that word means—"

"I know what it means. I'll see her later. I promise." Igrid hesitated. "Enough for today. Let's get you inside and clean up your elbow."

Thessa glanced down. Her eyes widened, then she smiled. "I didn't even feel it!"

"That's what happens when you're fighting," Igrid said. "I once saw a woman get her whole arm cut off and not notice until after she'd killed the Dhargot who did it to her."

"Really?"

"No, not really." Igrid plucked the wooden sword from Thessa's grasp and prodded her toward the manse. "Is that who you were talking about before? The Dhargots?"

Igrid had one hand on Thessa's shoulder and felt the child go rigid.

"They can't hurt you here," Igrid said, lowering her voice. "The ones who hurt you, they're all dead. Saanji killed them."

"But Saanji's a Dhargot, too!"

"But not like the others. He's our friend. He and his men don't… hurt children like that. We couldn't have won the war without them."

"Then who am I supposed to kill?"

Igrid resisted the temptation to pull the girl to a stop. Instead, she waited until they were inside the manse then gently but firmly turned her around. "You don't have to kill anyone. That's my point. The war's over."

"But what if I *want* to kill someone?"

Igrid was speechless for a moment. She remembered passages from the Codex Lotius, which she'd heard Rowen and the other Knights reciting, which cautioned against killing for pleasure. She was tempted to quote these to Thessa. Instead, she said, "I know the feeling. I do, child. But I've killed plenty of bad men, and the feeling doesn't go away. Better to get it in your head that you'll only fight if and when you have to, like to protect someone else that you love."

Thessa's expression indicated she was not listening. "Can I go? You said I had to go check on those weird new orphans today."

"So I did." Igrid sighed. "Go, sewer rat. And thank you."

Instead of running back outside, Thessa raced down to her room and slammed the door.

"Gods," Igrid muttered.

She tossed the wooden swords onto the floor. A moment later, a servant appeared as though from nowhere and scooped them up. Another came and offered her a towel and a cup of water. Igrid waved them off and went back outside.

She thought she'd go check on the orphans herself, but a commotion drew her gaze toward the chasm. Knights were shouting. One was calling for a Shel'ai. Igrid tensed. She remembered the dark-eyed boy and wondered if he'd escaped from confinement to hurt someone.

She turned to one of the Knights standing guard. Without a word, she drew the sword from his scabbard and rushed forward to see what had happened. Knights and squires drew aside to let her pass. A moment later, she spotted Sir Jontin hurrying toward her.

"The vault is secure," he said quickly, holding up his hands.

"Then what's wrong? Another rambling message from the Scion?"

Sir Jontin shook his head. "The guards at the vault…They found Zeia."

Igrid tensed, swallowing the sudden lump in her throat. She felt the silver key hanging around her throat, under her tight-fitting tunic. "Dead?"

Sir Jontin shook his head. "No, but near enough. No wounds that we can see, but she's pale as a ghost. Shaking, cold—"

Igrid turned, grabbed the nearest Knight, and shoved him toward the barracks of the Shel'ai. "Bring two sorcerers. Tell them Zeia's hurt." She paused. "Tell them she spent too much magic. They'll understand." She turned back to Sir Jontin. "Take me to her."

Sir Jontin led Igrid down a seemingly never-ending staircase that descended into the chasm, switching back and forth. Igrid noted that in addition to the Knight, a dozen other men with swords closed around her.

"Gods, I'm not marching into the breach!" she said. "Half of you, get back up there and guard the walls. Look sharp! And you two, take Thessa to the Shel'ai barracks. Put her with Sariel and stay with her."

Reluctantly, her bodyguards obeyed.

A chill crept down Igrid's spine as they descended lower and lower into Cadavash. She wondered if the chill was caused by the temperature or her memories of what this place had looked like when she'd gone there with Rowen after the war. The mad pilgrims and wailing dragonpriests were gone, of course, as were the great displays of unearthed dragonbones. But the shops and temples that had housed them remained, though they were frightfully dark, even at midafternoon.

"What's been done with her?" Igrid asked to break the silence.

"She's still where they found her, in an empty shrine near the vault," Sir Jontin answered. The way the white-haired Knight held one hand on his sheathed sword told her that he was equally unnerved by the place. "Looks like it happened last night, but the guards never heard her scream. They just happened to glance in and saw her lying there, shaking like…"

"Once the other Shel'ai examine her, I'll want her carried up to the surface." Igrid glanced around at the cold stone walls and floors, still stained in places with blood no amount of scrubbing could wash away.

"Of course, m'lady."

After a long, dizzying descent, they finally reached the bottom of the chasm. Despite torches burning in brackets along the walls, the shadows seemed to close in. Igrid felt as though she were running at night through a dense forest, tree branches raking her skin.

"Not much farther," Sir Jontin said, as though to reassure himself as much as her.

They passed down a long, narrow corridor, through one empty chamber after another, then descended a final, frightfully narrow staircase. The steps were dark and slippery. Igrid nearly lost her footing, but Sir Jontin caught her. A few Knights still followed them some distance behind. A scuffle and a curse told her that at least one had not been as lucky.

At the bottom of the stairs, she found herself in another long, dark corridor. That one was too narrow to contain bracketed torches, lest they burn the person walking by. Sir Jontin snapped a quick command, and one of the Knights behind them passed up a lit lantern. Sir Jontin held it before him and led the way. Igrid could tell by the swaying light that his hands were shaking.

Igrid could not blame him. At the end of the corridor sat an iron door, newly installed at Rowen's command, beyond which lay two of the most powerful and dangerous objects in the world: Knightswrath and Namundvar's Well.

Igrid scowled. "Where are the guards?"

"With Zeia, I think." Sir Jontin continued down the narrow corridor then stopped beside what looked like a crack in the right wall.

Faint blue light shone through the break. When Igrid reached it, she saw that it was in fact a stylized but narrow entrance into an ancient dragonshrine. There, the bones and artifacts had been left in place. Igrid turned sideways and eased herself inside. She nodded curtly at the Knights within then spotted Zeia lying in a corner. A single Shel'ai—the one assigned to stand guard with the Knights—hovered over her. Igrid could not remember the aged sorcerer's name, but he had a kind, tired face.

"I can't... do anything more," the Shel'ai said. "Others... need to help me heal her."

Igrid nodded. "They're on their way." She turned to the Knights.

"Get back and guard the vault. Open it up. I want you *inside* it, making sure nothing's amiss."

"We've already looked inside, m'lady," Sir Jontin said.

"Then look again. And Jontin, get back up to the surface and find out what's taking the Shel'ai so long."

When all the Knights had left, Igrid turned back to Zeia. The woman was pale as a sheet, her face damp with sweat. Zeia's eyes clenched as though in pain. Her maimed wrists were crossed over her chest, as though she were trying to shield herself from something.

Igrid glanced at the old sorcerer. "Has she said anything?"

"She's asked for you. But she keeps losing consciousness." The sorcerer lowered his voice. "The way we found her... Honestly, I'm surprised she's still alive."

Igrid looked around the room. Dragonbones still hung haphazardly from the walls and ceiling, along with the skull of a dragon that, while stunted, was as big as a pony. The skull hung on chains that creaked and swayed, causing the skull to turn slowly, as though of its own accord. A luminstone glowed on a table beside the place where Zeia lay, casting ominous shadows about the room.

"You were close by when this happened?"

"I must have been," the sorcerer said, "but I didn't hear or feel anything out of the ordinary."

"Do you think whoever did this is still down here?"

The sorcerer shook his head helplessly. "I don't even know what's been done to her, m'lady. But I don't see how anyone could have gotten down here and attacked her in the first place without—"

"He's not here," Zeia croaked in a raspy voice.

Igrid jumped. "You're awake. We have more Shel'ai on the way. They'll heal you. In the meantime, I need you to tell me what happened."

"I was... trying to find the Shel'ai I sensed earlier."

Igrid frowned. "You were looking for him down here?"

Zeia shook her head. "It's called divination. It's... a kind of trance that allows the soul to leave the body for a short time. I was doing it... and so was he. We met. Our spirits fought. He... beat me."

Something in Zeia's expression hinted that he'd done more than that. Igrid glanced at the other Shel'ai, but he sat on the floor, head sagged with exhaustion, and said nothing. She turned back to Zeia. "The vault's secure. Knightswrath is still here. You stopped him."

Zeia shook her head again. "He couldn't have taken it... in spirit form. He was just looking. He didn't... *need* to attack me. Do you understand? He did it for pleasure. He did it because he could."

Igrid heard the sounds of approaching footsteps, accompanied by the familiar metallic jingling of armor. Moments later, three more Shel'ai appeared, flanked by half a dozen Knights. Igrid drew back to let the sorcerers work. Zeia started to protest but stiffened and clenched her eyes. Tears leaked out.

Gods, what kind of pain does it take to make Zeia cry?

"Help her," Igrid said, "but I need to talk to her again as soon as possible."

She stepped outside, turned right, and saw that the vault door had been opened. Four Knights stood outside, swords drawn. All nodded as she passed them.

She entered the vault just as the Knights within were finishing lighting torches. The great chamber was bathed in yellow-orange light. She remembered Rowen saying that once, that room had been filled with beautiful murals and lit by strange luminstones unlike any other they'd seen. But Chorlga had burned all that away. Igrid took a deep breath and headed toward a dais, at the center of which sat a small stone well. Knights flanked the well. Beyond them, on a plain wooden altar, lay Knightswrath.

As Igrid passed the well, she glanced inside. She remembered stories about how the simple well had been built as a conduit into the Light, which Fadarah's Shel'ai had used to steal magic to help their doomed cause. But she saw only darkness. She forced herself to move forward, still clutching her borrowed sword, until she stood before Knightswrath.

It did not look terribly ominous at first: just an adamune with a long handle of carved dragonbone, sheathed in a scabbard of black leather banded in brass. But Igrid remembered the stories she'd heard, remembered how Rowen still spoke with awe and fear of the power he'd felt—so much power, flowing from the sword into him—power that could heal wounds or burn whole armies to cinders.

Too much power for any one man to wield, Rowen had said. *Always, I felt like it was going to burn me from the inside out. Still, part of me misses it.*

Igrid forced herself to reach out. She touched the scabbard. Then, she touched the hilt. The Knights guarding the sword tensed as though about to stop her, but Igrid pulled her hand back. She had not been burned. She knew that would change, though, if she tried to draw the sword. She wondered what would happen if she simply grasped it by the scabbard and held it aloft.

"Have any of you ever tried to pick it up before?" she asked the Knights around her.

Their eyes widened as though her question were blasphemy.

"Sir Locke was chosen, m'lady. Not us," one said.

Igrid smirked. "This sword once belonged to Fâyu Jinn. Are you sure? I could understand the temptation—"

"It would be an insult to the Light," said another.

Igrid had been about to grasp the scabbard to try to pick up the sword despite Rowen's past warnings, but that final statement stopped her. The last thing she needed was to anger the men she was supposed to be commanding. Instead, she scowled at Knightswrath's pommel—specifically, a carving of a woman with fire flying from her hands.

Silwren, you're still alive in there somewhere, aren't you?

She thought back to Rowen's story of how Silwren had awakened the sword's ancient, awesome power at the cost of her own life but, in some way, had poured her essence into the sword itself so that a part of her would live on forever.

You and I have unfinished business. She traced one fingertip down the sword. Its icy cold made her shudder. *You still haunt his dreams, you know. I don't think he'll ever forget you, no matter what becomes of us. I wonder, does that please you?*

Igrid shook her head at her own pettiness. She turned her back on the sword and faced the well instead. She wondered, not for the first time, how deep it was. She'd gone down there with Rowen once, drunk, and dropped a lit torch into the well before he could stop her. She remembered watching the darkness swallow the flame. She remembered how she'd listened for the sound of the torch striking the bottom but never heard it.

Sir Issa rushed into the chamber. "Lady Zeia wishes to speak with you."

Igrid nodded. She started to follow Sir Issa out of the chamber then glanced back at Knightswrath. *Another time.*

When she returned to the shrine, all the other Shel'ai had left. Zeia sat up, propped against a stone wall. Though a little color had returned to her face, something about her expression cast a chill down Igrid's spine, but she forced herself to sheathe her sword in her belt and approach Zeia anyway. She knelt.

Zeia spoke in a weak rasp. "First… I have to tell you… about divination."

Igrid frowned. "I'm not sure that's the most critical thing facing us right now."

Zeia ignored the comment and continued. "They say the Dragonkin used it once to spy on their enemies. But even for them, it was a skill that took years of practice. I've only ever known three Shel'ai who could do it… but not for long, and only once a month, if that." She winced as though in sudden pain. Then, Zeia took Igrid's hand, igniting a flaming hand of her own and squeezing so hard that tingling waves of heat and cold swept up Igrid's arm. Even though Igrid had seen Zeia use her flaming hands to grasp things without burning them, Igrid fought back against a rush of panic.

"There are… risks, as well. Like any expenditure of magic, if you spend too much, you die. Do you understand?"

Igrid stared down at the burning hand encircling her own, half-expecting to see her flesh blackening. She noted as well that the glowing luminstone beside Zeia seemed to change color, becoming violet instead of blue. Remembering Zeia's question, she forced herself to answer. "I've heard of Shel'ai casting so much wytchfire that they burn themselves out."

"That's… like this. Only this is easier, quicker. And far more painful." Zeia released Igrid's hand then closed her eyes and lay so still that Igrid thought she'd gone to sleep. Her flaming hands sputtered and died. Then, she opened her eyes and spoke again, weaker than before. "I tell you this… so you'll understand. There are no schools for Shel'ai. No teachers. Even we don't fully understand the limits and workings of our own powers. We learn through practice, through trial and error. That's how we get stronger." She sat up a little. "No one trains harder than I do.

But the Shel'ai... I encountered was... so strong, I thought at first he was a Dragonkin. It was almost like... being near Chorlga." Zeia shuddered, and tears welled in her eyes again.

"Whoever he is, he can't reach you here," Igrid said. "As soon as we found you, we armed everyone. There are so many guarding Knightswrath now that—"

"That's not what I mean!" Zeia leaned forward, reignited one burning hand, and reached for Igrid, but the hand sputtered and disappeared before Igrid could grasp it. "Someone's been teaching him, training him. What he did shouldn't be possible. Should have killed him. But when we were fighting, I could feel... all his hate. All that rage. Worse than Fadarah, worse than Shade. It's keeping him alive."

Zeia sagged back against the stone wall. Her eyes closed. Igrid started to withdraw.

A moment later, though, Zeia's words rang in her mind, as clearly as if spoken aloud: *Do not underestimate him. If you see him, kill him. If you don't... you're already dead.*

Igrid looked down. Zeia's head sagged to one side. Igrid sensed at once that Zeia had finally lost consciousness. She turned and left the shrine, rejoining the Knights and Shel'ai waiting in the hallway beyond.

Suppressing a shudder, she said, "I want her carried back up to the surface." Looking around, she saw the Knights had already brought down a stretcher made of sturdy leather stretched taut between poles of stout bamboo. Igrid considered waiting for them to place Zeia on the stretcher and following them as they carried her to the surface, but her nerve wore out. Suddenly, all she wanted to do was to be gone from that place.

She started back up on her own, ascending the stairs at a brisk walk. Somehow, the shadows of Cadavash seemed even more ominous than before. She thought, strangely, of all the dragonbones still trapped in the walls, buried there for eons, waiting to be unearthed. She had the feeling that they were laughing at her.

She quickened her pace, practically running. Relief flooded her when she felt sunlight pouring into the chasm, warming her skin, and she finally reached the surface. She turned and spotted Sir Jontin hurrying across the practice yard toward her, pushing aside anyone who got in his way.

Igrid scowled. "Sir Jontin, gods help you if you give me more bad news."

Sir Jontin stood at attention. "I'm sorry, m'lady, but… a raven just arrived from the Lotus Isles." Before Igrid could speak, he handed her the tiny scrap of parchment, bowed, and stepped back.

Igrid opened the message. She feared the worst, but her heart leapt at the sight of Rowen's handwriting. Then, when she read the few words he'd written, cold dread returned. She felt as if all the blood drained from her body as she read the message a second time. She stood a moment, unsure what to do, then passed the message to Sir Jontin. She had the slim pleasure of seeing his eyes widen when he read it.

"Send back a message telling him that Zeia's here, that she was attacked, and the Shel'ai he's looking for is right on our godsdamned doorstep." However, before Sir Jontin could leave, Igrid grabbed his arm. *If he sent it from Saikaido Temple, that means he's with Crovis…* "On second thought, the last thing I need is him charging back to protect me."

Sir Jontin frowned. "But… if the enemy is *here*, perhaps here is where Sir Locke should be!"

"Unless the Shel'ai has already fled."

"Begging your pardon, m'lady, but shouldn't we send out hunting parties to—"

Igrid shook her head, having already dismissed that idea since she'd been informed of Zeia's psychic assault. "We have a stronghold full of orphans. Half your men are squires, and half the Shel'ai are old men or midwives. Defending ourselves against Sons of Maelmohr is one thing, but we're not a field army." She let go of Sir Jontin's arm, stepped back, and considered the matter for a long time. She happened to spot a Knight with an empty scabbard, waved him over, and returned his sword.

Finally, she told Sir Jontin, "Tell Rowen everything. I think it's a mistake, but I don't know what else to do, so tell him anyway." She added, "And send *two* birds, one a few hours after the other, in case the Shel'ai burns the first one out of the sky."

Sir Jontin nodded, smiling in obvious approval of her orders, and started to go.

Igrid stopped him again. "Where are Thessa and Sariel?"

"They're well, m'lady. They're in the sorcerers' barracks, under guard, as you commanded."

"And the children we rescued last night? Gods, I was in the chasm, and I didn't even think to check on that boy. I didn't hear any screaming, though."

Sir Jontin's expression darkened. "The others are fine. Most are still sleeping. But the boy... took his own life."

Igrid felt another lump in her throat. "When?"

"Shortly after we locked him in the room, I think. He was unarmed, but he took a sharp stone and..." The Knight hesitated. "Given all that's happened, I was... waiting to tell you."

"You should have told me sooner."

"Apologies, m'lady. I did not think it as urgent as other matters." The Knight bowed. "We already buried him outside the walls. We didn't know his name or if he even had one, but Sir Issa carved a marker anyway. I'll show you the place if you like."

Igrid turned away. She knew she should say something, but no words formed. Sir Jontin waited a moment then turned and hurried off. Igrid glanced at the sorcerers' barracks in the distance.

She thought of Thessa and Sariel again. She hurried toward the barracks but stopped when she reached the doorway. Despite the noise of so many people milling in the courtyard, she heard a baby crying from within. She wondered if it was Sariel or the dragon-worshippers' child or one of the other orphan children. She reached for the door handle, saw her hand shaking, and pulled her hand back. A moment later, she headed back to the manse to arm herself.

CHAPTER NINE

THE AFTERNOON FOUND ROWEN STROLLING the streets of Saikaido Town with his companions. Having surrendered the impossible dream of privacy, he walked in full armor, nodding and shaking hands with everyone who greeted him. Though it seemed every resident of the small town wished to thank him for his service during the War of the Lotus, Rowen was grateful that at least the sizeable garrison at the summit of the hill had not come to do the same. A few Knights and squires milled about. Some greeted him shyly, but others kept their distance.

"Something tells me they favor Crovis," Maddoc whispered, nodding toward a group of middle-aged Knights—each bearing the insignia of the stag or the lotus—who stood at the far end of the market and cast cold looks in his direction.

"I'll try my best not to be offended," Rowen answered. "Besides, maybe it's *you* they hate."

Maddoc chuckled. "It probably is." He lifted his hand and waved at the Knights, as though they were old friends. Most looked away, but one or two nodded curtly.

Sang Wei blushed. "Don't antagonize them."

"Whatever do you mean, Sir Wei? I was just being polite." Maddoc batted his eyelashes innocently then spotted a loose thread on his cloak and conjured a tongue of wytchfire to burn it away.

"Enough of that," Rowen warned in a low voice. He noted how the townsfolk drew away at the sight of magic. He had specifically hoped to ease some of their fears by bringing Maddoc with him and letting everyone see that he was a trusted ally, but Maddoc was not making it easy.

Forcing a broad smile, Rowen stopped at a vendor's table to inspect a seashell necklace. Some of the shells had spots of deep blue on the inside, unlike anything he'd ever seen. He decided to buy the necklace for Thessa, along with a dragon-shaped ragdoll for Sariel. The vendor tried to give them to him for free, but Rowen forced a handful of coins into the old man's grasp.

They continued on through the market. Though Rowen was still full from the needlessly extravagant breakfast that the innkeeper had served them, he forced himself to buy three bowls of fish stew from another vendor then a fourth bowl when he saw a beggar in the distance. The beggar was a young man but walked with a terrible limp. His mouth was a mess of scars, as though everything between his nose and his chin had been sliced to pieces then improperly sewn back together.

"He can't talk, and we don't know his name," an old woman nearby volunteered. "A Jol did that to him."

The young beggar accepted the food and wine by bowing so deeply that he lost his balance. Rowen caught him, glad the steaming bowl of stew had not spilled on either of them, then glanced at Maddoc. "Is there anything you can do?"

All the mirth drained from Maddoc's violet eyes. The Shel'ai came forward, knelt, and inspected the young man's leg as the latter sat on a barrel to eat. Maddoc gently lifted the beggar's torn pants and touched a long, jagged scar running from calf to knee. The beggar watched Maddoc with wide eyes but shoveled stew into a small corner of his mouth—all that would open—without protest.

Maddoc glanced back at Rowen, his expression sour. "Bad healing, this. Looks like there was an infection. Probably some fool cleric smeared in thornroot, which only made it worse. I'm amazed he can walk at all." He turned back to the beggar. "Are you in a lot of pain?"

The beggar faced the Shel'ai with wet eyes and nodded.

"Believe it or not, that's good," Maddoc said. "It means the nerves aren't dead."

Rowen noted a hush had fallen over the market square. He felt the eyes of townspeople, Knights, and squires all watching to see what Maddoc would do. *If ever there was a chance to earn these people's trust, this is it!*

Maddoc inspected the man's leg a moment longer, then sighed and stood. He squeezed the man's shoulder, as though in apology. "The damage is too deep. The same's true for your face, I think." He gently touched the beggar's scarred face then nodded. "I can take away the pain for a while, but to really heal you, I'd have to slice you back open in both places, all the way down to where you were first hurt, then use magic to sew you from the bottom up." He paused. "No matter how painful that sounds, I promise you, it would hurt even worse."

The beggar blinked. He looked down at his stew then up at Rowen. He turned back to Maddoc. After another moment, he nodded. His small hole of a mouth moved as though he were trying to answer.

Maddoc's eyes narrowed. "Are you sure, friend? Once I start this, I can't stop."

The beggar nodded again.

Sang Wei touched his sword hilt. "Perhaps... we should do this elsewhere."

"Agreed." Maddoc helped the beggar rise and supported him under one arm. "I saw a temple on the other end of town. Besides, we'll need clerics to help afterward. He'll need to rest for at least a full day."

Rowen glanced around. The crowd drew in closer. Some looked appalled. Others appeared uncertain or merely curious. He imagined how horrified they would be when Maddoc began the process. He wondered if they would even try to intervene. Surely, the wiser course of action was to perform the ghastly procedure elsewhere then let the townspeople see the beggar once he had been healed.

"No," Rowen heard himself say. "We'll do it here, in front of everyone." He drew a curved, wickedly sharp knife from his belt and handed it to Maddoc, hilt first. Then, he turned and addressed the crowd. "Listen, all of you. My friend is not a god. Nor is he a demon. He is just a man with certain abilities that can be put to good use. But such help requires trust. This poor young man is already prepared to trust us, but I must ask that all of you watching do the same. If you do, I swear on my honor that, when this is done, you will see that the Shel'ai are our friends now."

Many of the townspeople stood frowning with their arms crossed, but no one raised a voice in opposition. In the distance, the Knights of the Stag and Lotus stood sternly, arms crossed, waiting to see what would happen. Rowen walked in one direction while Sang Wei walked in the other, gently urging the crowd back and creating a perimeter around Maddoc and the beggar.

Meanwhile, Maddoc helped the beggar lie down on the ground. The beggar's eyes grew wide with fear.

Maddoc said, "He will need to be restrained."

I was afraid you'd say that. Rowen returned to the center of the circle and knelt beside the beggar's head. "It'll be all right, friend." He grasped the man's wrists and pinned them down. Sang Wei gripped the man's legs.

Maddoc gently rolled up the man's pant leg and looked up. Though Rowen did not think the Shel'ai had ever trained with weapons, he held the knife with an odd grace. "Are you ready?"

The beggar hesitated then nodded.

With astonishing quickness, Maddoc sliced into the beggar's leg. The man jerked. To his credit, he did not scream, but his eyes widened even further, full of tears. Through what remained of the beggar's mouth, Rowen saw rotten teeth, gritting.

Someone in the crowd swore. A woman screamed. Rowen felt a wave of heat wash over his face and looked up. Maddoc had both hands pressed to the beggar's leg. Blood welled between his fingers. It had splattered Maddoc's clothes and face as well, but the Shel'ai did not seem to notice. Wytchfire danced along his hands. The Shel'ai grimaced and stared at the wound as though facing down some terrible adversary. Then he closed his eyes.

Rowen looked past his comrades, at the crowd. He noted that the old woman who had told them about the beggar had fainted. A father was shielding his son's eyes. Two burly fishermen had drawn knives as though they meant to rush in and stop what was happening but had not yet gotten up the nerve.

"Maddoc..." Rowen said.

"I know."

The Shel'ai opened his eyes, and the wytchfire brightened. Rowen turned away, tempted to let go of the beggar's wrists and recoil from the heat. Then, as suddenly as it had appeared, the heat faded. The beggar went slack. Rowen turned and saw Maddoc withdrawing his hands. His wytchfire had vanished.

Choking, Maddoc asked for water.

A vendor stumbled forward, speechless, and handed Maddoc a cup with shaking hands. Instead of drinking its contents, Maddoc poured it slowly on the beggar's leg, rinsing away the blood. All the original scars had vanished. In their place, the flesh was bruised but whole, with just one single thin scar—presumably left from Maddoc's incision. Rowen stared. Though he had seen such healings before, they still amazed him.

"Help him stand," Maddoc said as he sat on the ground, his head sagging against his chest.

Rowen and Sang Wei took the beggar by the arms and lifted him to his feet. The young man appeared to be in shock, but at the sight of his healed leg, he pulled out of the Knights' grasp and rushed forward on his own. He stumbled and fell. But a moment later, he pushed himself back up and took one small step then another.

Some of the townspeople cheered. But most just stared. Rowen turned to Maddoc. "Are you all right?"

"Just… tired." The Shel'ai smiled weakly. "I've gotten too accustomed to healing skinned knees and bloody noses. I can heal his face, too, but I'll need a moment to breathe."

"Perhaps the temple would be a good place to finish this," Sang Wei offered. He took Maddoc's arm and helped him to his feet. "Surely, we've proven our point by now."

"Agreed," Rowen said. While Sang Wei helped Maddoc, Rowen took the beggar's arm and guided him toward the temple in the distance.

The crowd parted. Rowen glanced around, looking for the Knights he'd seen earlier, but the shifting crowd blocked his vision. The beggar pulled away and raced ahead, laughing. He tried to hug several townspeople, but all pulled back as though still afraid to touch him.

Then, Rowen saw a glint of steel.

Acting on instinct, he threw himself in front of the beggar. "Stop! What are you doing? We're only trying to help!" A knife slashed Rowen's azure tabard but glanced off the kingsteel armor underneath. Rowen seized a fisherman's wrist, twisted, and wrenched the knife from his grasp.

A chorus of screams and shouts made him turn his head. The crowd closed in on them. Rowen could not tell whether they were coming to help him or the fisherman. He heard Sang Wei shout then lost sight of his companions. Somehow, the fisherman twisted out of his grasp.

Rowen reached for his sword, but someone grabbed his arm. He managed to break free of his captor, but something struck him in the back as a metallic ring told him that his armor had just saved his life again. He turned and saw an adamune coming toward him. He thought at first that someone had taken his own sword from him, but it was still sheathed at his side. Rowen twisted clear of the sword, but a scream told him someone else had not been so lucky.

Panic turned to rage. Rowen flung himself at his attacker. He could not see the man's face in the chaos but unleashed a savage flurry of punches that dropped him to the ground, then wrenched the sword from his grasp. But before he could bring the sword to bear, two men grabbed his shoulders from behind and dragged him off his feet.

As he fell backward, Rowen guessed where one of his assailants was and stabbed upward. A man screamed. Blood rained down on Rowen's face, blinding him. Someone kicked him in the ribs. His armor absorbed the force, but the blow distracted him enough for another man to get on top of him. A middle-aged fisherman with a scarred face hoisted a knife.

Rowen tried to stab this new attacker, but someone pinned down his sword arm. Then, almost as soon as his attacker had appeared, someone hauled him backward. Rowen was free. He rolled and rose to a crouch. He'd lost the sword he took from an attacker but still had his own, and he drew it.

"Listen, stop! All of you! We don't have to—"

Then, something struck the back of his head, and he tumbled forward, into darkness.

Long into the afternoon, as he had for days previous, Crovis Ammerhel stared at the scroll that the nameless Shel'ai had given him. What had at first looked like parchment seemed upon closer inspection to be skin—which, he suspected with awful dread, had once belonged not to an animal but a man. Even the ink had a strange look to it. The graceful characters seemed to writhe ever so slightly as though written in black fire that moved too slowly to be consciously discerned.

Crovis had already tested the authenticity of the message by trying to tear or burn the vellum. Like the most ancient works contained within the Scrollhouse, the message seemed impervious to damage.

Still, that doesn't mean it came from Nekiel!

The sheer impossibility overwhelmed him for a moment. Nekiel was a demonic creature of fairy tales, an antagonist surely as embellished and fanciful as the hero, Fâyu Jinn, who had banished him in the first place. Crovis knew little about magic, let alone the Dragonkin, but he doubted even their kind could survive so long.

Yet here the message sat, signed in Nekiel's name, challenging him.

Algol's final words returned, taunting him: *My master and I already know your answer.* Crovis shook his head. Even if the message were real, surely it was just some kind of trick. If those cursed by magic wanted Crovis to do one thing, that was just all the more reason to do the opposite. Still, Crovis looked down at the message again. A faint smile touched his lips. *The greatest enemy of the Knighthood knows my name. The vilest affront to the Light recognizes me—me—as a threat... and a worthy opponent.*

"Know the quality of a Knight by his enemies," Crovis said, reciting a passage from the Codex Lotius—one he had rarely considered before. For a moment, he permitted himself to believe that the stories of Fâyu Jinn's great battle against Nekiel were actually true. Steel against magic, Light against Dark—an epic contest, worthy of the gods' attention.

Isn't this what I've really trained for, all my life?

Crovis settled back in his chair, closed his eyes, and dreamt of battle. He was still dreaming when his ears faintly registered a commotion followed by someone pounding on his door.

CHAPTER TEN

ALGOL WOKE, AMAZED THAT HE was still alive—and amazed, too, that he could see. He ignited his flaming eyes, which improved his vision further still. What had at first been just a dark outline became the mouth of a cave, filled with night. The faint outline of trees shone beyond.

He took a deep breath, held it, and ignited more of his magic, testing himself. The weariness remained—a faint numbness in his chest that was half reality, half memory—but he knew he'd survived the worst of it. He looked around.

The place smelled of dead animals, which he suspected had something to do with the pile of bones in the corner. Some appeared to be the remains of prey—rabbits, urusks, wild dogs—but one larger corpse still had rotting flesh on the bones. He guessed that a greatwolf had once made its home there and died of sickness or old age.

Algol felt an unexpected pang of sympathy for the animal. Half-wolf, half-bear greatwolves had always been admired for their ferocity and strength. He could see why Shel'ai like Fadarah had adopted the greatwolf as their sigil—even though it had not helped them in the end.

Algol looked around and spotted the shaft of dragonbone lying nearby. Glad he'd not lost it in his blind stumble toward the cave, he seized the crude scepter and used it to lift himself up. He realized that he had lost something, though: the strip of cloth he tied over his empty eye sockets. He decided that was of little consequence. He could easily tear a strip off his clothing if need be.

Cautiously, he left the cave. The sounds of night surrounded him as he went farther and the smell of death faded behind him. He considered his next move.

He could hardly believe that the Knight had left the sword behind—though in a way, it made sense. *Locke didn't know what he'd find on the Isles, so he took his chances, for the greater good.* Part of Algol admired that even though it complicated matters. *Or does it? What if I were to take both the woman and the sword?*

Algol considered that. What seemed like a complication might very well have been an opportunity in disguise. But that presupposed that he wanted Knightswrath in the first place. He did not. After all, in the end, he needed it in Rowen's hands.

"Unless…"

He considered another option—a course of action he had always thought to avoid. It would surely cost his life but might achieve his objectives more quickly and with greater certainty. He glanced in the direction of Cadavash and thought of the Shel'ai whose spirit he'd battled. She had been weaker than he but still formidable. And Cadavash was home to other Shel'ai who would all be on their guard. In his current state, he could never get past so many, let alone defeat them.

I should not have fought the woman. I should have controlled myself.

He fixed his thoughts on finding a solution. If he could not get into Cadavash, perhaps he could lure the Knight's beloved out—with the sword. He might send a message, claiming the sword was needed on the Lotus Isles and begging her to bring it. Still, even if she believed the message, she would be cautious. She would not travel alone.

"I'll need help."

Algol chafed at the idea of returning all the way to the Lotus Isles. He doubted the Grand Marshal would assist him, anyway, and that meant he would have to hire mercenaries. He reasoned that plenty must have been milling about the Simurgh Plains, looking for work in the wake of the war's end. He simply had to find some whose ferocity was matched only by their lack of conscience.

Algol smiled. He knew that would not be too difficult. Turning east, he headed out to find the nearest town.

Rowen woke and found himself staring into the face of a weeping statue. He blinked. He took a few dizzying seconds to realize he was lying on a bed in the sparsely furnished anteroom of a temple, next to a statue of Armahg in one of her most common poses: weeping over the death of Zet the Dragongod, depicted at her feet as a cluster of multiwinged serpents torn in half.

Rowen turned in time to see Maddoc rising out of a nearby chair to approach him. The Shel'ai had dark circles around his eyes. His clothes still had blood on them. "Easy, Sword Marshal. You're safe. So's Sang Wei. He's in the next chamber, arguing with a squad of Knights who came to check on you."

Rowen listened and heard shouting in the distance, though he could not make out the words. What he took at first to be robed clerics in the distance were just more statues of Armahg and Zet. Only Maddoc stood with him, helping him as he sat up.

"Gods, my head…" Rowen said.

"I can help with that." Maddoc touched the back of Rowen's head, sending a pulse of heat into his skull. When the sensation passed a moment later, it took the pain with it.

"Thank you." Rowen glanced at the statue of Armahg again. "I take it we're not on Saikaido anymore."

"We thought it best to get you away. New Atheion was closest." Maddoc added, "The clerics of Armahg have been especially helpful once I hinted that you weren't the best of friends with the Grand Marshal."

Rowen thought of Matua, High Father to the clerics of Armahg, taken to Saikaido against their wishes. He nodded. "What happened?" For the first time, he realized he was wearing a thin, soft robe in place of his armor.

Maddoc pointed to a table in the distance, on which sat Rowen's armor and weapons. "We couldn't get to the horses. Basically, Sang Wei picked you up, and we carried you straight to a barge." He paused. "As you might have guessed, we were attacked in the street. There were six of them. I think so, anyway. It all happened so fast."

Rowen rubbed his eyes then tentatively touched the back of his head.

He felt a crust of dried blood, but the wound itself had vanished. "I remember an adamune swinging at me. I was afraid it was Sang Wei's."

Maddoc smiled faintly. "No, but it *did* belong to a Knight. He wasn't wearing armor, but he led the attack. The other five were failed squires, we think. The Knight tried to get to you. Sang Wei cut him in half." The smile broadened. "Gods, if you thought he was fast in the practice yard, you should have seen him there!"

"What happened to the other five?"

Maddoc's smile thinned. "You killed one. I wounded another. The crowd strangled him after, then beat the other three to death. If there were more, they got away." When Rowen was too speechless to answer, Maddoc said, "I didn't know if they'd help us or the attackers at first. But when one tried to stab you, they all went mad. They pleaded with us to stay. They said it wasn't their fault, but we thought we should get you away anyway."

That was a mistake. "I remember seeing other Knights in the square."

Maddoc nodded. "To their credit, they tried to help us once it started, but they probably just made things worse. One got confused and stabbed a fisherman who wasn't even part of the attack. I'm told he died shortly after."

"You're *told?*"

"As I said, Knights have been coming to New Atheion to check on you ever since the attack—which was only this afternoon, believe it or not. There are no windows here, but it's still the middle of the night."

"What about the beggar? Did you bring him with us? Were you able to heal his face?"

Maddoc's expression darkened. "I couldn't get to him before the attackers did. I'm sorry."

Rage boiled up inside Rowen. Despite some lingering dizziness, he waved off Maddoc's assistance and struggled out of bed. He paced, hardly noticing the cold flagstones chilling his bare feet. "My fault. All this is my fault. Eight men dead. I thought I was helping, but all I did was make a spectacle—"

"That riled up and flushed out attackers who otherwise might have crept into your room while you slept," Maddoc interjected. "Maybe if you'd taken our advice and had me heal the beggar in a temple, out of sight, you'd be dead right now."

But the beggar might be alive. "Gods, we didn't even know his name..."

"I'm afraid there's more."

"Lately, there always seems to be."

Maddoc cleared his throat as though bracing for rebuke. "Sang Wei sent word of the attack to Lady Igrid."

Rowen stopped. "He did *what?*"

Maddoc held up his hands. "I told him not to, but he did it anyway. There was nothing I could do."

"You could have burned the damn bird out of the sky!" Rowen turned away, clenching his fists. "You *know* what Igrid will do when she gets that message."

"Probably," Maddoc said. "Want me to send another, telling her to stay home?"

"No sense wasting a bird on a message she won't be there to read." Rowen was quiet for a moment. The thought of seeing Igrid brought a faint smile to his face. "I owe you and Sang Wei my life. And an apology."

Maddoc frowned then laughed. "I'm your servant, Sword Marshal. I did what I was supposed to do. Besides, if I hadn't, I'd probably be dead right now, too."

A door at the far end of the antechamber swung open. Sang Wei stomped in, slamming the door behind him. He blushed at the sight of Rowen and hurried forward. He fell to one knee. "Forgive me, Sword Marshal—"

"I will if you will." Rowen seized him by the shoulders and pulled him back onto his feet. "Now tell me what *that* was all about." He nodded toward the door that the young Knight had just slammed.

Sang Wei's face flushed again—in rage, that time. "The Grand Marshal has *requested* that you be brought back to Saikaido so that your wounds can be tended."

"Maddoc's already tended them."

"That's what I said. But they said it's also for your protection. When I wouldn't let them take you, they insisted on leaving a squad to guard the temple. But the Knights turned away all the clerics who live and worship here, and there's been fighting outside." Sang Wei rubbed his eyes.

Rowen noted that the young Knight still had blood on his armor and wondered if he had even washed or slept since the attack.

"Tell him what we learned about the Knight," Maddoc said.

Sang Wei nodded heavily. "The one who led the attack was Sir Onnai, a Knight of the Lotus."

Rowen whistled. *Gods, that's the man you killed?* "I've heard of him. When the Jolym invaded the Isles, they say he somehow killed six all by himself."

Sang Wei nodded again. He looked ill. "I've never killed another Knight before. Of course, I didn't have a choice, but... "

Maddoc stepped forward, squeezed Sang Wei's shoulder, and took over. "The Knights are already disavowing him. They say he acted completely on his own. But I think we all know that's unlikely."

Sang Wei tensed and stepped away from Maddoc. "We don't know that. I may not agree with the Grand Marshal's actions, but I would not be so quick to blame him for *this*."

"It doesn't seem particularly honorable, does it?" Rowen turned to Maddoc. "Have you recovered enough of your strength to read the thoughts of the Knights outside and—"

"Determine if they're hiding something?" Maddoc finished. "I already have. A few hate you. Some seem genuinely worried about you. All are loyal to Crovis, but I don't think any had any foreknowledge of the attack. And none know anything about Aeko."

Rowen wondered whether he should be relieved or disappointed. "That either means Sir Onnai and those squires were an exception, or else there's something sinister happening within the Order, right under Crovis's nose." He glanced at the others.

Sang Wei looked at the floor.

Maddoc said, "There's definitely... unrest. I heard some clerics from the Isles are talking about magic, how it's an affront to the Light, the way the Sons of Maelmohr say. A few rolled their eyes and walked away, but plenty of people stayed to listen. And there's argument over that Olg, too."

Rowen frowned. "What Olg?"

Maddoc blushed. "Forgive me. I forgot to tell you. We only just heard the story when we got to New Atheion. Apparently, an Olg—of all things—came to the Lotus Isles recently and tried to become a Knight!"

Sang Wei said, "He was turned away, but some are angry because technically, refusing to train someone based solely on their race is a violation of the Codex Viticus."

Rowen considered that. He had never known the Olgrym to be anything but savage killers, known for fanatic practices that included setting themselves on fire or smearing their bodies with the entrails of slain enemies. A few occasionally left their home at Godsfall to become mercenaries, but they behaved no better than the rest of their kin. Besides, Godsfall was on the far west side of Ruun. He had a hard time believing that an Olg would—*could*—travel all the way to the Lotus Isles to become a Knight.

"Maybe he was a half-blood," Rowen offered. "Plenty of Olgrym love rape as much as murder. Often, they sire children nobody wants. Fadarah was proof of that."

Sang Wei shook his head. "Everyone says he was a full-blooded Olg, big as a horse but mute. Didn't cause any trouble. He had a one-eyed sellsword with him who did all the talking. Apparently, the Olg got his tongue ripped out for speaking out against Doomsayer."

The mention of the infamous Olgish chieftain sent a chill down Rowen's spine. He remembered fighting the chieftain in the snow outside Hesod, Knightswrath in hand, raw magic overwhelming him. "Impossible. If he spoke out against an Olgish chieftain, they wouldn't just rip out his tongue. They'd rip out his guts while he was still alive."

Maddoc shrugged. "Either way, for a nation that survived a terrible war and absorbed New Atheion in the process, the Lotus Isles don't seem particularly docile these days."

"People are talking about Father Matua, too," Sang Wei said. "I didn't hear a word about him on Saikaido, but here, people are angry that he was carried off. And they know it was a Shel'ai who tried to kill him."

Rowen thought of Igrid's name, seared into the cleric's back with agonizing precision. *Not kill him. Just hurt him—and turn him into a living message.* "We need to combat that." He glanced at Maddoc.

Maddoc smirked. "I might make things worse if I go out for a stroll, so bring them back here, and I'll do what I can for them. Just promise you'll take the bodyguards Crovis sent you. And let us get some sleep first." He placed one hand on Sang Wei's shoulder.

The young Knight tensed but did not pull away.

"Agreed," Rowen said with a smile. "We could all use it." Nevertheless, he walked over to the table to gird his weapons and went out to speak with the Knights. As he walked, he thought of something else Maddoc had said: the Olg had been traveling with a one-eyed sellsword.

Could that be Dagath? He remembered encountering the brutish man on the road—that felt like a lifetime before—and barely escaping with his life. *No, the man must surely be dead by now, thank the gods!*

"If not, I wonder if he still has my sword," Rowen muttered, remembering the plain, waisted shortsword that had been a present from Kayden, his brother. Dagath had taken it. For a moment, Rowen thought only of getting it back.

Dagath glanced up from his third mug of ale in time to see a buxom barmaid leaning over to set down a bowl of stew for a customer. When the blushing customer handed her an extra coin as a tip, the barmaid winked and tucked it into her cleavage. Dagath's pulse quickened. He watched the barmaid head toward the kitchen and thought about following her. Then, he remembered he was not alone.

With a scowl, Dagath faced his companion.

The Olg had waved off slabs of charred meat but devoured four bowls of a thick stew made from spiced vegetables. He was working on his fifth. Dagath noted with revulsion that the Olg had hardly touched his ale. Instead of using the wooden spoon the barmaid had provided with the bowl, the Olg simply tipped the bowl and drank its contents then used his grubby fingers to scrape out what remained.

Who ever heard of an Olg that didn't eat meat? Gods, this one must have lost his brains when they took his tongue! At least he still knows how to fight.

Dagath touched his jawline. Half his face was still sore, reminding him of the blow the Olg had given him a week earlier. They'd stopped at a farm near the coast, seeking shelter. The farmer had a crossbow and might have turned away Dagath easily enough, but after one look at his companion—particularly at the Olg's thick arms and bare, gray torso crisscrossed with scars, not to mention his black eyes and long, dark hair braided with the skulls of rodents—both the farmer and his wife had told them to take whatever they wanted.

Dagath had assumed that invitation applied to their daughter, as well. The Olg felt otherwise. The blow Dagath had taken had been enough to knock him unconscious, though he suspected the Olg could have killed him just as easily.

"You're not much fun," Dagath grumbled. He grabbed a bone off his plate and waved it in the Olg's face. "Sure you're not hungry for something else?"

The Olg scowled then returned his attention to his vegetable stew. Dagath laughed. Since finding the Olg wandering the plains east of Hesod, he'd learned that unless he pushed too hard, he could get away with tormenting the gigantic warrior all he liked.

"You aren't still thinking of those Isle-men, are you? I told you you're wasting our time. Their kind don't like any but their own." Dagath paused. "Would have thought the same could be said for *your* kind."

The Olg ignored him.

When the barmaid emerged from the kitchen a moment later, she was carrying two more steaming bowls of stew and placed them before the Olg, careful to keep her rump just out of reach of Dagath's hand. "Free of charge, for helping me earlier." She leaned in and kissed the taut gray skin on his forehead.

The Olg turned and grinned, revealing rotten teeth. The barmaid's face soured. She flashed a strained smile then left, ignoring Dagath entirely. He watched her go.

The man who had groped the barmaid earlier, and whom the Olg had knocked unconscious with a thrown chair, had been carried out. A spot of blood was still visible on the floor.

"You shouldn't have done that," Dagath muttered. "That man and his friends were sellswords. They looked like they had some coins to rub together. We could have gone in with them." *Or pretended to, killed them in their sleep, and robbed them!*

The Olg lowered the bowl of stew, broth running from his lips, and frowned. He shook his head. As he slurped down his stew again, he lifted one massive arm and pointed in the direction of the barmaid.

116

Dagath snickered. "Women like her exist for two purposes. One is carrying bowls and cups. The other isn't." He winked with his remaining eye. When the Olg did not laugh, Dagath leaned closer. "No sense caring about somebody you don't even know. The gods made her pretty for a reason." He lifted his cup, drained the last of its contents, and shouted for the barmaid to bring him another.

When she did, unsmiling, Dagath took a coin and tucked it between her breasts. Then he sent her on her way by planting his hand firmly on her backside and pushing. He laughed at the look on her face. Then he turned his head, and his smile disappeared. His companion had risen from his chair, standing so tall that he had to duck to keep from scraping the ceiling. He had already picked up a gigantic mace of blackened iron and held it in the crook of his arm.

A silence fell over the tavern's common room. Dagath felt all eyes on him—including those of the barmaid. He fingered the hilt of his favorite weapon—a plain but elegant shortsword of Ivairian design—and wondered what he should do. Dagath was used to being the strongest man in the room. The Olg was probably twice as strong, but Dagath might still be faster.

Instead of drawing his shortsword, Dagath reached into his coin pouch, took out three copper coins, and placed them on the table. "For you, after we've gone," he growled in the barmaid's direction. Then, he asked the Olg, "Better?"

The Olg stared, unmoving.

Dagath cursed, took out two more coins, and set them down. In a low voice, he protested, "That's damn near all I've got! You gonna slice up some rich bastard and get me more?"

The Olg sat down, leaned his mace against the table, and went back to eating.

"Figures." Dagath looked around, scowling at every man who glanced in his direction until they looked away. "Not much point staying here. Too peaceful in these parts to find work. Better we head south to Nosh or, better yet, north to Dhargoth. Still plenty of fighting there."

The Olg finished his first bowl, started to drink the second, then set the bowl down. He looked up at Dagath. Then he pointed east.

Dagath scowled. "The Knights again? They already turned you away!

117

You're lucky they didn't fill you full of arrows as soon as they saw you. What, you want to crawl back and beg them to change their minds?"

The Olg took a small drink of ale then turned his attention back to his stew. Within moments, he'd drunk and scraped the bowl clean. He added both bowls to a neat but growing tower at the edge of the table. Then he looked down at the table, quietly tracing his fingertips over the grain in the wood.

"Listen," Dagath hissed, "there are *two* of us! You don't get to make all the decisions. If I say we're going to Dhargoth, we are." He leaned back and tapped the hilt of his sword. "You get me?"

For a long time, the Olg just stared. Dagath kept his hand near his sword, half expecting an attack. Instead, the Olg finally held up two fingers, one on each hand. He touched the fingers then slowly moved them apart. He pointed at himself with one finger and at Dagath with the other. He touched the fingers and moved them apart again.

Dagath's good eye narrowed. "You don't even have a name! Now, you want to split up… after all I've done for you? Those Noshans would have killed you if it weren't for me! And what about those Knights? You think they would have stood around waiting for you to make signs explaining what you wanted?" Dagath gestured wildly, mimicking the Olg. "No, they would have taken one look at you and cut you to pieces. *That's* the world we live in. Best you understand that." He snorted and took a long drink. "Gods, I can't believe I have to explain that to an Olg!"

Shaking his head, Dagath turned just in time to see someone new walk into the tavern. At first, Dagath took him to be a beggar, but something about the man set him on edge. He frowned and touched his sword again, easing the blade partway out of its scabbard.

The newcomer looked to be about Dagath's age—tall, lean, and fit—but was trying his best to look older. He was dressed in filthy rags and had a strip of cloth bound around his eyes, like any one of a hundred such wretches Dagath had seen in his travels. The man had a faint smile on his face. When the barmaid approached him, presumably to tell him that beggars were not welcome, he pressed so many coins into her palm that her eyes widened and she eagerly took his arm, guiding him to a table by the fire.

Dagath rapped his knuckles on the table to get his companion's attention. He nodded toward the blind man. "There's something about him. Don't know what it is yet, but..." Then, he noticed the blind man's cane. It had been bound in rags, but what lay underneath was not a simple tree branch, like he'd suspected. Instead, he saw a flash of ghostly white, intermingled with faint streaks of red.

Dragonbone! Gods, that staff could be worth more than the whole tavern!

Dagath considered the possibility that the blind man had simply found it and didn't even know its worth. However, the way he'd bound it in rags said otherwise. Dagath studied the man more closely. For the first time, he noticed that beneath an unkempt beard and sun-darkened cheeks, the man's features had a strange, angular quality to them. The tops of the man's ears, though rounded, looked scarred, as though they'd been cut or burned.

Dagath forced himself to look away, half afraid the blind man might notice the scrutiny. He whistled as he took another drink of ale. "I think I've found something, either our next employer or our next victim." He spoke in a low voice but did not bother checking the Olg's expression to gauge his reaction, deciding that he did not much care.

CHAPTER ELEVEN

IGRID KNELT ON THE MUDDY grass of the courtyard, bathing Sariel in a tin washtub. She'd wanted to visit the child and thought as well that it might be a good idea to let both Knights and Shel'ai see her performing a duty that was neither administrative nor related to fighting. However, so far, nothing was going as planned.

Sariel splashed immodestly in the tub, unleashing bright peals of laughter in the warm afternoon. The splashing had soaked Igrid's clothing, which attracted onlookers and only seemed to increase Sariel's amusement. Finally, forcing a smile, Igrid seized a towel and held it open. "Come on, little fish. The water's getting cold. Stand up."

Sariel started to rise out of the washtub, then laughed and collapsed back in the water, splashing even more water over the sides. Then she swiped one small hand and skipped soapy water right into Igrid's face.

Igrid bit back a stream of curses, reminding herself that she was being watched, and held the towel open again. "Out," she repeated more firmly.

Sariel stood, her smooth body streaming water, then laughed and collapsed again. That time, she ducked down. Igrid stayed back, expecting her to rise out of the water and repeat the game. When she did not, Igrid peered over the side of the washtub and saw Sariel in the fetal position at the bottom, completely submerged and holding her breath. A few tiny air bubbles rose from her lips.

"Out before you freeze," Igrid repeated. When the child did not obey, Igrid threw the towel over one shoulder, reached into the water, and tried to pull her out—then screamed and withdrew her hand. Though it looked placid, the water had suddenly turned hot, almost boiling.

Sariel rose out of the water, laughing, unhurt. Her small body steamed in the chill air.

"Nice trick." Igrid blew on her burned fingers. "Now, get out before I throttle you." She held the towel open a third time, glowering.

That time, Sariel obeyed. Igrid dried her hair.

Sariel laughed, squirming, then cried.

Igrid felt her nerves fraying. "What's wrong now?"

"Sampai…"

Igrid recognized the Sylvan word for *father*. "I told you, Rowen's gone," she snapped, forcing a smile for the benefit of those still watching. "But he'll be back soon. I promise. Now, hold still—"

Sariel screamed, and the towel burst into flames. Igrid cried out and fell backward. Violet flames coursed along the child's naked body. Sariel looked down at the flames, entranced. She laughed. Then she held out her hand to Igrid.

"I think not," Igrid said, wishing Maddoc were there. "Gods, this was a bad idea…" She looked around for another Shel'ai who could help. She spotted Thessa in the distance, practicing archery with Keswen. Sariel saw her, too, and started toddling toward her, her small body still awash in wytchfire. Faint tendrils of steam rose from the child's face as her tears steamed.

Seeing the girl, Thessa laid down her bow and ran to her. Without touching Sariel, she knelt in front of her. "Water," she said. "You see? Water." She held her hands before her, clutching a big imaginary bowl.

"Fire!" Sariel squealed. Her wytchfire brightened.

"Water!" Thessa insisted. She pretended to throw the bowl.

Sariel laughed and played along. Her wytchfire vanished as though extinguished. She collapsed onto the muddy ground and lay still. She played dead for a moment then started giggling. She rolled one way then the other until mud covered her body. "Dirt!" she cried.

"Water," Thessa said again. She pointed to the washtub.

Sariel's expression hardened. She crossed her arms. "Dirt," she said defiantly.

"Water," Thessa repeated. When Sariel did not move, Thessa

shrugged and started to walk away. Sariel screamed. Then she sprinted back to the washtub, crawled in, and sat. The water darkened, almost up to her neck.

"Thank you," Igrid managed.

"I better stay," Thessa said in a low voice. "If I go, she'll just get mad and do it again."

"Thank you," Igrid repeated. "I promise I'll make sure Keswen—"

Before she could finish, a Knight shouted from the walls. Igrid turned her attention to one of the watchtowers overlooking the walls and saw the Knight pointing. Sir Jontin appeared a moment later.

"A horse is approaching."

Igrid twisted and snatched up the tashi she'd left on the stone bench behind her, as well as a cloak that, mercifully, had stayed dry. She donned the cloak, held the sword, and tried to ignore Sariel's scream of protest when she walked away. Sir Jontin went ahead of her and ordered a squad of Knights to open the gates. Meanwhile, another squad armed themselves with polearms and bows and stood at the center of the courtyard, ready to repulse an attack if necessary. Keswen joined them, three arrows fitted to her bowstring.

Once the gates were open, Igrid spotted a single horse galloping over the hills. The horse's rider jerked unnaturally.

"The body's been tied to the saddle," Igrid muttered.

The horse had been draped in azure. The body wore azure and kingsteel, but Igrid could not see his face. Her pulse quickened.

Gods, please don't let that be Rowen…

Sir Jontin gave her a wide-eyed look as though he feared the same thing, and he ran through the open gates, holding up both empty hands. The horse saw him and angled toward Jontin's outstretched hand. When the horse was close enough, it slowed and turned sideways, allowing Sir Jontin to grab the reins, though the horse tossed its head in agitation.

Igrid took a deep breath, resisted the impulse to turn around and look at Thessa, and went out to join him. Sir Issa hurried past her. While Sir Jontin held the horse's reins and soothed the animal, Sir Issa drew a knife and cut the ropes securing the body upright in the saddle. The body sagged, and Sir Issa caught it, lowering it gently onto the grass.

The rider was a big man wearing a helmet with a facemask, but Igrid could not discern its design from that distance. She forced herself to draw closer and held her breath as Sir Issa removed the facemask.

The rider's face was a blackened wreck, save for the eyes, which were white and horrifically wide. Igrid recoiled, trying to speak, but no words came out.

"Somebody burned him," Sir Issa gasped. He tugged off one of the dead man's gauntlets, revealing a blackened hand. "Somebody roasted him in his armor."

"Look for a sigil," Sir Jontin interrupted in a stern voice.

Sir Issa blinked then nodded. The rider's tabard had been mostly burned away, but symbols still visible had been carved into his cuirass. Sir Issa took off his own cloak, balled it up, spat on it, and wiped away some soot. He stared a moment then looked up at Igrid.

"A crane. Not a lotus. It's not the Sword Marshal, m'lady." He turned to Sir Jontin. "I think... I think it's Sir Berric!"

For the first time, Igrid smelled burned meat. She realized what it was and almost gagged. "Rowen said the Shel'ai burned my name into Matua's back." She hesitated. "Take off his breastplate."

Sir Issa looked hesitant but obeyed. The young Knight's hands shook as he fumbled with the straps holding the halves of Sir Berric's cuirass together. A moment later, with Sir Jontin's help, he rolled Sir Berric onto his side and opened the cuirass like the halves of a cracked egg.

The smell of charred meat intensified.

Igrid's eyes watered, but she drew closer, forcing herself to look. Beneath his armor, all Sir Berric's clothes had been either removed or burned away. His chest was crisp and blackened, except for a long strip over his sternum that had been left pink, save for a single word—a name—that had been seared into it.

"Rowen..." Igrid choked.

Then, she heard the cry of a bird and looked up. A lone raven was winging across the sky, drawing closer and closer, lower and lower. Her heart rose in her throat again. The raven passed over the walls of the stronghold. Igrid turned, watching through the open gates, and saw it fly directly to the aviary.

Moments later, a flushed squire brought her a tiny slip of paper. Igrid accepted it without a word. Sir Issa had just covered Sir Berric's body

123

with his cloak while Sir Jontin prayed in Shao, but both men eyed the scrap of parchment in Igrid's hands. Igrid looked through the open gates again and saw Thessa, frightfully still, watching from a distance.

Finally, blinking back tears, Igrid forced herself to read the message.

The next morning, Rowen sent Sang Wei out on his own with orders to try to learn anything he could about the whereabouts of Aeko Shingawa. Then, fearful of what the people of New Atheion might do to a Shel'ai in their midst, he ordered half of the ten Knights to remain at the temple and guard Maddoc while the rest accompanied him throughout the city.

At first, they refused, saying their orders to safeguard Rowen had come from the Grand Marshal himself. But none wanted to disobey an order from their famed Sword Marshal, either. Finally, they consented.

After donning his armor, Rowen searched for the poorest-looking districts of New Atheion. That proved harder than expected. Though Rowen had visited the City-on-the-Sea once before, that had been while the massive skiffs supporting its many buildings had still been moored at the sea known as Armahg's Tears. Since the city had relocated to the Lotus Isles, much had changed. The order of the buildings was almost completely different. Likewise, much had been burned and rebuilt after the original city was attacked by the Nightmare, so Rowen felt as if he were seeing the city for the first time.

He decided to simply follow his nose toward the worst reek.

Beyond the Scrollhouse and what had once been the palace of Atheion's king—home presently to a puppet governor chosen by the Knighthood—he found an area that smelled of decay located upon a single, massive skiff at the outermost edge of the city. He guessed those were the parts of old Atheion most devastated by the Nightmare. Instead of being rebuilt, they had simply been relocated to the fringe and remade into the city's slums.

Rowen thought back to the Dark Quarter, the slums at the base of Pallantine Hill, where he'd grown up in the shadow of the rich citizens of Lyos. Despite the fact that the slums of Atheion floated on an unsinkable skiff designed eons before by the Dragonkin, they looked almost identical to the Dark Quarter. Houses were little more than shacks. The air hung thick with the pall of death and rotten meat. Burning garbage darkened the air with smoke. In the place of temples and libraries sat row upon row of crudely built taverns and brothels.

One of the young Knights pinched his nose. "Must we venture into such a place, m'lord?"

"Light have pity on these people," another Knight said solemnly. Then he added, "Might we not be better served inspecting the new gardens or the governor's palace?"

Rowen steeled himself and walked forward despite the smoke stinging his eyes. A chorus of coughs and metallic footsteps confirmed that his bodyguards had fallen in behind him.

Once Rowen's eyes grew accustomed to the smoke, he beheld a sea of wretched faces, dismal huts, and heaps of burning trash that reminded him of Dogbane Circle, the heart of the slums where he'd grown up. He made his way toward a muddy field encircled by shanties and taverns. A few beggars asked for coins, which Rowen freely gave, but most drew aside at the sight of so many fearsome Knights. Meanwhile, prostitutes—male and female alike, most of them gaunt, some of them frightfully young—tried to catch the Knights' attention with crude calls and provocative poses. Rowen motioned to one, handed him a pair of coins, and said, "I just want to know what this place is called."

The boy laughed. "Rich ones call this place the Privy. We just call it home."

Gods... "Thank you." Then, Rowen turned, his gaze falling on a dark pedestal at the center of the Privy. On the pedestal sat a blackened glass sphere. Everybody gave them a wide berth. Rowen had never seen such a thing before, but supposedly, one of these spheres sat at the center of each of the skiffs of New Atheion. They were used to compel the skiffs to move or stop without need for oars, sails, and anchors. According to Aeko, such a thing required great training and concentration, though, and only the clerics of Armahg were capable of it.

If these people could just find a cleric willing to help them, they could move this whole place somewhere better... but where would that be? Shaking his head, Rowen looked for the sick and injured. He did not have to search for long. Outside one tavern, he found an old man with a bloody, infected arm, lying next to a dog. The dog had been dead for days. The old man looked up, uncomprehending, still petting the dog's fur as Rowen tried to explain the healing he might find if he came along. Finally, giving up, Rowen told two of the Knights to carry the old man back to Maddoc. Though the Knights seemed reluctant to touch the old man or to leave Rowen alone, they were quick enough to accept any excuse to escape the Privy.

Not long afterward, he saw a little girl waving her hands before her as she walked. A quick glance at her eyes revealed that they were red and wet, nearly swollen shut. She was being helped along by a prostitute—presumably her mother—who had lost two fingers on one hand and looked as though she would soon have to cut off a third. Rowen told them where to go and assigned another Knight to see to it that they arrived safely.

By then, word had spread throughout the Privy, and soon, the sick and starving closed in, begging for help. With a start, Rowen realized Maddoc could not possibly heal that many. Apologizing, he selected only those who seemed the worst for wear, promising to return as soon as he could to help the rest.

When this is over, I have to come back here with all the Shel'ai at Cadavash to help these people!

He wondered how the Shel'ai would feel about that, though. If they refused his request for help, the only remaining option was to order them, and he had already gone to great lengths to clarify that the Shel'ai at Cadavash were not his subjects. Cursing, he pushed such thoughts from his mind and concentrated on simply getting the sick and injured back to Maddoc.

As he led the cluster of wretched people through New Atheion, he noted the looks of curiosity or contempt he received. He flashed back to what had happened in Saikaido and loosened his sword, but no one attacked them. By the time they arrived at the temple where Maddoc was staying, the Shel'ai was already busy tending those who had arrived before them.

"Sang Wei's come back and needs to speak with you," the Shel'ai said hurriedly, his face already lined with weariness.

Rowen nodded then turned to face his bodyguards. "All of you, take off your armor and help him in any way you can."

The armored men exchanged looks. Some were already pinching their noses or covering their mouths, anxious to leave the temple and wait outside since their Sword Marshal was safe.

"This is no fit duty for a Knight," one protested.

"This is the *only* fit duty for a Knight," Rowen countered. He took off his sword belt and laid it down. "Get to work. I'll come back and join you as soon as I can. Any man who's standing idle when I return will find me far less forgiving than the Light. Is that understood?"

The Knights nodded and reluctantly stripped off their armor. Maddoc smirked and nodded his thanks. Rowen nodded back and hurried off to find Sang Wei.

"Aeko came here right after Father Matua was attacked," Sang Wei said. Though they were alone in an adjoining room without windows and the door was closed, he barely spoke above a whisper. "Matua was in pain, of course, but the clerics say he and Aeko spoke for hours. When she left, she went straight to the aviary and drafted a message for you. But I spoke with the birder, and he said that instead of sending that message, at the last moment, she burned it and wrote another."

Rowen nodded. "What did the first message say?"

"He didn't know. He didn't see it, but he says the second message was much shorter."

"Do you believe him?"

"As much as I believe anyone."

Rowen considered what Sang Wei had just told him. "That means Aeko probably wanted to tell me more but decided not to. She knew I needed to know that Matua had been attacked, but she didn't say anything about the scroll or Knightswrath. Maybe she thought the Shel'ai who attacked Matua would see the message, or Crovis—"

"Crovis *did* see the message," Sang Wei interrupted. "The birder is sure of it. He says all the birds in New Atheion are trained to fly to Saikaido Temple before going anywhere else." He paused. "Aeko probably knew that."

"Maybe she just didn't want me rushing into a trap... which is exactly what I've done." Rowen remembered the sight of Igrid's name seared into Father Matua's flesh and shuddered. "Whoever attacked Matua just wanted me here."

"But why would he want Igrid?"

"To get to me, maybe." Rowen shrugged. "I don't know. Did you learn anything more about Aeko?"

Sang Wei shook his head. "Only what you already know. After Aeko sent her message, the Grand Marshal came to question Father Matua, who told him nothing. So he ordered the cleric taken to Saikaido instead. Aeko protested. I spoke with two clerics who say Aeko nearly drew steel over it. She finally backed down. Then, the next day, she disappeared. No one has seen her since."

"Did she have any friends in New Atheion, any who might be hiding her?"

Sang Wei smiled faintly. "It doesn't sound like Lady Shingawa had many friends left anywhere, sir. Most died in the war. After the Grand Marshal assumed control of Saikaido Temple, any remaining Knight she'd trained, worked with, or fought alongside was reassigned elsewhere."

"Except for the two of us... who were already half a continent away and no help to her whatsoever." Rowen shook his head. "She stayed here because of me, Sang. She endured Crovis and the disgrace of losing her position so that she could be my eyes and ears while I was off trying to play hero with orphans and graveyards."

"You got her promoted back to Knight of the Lotus again," Sang Wei protested. "Friends or no, she was powerful. Technically, she was sixth in line to be Grand Marshal if—"

"She should have been first. She would have made a better Grand Marshal than Crovis Ammerhel or me on our best days." Rowen hesitated, realizing he'd referred to her in the past tense. "Something tells me we're running out of reasons to stay here. And Igrid needs me. I should be back in Cadavash with her." *And the children. And Knightswrath.*

"Agreed. How soon should we leave?"

Now, Rowen wanted to say. "We'll stay in New Atheion another day or two so Maddoc can do his work. Then, we'll go back to Cadavash. If the Grand Marshal has a problem with that, he can send an army after me."

"Should I at least send a message to Lady Igrid, telling her you'll be returning?"

"No," Rowen said. "If the Grand Marshal finds out, he just might send that army after all."

"But you're the Sword Marshal! Surely he wouldn't risk—"

Rowen smiled. "Enough talk. Thank you. You've done well. Aeko was right about you. Listen, I'm going to go help Maddoc treat the sick. Stay here and rest."

But as Rowen removed his armor, stripping down to plain clothes so that he could work more easily, Sang Wei was already following suit, quietly volunteering to help.

He's a good Knight. Maybe one day, he'll make a better Grand Marshal than any of us.

CHAPTER TWELVE

IGRID WAITED UNTIL THE MIDDLE of the night before she visited the Shel'ai barracks. Careful to wash any thought of what she was about to do from her mind, in case one of the Shel'ai tried to read her thoughts, she checked on Sariel. The child was sleeping, apparently free of nightmares. Igrid leaned in and kissed her wispy golden hair—gently, so as not to wake her—and backed away.

Outside, she climbed the stairs to the battlements and slowly paced the entire wall encircling Cadavash, nodding at Knights and squires on patrol. She also made a point of greeting the various Shel'ai she'd assigned at Zeia's suggestion. She ran into Sir Issa and was impressed that, despite her low neckline, the young Knight managed to maintain eye contact while they spoke.

Finally satisfied, she descended from the walls and returned to the manse. She accepted the cup of wine given to her by a servant upon entering. She sipped only a little of it, though, then set the cup down and went to check on Thessa.

She could tell by the way the child whimpered in her sleep that she was having a nightmare. Igrid smelled a faint whiff of urine and guessed Thessa had wet the bed again—something she often did when she had nightmares about what had happened to her at Hesod. Igrid was tempted to awaken the girl and comfort her but knew that if she did, Thessa might guess what Igrid was planning.

Or worse, I won't have the heart to leave!

Blinking rapidly, Igrid closed the door to Thessa's room and returned to her own. She undressed, tied back her long red curls, and set about donning the armor of an Iron Sister: steel greaves and vambraces, a skirt of studded leather, and a stylized half cuirass of steel worn over a tunic of thick leather. She also took a small knife whose curved quillons were designed to let it rest discreetly between her breasts. Then, she girded a matching pair of tashi along with two straight, Hesodi-style stilettos. Like her breastplate, the stilettos bore the sigil of Hesod: a bare-breasted woman spearing a dragon.

Lastly, she donned a cloak, girded a quiver of arrows, and picked up a small but powerful composite bow that had been a gift from the new ruler of the Queshi. She stopped to look in the mirror. "I'm sorry, Rowen. But what can I say? You're not leaving me much choice."

She walked out of her bedroom, past a wide-eyed servant, then straight out of the manse. Ignoring the startled looks of every Knight she passed, she headed straight to the chasm. Quietly plucking a lit torch from the hands of a passing Knight, she began her descent. She hadn't gone far when a man called her name. She turned to see Sir Jontin rushing down the steps after her. His hair was tousled, and he still wore his bedclothes.

"M'lady... " He looked her over and trailed off, fuming.

"Sir Jontin," Igrid began formally, "I'm sorry that someone saw fit to wake you. I left a note tacked to the wall of the armory. The note leaves you in command during my absence. Please see to it that the children are taken care of—especially the dragon-worshippers. Also, I left a separate note for Thessa. It's on her nightstand. Make sure she reads it." Igrid felt a lump in her throat, swallowed, and continued. "I left an additional note in the aviary that you should send to the king of Lyos, requesting more supplies. With so many hungry mouths, we can't keep relying on donations. While I'm gone, you are to—"

"You aren't going." Sir Jontin shook his head firmly. "I'm sorry, m'lady. I know you're concerned about Sir Locke—"

Igrid smirked. "*Concern* isn't the word I'd use. But thank you for yours. I'll convey it to Rowen when I'm done throttling him for his stupidity." She started to turn.

Sir Jontin grabbed her arm then let go, blushing. "Forgive me, m'lady, but Sir Locke will have my head if I let you leave."

"Actually, I think he'll promote you to Knight of the Lotus, just for tolerating me as well as you did." Igrid paused. "I'm sorry, Sir Jontin."

Sir Jontin blinked. "No apologies are necessary, m'lady. If you'll just let me escort you back to the manse, we can discuss this—"

"I mean, I'm sorry for the headache you're going to have in the morning."

Sir Jontin's eyes widened. He backed away, bracing for an attack, but Igrid did not charge. Instead, she nodded to Zeia, who had crept up behind the Knight, silent as a cat. Zeia ignited her flaming hands and pressed one to each side of the Knight's head. Sir Jontin jerked then fell. Zeia caught him. His bedclothes smoldered as she used her burning hands to lower him gently to the ground.

Zeia said, "Actually, he'll wake in less than an hour. To do more would have risked singeing his brains."

"An hour is more than I'll need. Does Keswen have the horses ready?"

"She's waiting in the stables. I agree with the Knight, though. This is a mistake."

Igrid smirked. "Which do you mean: leaving or taking Knightswrath with me?"

"Both." Zeia's flaming hands disappeared. "We don't even know if you can carry the sword, let alone if it'll be any safer beyond these walls."

"No," Igrid conceded, "but it'll be safer in Locke's hands. That's why we're going to see that it gets there." *After I pummel him with it.* She started back down the stairs.

"What do you intend to do about the Knights and the Shel'ai guarding the vault?"

"Order them to one side. If that doesn't work, I'll leave it up to you."

Zeia said, "I am no longer at a place in my life where I want to kill Knights, let alone a fellow Shel'ai."

"Good. Let's hope they've come to a place in their lives where they don't feel like dying." She quickened her pace.

To Igrid's great relief, things at the vault went better than she had anticipated. She told the guards that the mysterious Shel'ai who had attacked Zeia probably knew the sword was down there—a truth—and for that reason, she wanted to store it elsewhere. She did not think the old Shel'ai, who happened to be the same one who'd found Zeia, believed them. But he glanced at Zeia then stepped aside without protest. The Knights were more hesitant, but Igrid's sternness won them over.

Igrid told Zeia to wait outside then opened the vault with her own key and hurried in. She held her torch before her, waving it against the darkness. Though she knew the way, she felt a pang of fear as the shadows closed in around her. Gone was the calm she felt the last time she'd visited this chamber. When she climbed the dais and found herself staring down at Knightswrath, she shuddered in cold dread.

Are you in there, Silwren? Are you listening? Igrid steeled herself.

"All right, wytch, you and I have some things to discuss." She thrust her torch into a bracket on the altar.

Torchlight glinted angrily off the brass trimmings of Knightswrath's scabbard.

"We never liked each other. Still, you didn't tell Rowen I tried to take the sword from him during the war. I almost didn't tell him, either. It wasn't that I didn't think he'd forgive me. It was that I *knew* he'd forgive me. That's always been our problem. Or mine, I suppose. There's nothing I hate worse than being forgiven."

Igrid stretched out her hand, hesitated, then grasped the scabbard. Nothing happened. She moved her hand to the hilt and closed her fingers around it. She thought she felt a faint tingling beneath the cold but couldn't have said whether that was real or just her imagination. She braced herself then grasped the scabbard with her free hand and lifted the sword off the altar. It felt so light, so perfectly balanced, that she almost forgot she was breaking Rowen's most emphatic rule.

"So what happens now? If I undress you, will you burn me alive?" She tightened her grasp on the dragonbone hilt, rubbing one thumb over the carving of a woman casting wytchfire at dragons. She eased the blade from the scabbard—just a finger's span.

A jolt of heat raced up her arm, searing her so deeply that she could not even summon the breath to scream. Somehow, she managed not to drop the sword. When she regained her senses, she was still standing, holding the sword, but it was fully sheathed. She wondered if she'd done that without realizing it or if Silwren's spirit were somehow responsible.

Igrid removed her hand from the hilt and looked at it. Though the hilt felt cool, her palm had been burned, as though she'd tried to grasp a fire-hot pan with her bare hand. She blew on it. Tears welled in her eyes, but she blinked rapidly, refusing to shed them.

"Fair enough. I guess I deserved that."

Igrid reversed the sword, holding it blade downward, so that the handle stood right in front of her face. She spoke to the carving of the woman. "I don't mind telling you, I feel stupid talking to a sentient sword. So let's get straight to it." She traced the crosspiece, which resembled a crane and a dragon rising to embrace the blade. "I'm taking you to Rowen. I'm going to find him and put you back in his hands. Personally, I don't give a winged damn about saving the Knighthood. I'm not even sure I care about saving Ruun. But I *do* care about saving Rowen. On that much, at least, we can agree."

The crosspiece glinted in the flickering torchlight, and Igrid realized that was as good an answer as she could hope for. She took off her cloak, wrapped it around the sword, and held it under her arm. "I hope that's not too warm for you, wytch. Let me know if it is." She stepped away from the altar, passed Namundvar's Well, and kept walking as the torchlight dimmed and the shadows closed in around her.

Rowen woke to the feel of cold steel pressing against his throat. A torch was blazing in his face. Blinking, he fumbled for the knife under his pillow. Steel pressed harder, turning from cold to hot.

"Please don't fight, sir. We don't wish to harm you."

Rowen recognized the voice as that of one of his bodyguards. He lifted one hand, but instead of grappling with his opponent, he tried to shield his eyes from the torch. "Sir Li, I'm surprised you aren't asleep. You worked as hard as I did."

Sir Li issued a sharp command, and the Knight holding the torch drew back. A few cinders had fallen on the sheets. Rowen crushed them out with his thumb and looked around. His room was filled with Knights. "Where are my friends?"

"Unhurt," Sir Li responded, "as per the Grand Marshal's orders."

"Orders he saw fit to issue in the middle of the night," Rowen said, "unless I slept a lot longer than I think I did."

"It's still the middle of the night, sir. Now, if you'll please rise…"

The Knights stepped back, though three held their swords drawn.

Rowen slid his legs out from under the covers and placed them on the floor, shuddering at the cold. "May I wear my armor?"

Sir Li shook his head. "You may not. We'll see that it isn't stolen, though. The Grand Marshal—"

"Would prefer to have me arrested in my bedclothes." Rowen laughed, despite the knot of panic rising within him. Judging by his weariness, he guessed that only a few hours had passed since they'd finished helping Maddoc tend the sick and injured. All those that Maddoc had treated had gone home. Still, Rowen had not expected Crovis's men to seize him without alerting his companions, who had been sleeping in the chamber just outside his own.

Feigning nonchalance, Rowen dressed. To his relief, he felt the small knife sheathed to the inside of his boot, meaning the Knights had not thought to search his clothes first. He did not draw it, though. The Knights closed around him. Two gently but firmly seized him by his arms. A third bound his hands. They marched him out of the room.

In the next room, a dozen more Knights stood with torches and drawn swords. None spoke. He expected to see Maddoc and Sang Wei being restrained—or feared to see them lying on the ground in pools of blood—but both men were absent.

"My friends—"

"You must not speak," Sir Li said.

"Every Knight has a right to know what he's being arrested for," Rowen countered. "Shall I quote the passages in the Codex Lotius and the Codex Viticus that agree with me, or would you prefer—"

"You must not speak!" Sir Li repeated. His voice suddenly sounded shrill and urgent. "Please, sir. It's the Grand Marshal's orders."

The Knights led him toward the doors of the temple then stopped.

"I'm sorry, sir." Sir Li placed a cloth sack over Rowen's head.

Someone else produced a thin cord and tied it around his throat, loose enough to let him breathe but tight enough to hold the sack in place.

Rowen felt night air on his arms as the Knights led him out of the temple. He half hoped the citizens of New Atheion would see what was happening and rally to stop him, but the sound of Knights' boots echoed on all sides a moment before they pushed him into what he thought must be a coach.

Rowen lay facedown in the coach, listening to the *clip-clop* of hooves on cobblestones, trying to breathe regularly despite his awkward position. A Knight sat down and rested one heavy boot in the middle of Rowen's back. A voice he did not recognize whispered, "You are a disgrace to the Light."

Rowen did not bother answering. The coach ride was mercifully short. When they lurched to a sudden halt, rough hands grabbed Rowen's arms and legs and dragged him out of the carriage. His ankle banged against something, and he cursed inside his hood. Someone struck the side of his head.

"Be quiet," the same cruel voice whispered.

His captors hefted him like a sack of potatoes then deposited him unceremoniously onto a rocking floor that he guessed belonged to a ferry. Once again, someone held Rowen down by resting his boot in the middle of his back. However, that time, the Knight ground his heel back and forth. Rowen winced inside his hood but did not cry out.

"Your friends are demons," the cruel voice said.

"You're no Knight," someone else added.

"Enough," Sir Li's voice called from a distance. "Sir Hiro, leave him alone."

Rowen heard indiscernible whispering followed by laughter, but the Knights did not taunt him again. After what felt like an eternity, the ferry ground to a halt on what he guessed must be the sandy shores of Saikaido. The Knights hoisted him back onto his feet.

"I'm going to have a hard time climbing a thousand steps when I can't see."

Someone punched him in the stomach.

Rowen had anticipated the blow and tensed. Nonetheless, he doubled over, feigning injury. He prepared himself to try and break free, intending to head-butt and kick as best as he was able. The hood would muffle his voice, but if he fought his way free—even for a moment—he could cry for help. He remembered what Maddoc had said: when he'd been attacked in the streets, the people of Saikaido had rallied to his defense. They might do so again.

But before he could act, someone pressed a blade between his neck and shoulder, where a simple thrust would push the blade straight down into his vital organs. He felt the tip draw a trickle of blood.

"Please don't try to escape," Sir Li said. "We don't want to do this, but we are prepared to obey our Grand Marshal's orders."

Rowen straightened slowly. "Give me a chance to face my accuser, as is my right, and I won't try to escape. I swear it."

"You're in no position to bargain, demon-friend," hissed the cruel voice of Sir Hiro.

"Enough," Sir Li repeated. "Just get him in the lift and take him to the temple."

Rowen swore. Too late, he remembered the baskets and pulleys that could be lowered from the summit and used to carry goods to the temple more quickly than carrying them up the steps. He had never seen them used to carry a person, but if they'd installed a bigger device, it would be possible.

Maddoc... Sang Wei... where are you?

Rowen heard nothing but the stomping of boots and the lapping of the surf until they reached the hill. There, they stopped. To his chagrin, they removed his boots, taking his hidden knife with them. The sound of creaking wood preceded his captors shoving him into what felt like a small bamboo cage. A door closed and latched.

"Don't struggle," Sir Li whispered. "Even if you break free, you'll just fall a thousand feet!"

Rowen did not answer. A moment later, he felt himself being lifted into the air.

Igrid feared they would emerge from the chasm to find all of Cadavash arrayed before the gates, determined to stop her. Instead, she saw just a few Knights and squires speaking in hushed, anxious tones as they passed. Sir Jontin still slumbered on the stone stairs. Igrid spotted Sir Issa, scowling down at her from the walls, and had half a mind to send him down to retrieve Jontin and carry him to bed.

Instead, she mounted the horse that Keswen offered her and headed for the gates. Zeia and Keswen fell in behind her, one on either side.

Igrid glanced back and saw Zeia holding the reins with her flaming hands. Then, facing forward, she told the Knights to open the gates.

They exchanged glances, but to her relief, they obeyed. Two removed the crossbeam while two more pushed on one of the gates. After propping the crossbeam against the wall, the first two guards pushed on the second gate. They swung open with a loud wooden creak. By the time Igrid and her companions reached them, an open path lay before them, extending into the starry eastern darkness.

Igrid wanted to glance back at the manse to see if Thessa had awakened and was watching them, but she kept her gaze fixed straight ahead. A cold breeze made her eyes water. Once they were clear of the gates, she flicked the reins.

"Let's go," she muttered to her companions. "The sooner we get this done, the sooner we can come home."

CHAPTER THIRTEEN

J ALIST HEWN, CAPTAIN OF THE Red Watch, blinked in the harsh
glare of daylight and wished he were still in bed. He'd hardly dressed
and left the barracks, walking through the streets of Lyos toward the
palace, but already his headache was returning. He wished he'd ignored
the urgency of the king's summons and stopped to get drunk first. After
all, early though it was, Lyos contained a number of taverns and brothels
between there and the palace that knew him by name and would gladly
welcome him—and his coin purse.

Of course, King Typherius would be disappointed, but that would not
be the first time. Over the past few months, Jalist had grown accustomed
to looks of disappointment, whether they came from the king, the many
clerics of Lyos, or even his own men.

"Not that they have a choice. I'm a hero, aren't I? They *have* to love
me." Jalist rubbed his eyes as he muttered.

A passing cleric frowned, thinking he was being addressed by a
madman or a beggar, only to turn and see the famed Captain of the Guard.
The cleric said something Jalist could not understand and kept walking.
As the cleric moved along, Jalist noted the color of the man's robes.

Jalist called after him, "Why is everything so damn red on this
continent? Red Watch, Red Steppes, Red Emperor, the Bloody Prince,
red greatwolves... even the Sons of Maelmohr wear red! Isn't it bad
enough we have to haul this red swill in our veins?"

The cleric kept moving and did not turn back.

"Good answer." Jalist shrugged. "Well, sooner I get this done, sooner

I can drink," he told a mother and her two small children as they passed by. The woman blanched and hurried her children along. Jalist laughed. "I *saved* those children!" He spat on the ground, reeled, and caught himself. "I helped save everybody... except my own damn people."

Jalist rubbed his eyes and kept walking. He took a moment to realize that he'd lost his bearings and was heading in the wrong direction. Then he spotted a familiar tavern and considered stopping after all until he remembered the realization he'd just had.

"Sooner I get this done... "

He turned, resolute, and marched toward the palace. Still, he'd gone only halfway when he spotted a squad of Red Watch riding toward him, just ahead of an empty carriage. Jalist tried to remember whether he was supposed to salute first or they were. He decided upon the latter. But when the horsemen reined up just in front of him, nobody saluted.

"Captain, the king awaits you. He wondered what was taking so long and sent this carriage to carry you."

Jalist frowned, staring up at the speaker. He lifted one hand, shielding his eyes from the glare of sunlight, but still did not recognize the man. "Thank you... " He shuffled over to the carriage and managed to climb inside. "Go slow," he told the driver. "I think Zet and the other gods are fighting for control of my head and bowels. Maybe if I—"

The driver snapped the reins, wheeling the carriage about and urging it toward the palace as fast as the horse could carry it despite Jalist's curses. Once they reached the palace, the driver climbed down and offered to help Jalist out. Jalist knocked his hand away and went to climb out himself. His foot caught, and he fell face-first into the street.

Two men—the driver and the man of the Red Watch who'd been sent to find him—hoisted him back onto his feet. Jalist grumbled his thanks. Neither man answered. Tugging at his crimson uniform, which lately had been growing tighter around his belly, Jalist threw himself at the stairs into the palace. His intention was to climb them so quickly that all his men would be impressed. Instead, he fell again. But he caught himself, feigned amusement at his skinned palms, and scampered up the rest of the stairs.

Two palace guards were waiting. They said something Jalist did not understand then half guided, half led him toward the king's solar. Jalist found the young king seated alone at a great oaken table. He did not rise to greet Jalist but instead scowled at him from across the table.

Jalist fell to one knee then struggled back onto his feet just as quickly. He looked around. "Where is everybody? I thought this was supposed to be an important council."

"The meeting was two hours ago," the king said, still scowling. He gestured for Jalist to sit. "Nice of you to join me, Captain.'

"My pleasure, sire." Jalist sat, rubbing his temples with his eyes closed. Then he opened them and looked around the table. "I trust this is about the Dwarrs. Another message from that new madman of theirs, demanding that we join in some holy crusade against magic? If you like, I can tell you how to tell him to go bugger himself in Dwarrish."

"That won't be necessary, Captain. This has nothing to do with the Scion."

Jalist pinched the bridge of his nose, trying unsuccessfully to drive off his headache. "Is there any wine?"

The king leaned closer and pushed a scrap of paper toward him.

Jalist frowned at the paper. "That's not wine."

"Read it, Captain."

Jalist picked it up. He stared at it a moment then rubbed his eyes and laid it down. "Forgive me, sire, but my eyes don't appear to be working. If I could just—"

"I'll give you a choice," the king said. "Either convince your eyes to start working again, or I'll organize a squad of your own men and have them toss you off Beggar's Drop. I don't think I'll have a hard time finding volunteers."

Jalist blinked. "Apologies, sire. I'll try my best not to make you throw me to my death." He rubbed his eyes again then picked up the parchment and squinted. He managed to read it once, frowned, and read it again. "Is this some kind of joke? How could Locke be arrested in New Atheion when he's still back at Cadavash?"

The king gave him a look of revulsion. "Sir Locke passed through Lyos over a week ago, on his way to the Isles. You spoke with him."

Jalist frowned. "I did?" He rubbed him temples again. "I think you should have a word with your birder. Whoever sent that message—"

141

"It didn't arrive by bird. One of my spies was in New Atheion when it happened. He brought me the message himself."

Jalist shrugged. "The man was probably drunk. I suggest you place less trust in spies." He added a belated "sire."

The king's eyes narrowed. "Then you don't believe it's true?"

Jalist shook his head. "Locke's a hero. These Knights worship him. They wouldn't so much as step on his shadow without..." He trailed off, unsure how to finish his sentence, and looked around the table for wine again. He spotted what he thought was a strangely thin carafe and tipped it, only to discover it was a candleholder whose candle had gone out. Hot wax poured onto his hand.

"At least that didn't go in my mouth," he muttered.

The king struck the table.

Jalist jumped. "What was that?" He set the candleholder down. "Is your hand hurt, m'lord?"

The king stared at him for a moment then shook his head and called for his guards. When they came in, the king stood and pointed at Jalist. "Take your mighty captain down to a jail cell and lock him up. Strip him naked and douse him in cold water every hour, on the hour, until I come down and tell you to stop." He retrieved the parchment and passed it to one of the men. "After you've doused him, each time, read that message into his ear. Understood?"

The guards smiled faintly. One said, "Understood, sire." Then they seized Jalist before he could protest and hauled him out of his chair.

Igrid stared at the sun-glazed plains and rolling hills before her and tried not to think about how much her hand hurt. The three women had ridden through the night then stopped at dawn for a few hours' rest. Igrid had hoped that the pain would subside. Instead, blisters had risen, and if anything, her hand felt worse.

"Gods, why didn't I bring wine?" she muttered.

"If Knightswrath did that, I don't know if I can heal it," Zeia said, "but if you want, I'll try."

Igrid realized that despite her wish to keep the injury secret, she'd not only forgotten to put her gloves on that morning but had also left her blistered palm turned upward. She closed her hand into a fist. "Don't bother. For all I know, the hand is Silwren's price for letting me carry this damn thing without being burned alive." She patted Knightswrath's hilt. The sword was still sheathed in her saddle, thoroughly wrapped and concealed by a cloak. "It'll heal."

Igrid glanced at Zeia's maimed wrists and wondered if she'd said too much. Zeia snickered but said nothing.

Keswen, who had been riding some distance ahead of them to scout for danger, reined in and turned around. "There's a village maybe half a mile ahead," she called back.

We should stop. An inn is safer than the wilderness, and a few hours' rest wouldn't hurt.

"We shouldn't stop," Zeia said. "Three young women—one of them a Sylv, one of them me—are going to attract too much attention."

Igrid scoffed. "We can defend ourselves. Any man dumb enough to try and stop us—"

"Will die," Zeia conceded, "but in my experience, the worst men have the most friends. I'd rather not be soaked in blood before we get halfway to the Isles."

Igrid bit back an angry reply and tapped a sword hilt with her burned hand. "You're not wrong," she said finally.

Zeia's tone softened. "We can stop a moment if your hand—"

"Better not," Keswen said. She'd returned and reined in her horse. "We're being watched." She feigned a yawn. "The copse of trees behind me, your left, maybe two hundred yards."

Igrid resisted the impulse to turn and look. "How many?"

"Not sure. More than one, though."

Zeia closed her eyes.

Igrid was close enough to feel the air around the Shel'ai begin to tingle.

"Five," she said a moment later.

Igrid pretended to massage a crick in her neck. "Are they just staring, or looking for trouble?"

"Well, they're hiding behind trees." Keswen idly touched an arrow in her quiver then withdrew it, pretending she only wanted to use it to scratch her back.

143

"I've seen boys hide behind trees so they could watch a girl bathe," Igrid said. "Might not be something the gods would applaud, but I'm not sure that warrants killing."

"They're armed," Zeia said. Her eyes were still closed. "Two crude spears, a pitchfork, some rusty knives."

"Highwaymen, then," Keswen said. She feigned another yawn, kept her back to the trees, and nocked the arrow to her bowstring. "We can take them, or we can steer north and hope they don't follow us." She faced Igrid. "Decide."

Locke would confront them. Not because he wanted a fight but because he'd consider it his duty to stop them from hurting someone else.

Taking her silence as indecision, Zeia said, "They could be from the village. If we kill them, we might end up with a much bigger fight on our hands." She smirked as she said the final word.

Keswen shrugged. "The wytch is probably right. If you want to get to Locke, this is a fight we don't have to fight."

Igrid considered the Sylv's choice of words. For the first time, she found herself wondering how Keswen really felt about Shel'ai. She'd been at Cadavash since the beginning, sure, but she was so taciturn that Igrid could not remember Keswen having more than one or two conversations with a Shel'ai before this.

"Agreed," Igrid said finally. "We'll steer north. Zeia, if it won't tire you too much, keep watch on them."

"I can do it for a while." Zeia cast a terse look at Keswen. "Maybe half a mile. But I won't be much use after that if there's a fight."

"Save your strength, sorceress." Keswen kept the arrow on her bowstring. "I'll hear it if they charge."

Igrid turned her horse and rode between them. "Fine. Let's go before I change my mind."

Algol stared down the hill at the women and wondered which he should kill first. He turned to Dagath, expecting the one-eyed sellsword to have an amusing opinion on the subject. Instead, he found Dagath scowling.

"I know them."

Algol asked, "Which ones?"

"*All* of them." Dagath pointed. "I fought the pretty redhead at Hesod. Almost had her, but she got away. Before that, I bedded the Sylv up north. She was a prisoner. I remember because she got free and killed my employer." He half smiled. "And that third one is a wytch. Same employer had me cut off her hands to keep her tame."

Algol smirked, certain the man must be lying. But a quick probe of his mind said otherwise. "You have had an interesting life, sellsword."

"Or else the gods are punishing me," Dagath grunted. "All three of those cunts are tough as greatwolves. Plus, *he* has a thing about hurting women." Dagath nodded down the hill toward the spot where his massive companion sat on a stone, a knife in hand, quietly sharpening tree branches into spears. "Weird for an Olg, I know, but I lay equal odds he won't help us when it comes down to it."

Algol frowned, adjusted the strip of cloth covering his hollow eye sockets, then turned back to the women riding below. "Do you have any special attachment to the Olg?"

Dagath chuckled. "You mean, like, would I mind killing him if it comes to it?" He shook his head. "No problem there, sorcerer. But you can guess what I'm about to say next."

"Of course," Algol said. "Coin will not be a problem. I'll make you a king, if that's what you desire."

"I'd settle for a harem and a solid-gold chamber pot." Dagath reached down and eased his sword from its scabbard. "I'm telling you, we'll need more men, though."

Algol glanced south. "Maybe not. Something tells me the gods are on our side."

"The gods aren't on *anyone's* side." Dagath snorted. "Least of all mine."

"Then how do you explain five bandits arriving just in time to help us achieve our objective?"

Dagath shrugged. "Three pretty women, two of them foreign looking, riding through the wilderness without any men to guard them? Doesn't take much to figure out what's driving *that* bunch." He nodded toward the five grubby figures following the women on foot, perhaps a mile behind.

Algol was quiet for a moment then laughed. "I've never had much use for the gods, either. I don't think they'll think too fondly of me by the time all this is over." He half expected the sellsword to ask him what he meant, but the latter said nothing.

Algol straightened then grabbed Dagath's arm and pulled him off the summit of the hill lest one of the women look up and see them. They descended the hill, and he faced the Olg. "I understand you don't like hurting women. But there will be no torture here, no rape. One of those women stole something of great value from me. The others helped her cut out my eyes while I slept. I seek only justice and the return of what was taken. It's a matter of honor." He paused. "Will you help?"

The Olg shifted and looked down then back up. Finally, he nodded. The bones braided in his hair clacked together.

Algol smiled and placed one hand on the Olg's massive shoulder. "Good. Thank you."

Dagath tested the edge of his sword then sucked the blood that blossomed from his thumb. "How do you want to do this?"

"Patiently," Algol said. "First, we wait."

No one spoke. A faint breeze blew, accompanied by a veil of shadow that darkened the sun on the grass. After a moment, the nameless Olg went back to sharpening spears.

CHAPTER FOURTEEN

ROWEN THOUGHT THEY WOULD TAKE him directly to see Crovis Ammerhel as soon as his bamboo cage shuddered to a stop. Instead, minutes turned into hours, yet still no one came to get him. He considered trying to break free but remembered Sir Li's warning and feared he might succeed only in plummeting to his death. The small size of the cage kept him hunched over, but with great effort, he managed to free himself of the hood.

Night air chilled the sweat on his face. He looked down and saw that he was indeed suspended high above the ground, at the very edge of the summit. Above him lay a massive pulley system. The bluff was only a few feet away, but the bars of his cage were too narrow to thrust his hand through. Lit torches blazed on the hill, beyond which lay a squat, dark structure that he suspected must be a storehouse. He could barely make out the outline of Saikaido Temple beyond.

Rowen waited, cold and angry, until he could stand it no more. Then, he started shouting. He half hoped some squire or cleric would come to rescue him. Just in case he was discovered by someone who had no notion what the Grand Marshal had done, Rowen mentally rehearsed a lie about being assaulted by townspeople, robbed, and thrust into the cage as a joke. But no one came. Finally, his throat raw, his back and legs cramped from hunching over, he gave up.

Rowen had just enough room in the cage to kneel. He closed his eyes and tried to meditate, but such concentration eluded him. He kept thinking of Igrid. By then, his written warning about finding her name seared into Father Matua's body must have reached her. Sir Berric had probably reached her as well. She could protect herself against a common assassin, certainly, but he wondered how she would fare against a Shel'ai. He wondered, too, if the children were still safe.

I should have left as soon as I saw what had been done to Matua!

He felt a surge of anger—first at himself, then at Aeko Shingawa for not fully warning him about the danger to Igrid in the first place. He took a deep breath and tried to calm his nerves, reminding himself that Aeko was still missing and he still did not know all that had happened. Then, he heard a throat clear.

Rowen opened his eyes. Wyn Kai stood before him, at the very edge of the summit, armored and expressionless. The two Knights faced each other in silence. Rowen straightened as much as he was able and gripped the bamboo cage. The motion caused it to shift and sway. Rowen looked down at a thousand feet of darkness then back up.

"Good evening, Sir Kai. I trust you haven't come here to set me free."

Wyn Kai regarded Rowen for a moment then withdrew a small flask from his belt, stepped perilously close to the edge, and passed the flask through the bars of Rowen's cage. Rowen accepted it and drank. Cold water cooled his parched throat. He intended to drink slowly and save some of the water, in case they decided to leave him there for days, but he drank it all instead. When he was done, he tossed the flask back between the bars.

Wyn Kai caught it and slipped it into his belt. He stared at Rowen a moment longer, still unspeaking, then turned to go.

Rowen said, "Wait. At least tell me what happened to Sang Wei and Maddoc. Whatever the Grand Marshal says I've done, they had no part in it. Set them free, and—"

"They're probably dead by now." Wyn Kai lowered his eyes to the ground. "Apologies, Sir Locke."

As he walked away, the Knight snapped his fingers. Four more Knights emerged from the shadows, two holding staffs fixed with hooks. They caught hold of Rowen's cage and dragged it forward. Another man unlatched it.

Before they could open the door, Rowen threw himself at it. He tackled one Knight in a tangle of arms and legs, but before he could get hold of the man's sword, the other Knights seized him by his arms and dragged him backward. The first Knight rose, scowled, and drove one gauntleted fist into the side of Rowen's head.

Wyn Kai's voice cut through the sudden fog of pain and vertigo. "Enough. Cover his head again."

Rowen struggled as best he could, but his captors bound his hands behind his back then succeeded in slipping the cloth bag over his head and lashing it with cord again. Rowen had thought they were using the bag he'd taken off and left in his cage, but this one smelled of onions. Also, his captors were not nearly as gentle as Sir Li. They tightened the rope around his throat until Rowen could barely breathe. Then, they shoved him forward. He stumbled but caught himself. He felt blood trickling from the side of his head where he'd been struck.

"Did any of you know Sir Wei?" No one answered. Given how quietly he had to speak, unable to draw a proper breath, Rowen wondered if they'd even heard him. "How about Aeko? Were you there when she died? Did you at least arm her before you killed her?" Despite waves of dizziness, Rowen laughed. "Of course not! If you had, she'd have cut you to pieces. Same with Sang Wei. I bet you stabbed them in—"

One of the Knights struck the back of his head. Rowen could tell he'd not been struck as hard as he could have been, but his assailant happened to hit the same tender spot where Rowen had been struck in the street. Pain washed over him—more than he could stand—and for a moment, the darkness of the cloth bag seemed to melt into his face.

Rowen woke to cold water raking at his face.

He sputtered and choked. Instead of quickly dousing him with a bucket, a Knight of the Stag was leaning over him, slowly pouring water from a pitcher. Rowen did not recognize the man, but he was young and handsome, with slicked-back hair and a cold smirk. He wore the armor of a Knight of the Stag. Rowen pursed his lips, holding his breath, but kept his eyes open.

When the pitcher was empty, the Knight of the Stag tossed it away, stood, and stepped back. "He's awake," he said easily, in the voice of Sir Hiro, the same man who had tormented him earlier.

Rowen tried to sit up. To his surprise, his hands were free, though thick iron chains attached his feet to the floor. Torches burned all around him, held in the hands of a ring of stoic armored Knights. He studied them as he touched the blood crusted to the side of his head and elsewhere on the back of his skull.

"Sir Rowen Locke, Sword Marshal and Knight of the Lotus, stand up."

Rowen recognized the booming voice of Crovis Ammerhel. Biting back an angry retort, he managed to rise. As he did so, he realized that the chains securing him to the floor permitted him to travel just a few feet in any direction. He turned and faced Sir Ammerhel, who stood before him in polished armor, plus a tabard and cloak of rich azure.

Crovis Ammerhel stepped a little closer. "Do you know what this is, Sir Locke?" He made a wide, sweeping gesture at their surroundings.

Rowen looked around. "Rock. Air. Metal. A bunch of bastards with no honor." He paused. "Am I close?"

Crovis started to smile then turned stern again. "Men sometimes turn funny when they're being interrogated. Always, it's because they're afraid. Tell me, are *you* afraid, Sir Locke?"

Rowen said, "Singchai ushó fey." *No courage without fear.*

That time, Crovis smiled openly. "Well said. But fear and courage are not the issue here. You have been summoned by this council to answer serious charges. I do not think I need to clarify the severity of your position. If you are found guilty, your life will be forfeit."

Rowen felt a lump in his throat. He swallowed it and said, "At the moment, I don't know why I'm here any more than I recognize your authority to detain me."

"I am your Grand Marshal. We are your fellow Knights. Our authority is not in question."

Rowen forced himself to meet Crovis's piercing gaze. "This is not the Hall of Assembly. No one here speaks for me. I have been taken and chained without first being told my crime. And worst of all, my companions, who did nothing wrong, have been slain… probably in their sleep." Rowen paused. "Shall we count how many laws you have violated, Grand Marshal?"

No one so much as murmured, but a few Knights shifted uneasily—

among them Sir Li. Others rolled their eyes. Sir Hiro spat on the floor, caught Rowen's eye, and tapped the hilt of his sword.

Crovis said, "I neither hide nor deny what you have said. Desperate times have led me to bend the very laws I have sworn to uphold. I regret this. Nevertheless, the principal threat facing the Knighthood is of *your* doing, Sir Locke. You and your admirers are like rotten flesh surrounding a wound. You must be cut out. It is not pleasant or glorious, but it is necessary."

"The war is over. Chorlga, Fadarah, and Shade are dead. The Dragonjol and the Jolym have been destroyed. For the first time in a thousand years, there is peace between Shel'ai and the other races." Rowen paused. "If all this constitutes rotten flesh, I suggest you never resign your Knighthood to become a healer."

Rowen hoped at least one Knight would laugh. No one did.

After a moment, Crovis said, "It's true that you ended the war, Sir Locke. But a peace achieved at the cost of our souls is no peace that can last."

Rowen felt a surge of pain and rubbed the side of his head. "Before I say anything else, I want to know exactly what happened to my friends. Aeko, Sang Wei, Maddoc…"

"Lady Shingawa is not dead—at least, not to the best of my knowledge." Crovis waved at Sir Li, who stepped forward. "Sir Li can speak to the final moments of Sir Wei and the sorcerer."

Sir Li hesitated again then drew closer to Rowen. At the look on Rowen's face, he flinched and kept one hand on his sword hilt. "Sir Locke, I was charged by the Grand Marshal with arresting both you and Sir Wei and bringing you to justice. The sorcerer was to be killed. At first, I could not find them. Eventually, I *did* find them elsewhere in the temple… in a rather compromising position."

Some of the Knights chuckled.

Red-faced, Sir Li said, "Upon delivering you in chains, Sir Locke, I informed the Grand Marshal that I approached these two men, alone and unseen, and shoved my sword through both of their bodies while they embraced." He hesitated. "That was a lie." Sir Li turned to Crovis and bowed. "I apologize, Grand Marshal."

Crovis scowled. "You told me—"

"A lie," Sir Li repeated. He looked ill. Slowly, he turned, addressing the entire circle of Knights. "Yesterday, I watched a sorcerer heal the meek and injured, asking nothing in return. I watched Sir Locke and Sir Wei help him. I helped him, too, as did all my men." His voice grew a little louder. "They are *not* what I was told. Despite my orders, I could not bring myself to stab good men in the back."

Crovis approached. Sir Li recoiled.

Crovis asked, "Where are they?"

Sir Li tried to meet Crovis's gaze then looked away. "Gone, Grand Marshal. I let them go."

A few Knights shouted with outrage. One even drew his sword. Crovis held up his hands, calling for calm. "Do you know what you have done, Sir Li?"

"I... I do, Grand Marshal. But honor will not permit me to do otherwise." Sir Li was shaking. Nevertheless, he drew his sword. "Sir Ammerhel, I question... both your honor... and your judgment." His eyes rolled, as though he could barely finish. "Thus... in keeping with the rules of the Codex Viticus, I challenge you to single combat."

A stunned hush fell over the chamber. *No*, Rowen thought, but he could not make himself speak. Meanwhile, Crovis faced Sir Li with an expression that melted from rage to sadness. He tapped the pommel of his sword but did not draw it.

"Sir Li, are you certain about this?"

Before Sir Li could answer, Wyn Kai stepped forward, holding up his hands. "I ask you to reconsider, Sir Li. You have committed a great and dishonorable offense, yes, but even great offenses can sometimes be forgiven."

"Some," Sir Li said, "but not all." He kept his eyes on Crovis as he lifted his sword with both hands. His blade trembled, as did the arms holding it.

Wyn Kai glanced at Crovis then stepped back. He folded his hands and looked at the floor.

Crovis sighed. Then, with lightning speed, he leapt forward. His adamune blurred from its scabbard. Sir Li's body tumbled backward. Men gasped. Crovis stood still for a moment then knelt and wiped his blade on Sir Li's tabard. He waved, and Wyn Kai stepped forward.

"Pack Sir Li's head in salt. When this is done, we'll place it on a spike in front of the temple, as a warning. In the meantime, burn the rest of the body with honor." Crovis faced Sir Li's body, which lay in a growing pool of blood, and bowed.

The other Knights stared, mouths agape. A few applauded.

Rowen watched the blood spread and spread, which caused some of the Knights to move out of the way. He said, "Damn you, Crovis."

Crovis sheathed his sword and stood before Rowen again, tauntingly close. "Sir Kai, I believe these procedures should be halted for the time being so that we may properly reflect on Sir Li's passing. Also, please immediately set to locating Sir Locke's missing companions so that they, too, may be brought to justice."

Wyn Kai gestured, and two Knights retrieved Sir Li's body, holding it by the arms and legs. Wyn Kai collected Sir Li's head, his own expression sour, and followed the rest of the Knights out of the chamber. Crovis closed the door behind them then returned to Rowen.

"What next, Sir Locke? Will *you* challenge me, as well?"

"I know I'd lose," Rowen admitted, "but it might just be worth it to escape your presence."

Crovis sighed. "I never wanted to be your enemy, Sir Locke. Perhaps you did not want to be mine, either. Yet here we stand."

Rowen gritted his teeth. "What happened to Aeko?"

"She fled," Crovis said. "Rather, she *tried* to flee, and I caught her." He slowly circled the chamber. "I saw the message she meant to send to you. In it, she told you what had happened to Father Matua and warned you to stay away. She did so in code, but I was not deceived. So I replaced her message with one of my own." He stopped in front of Rowen and smiled. "I see you were fooled... at least a little. I might be proud, had the action itself not been dishonorable. I had hoped you would bring me the sword, though."

Rowen gauged how close Crovis was and realized the Grand Marshal was taunting him, daring him to strike. "Take me to Aeko," he said instead.

Crovis stepped back. "I understand, you know. Why you didn't want me to know about the scroll, the one that describes what's inside the Dragonward. Thing is, Sir Locke, I already knew about that scroll. I knew because I'm the one who put it there."

Rowen stared, speechless.

"Why do you think none of your sorcerer friends ever knew about it, not even the Dragonkin?" Crovis snickered. "I found the scroll in a temple, years ago. In truth, I think I was guided to it by the Light. I took it with me to Atheion during the war. After the Scrollhouse was half destroyed, I hid the scroll in the wreckage."

"Why?" Rowen managed.

"I thought the Shel'ai would find it. I thought they'd use it to bring the Dragonward down."

"You... *wanted* that to happen?"

Crovis scowled. "Of course not! I am no fool, Sir Locke. I know the horrors this continent would face if the Dragonkin returned. But I also know the glories, how we could rise like dogblossom from the muck. Our people beat the Dragonkin once. They could do it again. But this time, it would be only their faith in the Light that would guide them. No magic. Just faith and steel." He smiled giddily and drew his sword.

Rowen tensed, certain he was about to die, but Crovis just inspected his blade as though seeing it for the first time.

"What about the Shel'ai, the one who attacked Matua?" Rowen asked. "Is he your ally, too?"

Crovis's eyes narrowed. "I do not care for that accusation, Sir Locke. Yes, the sorcerer approached me. Yes, he offered an alliance... but an alliance of enemies, not friends."

"Care to explain what you're talking about?"

"I don't think I have to." Crovis stepped to one side, held the unsharpened edge of his blade against Rowen's throat, and slowly pulled it back.

Rowen shuddered, despite his best efforts to keep still.

"You will be stripped of your Knighthood. You will be banished from the Lotus Isles. But you will *not* be killed, so long as you give me what I want. I swear it on my honor."

Rowen eyed the gigantic bloodstain on the stone floor. "You have an interesting concept of honor."

Crovis sheathed his sword and folded his hands behind his back. He stood close to Rowen, taunting him again. "If I swear an oath, that oath will be upheld. Hate me all you like, Sir Locke, but you know I speak the truth. But here is the other half of my oath: refuse to assist me, and I'll see to it that every woman and child in your ungodly little stronghold will face so slow and agonizing a death, even the Dhargots will pity you."

Rowen started to speak then lunged for Crovis's sword. Crovis easily stepped back, hands still behind himself, and kicked Rowen in the stomach. Rowen doubled over. Crovis sidestepped and drove his heel into the side of Rowen's head, where he'd already been injured.

Darkness nipped at Rowen's vision, but he pushed himself back up to his knees, refusing to lose consciousness. He could not tell where Crovis was standing, but he said, "Tell me, do all the Knights know you mean to bring down the Dragonward?"

"A Soroccan father does not explain what he's about to do before he throws his child into the sea. He simply does it. And because of this, because of kindness that seems at first like cruelty, his child learns how to swim."

Rowen thought of his Soroccan friend, Hráthbam, who had told him once that the story of Soroccan fathers teaching their children to swim was just a legend, and few if any fathers on the island would have condoned such a practice. He struggled to form that thought into words, but before he could speak, he heard a door open then slam shut.

Slowly, he sank back down onto the stone, half expecting Sir Li's blood to drift back and wash over him.

CHAPTER FIFTEEN

Igrid glanced south and touched her composite bow. "I say we stop here and fight them together. Enough running. With my and Keswen's bows alone, we can probably—"

"No," Zeia said. "As soon as they see we've stopped and we're ready to fight, they'll stop, too. Or they'll try and flank us. Better we draw them close then scare them off."

Keswen shook her head. "No need for that. We're talking about five men—half old, half just boys—with lousy weapons. You two keep going to lure them on. I'll circle behind and kill them myself."

Zeia frowned. "I don't care if they're armed with nothing but foul language. You can't kill all five by yourself."

Keswen snickered. In a blur, she nocked three arrows to her bowstring. "They won't see me coming. I'll hit two in the first volley, kill at least one. I'll hit another before they've even turned around. All five will have arrows in them before they're close enough to spit on." She added, "That's if half of them don't run as soon as it starts, which they probably will."

One of Zeia's hands burned to life. She touched the hilt of her shortsword, and a thin tendril of smoke rose from the pommel. "If even one gets away, he'll tell the village what happened. Then we might have twenty or thirty to deal with!"

"Then I won't let one get away."

Zeia shook her head. "If one runs while—"

"If one runs, he'll have an arrow in his back or his leg while he's doing it. He won't get far. If needs be, I'll track him."

Zeia eyed Keswen with contempt then faced Igrid. "If we scare them off *without* killing, they'll have nothing to avenge. That might be the end of it."

"Might," Keswen said, "might not. Why take that chance?"

Zeia blushed. "I'm still not... fully recovered. If the tide turns, I won't be of much help."

Keswen returned the arrows to her quiver. "That's why I said I'd handle it myself."

Igrid interjected before Zeia could reply. "Zeia has a point. I don't want them alive any more than you do, but if we just drive them off without killing, that'll probably be the end of it." She faced Keswen. "I don't want you fighting them alone, though. I'll stay on the hill with the horses and keep their attention. You circle around on foot. Take Zeia with you. The sight of her hands alone might be enough to drive them off."

Keswen shook her head. "If it's all the same, I'll go alone. I told you—"

"It's *not* all the same," Igrid snapped. "You'll take Zeia with you, or you'll turn around and ride back to Cadavash. If I have to say it again, you'll ride back to Cadavash with fewer teeth than you have now."

Keswen blinked then snickered. "Of course, Lady Igrid. Apologies." She glanced at Zeia. "Well, Burning Hands, let's get going."

Zeia gave the Sylvan woman a look of loathing then faced Igrid. "That one likes killing even more than we do."

"Now *that's* a frightful thought." Igrid sighed. "Just drive them off and hurry back. We have no time for this nonsense." She patted Knightswrath, where it still lay concealed in her saddle.

Zeia nodded then slipped after Keswen, quiet as a shadow. Igrid stood at the top of a high rocky hill, holding the reins of all three horses. The other two women descended the far side of the hill, swung wide, then slowly circled around to get behind the men. As much as they seemed to dislike each other, they moved in nearly perfect tandem.

Igrid glanced south at the five figures hurrying after her. They had switched to moving out in the open, barely three hundred yards away. Igrid doubted they had seen Zeia and Keswen leave, but any moment now, they would notice Igrid was alone. They might get suspicious, wonder why she wasn't running, and start watching their backs.

"Can't have that."

Igrid mounted her horse, stood high in the stirrups, and began taking off her clothes. The men stopped and stared then hooted with delight. They broke into a run. Igrid ignored the revulsion in her stomach and answered with a coy grin, tossing off article after article of clothing until she was nude from the waist up. She stood even higher in the saddle, arched her back, and waved. A cold breeze against her bare skin made her shiver.

"I hope you all die screaming," she hissed through clenched teeth.

"If you like, I'll see that they do," said a voice behind her.

Igrid dove from the saddle, rolled, and drew both swords. A man in a ratty cloak, a dirty strip of cloth tied around his eyes, was standing next to her horse. Somehow, he'd gotten so close to her that he could have easily reached out and touched her before speaking.

"Sorry to startle you." The man smiled faintly. He reached out and seized the reins of Igrid's horse. The horse did not recoil, though the beast's flanks heaved with frightful breaths.

Igrid pointed at the man with one sword and started forward. "I have a rule about killing blind men. Then again, I might break it if you try to take my horse. Now step back."

"I'm not here for your horse." The blind man patted the horse's neck in a comforting gesture. Then, he pressed one hand to the side of the horse's head. The horse reared up, screaming, then collapsed. The blind man looked down, as though appreciating the way the horse twitched. "Tell me, do you know—"

Igrid threw one of her swords.

The blind man's eyebrows rose, and one hand came up. Wytchfire sprang from his fingertips, struck the sword, and sent it flying. Instead of pressing the attack, though, he stood and simply stared at Igrid.

For her own part, Igrid picked up the tunic she'd tossed onto the grass earlier and pulled it over her head, covering herself. She clutched her remaining sword. "I trust you're the one who killed Sir Berric."

The Shel'ai said, "I have no idea what you're talking about. Now, kindly remove your weapons."

"Are those your men at the bottom of the hill?"

"No, just another of life's happy coincidences. Your weapons," he said again.

Igrid glanced down at her last shortsword, plus the stilettos at her belt. "I don't think so," she said finally. "I know a Knight who said she once managed to step around a gout of wytchfire and cut the sorcerer casting it in half. This Knight wasn't one to exaggerate. If she could do it, maybe I can, too."

"If you were going to keep fighting, you would have done it already."

"That depends on you. Walk away, and neither one of us dies. Press this, and maybe we both do."

The Shel'ai reached up and tugged the strip of cloth from his eyes.

Igrid flinched at the sight of his darkened eye sockets, then swore when violet fire bloomed within each of them.

He said, "I have no need to bargain with you, Iron Sister. Turn around."

Instead of obeying, Igrid took several steps to one side. Out of the corner of her eye, she saw that a big warrior had very nearly gotten behind her, followed by an even bigger, gray-skinned figure that could only be an Olg. Igrid swore then shifted her attention from the Olg to the warrior, who wore a patch over one eye. "I know you."

"Yeah, you do." The warrior spat on the ground then saluted with his sword. "Too bad we can't finish what we started three years ago."

"Life is cruel and unfair," the Shel'ai said.

Igrid turned back to face him and saw that he'd withdrawn Knightswrath from her dead horse. He left it wrapped in a cloak but held it as one might cradle a child.

Igrid held her second shortsword with one hand, drew her dagger with the other, and charged the Shel'ai. Before she had gotten halfway, though, something struck her, driving her to her knees. She looked down and saw a crude wooden spear. She guessed she'd been struck with the dull instead of the sharpened end. She turned and saw the Olg holding another such spear, his face stern and chiseled.

"Please stop fighting, Iron Sister," the Shel'ai said. A hint of smugness threaded his voice. "You won't get away, you won't kill any of us, and you won't die. But you *will* get yourself hurt for no reason. And I'll see to it that your companions down below suffer even worse."

The Shel'ai gestured, and his flaming eyes flared even brighter. As though plucked by invisible hands, Igrid's weapons flew from her grasp. The Shel'ai deftly caught each of them. Instead of keeping them, though, he discarded both onto the body of Igrid's horse. Meanwhile, the one-eyed sellsword collected the other horses. He led one to the Shel'ai and kept the other for himself.

The Shel'ai gestured. The massive Olg tossed aside his remaining spears and stepped forward, an enormous mace swinging from his belt. Expressionless, he seized Igrid and easily hoisted her over his shoulder.

"We must move quickly, I'm afraid," the Shel'ai said, mounting his new horse. "I am told that Olgrym can run nearly as fast as galloping horses. I do not think the ride will be quite so comfortable, though."

Igrid listened for some sign that Zeia and Keswen were rushing back to help her. Instead, all she heard was the warlike drumming of the Olg's heartbeat as he ran after the horses.

Zeia dragged her shortsword from a dead opponent, wiped the blood on the man's shirt, and scowled when it looked even dirtier than before. She stooped and wiped it on the grass instead. By the time she sheathed it, the flaming hand holding it had begun to sputter. She closed her eyes for a moment, fighting back a wave of nausea.

"Are you about to die on me, wytch?"

Zeia opened her eyes. Keswen had just finished using a knife to carve her arrows out of the dead and was inspecting each one for cracks in its wooden shaft. She returned five to her quiver but threw two away.

Zeia said, "We didn't have to do it like this."

Upon startling the men, Zeia had conjured her flaming hands, drawn both swords, and charged. It had worked. The men were so startled, so terrified, that all turned to flee. But Keswen had not let them. The twang of a bowstring signaled that the fight had begun, and Zeia had no choice. She managed to stun one man with a mind-stab, then finish him with her sword, but that was the limit of her strength. Keswen did not seem to mind. With frightful speed, her arrows had finished the rest.

The Wyldkin woman was searching them for valuables. As she did so, she muttered, "You said yourself what these men were, what they wanted to do. Do you really think they got less than they deserved?"

"No," Zeia admitted, "but Lady Igrid—"

"I never knew a Shel'ai to follow orders from a Human."

Biting back an angry retort, Zeia turned back toward the hill. She expected to see Igrid there, scowling from a distance, visibly enraged by what Keswen had done. Instead, she saw nothing. "Keswen…"

The Wyldkin caught the tone in her voice and spun, already fitting an arrow. She looked up at the hill then lowered the bow. 'Is she circling around to help us?'

"I doubt it." Zeia considered trying to locate Igrid with magic, but just the thought caused her nausea to return. "Maybe we missed someone. Maybe they circled around—"

"We didn't miss anyone." Keswen started forward at a quick jog.

Despite her weariness, Zeia followed. At the top of the hill, they found Igrid's horse—dead. Her armor and weapons lay scattered about. Keswen knelt and scooped Igrid's breast knife off the grass.

Zeia searched the remains of Igrid's horse. A dull sense of horror flooded her senses. "Knightswrath is gone."

Keswen looked around, scanning the grass with sharp eyes. "I don't see any blood." She pointed. "I *do* see tracks, though."

Zeia looked at the ground. "Two?"

"Three," Keswen corrected. "A man, a bigger man, and a godsdamned giant."

"Or an Olg."

"Whatever he was, the biggest one left on foot. The other two took our horses."

Zeia surveyed the scene. "No bandit could have snuck up on our dear Iron Sister like this."

Keswen studied the grass again. "No blood," Keswen repeated. "That doesn't make sense. If they just wanted to have some fun with her, they'd have knocked her out first. Otherwise, she'd have screamed and gotten our attention." She looked up. "Was it that Shel'ai?"

"Can't tell." Zeia sighed. "I could use magic to search the area for his residue, but it would probably kill me."

"Then don't. I'm probably going to need you." Keswen stood, turned east, and nocked an arrow. She held it in place with the same hand holding her bow. "They weren't riding very fast. If we're quick, we'll catch them when they stop for the night."

Zeia pressed a wrist into her stomach. *Gods, I can barely move! How am I supposed to recover my strength if we run until nightfall?* She glanced down at Igrid's composite bow, lying in a tangle with the rest of Igrid's possessions. She wanted to take it, in case weariness left her no magic with which to attack, but the magical strain of maintaining her hands made that impossible. She thought of asking Keswen to take it.

"Let's go," she said instead.

CHAPTER SIXTEEN

MADDOC SAT IN A CHAIR and looked out the window of his room at the inn. He could see the outline of Saikaido Temple, faintly visible through the fog of the Dragon's Veil, across the stretch of water known as the Burnished Way. "We can't stay here," he said at last.

Sang Wei sat at the other end of the room, obsessively sharpening a sword that needed no sharpening. "I know," he said without looking up, "but we dare not attempt a rescue until nightfall."

"A rescue?" Maddoc tried not to laugh. "We could talk to the governor..."

Sang Wei glanced up. "Phaegos is a protectorate of the Lotus Isles. We have no idea whether the governor here is loyal to Crovis or... or not."

Maddoc caught his meaning. While Rowen Locke was a popular and powerful man, he had never shown any interest in becoming Grand Marshal. Neither had anyone else, including Aeko Shingawa. That meant Crovis Ammerhel ruled unopposed. The governor of Phaegos might very well be one of Crovis's puppets, like whoever had been installed as ruler of New Atheion.

"We could send a message to Lyos," Maddoc offered.

"No need," Sang Wei said. "You heard what they're talking about in the streets. Everyone already knows that Sir Locke was arrested."

Maddoc could not decide whether that was a good or bad thing. Initially, he'd rejoiced when they reached Phaegos two days before and discovered that somehow, word of Rowen's arrest had preceded them.

Townspeople looked shocked. Those Isle Knights stationed within the city looked disheartened and confused. Maddoc had half expected Phaegos to rally an army.

Instead, they'd done nothing.

"What about Lyos?" Maddoc asked.

"You heard what Sir Locke said about Captain Jalist. The king did seem fond of him, though." The sharpening stone paused. "King Typherius has probably already sent a diplomat to talk to the Grand Marshal. That means he'll have to wait until the Grand Marshal responds before taking any action. We don't dare wait that long."

"Why not?" Maddoc stood up. "I don't want Locke in a dungeon any more than you do. But Crovis has, what, a thousand Knights at Saikaido, and squires besides? My magic and your steel aren't going to get him out of there."

Sang Wei examined his sword for a moment then jammed it into the floor, where it quivered as he stood and began to pace, shaking his head. "I'm not leaving him there, Maddoc."

Maddoc stepped into his path, blocked him when he tried to step around, and squeezed his arm. "We'll come back. But first, we get word to Igrid... and everyone else. I mean the Lyosi, the Dwarrs, the Soroccans, maybe even the Sylvs. Get everybody who owes their lives to Rowen Locke to send what they can spare... a dozen men, maybe a few hundred. By the time it's done, we'll come back with an army!"

Sang Wei grew quiet. Then he smiled faintly. "Like that army we put together to hunt down Chorlga."

Maddoc smiled back, remembering the sense of greatness of those days, the exhilaration of those nights. "By the time we return, Crovis will have no choice. He'll *have* to let Locke go."

Sang Wei nodded. Suddenly, though, he looked unconvinced. He stared out the window, at the mist. "No," he said finally, "*you* go. Find Igrid. Get word to Sir Locke's allies. In the meantime, I'll stay and talk to the governor. And while I'm at it, I'll talk to every Isle Knight I can find. Some have to be like the one that let us go. I'll put together a small army of my own if I can—not to attack, but to mass on the Grand Marshal's doorstep and make him nervous."

Maddoc opened his mouth to argue then thought better of it. "I think you'll make a handsome general," he said at last. He took the Knight in his arms.

Sang Wei blushed but did not pull away. "I always wanted to be a general," he confessed.

"I know."

They kissed.

Maddoc said, "When should I leave?"

"Not until nightfall."

Maddoc said, "I was hoping you'd say that."

Sang Wei stood outside the inn and watched as Maddoc moved quietly through the crowd. Like Sang Wei, the Shel'ai had changed his appearance as much as possible since Crovis surely had men looking for them. Sang Wei had reluctantly shed his armor in favor of the plain raiment of an aspiring merchant. He had even allowed Maddoc to take shears to Sang Wei's long hair.

As for Maddoc, the Shel'ai had opted for a different approach: disguising himself by becoming more conspicuous. He'd donned a brightly colored robe lined with tiny brass bells and spangles, covered his face with a veil, and wrapped the top of his head—including the tapered points of his ears—with a Soroccan headscarf. He looked, if anything, like an eccentric street performer. Even if someone noted the violet color of his eyes and the whiteness of the pupils, they might very well think they were somehow a part of his costume.

Sang Wei watched Maddoc disappear, blinked rapidly, and returned to the inn. He ignored the advances of the barmaid and the good-natured teasing from the innkeeper, and he walked back upstairs to his room. Once inside, he closed the door, undressed, and went back to sharpening his sword.

Sang Wei blushed. He hated lying—not just because lies were an affront to the Light, but because of how he felt about Maddoc. But what choice did he have? Sang Wei had no doubt that if the Grand Marshal's agents were anywhere in Phaegos, they would be cloistered around the governor. Likewise, Sang Wei could not risk speaking with all the Knights throughout the city, taking his chances on who could be trusted.

Most importantly, though, Sang Wei knew he could not leave Rowen Locke behind and simply trust that Crovis would be too fearful of reprisals to kill him. After all, as much as Sang Wei hated to admit it, the Grand Marshal had proven himself to be every bit as vile as Rowen and Igrid had always claimed. He was unpredictable as well. As far as Sang Wei knew, Rowen might already be dead.

But if he isn't, I have to get him out. It can't wait. Sang Wei paused. He had known that from the moment they'd fled New Atheion, though he'd been careful to avoid mulling on it, just in case Maddoc had been reading his thoughts.

Sang Wei looked down at the sharpening stone and realized his hands were shaking. He took a deep breath and let it go. "Singchai ushó fey," he whispered. He said it again and again, like a mantra, as he stared out the window and watched the sun go down.

For the first time in months, Jalist was sober. He was also angry. Morning light gleamed off cobblestones as he rode about the courtyard near the open gates of Lyos, having just donned his armor—and that only moments after having finally been released from prison.

Singling out a passing squad, he said, "You men, haul your asses back to the armory and trade those bows for poleaxes!"

The men comprising a squad of archers exchanged confused looks. "But Captain—"

"Bows don't look as frightening," Jalist explained. "Remember, this isn't about fighting. It's about looking mean and mad enough to gnaw the flesh off our grandmothers' bones." He turned in the saddle of his horse and waved at a passing line of smartly armored horsemen. "As for you bastards, you're too damn clean! Smear those faces with dirt or soot. Bug your eyes like you've just been smoking *fran-té* for a month. If you don't scare the piss out of me, you don't belong on this mission!"

A few men laughed, but all rushed to obey his commands. Jalist nodded with approval. Then he rode his horse outside the gates to supervise the marshaling of the slum-dwellers. Though the king of Lyos had initially resisted the idea, Jalist had convinced him otherwise, insisting that a host of armed men from the Red Watch was frightening, but such a host supported by gang members armed with hatchets and dressed in animal skins was positively terrifying.

Jalist watched crudely armed men moving in ragged lines out of the Dark Quarter, forming a chaotic, reeking mass in front of the city. He spotted their leader, a big man with a shaved head and a recent tattoo of a serpent coiling all around his bare chest. "Fen-Shea, good to see that pretty wife of yours hasn't split your skull with a cleaver!"

Fen-Shea laughed and shouted back, "I liked you better as a drunk, Captain!"

"Well, the sooner we rescue Locke and hang the Grand Marshal from a yardarm by whatever he has for a cock, the sooner you can get back to liking me!"

The resounding laughter echoing from the mouths of soldiers and slum-dwellers alike told Jalist he'd said the right thing.

A squad of horsemen approached him, riding up the hill toward the city. Jalist recognized the man leading them: the very corporal he'd sent to deal with the diplomats from the Lotus Isles. The king had ordered the diplomats banished from Lyos, but Jalist took it a step further and ordered the biggest, ugliest officer he could find to trundle the diplomats and haul them away in disgrace. Jalist imagined the diplomats returning to the Lotus Isles, outraged but unhurt. He wondered if Crovis would be angry. *Gods, I hope so!*

Jalist waved for the corporal and his men to join the others and moved to one side to allow a line of wagons to pass by, leaving the city to wait for him at the bottom of the hill. Each wagon contained a massive ballista that Jalist had ordered brought down from the city walls. Though their usefulness in a siege was limited, they looked terrifying.

Jalist lingered outside the walls a moment longer then returned to the courtyard in time to spot a burly Soroccan with a braided goatee, armed with a massive scimitar and riding toward him. Jalist returned his grin. "I thought you came here in a wagon."

"I left the wagon with Left." Hráthbam patted his horse's neck. "Right will carry me just fine."

As though intent on arguing with him, his mount—a simply named but spirited animal—reared up, nearly throwing him from the saddle.

Jalist waited until the merchant had regained control of his mount. "You sure you want to do this? I heard you have children—"

"And wives and a house and a ship that will probably run aground without me," the Soroccan cut in, "but I also have a friend who needs me. And I have a knack for looking frightening when I want." He widened his eyes and formed so serious an expression that Jalist laughed.

"We'll leave within the hour. Sooner, if I can manage it."

Hráthbam nodded. "Long enough for me to say a prayer of thanks that the gods saw fit to send me to your fair city in time to join you." He paused. "If I felt like praying, that is."

Jalist eyed the mace and longsword hanging on either side of Hráthbam's saddle. He tugged at the strap securing a kingsteel long axe—a gift from Rowen—to his back. His head hurt, which only made him angrier, which strangely, made him smile.

"I don't feel much like praying either." He waved at one of the passing archers, who had dutifully rearmed himself with a polearm. "You, send someone back to pick up those longbows. We'll bring them along just in case we need them."

CHAPTER SEVENTEEN

W YN KAI WINCED AT THE ache in his legs as he descended each of the one thousand steps. He remembered a time when he'd climbed or descended them at a far brisker pace without even breaking a sweat. But those days were gone, and he had the winter in his hair to prove it. He remembered hearing once that hair could whiten not just with age, but as the result of tremendous stress or trauma. He wondered what he would look like when the current crisis was over—if there was a paler shade than white.

Probably not, he decided, watching sunlight move along the steps, which were the color of bleached bone.

The sun had risen, meaning the steps should already have been crowded. Instead, they were deserted. Wyn Kai descended in the middle of the broad stairway and had the sense that he'd somehow been reduced in size. He told himself that most of the Knights and squires might still be in morning meditation, but he knew the truth.

As he neared the bottom of the hill, the noise of Saikaido Town washed over him. Fishermen were heading out with the rising sun, swinging oars and hauling nets. Tradesmen were loading wagons to be taken to New Atheion or across the Burnished Way to Phaegos. The ring of hammers meant that blacksmiths and carpenters had begun their day's labor. But to Wyn Kai's ears, all of it seemed subdued.

Everyone's heard about Locke. They want to know what's happening. But they're afraid to ask.

He spotted a Knight walking toward him. The Knight's eyes were bloodshot from spending the entire night on patrol. The Knight drew near and bowed.

Wyn Kai returned the gesture. "Report."

"Nothing of consequence, sir," the Knight said. "The people continue to show… discontent but no actual disloyalty. None gave any indication that they will take up arms against the Grand Marshal. However… "

Wyn Kai took advantage of the Knight's hesitation to seize his arm and pull him away from a passing group of merchants, out of earshot. "However?"

"As I said, sir, they are quite unhappy. And confused. Many are telling stories about Sir Locke's part in the War of the Lotus. Others are talking about his companions, how the sorcerer tried to heal that villager, only to be attacked—"

"What about Locke's companions? Has anyone seen them?"

The Knight shook his head. "We've searched everywhere, from the Scrollhouse and the Privy to all the temples or towns on the Isles. I suspect they've left the Isles altogether. No word from Lyos or Phaegos yet either, but there is a strange rumor. They're saying our ambassadors have been expelled from Lyos. They're saying the king heard about Sir Locke and drove them out. They'll arrive sometime today."

Wyn Kai nodded. He'd heard that as well. "Take ten men and go back to New Atheion. I know you're tired, but search the Privy again. That's where they'll be hiding, if anywhere." The Knight bowed and started to go. Wyn Kai stopped him. "And… what are *your* impressions, Sir Ulni?"

The young Knight blinked. "I serve the Council and the Grand Marshal, Sir Kai! If I have given the impression that—"

"Relax. That's not what I mean." Wyn Kai looked around. He lowered his voice. "Speak the truth, Knight. I'm not questioning your loyalty. I just want to know your heart."

Sir Ulni was quiet for a moment. He shifted uncomfortably then said, "To be honest, Sir Kai, I grow… uneasy. I am no friend to magic, but like some are saying, magic helped us win the war. Magic healed the sick and injured from the Privy. Our enemies use steel, and so do we. Steel is not evil. I mean, it depends how you use it. Maybe… maybe it's the same with magic." The young Knight blushed. "Forgive me, Sir Kai. Again, I do not mean to—"

"Stop apologizing. I asked a question, and you answered it honestly, as a Knight should. You're not in trouble. Carry on with your assignment."

Sir Ulni bowed again then hurried off.

I'll have to have him killed. He walked along the outskirts of Saikaido Town. He wondered how many other Knights were beginning to feel the same way as Sir Ulni or poor Sir Li. *And what would they say if they knew what we're really planning to do?*

Wyn Kai shook his head, trying to dismiss the thought as if it were an annoying housefly. He reminded himself of all the long talks he'd had with the Grand Marshal, all those speeches of honor and necessity. He mentally recited his favorite passage from the Codex Lotius: *Honor, like dogblossom, blooms best when mired in filth.*

He tried to tell himself that, in their current situation, the filth corresponded not to all the violence and horror that would result from the Dragonkin's return, but to the current sin of Shel'ai magic infecting the land and also the shame that only the magic of the Dragonward kept them safe.

After a moment, Wyn Kai glanced in the direction Sir Ulni had gone. "I have doubts, too, lad," he muttered.

He turned. Then he froze, one hand touching his sword hilt.

Another young Knight was approaching him. Like Sir Ulni, the Knight's eyes were heavy and bloodshot. He wore no helmet or facemask, but his armor had been polished to perfection. Head raised, the young Knight walked with grave dignity and slow, steely pride. He spotted Wyn Kai but did not turn away. Nor did he quicken his pace.

As the young Knight walked, his demeanor drew looks of curiosity. Townspeople began to gather in a circle, keeping their distance, as though they sensed that something great and terrible was about to happen.

The young Knight stopped in front of Wyn Kai. He bowed slightly. "Sir Kai."

"Sir Wei." Wyn Kai returned the bow but kept one hand on his sword and his eyes on Sang Wei's. "We were looking for you. Tell me, where is your friend?"

"That is not your concern." Sang Wei cleared his throat. "Please return to the temple and inform the Grand Marshal that I would like to

171

have a stern word with him." The young Knight stared straight ahead, unblinking, as though his eyes had been turned to painted stone.

Wyn Kai hesitated. "Sir Wei, don't—"

"Now, if you please." Sang Wei drew his sword. Sunlight washed its steely curve. Instead of striking, he stepped around Wyn Kai and moved with slow dignity to the temple steps. There, he stood, moving his naked sword to the crook of his arm.

Wyn Kai felt tears welling in his eyes. He stared at Sang Wei for a moment. Then, ignoring the murmurs from a growing crowd of onlookers, he hurried back toward the temple steps. He climbed them as briskly as he could, ignoring the ache that spread throughout his body.

Rowen woke to cold water being poured onto his face again. Blinking and sputtering, he looked up and saw the same Knight of the Stag with dark, slicked-back hair that he'd seen earlier.

"Good morning, Sir Locke." The Knight threw the pitcher away, and it shattered. "I have come to beg your forgiveness. I did not introduce myself to you before. My name is Hiro."

"I know."

Sir Hiro paused. "My older brother was a Knight as well. Perhaps you remember him."

"Sir Onnai," Rowen guessed.

Sir Hiro nodded, still smirking. He knelt. One gauntleted hand flexed in the torchlight. "My brother taught me everything there is to know about being a Knight. Honor, laws, writing... and of course, fighting." He made a fist and drove it toward Rowen's face.

Rowen caught the fist, pitched sideways, and pulled Sir Hiro off balance. They grappled for a moment, and Rowen managed to get a hold of Sir Hiro by the back of the neck and bash his face against the stone floor. He reached for the sword at Hiro's belt, but Hiro drove his elbow into Rowen's ribs and rolled away. Rowen tried to follow, but the chains held him back.

"Apparently, your brother wasn't much of a teacher," Rowen said.

Hiro rose slowly, blood streaming from his nose, trickling down to fill the lines of the stag carved into his breastplate. The smirk was gone. He fumed for a moment then drew his sword and started forward.

"Hold," Crovis Ammerhel's voice boomed. "I sent you to wake him, not kill him."

Sir Hiro froze, turned, and paled. When Crovis emerged from the shadows, Hiro hastily sheathed his sword and bowed. "Apologies, Grand Marshal. My temper—"

"Is the antithesis of your honor, as with all of us," Crovis interjected. "Your brother died because he acted rashly and against my orders. I did not think you so foolish. Was I wrong?"

Sir Hiro bowed his head but said nothing.

"Go," Crovis said at last. When Hiro was gone and the door closed, Crovis faced Rowen. "I apologize. Sir Hiro should not have done that. I apologize for his brother, too... and for myself, for not saying that earlier. That poor villager who allowed himself to be tainted by magic, he did not deserve to die. Sir Onnai and his men acted against my wishes. Their deaths were proper and justified."

Crovis stepped forward and placed a small wooden bucket on the floor. He nudged it closer with his boot. Rowen glanced down and saw his reflection.

"Drink," Crovis said. "I promise I'll think nothing less of you."

Rowen considered his faint dizziness and his parched throat then kicked the bucket away.

"A poor choice but yours to make." Crovis crossed his arms. "Something has happened. I'm told there's a certain Knight waiting at the bottom of the hill. I'm told he wants to challenge me. I am honor bound to accept."

"You seem to be fighting a lot of duels lately," Rowen said. "Well, good luck."

Crovis answered with a thin smile. "You speak with courage, but you lack the humility demanded for one of your station."

Rowen glanced beyond Crovis and eyed the spilled water soaking into the flagstones. "I apologize, sir. I'll try to work on that while you're gone."

Crovis's smile vanished. "The Knight who issued the challenge is Sang Wei."

Rowen momentarily forgot the chains again and started forward until he could go no further. "Crovis—"

"I see a fresh urgency in your expression, Sir Locke. Is this young Knight dear to you? I remember him, you know. He defended Lady Shingawa at Atheion. Though he acted foolishly, he showed courage. So I promoted him. Now he wants me dead, and I must answer for my mercy." Crovis sighed. "Strange, isn't it, how the Light presents us with such trials?" He turned to go.

"Wait, damn you! What is it you want? Why are you telling me this?"

"So that you will understand the severity of your actions," Crovis answered softly, still walking. "This young Knight is a good man. But he will die because you insisted on leading him down a path of dishonor and self-indulgence." He paused at the door.

Rowen's mind raced to find the right words. "Don't," he said finally. "Please, Crovis…"

"Are you prepared to grant my demands?"

Rowen straightened. "Of course not."

"Then I thank you for wishing me luck." Crovis opened the door.

"You'll need it," Rowen called, straining against his chains. "Sang Wei is better than you. He's better than me or Aeko or anyone else. He's the best there is. And he's fighting for the right reasons. Can you say the same?"

Crovis turned back. "Now you are trying to shake my confidence. You still do not understand that I am driven not by arrogance but by faith. But soon, I think, you will." He gave Rowen a pitying look then left the room, closing the door so softly that Rowen barely heard the lock click back into place.

For what felt like an eternity, Rowen struggled against his chains, but they held firm. Desperate, he tried calling for help, begging the guards to come in, hoping he might somehow overpower them. But no one answered. He paced in tight circles, barefoot, weak from thirst but burning with anger. Then, the door opened.

Rowen turned, hoping to see Sang Wei but afraid it would be Crovis. Instead, Wyn Kai entered. The white-haired Knight held a bucket in one hand. He came forward, expressionless, and placed the bucket on the floor. He nudged it toward Rowen, as Crovis had.

That time, Rowen accepted the water. He drank then asked, "Sang Wei?"

"I don't know," Wyn Kai said. He glanced back at the open doorway as though deciding whether to go back and shut it. "We need to talk." When Rowen did not answer, he said, "If Crovis falls, I will be next in line. I am willing to surrender, provided that I have your personal assurance that all Knights who followed Crovis will be granted amnesty. If it will seal the bargain, I offer you my life, to take or spare as you wish."

Rowen thought of Sir Hiro. He thought of the Knights who had been sent to kill Maddoc, and his lip curled with disgust. Nevertheless, after a moment, he nodded.

Wyn Kai continued. "Of course, if Crovis wins, we must assume that you are wrong and Crovis truly does fight with the Light on his side."

Rowen's eyes narrowed. "You don't sound too damn sure of that."

"Only a fool has no doubts when men's lives are at stake." Wyn Kai turned, took a step, then stopped. "You can stop wondering what happened to Aeko. She's here, in the temple—alive, though barely. Crovis seized her the moment she tried to contact you." He paused. "I'm not saying this to comfort you, Locke. I'm saying it to prepare you. If you don't agree to what the Grand Marshal asks, he'll kill her. He'll kill Igrid. He'll kill your friends back in Lyos. He'll march the entire Knighthood all the way across Ruun and go to war against the Sylvs. He'll kill those Shel'ai children you care about so much. He won't *want* to do any of it, but he'll do it nonetheless. If that doesn't frighten you, if that doesn't fill *you* with doubts, it should."

Rowen said, "Let me go. We'll march down the steps together. We'll stop the duel before anyone else dies. With all our influence combined, we can stop Crovis. I'll make you the godsdamned Grand Marshal if that's what you want!" Wyn Kai's eyes sparked with life, and for a moment, Rowen thought the white-haired Knight might agree.

Then, Crovis Ammerhel appeared in the doorway.

The Grand Marshal was breathing hard. His long dark hair had come unbraided and hung haphazardly about his shoulders. Blood dripped from his hair and covered his armor. As he moved into the chamber, Rowen saw that he was limping. Nevertheless, in one hand, he held the head of Sang Wei.

Rowen shut his eyes. Gritting his teeth, he screamed. Dimly, he was aware of Crovis speaking—first to Wyn Kai, then to him—but he refused to hear the words. Rowen turned, covered his face with his hands, and yanked vainly at his chains until he collapsed, tears streaming from his eyes. Only then did he open them.

By then, Crovis and Wyn Kai were gone. The door was closed. But in the ghastly, flickering torchlight, Rowen saw that Crovis had left Sang Wei's head behind.

CHAPTER EIGHTEEN

IGRID STARED AT THE RAGGED leader of her captors. While
the Olg had tied her to a tree, the sorcerer stood in the distance,
faintly smirking, in conversation with the one-eyed sellsword. Igrid
wondered how much magic the sorcerer must be expending so he could
see even when the strip of cloth covered his hollow eye sockets. She
thought of Zeia, how summoning and controlling her hands of fire took
both power and deep concentration.

That means he's weakening himself, even now. If I wait until—

The sorcerer turned and smiled at her, obviously having read her
mind. "Shall I tell you a secret, Iron Sister? Magic is a muscle. The more
you use it, the more you *push yourself* to use it, regardless of the risks, the
stronger it becomes. Most Shel'ai have forgotten this. The one you call
Zeia understands a bit of it, but still, she is like a child to me."

Igrid tested her bonds. To her surprise, the Olg had made them tight
enough to hold her but not so tight that they cut off her circulation. "Tell
me, are you still reading my mind right now?"

The Shel'ai nodded, still faintly smiling. "And a pleasant place it is,
full of sweet passions and—"

Igrid filled her mind with graphic images of her tackling the Shel'ai,
thrusting her fingers into his hollow eye sockets, cackling with laughter
as she clawed her way in. She imagined the warm wetness of his blood,
the squish of his brain, even the breath that accompanied his screams of
pain and panic.

The sorcerer recoiled as though struck, pressed one hand to the side of his head, and lost his balance. The one-eyed sellsword caught him. The sorcerer reeled for another moment then pulled away.

"Clever," he said after a moment. "Half a mind-stab, and you don't even have any magic."

"Stay out of my mind," Igrid said. "It's no place for you."

The sorcerer stalked toward her, uncovering his eye sockets. His flaming eyes blazed to life. He knelt so close that Igrid could feel the heat. Still, she forced herself to meet his gaze.

"I could hurt you for that, Iron Sister," he said. "I could make you feel like I'm peeling off your skin, one layer at a time, and rubbing you with salt—"

Igrid laughed. "Salt? How lovely! I recommend ants and lemon juice, as well."

The Shel'ai frowned. "I almost believe—"

"That I want you to tire yourself out so that my friends will have an easier time splitting you in half? Good for you. Perhaps you're not as dumb as—"

The Shel'ai struck her. When Igrid's bloody lip lifted into a lopsided smile and she winked, he struck her again. Then he straightened. "I have nothing to fear from your friends. Even if they care enough to pursue you, one ravaged sorceress and one Sylvan archer aren't enough to defeat *me*, let alone my bodyguards."

As the Shel'ai turned and stalked away, Igrid shifted her attention to his men. She had recognized the one-eyed sellsword from Hesod. Dagath was cruel, strong, and quick. Recounting her experience with him to Rowen, after the war, she was stunned to learn that Rowen had met the sellsword, too. Dagath was a survivor, though not especially bright.

As for the mute Olg, he was a puzzle to her. She'd met Olgrym before. All had behaved less like men than hungry greatwolves. But this one had not touched her beyond what was necessary to carry her. At the moment, he was tending the horses with surprising gentleness. She even thought she'd seen him smirk when she stunned the Shel'ai and grimace with disapproval when he struck her.

Turning her head, she looked for Knightswrath. It was leaning against another tree, uncovered but far out of her reach, next to a familiar shaft of dragonbone that the Shel'ai seemed to be using as a scepter. Moonlight spilled through the trees, gleaming coldly off the brass crosspiece and the buckles along the scabbard. Igrid imagined Silwren's face. *Well, wytch, if ever you wanted to make amends, now would be a good time to start!*

Igrid half expected Knightswrath to leap from the scabbard of its own accord. She imagined the blade ablaze, driving back the shadows, slicing her captors to ribbons. Instead, it continued to gleam, distant and aloof.

Some help you are.

The Shel'ai returned, snatched up both Knightswrath—careful to hold it by the scabbard—and his scepter, and faced Dagath. "I'll go and kill her friends. Guard the woman while I'm gone. Keep her quiet." He started away then added, "And leave her clothes on."

Dagath scowled with disappointment but nodded. "What about a fire?"

The sorcerer considered that and said, "If it draws her friends, all the better." The Shel'ai drew his tattered cloak about his body and vanished into the shadows of the forest.

Igrid considered screaming since they had not gagged her yet, but decided to wait. By then, the Olg had finished tending the horses. He returned to the center of camp with an armload of wood and built a fire. Dagath stood nearby, arms crossed, leering at her. She pretended not to notice. Meanwhile, the Olg moved about the edge of the camp, stooping and digging in the earth, producing handfuls of plants and roots. He placed them in a copper pot along with some water from his water skin and positioned it over the fire to boil.

Dagath snickered, shaking his head, but said nothing about the soup. Instead, he knelt on a fallen tree, just a few feet away from Igrid. "Better not cross that Shel'ai. I've seen others but none like that, and I don't just mean his eyes. He says his name is Algol and acts like that means something bad, though I'm not sure what." Dagath paused. "You're supposed to be dead, you know. That Dhargot took a shine to you while you were out cold. He paid me to kill you if he died."

Dagath formed a fist, showing her two rings he wore on one hand. Both were crusted with mud and dirt, but gold and jewels glinted faintly underneath. "He didn't want you raped and cut open once he wasn't there to protect you anymore." Dagath grinned, flashing her his rotten teeth.

"Tell me, pretty one... how does it feel to know you owe your life to someone they called the Bloody Prince?" He laughed. "I wonder where you'd be right now if he'd survived. Sure, you act all spit and fire now, but I bet you'd—"

The Olg picked up a rock and threw it, even as he calmly stirred the contents of the copper pot with a stick. The rock struck Dagath's shoulder. The one-eyed sellsword stood and drew his shortsword. The Olg stood, too. Expressionless, he unhooked the massive mace from his belt and gave it a few slow, menacing swings.

Dagath hesitated, fuming, then sheathed his sword. He spat on the ground and turned away. "I'm going to take a piss," he snarled. He pointed at Igrid. "Best gag her while I'm gone. I don't want to hear her smart mouth when I get back."

Igrid considered pointing out that she hadn't said a word to the sellsword. The Olg stooped and went back to stirring his soup. When Igrid caught the Olg's eye, he shook his shaggy head—not in rebuke, she thought, but warning.

"You're a curious one," Igrid said. "Nothing personal, but out of the three, I wouldn't have expected *you* to be the gentle one."

The Olg made a strange clicking sound that set Igrid's nerves on edge until she guessed it was laughter. A moment later, the Olg stood and approached her. At his heavy steps, she strained against her bonds, but the Olg simply knelt and offered her a drink. The feel of cool water against her parched throat made her realize how thirsty she was.

The Olg offered her more. When a little water spilled down her chin, trickling into her cleavage, he looked but made no move to touch her. Then he returned to the fire. However, Igrid saw an ominous tension in his gigantic shoulders as he turned away to stir the soup, as though he was forcing himself not to look at her.

Zeia ignited one flaming hand and grabbed Keswen's arm, pulling her to a stop so quickly that Keswen slipped, loosing an arrow into the darkness. The Sylv scowled. Instead of voicing a rebuke, though, she fell into a crouch.

Zeia crouched, too. She dismissed her flaming hand but projected her voice into Keswen's mind. *"The Shel'ai is close. He's hunting us. Don't talk."* A pause. *"Think your response, and I'll hear you."*

Keswen frowned then reached for another arrow. Zeia heard her think, *"We'd better move, in case the Shel'ai heard that arrow you just made me fire."* Keswen added a second thought: a colorful threat regarding what would happen if Zeia ever touched her again.

Zeia led Keswen through the trees. *"The Shel'ai's angry,"* she said. *"Something made him lose his focus. I think he's alone. We might be able to ambush him. Clear your mind. Calm your emotions. If we can—"*

Wytchfire blazed through the forest, scalding the shadows and hissing as it passed through the air. Zeia recoiled as the flames streamed by. Trees burned. Zeia winced in the sudden glare.

"Stay down," she told Keswen through mindspeak. *"I don't think he sees us. He's just firing blind."*

A second gout of wytchfire streamed through the forest, opposite the first. Keswen had three arrows on her bowstring, but instead of firing, she answered with a gruff nod. She took the lead, moving in a low crouch away from the flames. Meanwhile, the violet fire burning through the forest took on a red-gold hue. Smoke thickened. Sweat beaded on Zeia's forehead. She glanced back at a sudden, fitful screaming and saw that the flames had reached a bird nest.

Keswen stopped. Zeia glanced at her and saw her eyes streaming tears. Judging by the tension in her jaw, Zeia guessed the Sylv was trying to keep from coughing on all the smoke. Since Zeia suffered no such affliction, she took the lead again. She ignited one flaming hand but kept it low, out of sight. She touched Keswen's arm, leading her through the blinding smoke.

Once they were clear, Zeia signaled. Keswen crouched low, gasping for breath and doing her best to cough quietly. Zeia eyed her for a moment then made her decision. She stepped away. *"I'll take care of the Shel'ai. Find Igrid."*

Before Keswen could protest, Zeia stood tall, ignited both her burning hands, and drew both her shortswords. She did not cry out. Instead, she filled her mind with rage and let her opponent sense her as she moved steadily away from Keswen, skirting the edge of the burning forest.

A cruel voice rang in her mind: *"Are you looking for me, little one?"*

Zeia fought back a surge of panic and answered with defiance, *"You and I have unfinished business."* She walked a little farther then doubled back, in case the Shel'ai was trying to get behind her. As she moved through a kind of borderland between fire and shadow, she employed just enough magic to keep her eyes from losing focus. A pang of nausea reminded her that she was nowhere near her full strength.

"Where is the other woman?" the voice taunted.

Zeia filled her mind with an image of Keswen—burned, motionless, as blackened as the grass and leaves around her corpse. She even visualized the details of the Sylvan woman's bow, fire scorched, the string coiled and melted.

"Perhaps," the voice said, *"perhaps... "*

"Enough whispering," Zeia called out. "If you want to fight, I'm waiting."

The voice did not answer.

Zeia backed away from the fire. She turned slowly, scanning the darkness in all directions. She longed to use divination to try and locate the Shel'ai, but that would take time and weaken her too much. Besides, something told her he was so close that the slightest distraction could prove fatal.

What do the Knights say? No courage without—

A flash of movement made her turn. Wytchfire poured toward her face. Zeia dropped one of her swords and held a flaming hand before her, which absorbed the fire. Still, a wave of scalding heat swept up her arm. She reeled for a moment then pushed herself forward. Instead of retrieving her shortsword, she held one empty, flaming hand at the ready, in case she needed to absorb another blast.

A cloaked figure stepped through the wall of flames, his eyes blazing. Flames nipped at his clothes, but he hardly seemed to notice. In the crook of his arm, he held a scepter-like shaft of dragonbone. Knightswrath—still sheathed—was thrust into his belt. A cruel smile played on his lips. "Impressive," he said. "To be honest, I didn't know that was possible."

"I didn't know *that* was possible." Zeia pointed at his eyes with her remaining shortsword.

"You should have. It's not so different from what you do."

"But harder, I'd imagine."

The cloaked Shel'ai nodded. "True, but hatred is a powerful teacher. And I've had years and years to learn." He lifted his hands

Zeia braced herself for another gust of wytchfire. Instead, he plucked Zeia's discarded sword off the ground and threw it at her.

Zeia sidestepped, and the sword flew past her—then spun around and flew back at her opponent. The man waved again, and the sword's direction changed a third time, thudding into the earth.

"You're better than I thought," the man said, "but not good enough." He swaggered forward, grasped the sword, and plucked it from the earth. Wytchfire poured from his hand, sweeping up the hilt. The steel flared bright red. A moment later, the sword melted.

Go ahead, waste your strength. Zeia stood, waiting.

But the Shel'ai did not attack. Instead, he moved sideways, trying to circle around her. Zeia moved, too.

The Shel'ai said, "You knew Fadarah. I've always wondered—was he as strong as they say? I wish I could have fought him."

Zeia weighed her options. She could use magic to fling her remaining sword at him, but he could just as easily use his own magic to deflect it. Then, since she could not cast wytchfire herself, she'd be defenseless.

Unless…

Zeia imagined an invisible malice roiling in her mind, a terrible fog that she constricted and constricted until it formed a long, lethal needle. She imagined the needle quivering in the air, just in front of her forehead, tense as a drawn arrow. Then she fired the needle into her opponent's mind.

She'd used that attack before to stun Chorlga, the Dragonkin. She'd also used it to kill some of the worst men on the continent. But against the Shel'ai, it had no effect.

Her opponent winced then grinned. "Nice try, little one, but I've been trained to shield myself from such things." He took a step toward her.

Zeia fought back a surge of nausea and stepped back. "So who was this master of yours?"

The Shel'ai lifted both hands and unleashed twin streams of wytchfire. Zeia dropped her remaining sword and lifted both hands, bracing herself. Terrible heat washed over her, driving her off her feet. She tried, unsuccessfully, to keep from screaming.

Blind with pain, she heard the Shel'ai say, "My master and teacher was Nekiel himself, greatest of the Dragonkin. He who was banished, who must soon return. Does that impress you?"

The pain faded, and the Shel'ai hovered over her, his eyes blazing, both hands poised over her face. Wytchfire roiled at his fingertips. But instead of unleashing it, he kicked her in the face.

Igrid saw a faint smear of violet light on the horizon, and her heart sank. She smelled smoke a moment later but told herself that Zeia and Keswen might still be alive. She turned her attention back to escape. She'd already tried sawing her bonds against the tree bark, to no avail. She considered playing it either coy or insulting and trying to lure in the one-eyed sellsword so that she could trip him. She figured she had a slight chance she could wrap his neck in her hands and snap it before the Olg intervened, but that would get her no closer to freedom. Frustrated, she realized she had no choice but to wait for Zeia and Keswen to reach her.

When the Olg's vegetable soup was finished, he ladled some into a wooden bowl and brought it to Igrid. He did not free her hands. Instead, he knelt before her, his dark eyes unblinking and expressionless, and patiently spooned it into her mouth. Igrid had been all set to spit it out—perhaps even back in his face—but she decided that trying to earn the Olg's favor might help her escape. Besides, the soup tasted surprisingly good. When the bowl was empty, the Olg stood and tossed it to Dagath, but kept the spoon and made a motion for the sellsword to serve himself.

"Thanks," Dagath grumbled. "And here I was thinking of finally giving you a name!"

Ignoring him, the Olg picked up his mace and sat down on the fallen tree. His great weight caused the tree to sag, sinking into the earth. He turned, staring off into the forest. Then he hefted his mace with one hand and snapped the fingers of the other, catching Dagath's attention.

Dagath dropped his bowl and drew his sword. Removing a dirty cloth from his pocket, he said, "Gag her," and threw it toward the Olg, who made no move to catch it. Dagath turned—just as a bowstring snapped and an arrow skimmed past his throat.

Dagath's good eye widened as he pressed one hand to his neck. Blood welled between his fingers. He swung his shortsword once at the empty air, stumbled, then turned and ran. A second arrow sped into the darkness after him. Dagath grunted, but Igrid did not see him fall.

Meanwhile, the Olg hefted his mace with both hands and turned in the direction of the unknown archer. He sidestepped until he stood in front of Igrid and bellowed, swinging his mace.

Igrid spotted Keswen a moment later, slipping shadowlike through the darkness. She stood behind the Olg, two arrows gleaming on her bowstring. She pulled them back. Igrid resisted an odd impulse to warn the Olg. Somehow, though, the Olg seemed to sense his danger and turned—just as Keswen fired.

One arrow struck the Olg's chest, well below the heart. The other glanced off his shoulder. The Olg jerked, as though merely startled, then started forward. He bellowed again and swung the great mace.

Keswen dove, and the mace narrowly missed her head. Then she rose. Steel flashed. The Olg howled. Three bright-red lines formed on his leg. A moment later, blood poured from the slashes, soaking his pants.

The Olg answered with a swing of his own, but Keswen rolled clear again. That time, as she rose, she threw her sword. To Igrid's amazement, the Olg swung his mace and met the sword midair, and its blade shattered like glass. Despite his wounds, the Olg charged.

Keswen dove again, narrowly dodging the mace, and nocked an arrow as she rose. She aimed for the Olg's throat, but the Olg twisted, drove at Keswen with a murderous backhand, then jerked as Keswen's arrow found his thigh instead.

Igrid finally found her voice. "Keswen, damn you, quit dancing and cut me free!"

Instead of answering, the Wyldkin woman nocked two arrows and moved backward until she stood next to the tree where Igrid had been tied. She let go of her bow long enough to draw a knife, slice through Igrid's bonds, leave the knife for Igrid, and return her hand to her bowstring—all in the blink of an eye.

But the Olg had not charged. Nor had he retreated. Instead, he stood at the far end of the camp, numerous slashes and three arrows in his body. He breathed hard, though Igrid could not tell whether it was from pain or rage. She stood, holding Keswen's knife, massaging her sore wrist.

"Keswen, don't."

The Wyldkin woman had drawn back her bowstring, prepared to send two more arrows into the Olg's body, but had yet to fire. She whispered, "If he charges, this might not be enough to stop him. You get behind him with that knife and—"

"He won't charge." Igrid faced the Olg. "Enough," she called. She glanced at Keswen's shattered sword. "Easy, Breaksteel. We'll go one way—you go the other. Agreed?"

The Olg's dark eyes narrowed. After a moment, he nodded. He shuffled backward with labored breathing, favoring one leg. The darkness closed around him, blending into his ash-gray skin.

"Well done," Keswen muttered. She drew back her bowstring and sighted along the topmost arrow. "He's far enough that—"

"Don't," Igrid said. "I told you—let him go."

Keswen gave her an incredulous look. Then she turned back toward the Olg and cursed. "He's gone." She lowered her bow a little. "Don't see the other one, either. We better go."

"Where's Zeia? Algol has the sword. We have to—"

Keswen answered by pushing Igrid toward the horses. "Just move," she whispered. "We'll sort the rest out later."

CHAPTER NINETEEN

For two days, Jalist's army had camped along the coast of Ruun. Each day, dozens of men sounded trumpets, the noise spilling across the Burnished Way, while Jalist and his officers continued seeking boats. Before long, they'd purchased every ferry, barge, and fishing boat for miles, and still they had nowhere near enough to carry his entire force to Saikaido. So Jalist ordered his men to start building boats instead.

As the sounds of hammers and axes echoed along the shore—mingling with the chaos of an angry, filthy army hungry for blood—Jalist paced, awaiting a visit he knew must eventually come. Finally, on the morning of the third day, just as sunrise glinted off Hráthbam's new bronze breastplate, the Soroccan woke him and directed his attention to the east.

"A ship's approaching," he said, "steered by an unhappy-looking Knight with a white flag."

Jalist rose quickly, donned his armor, and was still buckling on his sword as he raced along the beach. Word spread. Weapons glinted. While the men of the Red Watch fell into neat ranks, the slum-dwellers were another story. Men rose from their tents or from the bare sand on which they'd been lying, some of them still drunk, and shouted curses at the eastern sky.

Jalist decided not to order them to be silent, uncertain whether they'd obey, anyway. He winced in the glare of sunrise, shielded his eyes with his hands, and spotted a finely hewn ferry skimming along the waters, drifting out of the mist toward the shore. He fixed a scowl to his face, moved to the edge of the harbor, and crossed his arms, waiting. A cloaked man joined him a moment later.

"Are you sure you want to be here?" Jalist asked without turning.

Maddoc nodded.

Jalist noted the tendrils of wytchfire leaking from the Shel'ai's clenched fists. "No killing," he said. "That's not why we're here."

"Speak for yourself," Maddoc said in a low voice.

Jalist traded worried looks with Hráthbam, who had huffed up just a few steps behind them, then faced the Shel'ai again. "Listen, lad. You want revenge, fine. I understand. But it'll have to wait. We're here for Locke. After that, you want to sneak into the temple and turn the Grand Marshal into kindling, that's your business."

Maddoc said nothing. Jalist tapped his sword hilt, wondering if he'd find himself in the position of having to kill an ally to protect an enemy. He glanced at Hráthbam in time to see the dark-skinned merchant loosening his scimitar. He guessed they were thinking the same thing.

"Easy, lad," Hráthbam said to Maddoc.

"I'm probably twice as old as you are, Soroccan." Maddoc gave Hráthbam so cold a look that the latter drew back a step. Then, to Jalist's surprise and relief, Maddoc turned his back on the approaching ferry.

Jalist stepped forward, walking down the pier to the very edge. He deepened his scowl and waited for the ferry to come to a stop. He crossed his arms, watching as a dozen Knights stood in the ferry, hands on their swords. One white-haired Knight with lotuses carved into his armor stepped ahead of the rest. Unlike the others, who glared at Jalist, he glanced along the shore, at all the armed men arrayed before him.

"I am Wyn Kai, Knight-Captain of the Order. I have been sent by the Grand Marshal to inquire as to why—"

"We're here to pick a fight," Jalist interrupted. "I'm Jalist Hewn, Captain of the Red Watch. I am also Rowen Locke's friend. You're holding him prisoner. You'll release him, or your precious Order will find its rosters greatly culled."

Jalist waved, and squad after squad of crimson-clad spearmen marched in double time toward the shore. Slum-dwellers followed in loud, disorderly waves. A deafening cacophony of vile insults issued from their mouths.

Jalist smothered a grin as Wyn Kai blanched.

"Captain, there is no need for such threats. Despite whatever rumors you've heard—"

"We've already given you a few days to come to your senses," Jalist interrupted. "We'll give you two more. Either you meet our demands, or you'll find your precious temple under siege."

Wyn Kai shook his head. "Captain, with respect—"

"Save your respect. I don't respect you any more than you respect me."

Wyn Kai frowned. "I only meant to tell you that we both know your forces are far too small to pose a threat."

"We'll find out in two days." Jalist turned to go.

Maddoc stepped forward before Jalist could stop him. Wytchfire flitted about his fists. "Sir Kai, I believe you were looking for me."

Wyn Kai shifted uncomfortably. "Lord Maddoc…" He turned back to Jalist. "Captain, perhaps we should speak in private. I am sure that—"

"I've already been to the Isles," Maddoc said in a low, lethal voice. "I saw…" He choked. "I saw what you did." Wytchfire flared up his arms, engulfing half his body, bright and hot. Isle Knights recoiled, drawing swords. Somehow, Wyn Kai held his ground, though Maddoc towered over him on the dock. "I think I'll send *you* back without a head, to balance things. What do you say to that?"

Jalist placed one hand on Maddoc and pulled the Shel'ai back, half afraid of being burned alive in the process. "As you can see, Sir Kai, your Grand Marshal is not a well-loved man at the moment. And your Order has not always been widely loved in Lyos anyway."

"But we defended you from the Throng—"

"Did you? I remember it differently." Jalist decided not to mention that he knew that because he himself had been with the Throng at the time of the attack. "Also, I seem to remember stories of the Order bleeding Lyos's coffers dry for, what, ten generations? Same thing happened at Phaegos. Maybe if we wait long enough, they'll send an army to help us, too."

Wyn Kai opened his mouth, as though to protest, then fell silent.

Jalist said, "But I don't think you want a war as much as we do.

So release Locke at once… and Father Matua and Aeko Shingawa and anybody else you're holding… and maybe we'll let you smug bastards go back to meditating over blossoms and fighting with sticks."

Wyn Kai cleared his throat. "Captain Jalist, as I said, there is no need for any of this. You and I must prevent bloodshed if we want to—"

"To survive the return of the Dragonkin?" Jalist glared at the Knight then nodded toward Maddoc. "The Shel'ai told me. But I wonder if all your Knights know." He raised his voice, addressing the rest of the Knights on the ferry. "Well, do you? Are you aware that your Grand Marshal is trying to bring down the Dragonward? That he's prepared to—"

Wyn Kai drew his sword.

Jalist leapt back, fumbling for his own blade, but Wyn Kai made no move to clamber onto the pier. Instead, the white-haired Knight pointed at Jalist. "We have a thousand Knights on Saikaido and twice as many squires. We can double that number in a few days. I only see a few hundred men here. I sought to avoid bloodshed, but if that's what you want, sail through the mist, and you'll find us waiting." He sheathed his sword, turned, and ordered his Knights to push off.

"Two days," Jalist called after him.

The slum-dwellers intensified their insults when they saw the Knights leaving. Men of the Red Watch joined in, cheering and sounding their trumpets.

Hráthbam stepped closer and still had to shout to be heard. "He's afraid."

Jalist nodded. "But not of us." He glanced at Maddoc, only to find that the Shel'ai had already stalked away, wytchfire leaking from his fists, his clothes smoldering.

"Him?" Hráthbam asked.

Jalist considered the question then shook his head. "I don't think so… but someone like him." He returned to the camp, gesturing for his officers along the way. "Since it looks like everybody's already awake, tell them to get to work on those damn boats!"

Then, his gaze fell on a line of wagons parked in the distance, each one laden with a ballista. He remembered Maddoc's description of the hill on which Saikaido Temple sat. He stared at the ballistae for a moment then turned back to Hráthbam.

"Get that damn Shel'ai back here. I have something absurd that I think he'll want to hear."

Rowen woke at the sound of the door unlatching. Despite his thirst and weariness, he stood. Sir Hiro swaggered into the cell. Rowen shifted, trying to ignore the weight of the shackles binding his hands. Since his last meeting with Crovis, his hands and feet had been chained, and he'd been taken to another room, deeper within the temple.

"Strange that all these rooms are here." Sir Hiro struck the wall with his fist—a signal for the guards to close the door behind him— and approached Rowen. "Did *you* know they were here? I didn't. I must have spent half my life in this temple, and I never knew what was right under me."

"Fitting."

Sir Hiro seized the bucket that had been left in the cell to attend to Rowen's bodily functions, turned it over, and placed one boot on it. He leaned on his knee. "We just burned Sang Wei's body. What was left of it, I mean." He snickered. "I wish he'd challenged me instead. It would have been a great honor to slice through the neck of my brother's killer, to smell his filth as he collapsed on the ground."

When Rowen did not reply, the dark-haired Knight drew his sword and displayed it. Rowen noted a long line of chrysanthemums etched into the blade.

"Recognize this?" Sir Hiro asked. "You should. It was your pupil's." Sir Hiro gave the blade a few slow swings, as though appreciating its balance.

Then he jammed the tip into the ground, working it between two flagstones. He leaned and leaned on it, bending the sword back over his thigh. Finally, the blade snapped.

Sir Hiro eyed the hilt with exaggerated surprise. "Oops." He tossed the hilt away, and it sparked off the wall and landed on the floor. "There's something else I want to tell you, Sword Marshal. Do I have your attention? Are you listening?"

Rowen glanced at the broken shaft of kingsteel lying at the Knight's feet and said nothing. Sir Hiro followed his gaze and picked up the broken blade then the hilt. Holding a piece of the sword in each hand, he approached Rowen.

"There's something I want you to know. I killed Sir Berric. It wasn't just me, though. I had help from a certain people with big muscles and gray skin." Sir Hiro laughed. "What, you didn't see that coming? You should have." He stepped closer. "We caught him outside the Isles. Only we didn't kill him first, like the Grand Marshal ordered. He was still alive when we tied him down and roasted him in his armor like a pig. Believe it or not, it was the Dwarrs' idea. We even burned a message into him, for that pretty woman of yours. Gods, you should have heard him screaming! You would have wept. Or maybe you would have laughed, like we did."

Rowen started forward then stopped himself.

Sir Hiro laughed. "I'd love to fight you, Sir Locke... especially now that you don't have a wytch or a godsdamned burning sword to help you. A *fair* fight. But the Grand Marshal says no." Sir Hiro dragged the broken blade along Rowen's cheek, drawing blood.

Rowen jerked his head back, hissing with pain. He retreated until his back pressed against the wall. Sir Hiro followed.

Rowen lowered his head. "Stop," he whimpered. "Please... "

Sir Hiro chuckled. "Now *that's* a surprise. I thought you were a great man!"

"Stop hurting me," Rowen repeated, keeping his eyes on the floor.

"Oh, come now. Don't be afraid." Sir Hiro leaned closer. "I won't hurt you, as much as I'd like to. Actually, I just came to ask a question. This woman of yours, the Iron Sister. They say she's got—"

Rowen drove his head into the Knight's nose. The Knight reeled backward, dropped the broken blade, and pressed one hand to his face. Blood poured through his fingers. Rowen followed, grabbed the sword still sheathed at Sir Hiro's belt, and drew it.

The Knight's eyes widened as he moved the hilt of the broken sword—Sang Wei's sword—to defend himself. Rowen stabbed around it. Holding the sword with both his shackled hands, Rowen drove it hilt-deep into the Knight's chest, just below his throat. He gave it a sharp twist.

"What, you didn't see that coming?" Rowen whispered in Hiro's ear, then dragged the sword out.

The cell door opened, and a Knight rushed in, sword drawn—then recoiled as Rowen scooped up the hilt of Sang Wei's broken blade and threw it at his face. Rowen followed, moving as fast as he could with his shackled feet. Despite his thirst and exhaustion, he pressed the attack. They traded a series of frantic blows. Rowen found himself being driven back. Then he ducked beneath a whirling blade and stabbed the Knight in the foot. The Knight howled and limped backward.

Spotting a third Knight in the hallway, Rowen let the man go. Rather than attacking, the third Knight supported the other on his arm and helped him get away. As they vanished down the hallway, Rowen heard them shouting for help. Rowen stepped out into the hallway, where the ceiling was higher, and attacked the shackles binding his feet. Though they were made of crude iron, not kingsteel, he had to swing a dozen times before he could break free. By then, three more Knights had gathered at the far end of the corridor. All three held polearms.

Rowen considered the shackles still binding his wrists and knew he had no choice but to run. He made it to the far end of the corridor, where he found himself facing a narrow stairwell leading down. He'd hardly started down the steps when he met another Knight, charging up. Rowen threw himself forward. The Knight's eyes widened, but he managed to raise his vambrace to ward off the blow. Rowen's blade sparked off armor. The two struggled. Rowen lost his sword. A moment later, both men lost their footing and fell backward into darkness.

Hráthbam winced as one of the men forgot his advice and lifted his oar out of the water. "Quiet," he hissed. He turned back toward shore.

The entire island of Saikaido had been transformed into a fortress. Some men were digging trenches in the sand while others labored on a massive row of palisades and sharpened stakes. Torches burned in the distance, mingling with the glint of drawn steel. Hráthbam peered through his spyglass and saw dozens and dozens of Knights and squires swarming along the beach.

He lowered the spyglass to survey the rest of the flatboat's inhabitants. Though Jalist had originally planned to send a dozen of his best swordsmen, that plan had changed as soon as Fen-Shea heard and proposed that they send just six of his own. Hráthbam studied those six. Four men and two women, they were without doubt the leanest, most frightful bunch he had ever seen. And one was Fen-Shea's wife.

As for the other two inhabitants of the flatboat, one was Maddoc, who everyone fully expected to get himself killed once Rowen had been rescued. The other inhabitant was a ballista.

And me, of course. Hráthbam shook his head. As the only person on the boat who actually knew how to operate a ballista. Hráthbam looked over his shoulder. By then, Jalist's ragtag army was already on the water, preparing to feign a night invasion of Saikaido's southeastern shore, thus providing a distraction for Hráthbam and the others.

Fen-Shea said, "Don't worry, my dark friend. I've gotten into tighter places than this. Haven't I, Cadney?" He squeezed his wife's thigh.

She answered by elbowing him in the jaw. Fen-Shea laughed, despite the bruise already forming.

"Gods," Hráthbam said, loosening his scimitar.

"Quiet," Maddoc warned everyone. His icy tone washed away even Fen-Shea's smile.

Hráthbam continued whispering directions to the men with oars. The flatboat passed the beach then circled in closer, to the northeast edge of the island. There, the hill broke off into a rocky bluff that ran right up to the coast, crested by the dark outline of the temple.

Hráthbam trained his gaze upward. A few lamps flickered from temple windows, but on this side of the island, Saikaido's defenses were practically nonexistent. After all, no sane man would ever attempt to scale not only the rocky bluffs but also the sheer face of the temple above.

Good thing this boat is full of madmen. Hráthbam turned to Maddoc. "How far—"

The Shel'ai hissed through his teeth for Hráthbam to be silent. A moment later, his voice echoed in Hráthbam's mind. *"There are three archers patrolling that parapet. You can't see them, but I can. Wait a moment for the last to leave."* A pause. *"There."* Maddoc pointed.

Hráthbam nodded. He turned to Fen-Shea. "You'll have to do some climbing, not to mention a fair bit of shimmying along a cord overlooking an unlit mass of rocks and ocean. Sure you're fine with that?"

Fen-Shea started to laugh, glanced at Maddoc, and grinned instead.

"I was born for this, Soroccan. Just aim true and guard the boat. And don't you leave without us!"

"Wouldn't dream of it, my friend." Hráthbam cast a worried look at the temple parapets as he moved to load the ballista. As he turned the lever, he winced each time the mechanism clinked. He winced again when the spear scraped against the flatboat as he lifted it. Two of Fen-Shea's men quietly bound one end of the spear to a tough, thin cord. Hráthbam listened for shouts of alarm but heard nothing other than the lapping of waves and the distant commotion on the beach. When the spear was ready, he set to aiming the ballista, muttering under his breath when the sway of the boat made the difficult process that much harder.

"If you miss…" Maddoc trailed off meaningfully.

"I won't miss." Hráthbam reached for the firing lever then stopped. He'd aimed for a spot on the bluff that seemed more dirt than rock—soft enough for the spear to sink in without much noise. But just above, a sudden wisp of lamplight illuminated a thin crack in the temple wall. He swore. "Whoever's there will hear," he whispered.

Fen-Shea squinted. "The wall looks weak. Maybe the spear can break through."

Cadney rolled her eyes. "You can tell that from here, can you, love?"

Maddoc said, "Weak or no, you and your men can't get all the way inside before the alarm's raised."

"Don't bet on it," Fen-Shea grunted, but without much conviction.

"I'll aim lower," Hráthbam said. "You'll have to do more climbing, but at least you'll have a chance." He had hardly begun to swivel the ballista, searching for another ripe target in the darkness, when Maddoc touched his arm.

For the first time, the Shel'ai was smiling. He pointed toward the crack in the temple wall. "Plan's changed. Get another spear ready. Forget the cord." Before anyone could reply, the Shel'ai pressed his fingertips to the cord tied to the spear, and a flare of wytchfire burned away the cord, which collapsed back onto its coil.

Fen-Shea snarled and started to draw his knife, but Cadney stopped him.

Hráthbam frowned. "Why did you do that?"

195

"Because the cord would weigh down the bolt, and you'll need it to be as strong as possible if you're going to break down that wall."

"And why in Dyoni's name would I want to do that?" Then, Maddoc's voice echoed in his mind, answering his question, and Hráthbam grinned.

Rowen struggled to his feet. He glanced up and saw torchlight playing off the walls of a stairwell. A Knight lay on the ground nearby, moaning faintly. Rowen looked for his sword but could not find it. He took the prone Knight's blade instead. He considered killing the man but let him be.

That corridor was even narrower than the last one, with only one torch burning in a soot-stained bracket along the wall. Rowen grabbed the torch and hurried down to the end of the corridor, where he found two stairwells, one descending in either direction. He chose the left stairwell but flung his torch down the right. He edged along the wall, feeling his way until he reached the bottom.

Shouts and metallic footsteps told him the Knights had chosen the other stairwell based on the flicker of the torch. Rowen pushed on in darkness, half afraid he would reach a dead end and have no choice but to turn back and surrender. Instead, he felt a cold, metal door. Instead of a lock, a thick wooden crossbeam held the door in place. He removed the beam. Though he opened the door slowly, the hinges shrieked.

A cold draft of air touched his face. The room before him was nearly as dark as the corridor he'd left behind, except for a faint spark of light in the distance. He moved toward it as cautiously as he could, inching along in the darkness. Finally, he reached what felt like a small wooden table with a lamp on top of it. The lamp had nearly burned out. Rowen turned up the wick until yellow light shone through smoke-stained glass. He lifted the lamp and turned slowly, surveying the room.

The room was small, with worn stones that spoke of great age. One wall bore a long crack, which, judging by the fresh night air streaming in, led outside. Next to the crack, chained to the wall, was Aeko Shingawa.

At first, Rowen hardly recognized her. She wore no armor. Her clothes were tattered and bloodstained. Dried blood covered her lean, bronze limbs. Her hair hung in her eyes, filthy and matted. Her head hung, too, so that he feared she was dead. At the sound of her own name, though, her head lifted.

Her eyes opened. "Squire..."

Rowen embraced her for a moment then attacked the chains holding her hands to the wall. They were made of sterner stuff than those that had bound his feet, and he winced as the shrill metallic scream of each strike echoed through the cell. Finally, the first broke free. Aeko's arm sagged, and she dangled from the last chain like a dead animal.

Shouts echoed from the corridor beyond. Cursing, Rowen attacked the final chain with renewed strength. The moment he freed Aeko, he feared she would fall, but to his surprise, she straightened.

"Give me the sword." Her voice rasped.

Rowen obeyed.

Aeko stepped to one side and lifted the blade. "Hold out your hands." Aeko lifted the sword with both hands.

Rowen was about to protest, doubting Aeko's strength and aim after so long in captivity. But before he could speak, Aeko swung.

Rowen's chains shattered.

Aeko collapsed to her knees then pushed herself back up before Rowen could move to assist her. A wild look filled her eyes. "Run, Squire... Crovis will be here soon... He visits me every night..."

Rowen took her arm and eyed the crack in the wall. For a moment, he thought he might widen it with his sword so that he could push Aeko through to freedom, but a glance told him that was impossible. He turned back to the door.

"No way out," he said.

Aeko stared ahead, a blank look on her face, as though she had not heard him. Then she sighed. "Sorry, Squire. I'm not giving the sword back. You'll have to pick one up off the floor." She moved to the center of the room and slipped into a fighting position. Though she was visibly weak, her limbs spoke of lethal tension.

Rowen smiled. Armed with just the lamp, he joined her. "How long have you been here?"

"Long enough to forget what a bath feels like."

"But not long enough to forget how to hold a sword?"

"Not quite."

197

"I'm sorry I couldn't get you out of here."

Aeko answered with a thin smile. "Sorry I couldn't get *you* out of here."

"We'll call it even."

The Knights were close enough that Rowen could distinguish the orders being shouted in the hallway beyond. Rather than just charge into Aeko's cell, the men were gathering reinforcements, forming ranks. Rowen heard Wyn Kai's voice over the din.

"They'll offer to let us surrender," Rowen said.

Aeko nodded. "Not interested. But feel free if you like."

"Considering what Crovis wants me for… " Rowen hesitated. "He knows I'll tell him no. But if he gets Igrid, he'll torture her right in front of me."

Aeko turned to him. "Everyone has their limits. You love her. I wouldn't blame you—"

"No." Rowen shook his head. "I can't give him what he wants. Not for Igrid, not for anyone. Better I die now."

"Your death *would* have the advantage of saving the entire continent from certain doom." Aeko's smile broadened. "Not many men can say that."

"I already saved it once. I was hoping to live this time." Rowen adjusted his grip on the lamp when it began to burn his hand.

Aeko said nothing.

No courage without fear. Rowen waited.

A moment later, he jumped as a shrill, metallic crack erupted just behind them. Bits of stone skittered across the floor.

"What in the gods… " He lifted the lantern, and his eyes widened.

Before him, the tip of a spear gleamed coldly, protruding from the crack in the far wall. He stared, uncomprehending, until Aeko grabbed his arm and pulled him to one side. A moment later, a second impact filled the room. One stone fell, followed by another.

Choking on dust, Rowen forced his way forward. A larger gap had been opened in the wall, revealing a world of stars and darkened ocean beyond. He lowered his gaze and saw someone frantically waving a torch, far below, on the water. He stared in disbelief again.

Aeko asked, "Friends of yours?"

Just then, Maddoc's voice resounded in Rowen's mind, calling him outside. Speechless, Rowen pushed Aeko through the gap then turned and flung his lamp at the far wall. It shattered, plunging the cell into darkness. He moved to follow Aeko, but the fit was tighter than he'd expected.

Aeko grabbed his arm, pulling from the other side. Rowen had his head turned sideways, facing Aeko's cell door—just as Knights poured into the cell, swords and torches in hand. He braced his foot against the floor and pushed. The wall tore at his chest and back, and blood trickled between his shoulder blades. Still, he made it through just as the Knights turned and spotted him.

Night air chilled the sweat on his face as Aeko dragged him to the edge of the bluff.

He looked down. "That's a long climb." He turned to Aeko. "Listen, give me the sword. I'll hold them back while—"

"I have a better idea." Aeko jammed her sword in the earth and left it there. Then she took Rowen's hand and dragged him with her as she leapt off the edge into a long, heart-stopping free fall.

CHAPTER TWENTY

IGRID FORCED HERSELF NOT TO back up as Keswen took a menacing step toward her.

"Are you mad? We're riding back to Cadavash," the Sylvan huntress insisted. "Say *no* one more time, and I'll knock you out and tie you to that damn horse."

Igrid fought back a grin and touched the knife Keswen had loaned her. Keswen had returned Igrid's breast knife as well, though Igrid kept that hidden.

"Feel free to try," Igrid said. "But while we're killing each other, Algol could be doing the same to Zeia."

Keswen reined in her horse. "No offense, Iron Sister, but I don't give a damn what happens to Zeia. Knightswrath is what's important. She'd say that herself if she could. We can't get it back on our own. So we ride like mad back to Cadavash, rouse every Knight we can find, and—"

Igrid smiled at the thought of seeing the children again, even if that meant sparring with Thessa and stamping out Sariel's fires, but she shook her head. "That will take too long. Algol will be back on the Lotus Isles by then."

"So what if he is? Whatever danger your man is in, I'm sure his own Knights will protect him against—"

"I think Crovis and this Shel'ai are working together. Don't ask me why, but I think they want the same thing: the Dragonward brought down."

Keswen frowned. "What in the gods' names are you talking about?"

Startled, Igrid realized Keswen still did not know about the scroll taken from the Scrollhouse. She divulged the secret as quickly as she could then repeated most of it when Keswen simply stared, speechless. "So we have to get Knightswrath before—"

"Do you really think Locke would help this Shel'ai, whatever he calls himself?" Keswen shook her head. "Obviously, they wanted you so they could use you against him. They don't have you. Instead, they have a sword they can't use. I don't think we're in half as much peril as you think."

"Unless they find a way to use the sword *without* Rowen."

"Is that possible?"

"Honestly, I don't know."

Keswen frowned again. "I hate magic."

"I don't blame you. But we need to get that sword back. Otherwise, whatever happens is my fault."

"No, it's Locke's fault for not taking the damn thing with him. I've met wild dogs that have more sense than men." Keswen sighed. "Where do you want to start? We have horses. They don't. That means we're faster, but they'll have an easier time hiding—not exactly a good thing, when one of them can burn us to ashes with a wave of his hand."

"We'll start at the camp." Igrid turned northeast, where smoke from the burned-out forest still smeared the horizon. *With a little luck, we won't become smoke ourselves.* She urged her horse onward before she had time to change her mind.

Dagath scowled at their newest prisoner as they made their way through a nameless patch of forest.

She'd been unconscious when Algol brought her to him. Dagath laughed at first, remembering the fearsome wytch whose hands he'd cut off years before, leaving her powerless. Then, she regained consciousness, and he realized she was not so powerless after all.

Her scarred, hideous stumps blossomed into terrifying hands of fire that plucked the sword from his belt and very nearly cut him wide open before Algol's magic had driven her unconscious again. She lay across the back of a plow horse they'd stolen from a farm and had not stirred for almost a day. Still, Dagath was keeping his distance.

"We should just kill her now," he said.

"Perhaps," Algol said, "but she might be useful later. She's Locke's friend. Besides, you're the one who cost me the Iron Sister." He held the reins of the plow horse as he walked. He seemed careless, utterly unconcerned about who might have been following them.

Dagath glanced back for signs of pursuit. He hated traveling through forests. *Too many shadows.* He rubbed his shoulder then gingerly touched his neck. Though Algol had mostly healed Dagath's wounds, he still remembered the awful kiss of the Sylvan woman's arrows. He glanced at his new employer. "What was so important about her, anyway?"

"So far, you've impressed me with how you refrain from asking troublesome questions. Don't spoil that now."

Dagath fell silent and fixed his gaze on the eastern horizon. Before him, the Simurgh Plains gave way to hills that gradually sloped down toward the sea. Sunset filtered through a distant fog. He could already smell a faint whiff of salt in the air. He had the awful feeling that he was simply retracing the path he'd taken weeks earlier with that nameless, foolish Olg.

Dagath found himself wondering if the Olg had survived his fight against the Sylv. He doubted it but thought it over and decided he did not care. After all, the Olg had been a miserable traveling companion. However, the Shel'ai was more to his liking and reminded him of some of his previous employers, Brahasti and the Bloody Prince.

Dagath sighed, remembering the pleasures of those days. He glanced over his shoulder at the smoking western sky. If the Iron Sister and the Sylv were indeed following them, he wondered if they had come upon the farm yet. He smiled, imagining the looks on the faces of those he'd slaughtered. Then he faced ahead, still smiling.

A moment later, his smile vanished as the forest came to life. Strong, gray-skinned warriors emerged from the shadows and encircled them, drawn steel glinting in the setting sun.

"Move and die," someone called.

Igrid said, "Keswen, stop."

The Sylvan woman ignored Igrid's order and dismounted her horse, fitting an arrow to her longbow as she strode forward. Lying on the grass, a mass of dark hair and gray, blood-crusted muscle, the Olg turned his head to look at her. His powerful chest rose and fell with labored breathing. The Olg had dragged Keswen's arrows out of his body but had not bandaged the wounds. His mace lay beside him on the blackened grass, but he did not reach for it. Instead, he stared up at Keswen with dark, unblinking eyes.

"Stop," Igrid repeated, leaping down off her horse.

Keswen still did not answer. Instead, she pulled the bowstring back to her cheek. Her shoulders tensed. Igrid cursed, drew her knife, and threw it. The pommel struck Keswen's bow just as she released the bowstring. The arrow thudded into the grass next to the wounded Olg's face. The Olg did not even blink.

Keswen whirled, already reaching for another arrow. Igrid drew the breast knife from her clothing and stepped forward. She knocked the bow aside with one hand and pressed the small knife to Keswen's throat with the other. "I said stop," she said in a low voice.

Keswen frowned as her confusion turned to anger. She slipped to one side, swung her bow like a quarterstaff, and knocked Igrid off her feet. Igrid rolled away as quickly as she could. Nevertheless, by the time she rose, Keswen already had another arrow nocked and drawn. That time, the arrow was aimed at Igrid's heart.

"Enough, Iron Sister. From now on, I'm the one giving orders. And my first order addresses how we treat wounded enemies who delight in rape and murder." She stepped back and swiveled her bow aiming at the Olg again.

Igrid stepped in front of the Olg, blocking her shot.

Keswen's eyes narrowed dangerously. "What in Fohl's hells are you doing?"

Good question. "He's already down. He's no danger to anyone. The fight's over."

"Begging your pardon, Iron Sister, but I've been fighting Olgrym all my life. I know a bit more about them than you do. See those scars all over his body? He didn't get those from picking vegetables." Keswen tried to step around Igrid.

Igrid moved with her, still blocking her shot.

Keswen snickered. "Do you really think I can't put this arrow past your ear, right into his eye?"

"I bet you can," Igrid conceded, "but can you nock another before I cut your throat?"

Keswen's snicker vanished. "You'd really kill me over an Olg?"

Rowen might. "I'd rather not, but that's up to you."

Keswen lowered her bow. "You're an Iron Sister, not an Isle Knight. That means you're smart enough to know that killing an enemy while they're down isn't an affront to the Light or the gods or anything else. It just keeps you from getting stabbed in the back."

Igrid sidestepped, turned, and looked down at the Olg. "If Breaksteel followed that advice, I'd be dead right now."

"Perfect," Keswen groaned. "He gave you some soup, and you gave him a nickname! How delightful. The minstrels will be pleased." She snatched the arrow off her bowstring, flipped it between her fingers, and jammed it back into her quiver.

Igrid edged closer to the fallen Olg, keeping her breast knife drawn. "It would be a poor reflection on my kindness if you tried to kill me as soon as I get close."

The Olg lifted his head and almost smiled. Then he shook his head. His hands moved slowly to his chest. He made three quick, strange motions with his fingers.

Igrid frowned. "What…"

The Olg repeated the gestures.

"Hand-speech," Keswen said, her voice laced with disgust. "Wyldkin and Shal'tiar use it when they have to keep quiet. Some Olgrym know it, too. If you like, I'll tell you how they captured our hunters and tortured them into teaching—"

"What did he just say?"

Keswen shrugged. "Just what you'd expect. He says the sorcerer left him here. He says he was tricked, he won't hurt you, he likes the color of your hair because it reminds him of blood, and he wants to fill your belly with—"

"Enough." Igrid turned back to the Olg. "I trust most of that was an embellishment."

The Olg smiled again.

"What's your name?"

The Olg answered with a flurry of signs then shrugged.

"He doesn't have one," Keswen said. "Olgrym don't get names until they've killed their first victim, and he *claims* that—"

"All right, Breaksteel will suit him fine for now. Where did the sorcerer go?"

The Olg shrugged his massive shoulders again then winced with pain. He made another complex series of gestures.

Keswen said, "He says he went east. The other sellsword is still alive." When the Olg made another series of gestures, Keswen laughed. "He says he doesn't like the sorcerer. He doesn't fight with honor. He says if we help him with his wounds, he'll help us kill him." Keswen faced Igrid. "Before you consider that, let me tell you a thing or two about the Olgish concept of honor."

"I'd rather you didn't." Igrid frowned down at Breaksteel. "As you can see, my friend doesn't trust you. I don't either. She's right. You gave me soup. You also helped kidnap me and tied me to a tree. I've known your kind before. As the saying goes, a snake is still a snake."

With great effort, the Olg sat up. He reached for his mace. Igrid and Keswen recoiled. Keswen nocked three arrows, but instead of attacking, the Olg simply used his mace as a crutch then dropped it as soon as he was on his feet.

He made a longer series of gestures then waited for Keswen to translate.

Keswen rolled her eyes. "He says he's not like the others. He says he's one of the Tongueless."

"What are they?"

Keswen shrugged.

Breaksteel answered with more gestures. Keswen frowned and said nothing. The Olg repeated the gestures with greater urgency.

"Well?" Igrid asked.

Keswen shook her head. "Just a bunch of nonsense."

Breaksteel shook his head. The tiny skulls braided through his hair clacked together.

Igrid said, "Tell me anyway."

Keswen sighed. "He says his clan rejected the old ways. They fought Doomsayer when he was trying to unite the clans for war. Most died.

He and a few others were caught. Doomsayer let them live as a sign of disgrace, but he ripped out their tongues. They've been living on the Dead Shores ever since." Keswen gave the Olg a look of loathing. "Too bad he's lying."

"How do you know?"

"Because *no* Olg rejects their ways and lives!"

"Are you sure?"

Keswen blinked. "There are rumors. Sometimes, a captured Olg will rant about the Tongueless, how they've gone soft, but it's all nonsense. I've spent my whole life on the Ash'bana Plains, and I've never seen—"

Igrid turned back to Breaksteel. "Let's say I'm dumb enough to believe you. What are you doing this far east?"

The Olg started to gesture, but before he could finish, his strength gave out. He collapsed with a heavy crash, and fresh blood streamed from his wounds. Igrid started forward, but Keswen grabbed her arm. "Careful with that soft heart, Iron Sister. It'll get you killed. I've seen this trick before."

The Olg gestured weakly, then his head sagged back onto the grass. His eyes closed. His chest rose and fell, more labored than before.

"What did he say?" Igrid demanded.

Keswen laughed. "He says he went east because he wanted to become a Knight! He says they turned him away, though." She faced Igrid. "Are you done wasting time with this?" She touched her shortsword. "If you like him so much, let me put him out of his misery. Unless you'd rather I leave him for the wolves." She faced the Olg. "Or the vultures. Or ants."

Igrid looked east. She wondered how far the Shel'ai had traveled. She wondered, too, what Rowen would do in her place. She had an awful feeling that she already knew. She turned back to Keswen. "You have a choice, Sylv. You can either ride back to Cadavash alone, or you can help me clean and sew his wounds. Whichever choice you make, do it quietly, and make it now."

CHAPTER TWENTY-ONE

CROVIS GAVE SERIOUS THOUGHT TO executing a dozen Knights—publicly, at the foot of the temple steps—as punishment for permitting both Rowen Locke and Aeko Shingawa to escape. In the end, though, he decided to show mercy. He chose only one Knight: the man who had fled after Rowen stabbed him in the foot. He had that Knight brought to the base of the temple at dawn, supported on both sides since he could barely walk.

"Return his sword," Crovis said.

The young Knight's eyes widened. Speechless, he accepted the blade Wyn Kai handed him. The other Knights backed away. The young Knight tried to take a step on his bandaged foot and collapsed. Crovis waited until he'd pushed himself back up, using his sword as a crutch.

"Grand Marshal, wait. I didn't—"

Crovis drew his sword, stepped forward, and ended the fight in three lightning-fast cuts. He saluted as the corpse fell onto the sand. Then, he turned to face the crowd of onlookers, which was composed of not only Knights and squires, but also townspeople. A few nodded with approval. Others shook their heads. Most stared straight ahead as though their features had been carved from stone.

"This was not punishment," Crovis said. He wiped his blade on his sleeve. "Earlier, this Knight showed cowardice in the face of a superior enemy. Facing me was his chance for redemption. Had he looked within, had he found courage and fully embraced the Light, he would have defeated me, despite his wound." Crovis turned, saluted his fallen foe, and sheathed his blade. "Our entire Order is founded upon this principle. We will not abandon it now."

Stepping back, Crovis waved. Three Knights came forward. One retrieved the dead man's head while the others gathered the rest of the body. Crovis stood at attention until the body had been carried away and the head placed on a spear—another in a growing row along the base of the temple steps.

Then, he turned. "You wished to speak with me, Sir Kai?"

Wyn Kai cleared his throat. He stepped closer and lowered his voice. "Grand Marshal, I was able to obtain a more accurate count on the number of enemies surrounding the island. As you surmised, their force is smaller than ours. But they have twice as many ships. And—"

"Ships are of no consequence," Crovis said. "Besides, when word of Locke's and Shingawa's treachery spreads throughout the islands, the other temples will lend us their assistance."

Wyn Kai's face turned red. "Grand Marshal, did you read the letters I left on your desk? The rest of the Council is starting to turn against you. There's talk that you've allied yourself with the Dragonkin. Now that Locke and Shingawa are free, they might—"

"They will attempt to spread lies as false Knights always have. But true Knights know the truth when they hear it." He added, "Do not fear, Sir Kai. Even if a few in our Order turn against us, we are not without allies. There are countless others throughout Ruun who understand the evils of magic. All will join us before long."

Crovis turned, surveying the defenses along the shoreline. His Knights had already erected a bristling wreath of sharpened stakes all along the beach, and they were busy transporting all the siege weapons atop the temple to the bottom of the hill, to defend the shoreline instead. Crovis frowned. "I don't hear as many hammers as I should. Why has the palisade not been completed?"

"Grand Marshal, we've run out of building materials. Since the southeast edge of the island is the most accessible, might I suggest we redeploy what we've built so far to guard that approach?"

Crovis turned back to face the hill. He looked up and up, to the temple. "No, we'll guard it all," he said finally. "The garden is full of trees. Cut them down."

Wyn Kai was speechless for a moment. "Grand Marshal, many of those trees are centuries old! Some might even be—"

"They're *trees*, Sir Kai. The last time I checked, trees were made of wood. So are the fortifications you're supposed to be building." Crovis started to walk away then changed his mind. He placed one gauntleted hand on Wyn Kai's shoulder. "These are dark times, old friend. I pray we are not asked to sacrifice more than we already have, but if that prayer is not answered, I know that I can depend on your sense of honor as I always have."

Wyn Kai bowed. "Of course, Grand Marshal."

"Good." Crovis turned. "If I don't hear axes by the time I sit down for breakfast, I will be very disappointed." The Grand Marshal considered starting back up the temple steps, but the sea air felt good on his face, so he toured the island's burgeoning defenses instead. As he walked, he thought of the blind Shel'ai he'd met before. He had not seen the man since then. For all Crovis knew, he could be dead. However, Crovis doubted it.

Perhaps the Light is keeping him alive. Surely even evil men have a part to play in the Light's grand design. As he continued to survey the island's defenses, nodding to all those who cheered or bowed at his approach, Crovis contemplated his own part in the Light's plan. He prayed that whatever his role, he would fulfill it well.

Algol watched, unsurprised, as the Dwarrs closed in.

Though they moved stealthily from tree to tree, hugging the shadows, he counted at least twenty of them. His heightened senses had detected them moments earlier, but they carried bows as well as axes and swords, so running would have been futile. He felt a moment of panic when he thought back to the three Dwarrs he'd caught in the wilderness shortly before making his way to Cadavash. For no reason besides his own amusement, he'd killed them. Surely they'd been discovered by then. But the newly arrived warriors would have no reason to suspect him. To them, he would appear as just a blind beggar.

Algol moved his cloak to cover Knightswrath's hilt and turned toward Zeia. He might have moved her hair to cover the tapered points of her ears, but her hair was too short. He considered covering her head with a cloth, but that would look too suspicious. Besides, the Dwarrs had already encircled them. He could feel their tension and suspected they were trying to decide whether Zeia was a wytch or a Sylv. A moment later, they stepped out of hiding.

Though he'd seen them coming, their drawn steel and taut bowstrings made Algol's heart leap into his throat. Meanwhile, Dagath cursed and drew his sword. With great effort, Algol restrained himself from burning the closest Dwarrs with wytchfire. Instead, he feigned confusion. "Dagath, what's happening?" he cried, deliberately making his voice sound shrill and afraid.

Luckily, the sellsword guessed his game and played along. "Trouble, Master. Bandits, I think. A lot of them." He added, "They're Dwarrs, believe it or not."

Algol opened his mouth, feigning amazement. "Dwarrs, this far north?" Still holding the reins of the plow horse, he swung his scepter like a cane before him, as though trying to get his bearings. "How many? Are they armed? Gods, where are they?"

"They're all around us," Dagath growled.

Algol looked through the cloth tied around his eye sockets at the man he suspected of being the Dwarrs' leader: a powerfully built man with salt-and-pepper hair and cautious eyes. While the other Dwarrs seemed like either young or old men who had only recently taken to soldiering, that Dwarr had the look of an experienced warrior. He held an impressive long axe with both hands. Though he spoke to Dagath, he kept his eyes on Zeia, ready to swing.

"Sheathe your blade, sellsword. We aren't killers, and we certainly aren't robbers. We'd just like to know why you have a woman tied to your horse… and more importantly, what she is."

Dagath hesitated then sheathed his sword. He glanced at Algol. "A strange tale, that. I'd best let my master explain."

The Dwarrs' leader turned to Algol. "Well?"

Algol bowed. "I am Father Arddu. As you can see, I am but a poor priest. This man, Dagath, is my guard. We found this woman on the plains. I thought at first that she was some poor daughter of the gods, ravaged by men who craved nothing but pleasures of the flesh. But we could not wake her. Then, Dagath noticed her ears. He tells me they are pointed… and that, curiously, she has no hands. A Sylv, I believe they call her kind. We thought to take her to Lyos, to see what should be done with her."

The Dwarrish warrior's eyes narrowed. He reached out and lifted Zeia's head by the chin. He waved another Dwarr closer and handed the man his axe. Then, he used his free hand to pry open one of Zeia's eyelids. He let go of her head and leapt back, reclaiming his axe. "That's no Sylv, priest. That's a wytch!"

Algol looked about, feigning confusion. "I don't understand… "

The Dwarrish warrior seemed undecided whether to ask questions or simply to order them killed. But when moments passed and Zeia did not stir, he returned his attention to Algol. He stepped forward and used the butt of his long axe to move Algol's tattered cloak, revealing Knightswrath's hilt. "A poor priest who wears no divine sigil but carries a sword and a cane made of dragonbone?" He stepped back. "It's bad enough, the company you keep. I'll give you one last chance to tell us the truth."

Dagath tensed, reaching for his sword, but three Dwarrs with nocked arrows stepped closer and dissuaded him.

Algol thought quickly. "May I have your name, sir?"

"Keidu," the Dwarr said. "I'd ask for yours, but frankly, I'm more interested in hearing about this wytch."

"Keidu," Algol said, bowing again, "I understand how strange this must appear. But you said you and your men are neither killers nor robbers, and though I hear fierceness in your voice, I hear kindness, as well."

Keidu snickered. "And here I thought the blind had superior hearing."

Algol feigned insult. "Please, my child. If I could just explain… "

"I wish you would."

Algol held up his scepter. "This is a relic of my order, like the sword. I serve Tier'Gothma. We are bound to Lyos to present these relics to the head of my order. As for sigils"—he smiled—"the blind have little use for symbols. And in truth, I thought traveling in rags would make it easier to conceal these relics."

The Dwarrs exchanged looks. Keidu frowned, unconvinced. He turned to Zeia. "And the wytch?"

"As I said, we found her on the plains. My guard noticed her ears. But I did not think to have him examine her eyes. I assumed she was just a Sylv, though the gods only know what she'd be doing on the Simurgh Plains, so far from her homeland." He shrugged helplessly. "To be honest, I know little of such matters. To me, magic has always seemed like the work of demons. I did not think to encounter it in this lifetime." To emphasize his words, he drew away from Zeia, holding his scepter before him, as though to ward off some great evil.

The Dwarrs spoke in whispers. Keidu stood in silence, glaring at everyone. Finally, he sighed. He gestured for his men to be quiet and faced Algol again. "You're a lucky man, Father Arddu. The world is a harsh place. It's good we found you before this wytch regained consciousness. But have no fear. We'll accept responsibility for her."

He snapped his fingers and gestured. With great reluctance, four Dwarrish warriors came forward, untied Zeia from the plow horse, and dragged her roughly to the ground. They looked as though they would rather stab her than touch her but were not about to disobey their commander. One of the men glanced at Algol then back at Keidu.

"What about all that dragonbone?"

Keidu said, "Let them keep it." He glanced at Algol. "As I said, priest, we are not thieves. We are the Sons of Maelmohr. May the gods protect you." He nodded in farewell and vanished into the forest. His men followed, dragging Zeia behind them.

Igrid blinked as the smoke stung her eyes.

Before them lay a farm. All was quiet. A dirt path led between a charred wheat field and a pasture full of dead cattle, up to the dark, open doorway of a burned-out farmhouse. She approached slowly, both knives drawn, eyeing the shadows for hidden enemies. Keswen moved beside her, prodding Breaksteel ahead of them.

The Olg limped, gritting his teeth with pain, but did not refuse. Igrid had permitted him to keep his mace, though weak as he was, he used it as a cane. He'd slept little since they'd washed and sewn his wounds. Despite her reluctance, Keswen had agreed to use her substantial knowledge of herbs to treat him. She insisted that without time to rest, though, he would most likely keel over any moment. She sounded as though she welcomed the thought.

So far, though, the Olg had kept pace with their horses, steadfastly signing his refusal each time Igrid tried to make him ride her horse instead. The Olg was limping weakly toward the farmhouse, occasionally glancing spitefully at the arrow Keswen kept trained on his back.

The Sylv glanced at Igrid. "You think this was the sorcerer?"

"Could be bandits, but I don't think they'd waste time with fire."

"Agreed." Keswen pointed.

Igrid turned to see a young man propped against a charred scarecrow. The man's eyes were wide. A spear—probably his own—had been shoved clean through his chest, pinning him to the pole. Everything below his neck was charred wreckage. Everything below his waist was ash. Near him lay a burned plow. She saw no sign of the animal to which it had once been harnessed. Igrid shuddered and turned back toward the farmhouse.

Keswen said, "There's no need to go in there."

Igrid caught her meaning. If the Shel'ai and the sellsword had left anything behind, it would just be a cruel message designed to taunt and dissuade them. They might as well press on. Still, Igrid hesitated. *They killed these people for no reason.* But as soon as she had the thought, she realized she was wrong. Everything she'd seen from that Shel'ai, from his attack on Father Matua to his savaging of Zeia, spoke of deliberate malice, of cruelty for cruelty's sake.

"He's mocking us," she thought aloud. "Rowen's honor, what he's trying to make out of his Knighthood. What both of us are trying to make out of the world…"

Keswen grunted her agreement. She moved over to the scarecrow, said something in Sylvan, and wrenched the spear from the charred man's chest. She caught what remained of his body and lowered it gently to the ground. Then she bowed and walked away, keeping the spear.

"We should look for weapons," Igrid advised. She thought of those she'd left behind, including her expensive composite bow, and wished they'd had time to go back and retrieve them. Then she heard a scratching sound from within the farmhouse.

She stuck one of the knives into her belt and reached out to take Keswen's sword. She strode ahead of Breaksteel toward the doorway.

Keswen hissed for her to stop, but Igrid ignored her, thinking instead of Sir Berric. Then she thought of Thessa and Sariel. She thought of Rowen—wounded, far from her protection. She considered the possibility that one or both of her enemies might still be within the farmhouse. Trap or no, she decided that no matter what happened to her, no amount of steel or wytchfire could stop her from splitting her enemy in half.

But the moment she set foot inside the farmhouse, she stopped in her tracks. A smell filled her nostrils: not just the smoke from fire, but the saltiness of blood mixed with the sour musk of bodily filth. Her eyes narrowed in the darkness. She discerned the outlines of crude, burned furniture and toppled cupboards. Seated on the floor in the center of the farmhouse, propped up facing the door as though to greet her, were three more bodies—one of them a child—all charred beyond recognition.

Igrid stared for a moment then looked away. A flash of color caught her eye. She edged toward it. On the floor, folded with mocking neatness, lay a little girl's dress. Igrid lifted her gaze and saw a red-haired ragdoll placed in the window, staring out with dark eyes.

Igrid's stomach lurched as she realized what that meant. The shadow of her own sword quivered on the floor as she began to shake. Then, she saw something move out of the corner of her eye. However, she turned slowly, as though mired.

Dimly, through a slant of light streaming through the open window, she saw a greatwolf emerge from the wreckage of a larder. Yellow eyes narrowed. Teeth bared. The huge thing snarled for a moment then came at her—but stopped as the head of a mace drove its long, sharp teeth to the floor.

The mace struck again. The greatwolf twisted, somehow still alive. Its jaws snapped. Claws raked the empty air. The mace rose a third time, higher than before. It hung there a moment, so black that it looked like it was made from shadows, then fell.

The greatwolf's head shattered.

Only then did Igrid realize she could move. She lurched toward the greatwolf and thrust her sword—first into the wreckage of its skull, then between its shoulder blades. She stabbed with her knife, too, howling.

Then, Keswen's voice cut through the fog. "Enough, Iron Sister. Outside. Now."

The sternness reminded her of Captain Ailynn, her late commander in Hesod. Igrid blinked. Then she stiffened to attention. "Yes, Captain." She looked back at the window, snatched up the girl's ragdoll, and backed out of the darkness.

CHAPTER TWENTY-TWO

FOR THE FIRST TIME IN as long as he could remember, Father Matua woke without pain. Sunlight streamed through a window, making him wince. Salty air filled his nostrils. He vaguely remembered being in a different room—a closed, stifled room without light—but that seemed like a bad dream, as did the pain.

Matua glanced down and saw his body still wrapped in bandages. He pressed on the bandages, and pain raced through his body. *Not a dream after all.* He tried to sit up. No one appeared to help him. He looked around and realized he was alone in what appeared to be a study filled with bookshelves.

A washbasin sat on a table beside his bed, along with a pitcher of water. Matua saw no cup, which suited him fine. Gripping the pitcher with his only hand, he drank. The water was cold. He spilled a great deal down his chest, but he smiled at the thought that, judging by the smell, that was the closest thing to a bath he'd had in days.

When he'd drunk his fill, he set the pitcher down, gathered his strength, and got out of bed. The feel of the cold stone against his bare feet stunned him almost as much as the soreness in his muscles. Nevertheless, he managed to stumble toward the window.

Instead of stained glass, the window itself was just a thin opening in the stone wall, like an arrow slit. He stared out at blue water and seagulls—no skiffs. *I'm not in Atheion, then.*

He pressed his face to the arrow slit, hoping to lean out and look down, but his head was too wide to pass through the opening. Instead, he took a few deep breaths then turned to more closely inspect his room. The door was closed. He had yet to check it, but something told him he would find it locked. He approached the closest bookshelf, inspecting its contents for a clue as to his whereabouts.

"Treasury reports," he muttered. He set down one book and selected another, which contained a tedious tome of laws. He traded that for a thin, brittle scroll. "A roster of names more than two centuries old. It appears I'm on the Lotus Isles."

"So you are."

Matua turned. A lean, dark-haired man sat in a chair between two bookshelves, so gowned in shadow that Matua had not noticed him before. The man stood. His dark hair fell past his shoulders. Armor shifted beneath his white cloak, brightening in a slant of window light.

Matua resisted the impulse to dive for the pitcher and hurl it at the armored man. "Good afternoon, Grand Marshal. How kind of you to keep vigil. I wish you'd woken me earlier."

"Believe me, I tried." Crovis stepped to the center of the room. Sunlight sparkled off his gauntlets as he flexed his fingers. "You've been as good as asleep for longer than I can recall. Much has happened. We must talk."

Matua felt a surge of vertigo, though he could not tell whether it came from his injuries or from fear. Faintly, he recalled the cruel, not-so-blind Shel'ai who had tricked his way into the Scrollhouse. Matua thought he remembered speaking with Aeko, too, but wondered if that had simply been part of his delirium. He glanced at Crovis and wondered how much the Grand Marshal knew.

"Perhaps we should begin with what I'm doing here. I would have thought my brothers and sisters in Armahg would have been willing to treat my injuries themselves."

"They were, but I feared for your safety."

"I trust I'm on Saikaido, then." Matua paused. "Tell me, have there been many attempts on my life?"

Crovis's lips broke into a thin, wolfish smile. "Many have died, if that's what you're asking."

"I'm not sure it is."

"Then perhaps you're asking the wrong questions." Crovis retrieved

217

a different pitcher from a shelf, along with a goblet. He filled the goblet with a thick, red wine and offered it to Matua. When the cleric shook his head, Crovis took a drink, and the wine reddened the Grand Marshal's lips. He emptied the glass then filled it again. "I know you conspired against me," he said finally.

Matua feigned bemusement. "Grand Marshal, are you really this threatened by a one-armed bookkeeper with white hair?"

"I've known kings who were less threatening." Crovis set the cup down. "I know about the scroll. I know because I put it there after I found it on the Isles." He paused. "What, nothing to say?"

Matua shook his head. "I always thought it strange that the Dragonkin would hide a scroll in a wall when they left everything else out in the open. But Rowen said he could understand why Fâyu Jinn's allies would want to keep something like that hidden. I guess he was right. They hid it, but not in the Scrollhouse. May I ask where *you* found it?"

Instead of answering Matua's question, Crovis grimaced. "Fâyu Jinn's allies were demons. Their motivations do not concern me. I simply want to do what I can to safeguard Ruun."

"I'm very glad to hear that, Grand Marshal. Then I suggest you leave a garrison of Knights outside Shigella's Tomb. While they're guarding it, Sir Locke can continue to safeguard Knightswrath. If you send supplies to him at Cadavash, he can maintain—"

"Locke is a traitor, Father. Like you. The reason why he's the only one who can wield Fel-Nâya is because, like Locke, Jinn's sword is infected by devilry. It recognizes one of its own."

Matua stared for a moment, uncomprehending. "Grand Marshal, just what are you proposing?"

Crovis picked up his wine goblet again and moved toward the arrow slit. Matua stepped out of the way.

Crovis took a sip of wine as he stared through the window at the sea. "I told you, I'm here to safeguard Ruun. I was chosen for this. Even Nekiel understands. Even Nekiel recognizes me as his true enemy." He turned and continued with a strange, giddy light in his eyes. "It's true, cleric. Nekiel lives! Through the sorcerer who attacked you, he has spoken to me. He has challenged me to single combat. And I will meet him." He faced out to sea. "And, by the Light's grace, I shall prevail."

Matua felt weak, and the room spun. He leaned against a bookshelf for support. "You mean to bring down the Dragonward…"

"When a bone heals poorly, it must be broken again before it can heal. Long ago, Fâyu Jinn faced a great challenge. With faith and courage, he united the people. But in the end, his courage faltered. He won not through faith, but magic. That tainted his victory, and the repercussions have troubled our land ever since."

Matua looked about the room for a weapon. His gaze fell on the wine pitcher. Despite his dizziness, he moved toward it. He seized it with his remaining hand, leaned against the shelf for a moment, then moved toward the Grand Marshal.

The Grand Marshal still had not turned. Matua swung the pitcher, aiming for Crovis's head. But Crovis twisted at the last instant, raising one mailed fist. The pitcher exploded. Wine and ceramic shards went everywhere. The Grand Marshal shoved Matua to the floor even as he continued to hold his goblet without spilling a drop.

"For a long time, I thought about killing you. But despite what you think, I am a man of mercy. Rowen Locke is out there right now, attempting to start a rebellion. If he succeeds, hundreds of Knights will die. Worse, every Knight who perishes here means one less disciple of Light to fight the Dragonkin when they return."

Matua wiped wine from his face. "I won't help you."

"Father, I don't think you want to see bloodshed any more than I do."

Matua considered arguing that Crovis's end goal would bring about a degree of bloodshed unseen since the Shattering War. "Even if that were true, what you want is impossible. Rowen is free. You don't have Knightswrath. You can't open Shigella's Tomb."

"That's not entirely true," said another voice.

Matua turned to see that during his brief, failed attack on the Grand Marshal, the door had opened. A familiar figure strode in. The sunlight streaming through the arrow slit seemed to wither before the darkness of his hollow eye sockets. Matua lowered his gaze to the sorcerer's belt, and his heart fell at the sight of Knightswrath. Matua looked past the sorcerer and saw a white-haired Knight waiting in the hallway beyond, next to a grubby warrior with a patch over one eye.

The Shel'ai studied the fallen cleric then turned to face Crovis.

"Grand Marshal, it seems you have not upheld your end of the bargain. No matter. Even without Rowen Locke, we can still open Shigella's Tomb and bring down the Dragonward."

At the sight of the sorcerer, Crovis had half drawn his adamune. Then his gaze fell on Knightswrath. He let his sword slide back into its scabbard. "How?"

"Just get me there. I'll take care of the rest. Given the mess you've made of things, though, I suspect that will cost you many followers."

Crovis smirked. "I have made arrangements, sorcerer. Be patient. Reaching Shigella's Tomb will not be a problem."

The Shel'ai gave Crovis a quizzical glance, falling so silent that Matua wondered if he were reading the Grand Marshal's thoughts. Finally, the Shel'ai laughed. "Forgive me, Grand Marshal. I underestimated you. But I suspect I am still correct in my assertion regarding bloodshed. All the better."

Crovis gave the Shel'ai a long, cold look. "How much must you hate this world, that you would do this?"

The Shel'ai answered with a cold smile. "Knight, you have no idea. But soon, I think, you will."

Crovis eyed the Shel'ai for a moment then looked down at Matua. "Apologies, Father. It seems I might not need your assistance after all." He directed his gaze at the Knight waiting in the hallway. "Take the cleric down below. If I need him later, I'll come get him myself. If not"— he glanced at Matua again—"we'll tie him up in front of the temple and burn him as a warning of what's to come."

The white-haired Knight's eyes widened. "But, Grand Marshal, he's a High Father! Surely the clerics will—"

The Shel'ai spoke before Crovis could interject. "Soon enough, the clerics will have far more important matters demanding their attention. Don't you think, Grand Marshal?"

Crovis said nothing for a moment. Facing Matua, he bowed slightly. "Apologies," he said again and gestured for him to be taken away.

Jalist stood on the beach and stared out at the massive, disorderly flotilla bobbing in the moonlit tide. The boats were empty. Instead, his men had dug trenches and raised palisades along the beach, as quickly as they could build them. A full day had passed since he'd feigned his attack on Saikaido Temple, only to withdraw back to the shore. Since then, he'd been working frantically to prepare for the Knights' reprisal.

So far, the Grand Marshal had not attacked, but Jalist's scouts had reported a seemingly never-ending armada of boats streaming off the other islands, toward Saikaido. Each boat carried dozens, even hundreds of Knights and squires from the other temples. All, apparently, had been summoned to Saikaido's defense.

But will they fight for him, knowing what he did to Locke and Aeko, or against him?

Jalist was not so sure. They had already sent messengers to each of the other temples, detailing Crovis's secret crimes and warning them what the Grand Marshal planned to do. Jalist seriously doubted that many would believe him—he hardly believed it himself—but as Rowen pointed out, they did not have to believe them. They only had to mistrust Crovis enough to refrain from rushing off to war.

Maddoc joined him. His violet eyes were raw and bloodshot, as they had been every day since his arrival in the camp. "Still no word from the others."

Jalist wondered whether he meant Hráthbam, who had raced back to Sorocco to rally as many ships as possible, or Rowen and Aeko, who had not even waited long enough to change into dry clothes before they insisted on taking Jalist's fastest ship to New Atheion.

"Still glad you didn't insist on getting yourself killed in that temple?" Jalist asked.

"There might still be time for that."

"Maybe." Jalist took a moment to appreciate how handsome the Shel'ai looked, then reminded himself that Maddoc was still in mourning. Jalist studied the eastern horizon instead, scanning the distant mist for signs of movement. "If we can get enough ships to surround the island and we can keep the other Knights from siding against us, Crovis will be trapped. He won't be able to leave, let alone reach Shigella's Tomb. He'll have to surrender." He paused. "If you want to kill him then, that's between you and Rowen."

Maddoc's lip curled with disgust. His breath fogged in the night air, matching the color of his pupils. "I'm all for trapping that bastard on his little island, but we should be guarding the tomb, too."

Jalist shook his head. "Until I get reinforcements, I don't have the men."

"If Crovis attacks, you can defend the tomb as well as this worthless beach."

"Sure," Jalist said, "if I had enough boats to *get* all my men to the tomb—which I don't. At least here, we're fortified."

"A few thousand Knights and squires would wash over this army like a tide."

Jalist looked around at the men patrolling their paltry fortifications. "Keep your damn voice down," he hissed. "I'm betting it won't come to that. Crovis doesn't even have Knightswrath. Or Rowen. He's finished. He just doesn't know it yet."

"Maybe," Maddoc said. "Maybe not."

"Well, if Crovis *does* send an army to crush us, it'll be your job to set his godsdamned boats on fire before his men reach the shore. You up for that?"

Maddoc nodded slightly.

Jalist grunted. "Maybe you'd do better if you get some sleep first. Go on. I know what's on your mind, but if you can't quiet it, drink a pitcher of nightwine. I'll send for you if—"

"Too late." Maddoc pointed.

Jalist's heart leapt into his throat. He followed the Shel'ai's gesture but saw only moonlit fog. Then, he spotted a faint smear of orange far out to sea. "Probably just a fishing boat."

"You've already bought, borrowed, or stolen every fishing boat that Crovis didn't already have. Besides, this is bigger. You better tell your men to stand ready."

Jalist gestured to one of his men, a frightened young page clutching a trumpet, then hesitated. "Let's wait a moment. Maybe it's just a messenger. Maybe they just want to issue some more threats." His eyes widened.

In just the space of a few moments, the orange smear had broadened, spreading across the eastern horizon. What he had taken at first for a handful of ships actually appeared to be an entire armada, sailing toward them at great speed.

Cursing, he gave the order, and the page sounded his trumpet. Others repeated the alarm until the shrill cry echoed along the beach. Someone from the slums pounded on a drum. Men shouted as the camp came to life. Soldiers and common brawlers swarmed down the beach, taking up position. Some cheered. Some, particularly Fen-Shea's men, hurled insults across the water. Many laughed. Behind their bravado, though, they seemed as afraid as he was.

Jalist loosened his sword then hefted his long axe. Someone brought his horse. Blood pounded in Jalist's ears as he rode along the beach, waving his long axe over his head. Men cheered at the sight of him. Jalist laughed, pretending his fear was nothing but a figment of a child's imagination. For a moment, he felt like a Housecarl again.

Then, he turned east.

By then, the glow had broadened further still, impossibly huge. Jalist shook his head in disbelief. It looked as though all the galleons of all the island people on Ruun had massed together in tight formation and were driving right at them, burning out of the darkness. All around him, men began to panic.

"Hold your ground," Jalist shouted. "It's just a bunch of wood and lanterns, boys. Fifty gold coins says all those ships are half empty!"

"Half air, half dung," Fen-Shea shouted. His men laughed and cheered, but Jalist saw uncertainty in Fen-Shea's expression as the gang leader rode past.

Maddoc joined him a moment later on a horse of his own. The Shel'ai said something Jalist could not hear over the din. Before Jalist could ask him to repeat himself, officers from the Red Watch hurried up, requesting orders. Jalist restrained his impatience, supervised the arming of his ballistae, then cursed himself for disarming most of his archers. He took up position at the center of the beach, still brandishing his long axe.

Maddoc followed. The Shel'ai had given up shouting. Instead, he projected his voice directly into Jalist's mind: *It's an island, not an armada.*

Jalist straightened. He faced the Shel'ai, incredulous. "Are you sure?"

Maddoc nodded, his face unreadable in the dark.

Jalist glanced back at his ragtag army then dismounted his horse. He handed his long axe to his page, pushed through his men, and clambered onto the pier. He raced to the end of the pier, where a small boat was waiting, and jumped in without waiting for Maddoc to catch up. Seizing the oar, he pushed away from the dock, rowing frantically toward the approaching armada.

Men cheered, thinking he was so anxious to fight that he was rushing ahead to meet the enemy single-handed. Jalist ignored them all and rowed until his muscles ached. The armada grew until he could distinguish individual torches and lanterns, framed by the glint of drawn steel. Then, someone shouted at him from the direction of the armada.

Jalist could not tell what was said, but he swallowed his panic and kept rowing. Moments later, the fog lifted, and Jalist beheld not an armada but a single, floating island. Armed men crowded the island. Most wore rags, but some wore azure silk and glittering kingsteel. Jalist continued rowing toward the island. Archers appeared, training their arrows on him, but no one fired. A moment later, his boat struck the edge of the island—which appeared to be a section of city, floating on a thick slab of steel. Jalist stood, held up his open hands, and waited.

A single Knight moved ahead of the rest, dressed in a wolfish facemask and armor covered in lotuses. The Knight pulled off the steel mask and helmet. Dark hair tumbled out. Aeko Shingawa had washed since Jalist had last seen her. Though her face remained gaunt from her long captivity, a terrible fierceness shone in her eyes. She bowed.

"Good evening, Captain Jalist. We've managed to find three hundred Knights and five hundred people from New Atheion who would like to have a stern word with the Grand Marshal. Do we have permission to join your host?"

Jalist grinned. "I think I could agree to that."

Another Knight joined her. Unlike Aeko, he wore mismatched armor and no helmet or facemask. He said nothing but held out his hand. Jalist took it. Rowen helped him out of the boat, onto the enormous skiff. Rowen embraced him then gestured, indicating the great, floating vessel around them.

"Welcome to the Privy, my friend."

CHAPTER TWENTY-THREE

ZEIA WOKE BUT KEPT HER eyes closed.

Her head ached—not just from the blows she'd taken, but from the successive jolts of magic the Shel'ai had used to keep her subdued. Though she doubted she'd given any indication of consciousness that a non–magic user would discern, she fully expected to be jolted back into unconsciousness as soon as she woke. But the moments wore on, heady with pain and a building sense of confusion.

Gradually, she realized she was sitting on the cold ground, her back pressed to something hard and gnarled. Her wrists were tied behind her, bound so tightly that tendrils of pain raced up and down her arms. An orange glare buffeted her eyelids. She guessed she'd been bound to a tree in front of a campfire.

Then, she heard voices. For a moment, the pain clouded her senses so that she could not distinguish the words. She took a slow, deep breath and imagined the pain as an illusion, a meaningless fog that dissipated from her mind. As the cloud rose, she expected to hear the Shel'ai or the one-eyed sellsword who had cut off her hands years before and—somehow—was nearby. Instead, she heard Dwarrs.

Zeia listened in disbelief. She spoke only a little of their language but could tell the men were discussing what to do next. Apparently, their group was the vanguard for an army moving up from the south. They'd been charged to scout the surrounding lands for danger. Some thought that included the responsibility of attacking any Human settlements in those parts unless they agreed to help. Their leader felt differently.

Zeia tried to discern how many men she was dealing with, but the voices overlapped, and the stern voice of their leader was the only one she could distinguish clearly. Adding to the difficulty was the fact that from time to time, a Dwarr would check to see if she was still asleep by jabbing her in the ribs with the butt of a weapon. Zeia had anticipated that, though, and took the blows without response.

"She's kind of pretty," said a voice near her face. "I mean, except for the hands."

"And the ears, and the eyes." Another voice laughed. Someone grabbed her face, tipped it upward, and pried open one of her eyelids. A face with gray skin and a full beard scowled at her. With great effort, Zeia stared blankly ahead until the hand let go of her chin. Then, she let her head fall back to her chest.

A third voice joined the other two. "Do you think the general will let us have some fun with her?"

The first voice answered with disgust. "I'll forget you said that." Zeia heard the shuffling sound of someone walking away.

"I doubt it," said the second voice. "If he's smart, he'll cut her throat before she wakes up."

"Why?" asked the third voice. "Without her hands, she can't do nothing."

"You an expert on magic, all of a sudden?" Steel scraped on leather. Zeia managed to keep from tensing as someone pressed the edge of a knife to her throat.

"That's more than she deserves," said a new voice. "After all her kind have done to the world, I say we should—"

"You men," the leader called, "get away from that prisoner before I wring your necks!"

Zeia heard rapid footsteps as the men hurried away. She was tempted to open her eyes a little and gauge more of her surroundings, but more footsteps told her someone else had come to look her over.

A moment later, the leader spoke: "You may as well open your eyes, wytch."

Zeia did not answer.

"I said open your eyes," the leader repeated.

Steel scraped against leather again. That time, a blade pressed so hard against her throat that she felt a thin trickle of blood. She opened her eyes and had the satisfaction of seeing the leader draw back, his own eyes widening.

"Want to tell me what you're doing on the plains?" he asked.

Zeia glanced past the leader and saw the other Dwarrs watching tensely, most clutching their weapons. "I was attacked."

"By who?"

"Another Shel'ai and a one-eyed sellsword." She smiled at the look on the leader's face. "I take it that's who you bought me from."

"We didn't *buy* you," the leader snapped. "We aren't slavers. We took charge of you as a kindness—"

"To another Shel'ai who hadn't gotten around to killing me yet," Zeia finished. "How good of you."

Another, younger, Dwarr joined the leader and brandished a knife. "Guard that tongue, wytch, or we'll cut it out! You're talking to General Keidu, the last of the old king's Housecarls!"

Zeia glanced from the younger Dwarr to the leader. "Actually, you're the second Housecarl I've met. There's another one living in Lyos."

General Keidu struck her. "Jalist Hewn is no Housecarl. Say otherwise again, and you'll wish you hadn't."

Zeia traced the inside of her lip with her tongue, tasting blood. Something told her the Dwarrish general had not struck her half as hard as he could have. Still, her self-control began to unravel. She was having trouble restraining herself from summoning what little magic she could eke out to turn the Dwarrish general's brain into mush.

As though sensing his peril, General Keidu stepped back. "Believe it or not, wytch, depending on how you answer our questions, there's still a chance you might survive this."

"What questions?"

"That's between you and the Scion."

Zeia nodded. "Is he close by? I'd very much like to meet him."

Keidu raised one eyebrow. "Don't mock me, wytch. We may not have magic, but we have hands. From what I hear, a wytch isn't much use without those."

If you only knew. "My name is Zeia. I am an ally of Sir Rowen Locke. I was on my way to the Lotus Isles when I was attacked by the very

227

same Shel'ai you met earlier. Why you've decided to help him is beyond me, but—"

"We do not help Shel'ai," Keidu interrupted. "Assuming you're telling the truth, had we known what he was, he would not have gotten away so easily."

Zeia noted how the Dwarr's eyes had widened at the mention of Rowen. She wondered if they'd met earlier. "Tell me, General, are your kind and mine at war now?"

Several of the general's men muttered their responses. Keidu gave them a cold glance that called for silence then turned back to her. "The Scion has taken steps to protect our borders and form alliances. We will no longer tolerate your kind within our lands."

Zeia was tempted to ask when in recent history the Dwarrs had ever allowed the Shel'ai to live near their lands, let alone within them. "My kind did not send the Jolym. We had nothing to do with Chorlga or his Dragonjol. We have suffered as much as your race, perhaps more. Instead of reverting back to the old ways, bickering and—"

Keidu struck her again, harder that time. "A while back, I met your friend, Locke. He had a Shel'ai with him. I let them go. Then, a few days after, I found some of my men lying in the woods, charred stiff. For all I know, *you* did that. Or Locke's pet did."

Zeia tongued the blood from her lip and smiled. "Without my hands?"

"You could have lost them in the battle."

"Are you sure? Losing one's hands isn't like losing one's cloak." Zeia noted the bitterness in her own voice and took a deep breath. "The Shel'ai traveling with Rowen is called Maddoc. He's one of the gentlest men I've ever known. If anybody killed your men, it was the Shel'ai you met on the road earlier." She paused. "Face it, General. You had the chance to avenge your men, and you let it slip through your fingers."

Keidu looked like he was about to strike her a third time then decided otherwise. He glanced at the young Dwarr holding a drawn knife. "Haydn, keep a close watch on her. If she tries anything, kill her. If she doesn't, see that she's left alone." He turned back to Zeia. "We'll keep you here until the Scion catches up with us. A day or two. I suggest you soften that tongue if you want to live, wytch."

He turned and stalked away.

Zeia met the cold stares of her guards then feigned exhaustion and let her head sag to her chest. Closing her eyes, she tried once again to gauge what magic she'd recovered. She guessed that she could summon her hands and burn herself free then execute one or two mind-stabs, but that would not be enough to help her get away—especially if she barely had the strength to run. Nor did she have anywhere near the strength necessary to find Igrid and Keswen and guide them to her using only her mind.

Instead, she tried to puzzle through all that had happened over the last few days. She still knew next to nothing about the Shel'ai that had been tormenting them, beyond the fact that he was powerful, that he somehow used his magic to see, and that he was even more bloodthirsty than Shade. He was obviously planning something, probably manipulating all of them and turning them against each other—as Fadarah had done and as Chorlga had done to Fadarah.

Gods, why must we treat each other this way?

She thought of Saanji and wondered how he was doing without her. As the campaign against the Red Emperor was at a standstill, she doubted he was in serious danger. Besides, his men worshipped him, and the renegade prince knew how to take care of himself. He'd needed cunning to survive his brothers. And he'd learned even more in the past year, relying less and less on Zeia's advice until she became more like a cross between a lover and a bodyguard.

If I die here, he'll never know what happened to me. I guess I'll just have to make sure I don't die here. Zeia opened her eyes. Ignoring the Dwarrs milling about the camp, she eyed the shadows beyond.

Then she spotted a familiar figure in the distance, moving through the darkness, effortlessly evading the sentries: a lean figure with feathers in her hair. Zeia was quick to look away—not just to avoid giving away Keswen's position, but also because she did not want to give the Sylv the satisfaction of seeing her smile.

Keidu paced along the outskirts of the camp and thought once again about letting the woman go. He'd mentioned finding his slain men as a test, and her reaction satisfied him that, wytch though she was, she had not been their killer. Part of him wanted to pursue the supposedly blind man they'd met earlier, in order to ascertain if he really was a Shel'ai, but they'd been ordered to wait there, and he doubted his men would move until the Scion arrived.

Father Gaulgodd will probably kill her.

Keidu tried to decide whether he thought that was a good or a bad idea. Yes, the Scion considered all magic users to be abominations—and to some degree, he had a point—but nothing would be gained by making Rowen Locke their enemy. Then again, if they allied themselves with Crovis, wasn't that an inevitability?

Keidu shook his head. He remembered telling Father Gaulgodd that he was no friend to magic. That had not changed. But the handless woman was defenseless, exhausted. They were not in battle.

He entertained the possibility of letting her go. He wondered how the men would react, if they'd even go so far as to defy him. The Scion's sermons had set a fire in their guts, and all seemed eager to spill Shel'ai blood. That was especially true of Haydn, who thought it would increase his esteem in the eyes of Father Gaulgodd—which it probably would.

There's still time, though. If I can teach him some compassion, I might even make him a Housecarl, provided we can—

A cry of alarm brought Keidu spinning around, drawing his sword. He started to turn toward the captive wytch, but the cry diverted him toward the horses instead. Somehow, they'd gotten free. Most of the men had already taken off, trying to catch them.

Keidu sensed the deception at once. "No, forget the horses! Guard the wytch before—" An arrow skimmed his shoulder, scratching one of the scales in his armor. Keidu turned then dove, narrowly avoiding two more arrows that thudded into the ground where he'd been standing.

Keidu rose, shouting to his men again, trying to get their attention, but chaos reigned in the camp. Some had already taken off into the woods, either to fight or run. Some pursued the horses. Others hid behind shields. Keidu saw the wytch on her feet, free, and barreled toward her. She turned to face him, and her arms came up.

Keidu slowed, dumbly wondering if she could throw wytchfire from her wrists. Instead, hands of flame blossomed from her scars. The Shel'ai scooped up a sword off the ground and swung. Keidu held her in sword block. Then, the wytch reached out with one blazing hand and touched his shoulder.

Keidu bit back a scream of pain as wave upon wave of heat heated his armor. He shoved the wytch back and aimed his sword for a killing blow but then narrowly managed to reverse the blow to keep a red-haired woman from chopping his head off. Facing two opponents at once, he considered retreating. Instead, he drew a dagger and stabbed at both of them at the same time.

The red-haired woman's shortsword blocked his, then she plucked a knife from her cleavage and deftly parried Keidu's dagger. As they fought, the wytch turned and ran into the forest. The red-haired woman blocked two more swings from Keidu then sidestepped and struck another charging Dwarr across the face with the flat of her blade.

"Stop them!" Keidu cried.

The Dwarrs had given up on the horses, but only half rushed to help Keidu. The rest were busy trying to locate an indeterminate number of archers who were raining arrows on them. A few men screamed, struck in the leg or shoulder, but most of the arrows thudded harmlessly into the mud.

Keidu waved at the red-haired woman, who was backpedaling into the forest after the wytch. He started after her, but three arrows thudded into the dirt, each barely a finger's span from his boots. Instead of retreating, Keidu charged—then stopped short as a gray wall appeared in front of him.

Somehow, the wall was armed. A massive black mace swung at Keidu's head. He managed to duck at the last instant, but before he could answer with a blow of his own, yet another arrow sliced the air. That one glanced off his sword blade, stunning him. By the time he recovered, the gray wall was gone.

"General!"

"Follow them," Keidu said, even as he turned toward the speaker. One of his men was kneeling beside another. The latter lay facedown in the mud. Keidu saw no arrows protruding from the warrior's body. He helped the first warrior roll him over. Wide, unblinking eyes greeted him.

"Haydn… " Keidu searched but saw no wounds. Nevertheless, when he pressed his fingers to Haydn's throat, he felt no pulse.

"The wytch just touched him, and he fell over dead," the first warrior whispered.

Keidu stared for a moment then stood. "Get the horses," he snarled. "We're going hunting."

"I hope you feel like running," Igrid said.

Zeia answered with a Sylvan curse. Then her eyes widened at the sight of Breaksteel, and she lifted one flaming hand.

Igrid grabbed her shoulder. "Don't. Just run. I'll explain later."

To her relief, Zeia obeyed.

Igrid looked over her shoulder. She could not tell how many Dwarrs were pursuing them, but a quick glance told her they were too numerous.

Then Keswen's voice seemed to speak to her from all sides at once, though Igrid could not find the Sylvan huntress in the trees. "I can't just keep wounding them! If you want to get away—"

Igrid missed the rest, forced to duck beneath a hastily flung spear. Wrenching it from the tree where it stuck, she swung it like a quarterstaff, sweeping a charging Dwarr's legs out from under him. She backpedaled, used the spearhead to parry a sword, then lost the spearhead to a cleaving blow from a long axe.

She backpedaled again, drawing her sword with one hand, swinging the remains of the spear with the other. She managed to club the Dwarr wielding the long axe when he overextended his swing, but the one with the sword was quicker. She sensed her opponent was skilled but untried. She risked a bold thrust at his face, which left her body open, then kicked him in the groin when he moved too quickly to block. He crumpled, and she was running again.

She spotted another Dwarr angling beside her, a mace in hand, his young face livid. An arrow narrowly avoided the bridge of Igrid's nose and struck the Dwarr in the throat. Igrid turned in the direction of the arrow, unsure whether to berate Keswen or thank her, then just barely raised her sword in time to block an incoming long axe. The force of the blow jarred her down to her bones. Before she could recover, her latest opponent twisted his axe, hooked her blade, and wrenched it from her grasp. Igrid reached for her breast knife. Before she could draw it, though, Breaksteel hurtled out of the shadows and brought his mace down with both hands.

Igrid looked away. Nevertheless, she felt the Dwarr's blood splatter her neck, intermingled with the small sting of skull fragments. *This wasn't supposed to happen.*

Breaksteel hovered near her, stoic and blood splattered. The other Dwarrs hung back, staring fearfully at his massive mace. Then, they fled. However, Igrid could already hear horses in the distance.

"This isn't over," Igrid warned.

"Yes, it is," Keswen said easily. Igrid turned and saw the Sylvan huntress picking her way through the forest, finally out in the open. She still had two arrows nocked to her bowstring. "I shot two more riders. The rest are falling back. If you listen, you'll hear their leader screaming at them. If we're lucky, he'll hang them for cowardice."

Igrid sensed the joke but did not laugh. Instead, she glanced down at the dead Dwarr at her feet. "We weren't supposed to kill anyone."

Keswen followed Igrid's gaze. She took the arrows off her bowstring and returned them to her quiver. "I think we're all well past that point, Iron Sister." She nodded to Igrid's left.

Igrid turned in time to see Zeia rejoining them, eyes locked on Breaksteel, her features pale and taut.

"I have questions," Zeia said.

"You're welcome for the rescue," Igrid said. "The questions will have to wait. Let's cover some distance before the Dwarrs change their minds."

CHAPTER TWENTY-FOUR

"H AS SHE LOST HER DAMN mind?" Rowen spoke with such vehemence that all the surrounding officers and soldiers looked up in alarm. He read the message one last time, hoping he'd mistaken it somehow, then cursed and passed it to Aeko.

The two stood at the edge of the Privy as it bobbed on the sea, just out of range of Crovis's trebuchets. For three days, Rowen had made the gigantic skiff his base of operations, alongside Aeko Shingawa and her officers. The Privy was the centerpiece of their siege against Saikaido. Meanwhile, Jalist's ragtag armada of ferries and fishing boats had fanned out, joined by a growing number of galleons sent by those Knights loyal to Aeko, and formed a tight circle around the island.

Aeko read the message from Cadavash. A moment later, she laughed. Passing back the message, she asked, "How is this in any way a surprise?"

"Which part—that she defied my orders or that she took Knightswrath with her?"

"Take your pick," Aeko said.

"Not really," Rowen admitted, "but I would have preferred to hear this from her instead of in a message from Sir Jontin."

"You're just lucky they knew enough to send it to Lyos so the king could send it to you by messenger. If they'd sent it by raven—"

"It would be in Crovis's hands now," Rowen finished. "And that's exactly where Knightswrath will be, if he learns it's anywhere but Cadavash."

Aeko shook her head. "He's trapped in the temple. Even if he knew, he couldn't get his agents past us."

Jalist, who had been leaning against a railing, holding his stomach, glanced back and spoke for the first time. "You almost sound convinced."

"We could send some Knights to intercept her," Aeko offered. "She's probably already almost here, but they could give her safe escort the rest of the way."

Rowen considered the reports they'd heard lately of the Sons of Maelmohr marching north of Stillhammer, in even greater numbers than they'd seen a few weeks prior. He had not been particularly concerned before since a few hundred untried warriors could not pose a serious threat to the well-fortified walls of Cadavash. But the thought of Igrid traveling through the wild filled him with panic.

"She's not alone," Aeko reminded him. "Sir Jontin says she has Zeia and Keswen with her."

"Exactly," Rowen answered darkly. "The Scion's fanatics might not react well if they catch her with Zeia."

Jalist spat over the side of the skiff, wiped his mouth, and straightened. "You've got that right. But Igrid's not dumb. She'll avoid a fight if she can."

"When have you *ever* known Igrid to avoid a fight?" Rowen smiled faintly despite his concern. "Send the Knights anyway. Send Maddoc with them. Find her—and the sword—and get them here while I still have some semblance of sanity left."

"I will," Aeko promised, "but you're staying here."

"I never suggested otherwise."

"Like hell," Jalist muttered. He nodded toward Aeko. "She's right. We need you here. The Red Watch and the slum-dwellers will follow me. The Knights will follow Aeko. But *you're* the one holding this foolish mess together."

Rowen fixed his gaze on Saikaido, the temple faintly visible through the distant mist. *Even if Igrid's all right, what about Zeia and Keswen? What about Sir Berric? Gods, I'll have to tell them about Sang Wei.* Rowen shut his eyes. "Why is it that every time one war ends, some fool has to go and start another?"

"I don't know," Aeko said. "Once we get Crovis in chains, we'll ask him."

"If he lives that long," Jalist said. "Not that I blame him, but the way Maddoc's been acting, I wouldn't be surprised if he—"

A war horn blared, drowning out the rest of Jalist's statement. The companions exchanged glances. Rowen scanned the waters around Saikaido for Crovis's ships, thinking they were attempting to run the blockade. Then, the horn sounded again.

"That's coming from the shore," Aeko said.

Rowen faced the mainland. In the distance, barely visible along the beaches, lay about half of Jalist's army: mostly Fen-Shea's men, all those that could not fit onto the ships currently encircling Saikaido. Jalist had left Fen-Shea in charge and tasked the camp with keeping the ragtag armada fed and supplied.

"Might be somebody's idea of a joke." Jalist did not sound convinced.

Aeko raised a spyglass and trained it on the beach. She swore. As she passed the spyglass to Jalist, Rowen narrowed his eyes on the distant beach and made out a red-black smear descending the hills, sweeping toward the camp. Just then, a new chorus of low, unfamiliar horns split the air.

Jalist blanched. "Those are Dwarrish horns." He passed the spyglass to Rowen. "Get me to the shore. Now."

Rowen did not look through the spyglass. Instead, he followed after Aeko as she began shouting orders. Grabbing a stunned cleric of Armahg, Rowen shoved the man toward the center of the Privy. A few more priests went to help, and three pressed their hands to the glass orb. The entire skiff trembled as though alive and gradually turned. However, Rowen could tell at once that they would never reach the shore in time.

Then, yet another trumpet split the morning air. Rowen turned northwest as the bottom dropped out of his stomach.

Jalist joined him, dark eyes fixed on the distant stirring of ships. "Crovis?"

Rowen nodded, speechless.

Aeko drew closer. "If we steer the Privy toward the shore, we won't have enough ships to keep Crovis penned in. He'll break through."

"And if you stay and fight Crovis, all my men will be slaughtered,"

Jalist snarled. "He doesn't have Knightswrath. If he wants to go sit in front of Shigella's Tomb and count his toes, let him!"

Aeko looked at Rowen. "It's your choice, Squire."

Rowen hesitated. A feeling of dread surged within him. Something told him that no matter what he chose, the consequences would be terrible. He looked toward the south. Already, the wind was carrying the clatter of steel and the screams of the dying across the calm waters. "Make for the shore," he said finally. "I'll stay here and command the ships against Crovis."

Before anyone had a chance to argue, Rowen turned to a signalman. He chose two flags from the man's stack of pennants. The first corresponded to a galleon that had been affectionately rechristened *Rowen's Wrath*, which happened to be the closest ship. The second flag informed them to prepare to receive a passenger. He waited an anxious moment for *Rowen's Wrath* to reply. Then, he ran to the edge of the Privy, climbed over the railing, and waited for the ship to pull up alongside.

Fen-Shea picked at the scabs covering his newest tattoo: a three-headed serpent with roses for eyes and daggers for teeth. He liked the coloring— especially the scales—and the blend of beauty and fierceness, plus how it looped around his kneecap and wound down his calf. Cadney herself had finished it just two days before, a parting gift before she left the camp. By then, Fen-Shea figured, she'd returned to the Dark Quarter and picked up their child from her sister's care. He longed to be with them but had steadfastly resisted the temptation to abandon his post. After all, he had made a promise to Jalist Hewn, and it would not do for a reputable gang leader to anger the Captain of the Guard.

Besides, Locke still needs me, and I owe that ginger bastard my life.

Fen-Shea yawned. Sitting on the edge of the dock, dangling his bare feet over the surf, he listened to the men brawling with each other. With Captain Jalist and most of the Red Watch either on the Privy or manning the small armada of boats swirling around Saikaido like hornets, what remained of the camp had naturally devolved into chaos. The latrines had overflowed. The men stole or wrestled for sport. A fourth of them were drunk.

On the other hand, a fourth was better than half, which it had been the day before, when Jalist personally threatened to lop off Fen-Shea's head if he didn't get the camp in line. Fen-Shea snickered. He doubted the captain expected much from him, and the Isle Knights expected even less. Thanks to Fen-Shea and his men, with a little help from that Soroccan, they'd rescued Locke and his pretty, dark-haired teacher from captivity. But any future fighting would take place on the water.

Crovis can't win by sea, and we can't win by land. So we wait. "Rather, they wait," Fen-Shea muttered. Though he had only been awake for a few hours, he considered finding a warm spot in the sand and taking a nap.

Then, he glanced westward and frowned. The sun appeared to be setting.

"A little early for that... " He rubbed his eyes and stood staring for a moment, then his eyes widened. "Damn... " Barefoot, he turned and grabbed the nearest warrior. The man was drunk. Fen-Shea shook him. "You, go find that boy with the trumpet—Jalist's page. Find him and bring him back here."

The man blinked then belched. Fen-Shea repeated his orders and gave the man a hard shove. He gave the same orders to two other men who happened by. Then, he tugged on his boots and snatched up his mace. "Arm yourselves, you fools!" He pointed at the western hills, already bristling with horsemen and spears. "And say some prayers, if you know any good ones."

Igrid took both the first and the last watch before dawn. Tired as she was, she knew Zeia needed rest more than anyone—and Keswen had steadfastly refused to trust Breaksteel with a watch of his own. Igrid could not blame her. The mere sight of the hulking warrior was unnerving. But so far, the Olg had proved trustworthy. He'd saved Igrid from the greatwolf, fought the Dwarrs, and cared for the horses, all without complaint. Despite his scowl, he'd even permitted Keswen to keep hold of his weapons while he slept.

More than once during Igrid's watches, Keswen would sit up, palming her sword, scanning the darkness with her sharp gaze, and relax only after she spotted the Olg slumbering peacefully at the far end of the camp. Igrid was more than a little surprised that Keswen had not taken advantage of the chaos of battle and simply killed him during their fight against the Dwarrs.

Of course, if she doesn't, Zeia still might.

Igrid's statement that Breaksteel was their ally had left the Shel'ai speechless, as though Igrid had just declared her love for the very same Dhargots who had ravaged her city of Hesod. But Zeia had been too tired to argue. Igrid hoped that by the time the Shel'ai regained her strength, they would have Rowen by their side.

She wondered if Rowen would defend the Olg or kill him. After all, he'd been in the Wytchforest when the Olgrym overwhelmed the Sylvan armies and nearly tore the kingdom asunder. He'd seen them rape and murder indiscriminately, like feral dogs. Rowen himself had used Knightswrath to strike down Doomsayer. For all she knew, he would kill Breaksteel as soon as he appeared, before Igrid had a chance to explain.

"No," she muttered, "not Rowen." Another Knight might, but Rowen had once been deemed a failure and dismissed from the Lotus Isles. He knew what it was like to be derided for his appearance. Maybe that was why he'd always been so sympathetic to the Shel'ai.

Igrid considered that as the pink rouge of sunrise blended into the eastern sky. She stood and stretched. She liked how quiet it was, not to mention the fact that they weren't running for their lives. Whatever the Dwarrs were doing in those parts, they'd apparently decided not to follow them. That suited Igrid fine. She had foul memories from the last time she'd passed through the Red Steppes, and she preferred not to add to them.

Returning to the heart of the camp, Igrid added the final two pieces of wood to the dying fire then went to wake Zeia and Keswen. Both opened their eyes before Igrid had even gotten close enough to touch them. Zeia still looked pale, with a swollen lip, but she answered Igrid's concerned expression with a faint nod.

Keswen cast a loathing glance in Breaksteel's direction then used both hands to give Igrid the heavy mace. Igrid wordlessly carried the mace to the Olg. Like the others, he woke without needing to be shaken. He rose and held out his hands, head bowed. Igrid swallowed her fear at the familiar realization that the Olg towered over her. She placed the mace in his hands. He stepped back and made a hand-sign to indicate his thanks. Then, without waiting for orders, he went to ready the horses.

"Handy little pet you have there," Keswen said when Igrid returned.

"Reminds me of a Jol," Zeia added, "except that this one will eventually turn on you and rape you to death."

Igrid spent a moment formulating a retort then decided against sharing it. "We're almost to the coast. With a little luck, we'll be at Saikaido by this afternoon."

With a Wyldkin's sense of immodesty, Keswen had just ducked behind a tree to do her morning duties. She returned and started gathering her weapons. "I wonder what Locke will say when he hears we've lost Knightswrath."

Zeia said, "You might not have lost it if you hadn't wasted time on me."

Keswen snickered. "Not my idea, wytch." She went to take one of the horses from Breaksteel.

Zeia turned to Igrid. "I could have gotten away on my own."

"Or maybe you would have gotten yourself killed."

"Maybe," Zeia conceded, "but Knightswrath is more important than—"

A distant war horn interrupted her.

Zeia frowned. Igniting her hands, she reached for a sword but did not draw it. "That's coming from the east."

Igrid hurried toward the horses. Zeia followed. Mounting the remaining horse, Igrid extended her hand. She braced herself but still shuddered when Zeia's flaming hand seized hers, sending an electric tingle sweeping up her arm. Despite her lingering weakness, Zeia leapt easily into the saddle behind Igrid.

On foot, Breaksteel made a series of gestures then turned east and took off at a brisk jog. Keswen said, "He's running ahead to scout. He says that's a Red Watch horn."

Igrid asked, "How in the Undergod does he know that?"

Another horn sounded, then another, then another. Those sounded closer. Unlike the first, they had a low, ominous tone, like the rumbling of thunder.

"Dwarrs," Zeia whispered in Igrid's ear.

"How do you know?"

"Do you have any other ideas?"

Igrid glanced at Keswen. She guessed they were all thinking the same thing. "Why would the Dwarrs be fighting the Red Watch... and why this far south?"

Keswen drew two arrows and nocked them to her bowstring. "Well, Iron Sister, if you want to find out, lead the way."

Zeia asked, "Do you think this has something to do with Rowen?" She gripped Igrid's waist with her flaming hands, sending tiny jolts of power throughout Igrid's body.

Igrid was tempted to pull away but decided the disquieting sensation might be just what she needed to wake up.

"Has Locke ever gone anyplace without getting in some kind of trouble?" Igrid waited.

Keswen and Zeia did not answer.

"I didn't think so." Igrid flicked the reins.

CHAPTER TWENTY-FIVE

CROVIS AMMERHEL WATCHED SUNRISE GILD the bristling defenses along the shoreline. He smiled. The palisade had been completed. Archers and siege engines guarded the island at every turn. Furthermore, Crovis's ships sat menacingly in the harbor, swarming with armed men, eager to be unleashed. True, Crovis had far fewer ships than those faithless wretches sailing circles around the island like a fleet of slow-moving vultures, but that was of little consequence. When the time came, Crovis had every confidence that faith would matter more than wood and steel.

Wyn Kai joined him, speaking in hushed tones about a lack of supplies, something about a handful of deserters, but Crovis paid no mind. He could feel that the time was fast approaching. Then, he turned and spotted the Shel'ai who called himself Algol making his way along the shoreline.

The Shel'ai had shed his tattered clothes in favor of the snow-white raiment of a cleric of Light. A drawn hood concealed his features, though Crovis could still see a fine silk handkerchief tied around the sorcerer's eyes. A bare, polished shaft of dragonbone rested in the crook of his arm. The sellsword, Dagath, followed a step behind. In place of his old clothes, the sellsword was wearing the brigandine of a squire. A gleaming tashi hung at his belt, opposite his usual shortsword.

Crovis tensed, somewhat concerned about where the Shel'ai had left Knightswrath unguarded but even more afraid of what would happen if it was spotted. Then, he noticed a sword bag of white silk hanging from

Algol's shoulder by a white cord, the color so perfectly matching Algol's robes that it was nearly invisible. Algol joined them, smiling as he bowed. "May the Light's blessings be upon you both. Would either of you like to confess any sins this fine morning?"

Wyn Kai backed up, touching his sword hilt and snarling something under his breath. Dagath reached for his own swords in answer, but a look from Crovis sent the sellsword back a step.

Crovis glanced around to make sure no other Knights were within earshot. "You were not to leave the temple."

Algol feigned surprise. "Have I left the temple? A thousand apologies! Alas, I cannot see… " He reached toward the band of silk covering his eye sockets.

Crovis seized his arm. "I doubt that, sorcerer. I doubt that very much."

Algol snickered. "Fair enough. In truth, though, I *do* see much better when my eyes are burning. And uncovered—"

Wyn Kai stepped closer. "Leave them covered, demon, or the next thing you'll see is my sword through your heart!"

Crovis studied the fearless smile on Algol's face and decided that the mad Shel'ai was probably about to remove the cloth anyway, daring Wyn Kai to strike him. Crovis placed a hand on Wyn Kai's shoulder, urging him to step back. Facing the Shel'ai, he said, "You truly are mad."

Algol's grin remained unfazed. "Have I given you cause to think otherwise?" He stepped back and fumbled for Dagath's shoulder, as though truly blind. "Come, my son. Let us feel the breeze on our faces a little longer before the battle starts."

Crovis frowned, tempted to ask what the Shel'ai meant, but then, the sound of a trumpet drifted across the water. It was so faint that he might have dismissed it as a trick of the wind, had his instincts not told him otherwise.

Crovis turned southward. Wyn Kai spoke, but Crovis ignored him. All along the shore, men stopped whatever they were doing, sensing something amiss. Hammers froze midswing. Swords were drawn. Then, a new chorus of trumpet blasts filled the air, louder and stronger than the first.

Crovis grinned. "Sir Kai, get my horse." He turned to face Algol. "The time has come to put your allegiance to the test."

243

Algol's smile vanished. He bowed with almost believable humility. "Choose your ship, Grand Marshal. I shall do the rest. I swear it."

Fen-Shea watched as a broad, muscular wave of men and horses surged downhill, toward his disorderly camp. He had never known Dwarrs to be accomplished horsemen, yet they came on like an avalanche. When they were almost within bow range, they began shouting—not the individual shouts of the reckless, but the low, ominous, unified rumbling of men prepared to fight and die in perfect synchronicity.

I thought the Dwarrs lost their army! How in the gods—

Beside him, the leader of a smaller gang threw down his spear and ran, shouting for his men to follow. Fen-Shea called out a command to wait. No one listened.

All along the beach, men blinked away sleep or stared in amazement at the wall of death thundering down on them. Chaos increased tenfold. Men fled by the dozens. Fen-Shea saw a Red Watch sergeant a hundred yards away, shouting orders, trying to prevent a rout. A slum-dweller stabbed him in the back and kept running.

"I should run, too," Fen-Shea muttered.

Then, he spotted Wiglaf, the lean, wild-eyed leader of the Crazy Knifemen. The gang leader was running for his life, surging well ahead of his men. Before he realized what he was doing, Fen-Shea stepped into Wiglaf's path. He dropped to one knee and swung his mace. Wiglaf howled in pain and tumbled over Fen-Shea's shoulder. Fen-Shea stood, twisted about, and swung a second time. Then, he turned to face the rest of the Crazy Knifemen.

They slowed, stunned, momentarily forgetting the charging horsemen as they stared at the caved-in skull of their leader. Fen-Shea's men, equally startled, rushed forward and formed a protective ring around him. For a moment, no one spoke.

Then, Fen-Shea lifted his bloody mace and pointed at the Crazy Knifemen. "I killed Wiglaf. That means you follow me now. And I say there's no way in Fohl's hells we're letting a bunch of gray-skinned bastards drive us from our own camp!"

He gestured for his horse. The one they brought was not his own, but Fen-Shea accepted it anyway. As he hoisted himself into the saddle, the raised vantage point allowed him to see the approaching, thundering horsemen with fresh clarity.

Fen-Shea felt all the blood drain from his face. Nevertheless, he spurred his horse forward, shouting and waving his mace. Slum-dwellers leapt aside to let him pass. He hoped that at least some of them were following him, but he dared not look back to find out.

The clerics of Armahg brought the Privy so close to the shore that it ran aground. Nevertheless, fifty yards of water separated Jalist from the fighting. He leapt over the side, swore as the water rose up to his thighs, and waded toward the shore. Men of the Red Watch followed. Jalist glanced back and saw Aeko still furiously trying to get all her Knights on horseback. He glanced beyond, hoping to catch sight of the sea battle between Rowen's ships and Crovis's, but the skiff and the mist obscured his vision.

Jalist fixed his gaze on the battle ahead. He'd lost sight of the gray wall of Dwarrish horsemen, but the screams told him they'd already torn into the western edge of the camp. Dozens of men fled along the beach. Splashes of red shone amidst the chaos. With a sickening rush, Jalist realized his whole army was being routed.

Jalist pushed ahead through the water until he felt dry sand beneath his boots. Then, he saw the stakes. Originally stuck in the sand to defend the beach against an attack by sea, the sharpened stakes ran all along the eastern edge of the camp. That meant they were useless in defending against a charge from the west.

Jalist had an idea. Before he had time to contemplate its sheer lunacy, he began barking orders. For a moment, men of the Red Watch glanced at him as though he'd returned to drinking. Then, as the noise of battle raged just in front of them, they hurried to obey.

Keidu fought on foot. His horse had been cut out from under him, and a deep gash leaked blood from his forehead, but his long axe sang

through the morning air. Men fell before him. Other Dwarrs who had been unhorsed hurried to join him. Despite their lack of experience, they fought with savage fury.

Keidu led them past tents and scattered campfires, through a forest of Human bodies. Despite its weight, his axe felt light in his hands, as though Maelmohr himself had lent him strength. Keidu laughed. He felt like a Housecarl again.

Finally, near the center of the camp, he slowed.

Turning north, he saw to his surprise that a small force of Humans had found their courage and were actually standing their ground. Against them rode a great column of Dwarrish horsemen, led by Gaulgodd himself. The Scion rode as though he'd been born in the saddle. He led his horsemen in fast, deadly circles around the smaller Human force, tightening and tightening like the coils of a snake. Forgefang glinted in the Scion's grasp, the great sword trailing blood in the morning air.

Despite his lingering mistrust of the man, Keidu shouted in exaltation. His men echoed the cry. Then, the strategist in him took over. Keidu saw that Gaulgodd's riders would easily slaughter the Humans they were encircling, but in the process, they'd left their flanks vulnerable to a countercharge. Keidu rallied all those Dwarrs fighting on foot—nearly a hundred—and moved to close the gap.

A handful of Humans tried to stop them and were mowed down. Keidu wiped the blood from his face and laughed again. Then, after what felt like an eternity of easy victories, he saw something curious. Just ahead lay the wall of stakes that fortified the eastern edge of the camp. While most of the stakes were still aimed harmlessly out to sea, a portion of the wall—maybe fifty yards' worth—had been reversed. Behind the stakes, a great knot of fighting men waited. Some wore the scarlet uniforms of Lyos. Others were dressed in the light blue of New Atheion.

Keidu signaled a halt. Despite the blood pounding in his ears, he knew better than to charge such a well-fortified position. He considered circling around and attacking them from behind, but that would mean leaving Gaulgodd's flank open.

Then, ahead of him, a single man stepped ahead of the rest, moving beyond the sharpened stakes. Though he was dressed in scarlet, he was shorter and broader through the shoulders than the rest, with gray skin and dark eyes. He pointed at Keidu.

Keidu stared. Then, he laughed. Ordering his men to stay where they were, he walked ahead alone. The enemy Dwarr did likewise. The two met halfway between their separate forces.

Instead of attacking right away, Keidu rested his long axe on the ground and leaned on it. "I didn't know you were still alive."

Jalist asked, "Why have you done this?"

"First, we weep. Then, we rage." Keidu hefted his long axe again, turning it in circles from hand to hand, faster and faster. "You, who corrupted our prince... who bed down with demons... who serve the same forces that brought Stillhammer to its knees!"

Jalist shook his head. "You serve Crovis?"

"I am a Dwarr. I serve no one. But I fight alongside those who know evil when they see it."

Jalist sighed. Then, without another word, he unslung a long axe from his own back and strode forward.

CHAPTER TWENTY-SIX

ROWEN HAD NEVER BEEN IN a sea battle before. He wondered for a moment if he'd made a terrible mistake, if he shouldn't have taken command of the land forces and left Aeko in charge of the boats instead. However, he had little time to ponder that before he heard himself ordering the crew of *Rowen's Wrath* right into the heart of the fighting.

Crovis's fleet consisted of two galleons, four longships, and half a dozen ferries that had been converted into troop carriers. Rowen had thrice as many ships, but nearly all were ferries and fishing boats. *Rowen's Wrath* was the only galleon. Without the Privy, which had been swarming with archers and ballistae, he doubted they had much chance of defeating Crovis's fleet.

We don't have to defeat them. Just hold them.

Rowen stood beside the captain, a dark-skinned, one-armed Knight of the Stag named Koroquin. Rowen had never exchanged more than a few words with the man, but he was an old friend of Aeko's and had been the first to change allegiance.

"The Grand Marshal will be on one of those galleons," Koroquin said.

Rowen nodded in agreement. Then, wide-eyed, he dove in time to avoid a ballista bolt that sank into the deck planks. Koroquin issued orders to his own men, unfazed. Half a dozen ballistae fired at one of Crovis's passing longships. Archers traded fire. By the time Rowen was back on his feet, the enemy ship was ablaze.

"Left or right, sir?" Koroquin asked.

Rowen blinked then realized the Knight was referring to the two galleons driving across the water, straight at them, each one sporting a great bronze battering ram identical to the one at the head of *Rowen's Wrath*. "Left," he said.

Koroquin shouted an order to the Knight manning the helm then calmly replaced him when a ballista bolt punched through the side of the man's cuirass. Rowen winced as an arrow glanced off one of his kingsteel pauldrons. A second arrow struck his cuirass, just half an inch below his throat. Rowen held one arm in front of his face, thinking ruefully about the helmet and facemask he'd left on the Privy.

Then, he looked up and saw both of Crovis's galleons still sailing straight at them. With numbing dread, Rowen realized Koroquin intended to ram one of them. He was about to shout a different order when he changed his mind. Instead, he turned to rally as many Knights as he could. A moment later, he looked up in time to see the target of *Rowen's Wrath* trying to steer out of the way—too late.

Rowen's Wrath shuddered as its great ram tore into the hull of Crovis's first galleon—a moment before the second galleon drove headlong into *Rowen's Wrath*. The sound of splintering wood filled the air, followed by men's screams and the shudder of bowstrings. The force of the impacts threw Rowen off his feet.

Koroquin grabbed Rowen's arm and hauled him upward. The dark-skinned Knight ignored an arrow that glanced off his shoulder. "I'll go right. You go left. Don't die." Before Rowen could answer, the Knight howled and rushed the second of Crovis's galleons, so close that the Knights on board were clamoring to cross to *Rowen's Wrath*.

Shaking off his daze, Rowen fixed his gaze on the first galleon. Knights bristled along the railings, a few armed with bows. A ballista fired a bolt that fell just short of Rowen's feet, thudding halfway through the floor. Rowen looked for Crovis but could not see him on the decks of either galleon.

He drew his sword anyway. "Follow me," he told anyone who was listening and charged.

Crovis's Knights rowed his longship right past the heart of the fighting. Though his face burned at the thought of leaving his embattled men behind, he reminded himself that it would not do to win the battle if they lost the war. Thanks to the timely arrival of his newest allies, half the enemy's forces were busy fighting on the mainland. He would never have such a chance again.

Algol, however, sat next to him and smiled openly as Knights fought each other, and Crovis fought the impulse to kill the wretched sorcerer right there and then. The sorcerer's one-eyed bodyguard sat right behind them, next to Wyn Kai. Crovis sensed the bodyguard was a dangerous man but one Crovis could kill if he had to—which he would if he decided to kill Algol.

No, we still need the Shel'ai. Besides, he'll be dead soon enough.

Crovis turned to Wyn Kai, who was pale and grimacing. Since he was no stranger to the sea, Crovis guessed the Knight was equally unhappy to be leaving the battle. *No,* Crovis realized, *it's more than that.* Wyn Kai understood the necessity of what they were doing as well as Crovis did, but Knights fighting other Knights was not a cause for celebration.

Soon, though, we will all be on the same side again, fighting a common foe.

Crovis glanced at Algol. As powerful as the Shel'ai was, Nekiel was stronger still. Crovis knew he would need unshakable faith in the Light in order to prevail. He could suffer no hesitation, no doubts, no uncertainty, or all was lost.

"I believe," Crovis muttered. "I believe."

Wyn Kai looked at him questioningly. Crovis shook his head. A moment later, Wyn Kai pointed. Crovis turned in time to see a flatboat moving to block their path. In place of Knights, the flatboat was crowded with mere squires armed with bows, along with others manning a ballista.

Crovis wondered if the squires knew who he was or were simply trying to prevent a handful of enemies from escaping. Either way, the challenge irked him. He turned to Algol. He said nothing. Nevertheless, the Shel'ai nodded. He laid aside his dragonbone scepter and stood.

"Right away, Grand Marshal."

The Shel'ai stood and moved to the head of the boat. Just then, the squires fired their ballista. Its steel-tipped bolt tore through the air. The squires' aim was flawless. The bolt arced perfectly toward Crovis's boat. Algol waved his hands, though, and an invisible force batted the bolt to one side. It splashed into the sea and vanished below the water, just off the port side.

Unfazed, squires crowded along the edge of the flatboat, nocking arrows, drawing back their bowstrings. Before they could fire, Algol aimed his fingers at them. Wytchfire roiled from his hands, billowing through the air. A few squires cried out and leapt to one side. A handful managed to loose their arrows before the flames washed over them.

Crovis forced himself to watch despite the sickening feeling in the pit of his stomach. Yes, those squires were upstarts—and traitors, besides—but they were still Isle-men. They deserved better than to die at the hands of magic.

Algol laughed, scouring and scouring the flatboat with wytchfire until nothing moved. Finally, he stopped. Crovis watched the burning flatboat drift past, occupied by just a few indiscernible figures, twisted and charred. He turned his attention back to Algol.

The Shel'ai had pulled the silk cloth from his eye sockets. Eyes of violet flame burned in his skull. His face was pale, though, and two arrows had pierced the sorcerer's body—one in his shoulder, the other in his side. Blood soaked his white robes.

"Save your concern, Grand Marshal," the Shel'ai said mockingly. "I assure you, I have hate enough to see this through to the end." Removing Knightswrath from its sword bag, he used the sword as a crutch and returned to his seat.

Rowen saw a flash of purple flame in the distance. Momentarily distracted, he just barely blocked an adamune swinging at his neck. Stepping in, he grasped his opponent's wrist and held it. He might have shoved his blade into his enemy's neck, but the young Knight's eyes went wide with panic as he recognized his peril. Instead, Rowen shoved him over the side of the boat, into the water. Then he turned to reassess the battle.

Across a short span of water floating with burning wreckage, Koroquin and his Knights were still battling on the deck of the other galleon. Despite being outnumbered two to one, Rowen could tell that his and Koroquin's forces were winning. However, all three galleons were hopelessly locked together in a mass of smoke and splintered wood.

Rowen cursed, looking for another ship he could take in pursuit of Crovis. He saw none.

For one wild moment, he considered leaping off the side of the ship, into the water, and swimming. But his Knights were still fighting, and he could not bring himself to abandon them. *Besides, Crovis doesn't have the sword. He doesn't have me. Even if Algol's with him, what will he gain by slipping past us and reaching Shigella's Tomb?*

One of his Knights staggered and fell, wounded. Rowen launched himself forward, stopped the other Knight from delivering the death blow, and cut the Knight's legs out from under him. He said a quick prayer for the Knight's soul before pressing on toward his next opponent.

He knew they had to finish the battle as quickly as possible, but that was easier said than done. Many of Crovis's men lacked spirit, but they were still Isle-trained. Rowen needed more men. Then, through a thin mist that hung like a shameful pall over the battle, he spotted another line of ships sweeping toward them.

For a moment, he feared they were galleons from another isle, rushing to Crovis's defense. But as they drew nearer, he realized that they were shorter, sleeker vessels with a strange configuration of sails. The sails themselves were not white, like Isle ships, but red, emblazoned with a golden chalice.

Rowen laughed. Fighting back a Knight and a squire who tried to attack him simultaneously, he shouted Hráthbam's name across the waters then hefted his sword and drove at his enemies with renewed fury.

Jalist blinked the sweat from his brow, ducked beneath Keidu's whirling long axe, and answered with a swing of his own, but Keidu was faster. Somehow, he recovered his balance, stepped forward, and caught the shaft of Jalist's axe on the shaft of his own. Before Jalist could strike again, Keidu drove his knee into Jalist's stomach.

Jalist doubled over and fell to his knees, dropping his axe. Keidu lifted his own axe to finish him. Jalist waited, waited, then rolled forward. Drawing a dagger, he stabbed blindly. He felt the blade sink through flesh and jar off bone and then stood and turned.

Keidu straightened slowly. He frowned at the dagger in his side then plucked it out and threw it away. He still held his long axe but struggled to lift it.

Jalist drew his shortsword and stepped closer. With a sudden burst of strength, Keidu swung his axe. Jalist stepped in, held his sword with both hands, and blocked the blow. Then he twisted, dragging his blade down the space between Keidu's neck and shoulder. He stepped clear before Keidu could grab him. A hard shove sent Keidu to his knees.

Jalist took a moment to catch his breath. Looking up, he saw Aeko leading a flashing column of Knights up the beach, around the sharpened stakes, toward the Dwarrish horsemen. Keidu's footmen rushed to block them. Jalist gestured. His own men cheered and streamed past him, swords glinting. A moment later, Keidu's men had no choice but to turn and face them.

Jalist stood virtually alone at Keidu's side. Keidu still knelt, merely grimacing as blood streamed from his wounds. He managed to draw his shortsword, but Jalist circled to his other side, out of range. Keidu tried to stand but fell back to his knees.

"That was a cheap shot," he muttered, grinning through a mouthful of blood.

Jalist nodded. "Sorry." He stood in front of Keidu and thought of Maddoc, realizing for the first time that he had not seen the Shel'ai since the fighting started. But if Jalist could find Maddoc, they might be able to heal Keidu before—

Keidu snarled and launched himself forward. The tip of his sword jabbed toward Jalist's stomach. Jalist twisted sideways. Keidu's sword sliced through his tunic and brigandine but missed his flesh. Jalist tried to move his sword out of the way, but Keidu caught his wrist with an iron grip. Jalist watched in horror as his sword sank into Keidu's throat.

Keidu shuddered mightily. Then, slowly, he pulled himself forward. He stopped only when he rested against the quillons of Jalist's sword. "For the prince," he choked. Then he sagged to the ground.

Jalist let go of his sword and stood there a moment, shaking. Then, he sank to his knees and wept.

Maddoc sat alone in a fishing boat, rowing as fast as he could. He'd been standing on the Privy, apart from the others, when the fighting started. He'd sensed at once how things would unfold: Rowen would lead the attack on Crovis while Aeko and Jalist took the Privy to the shore and led their forces to help the camp. Since the latter was more urgent, naturally, they would expect Maddoc to assist them.

But Maddoc had other plans. So he'd hurried to the edge of the Privy, where a fleet of small boats had been secured, and took the closest. None of the commanders saw him go, which suited Maddoc well. He was not about to ask their permission.

Maddoc shied away from most of the fighting, biding his time until he spotted the glare of purple flames. His pulse quickened. If Algol was there, Crovis had to be close, too. Maddoc hesitated only a moment then started paddling. He knew it would be prudent to seek out Rowen and get help—after all, Algol was powerful, and Maddoc would have to get through him to reach Crovis—but he dared not wait.

Maddoc rowed, ignoring the exhaustion in his arms. He imagined Sang Wei in the boat beside him, rowing with him, lending him his strength. Smoke stung his eyes. Maddoc wept, but the sea air dried the tears against his face.

Crovis's ship lay just ahead, its escape blocked by another flatboat crowded with Knights and squires. Wytchfire flashed across the water. Men screamed, but no one retreated. The boats collided. Knights fought, so identically armored that Maddoc could not tell one side from the other. In their midst, a white-robed priest laughed, lifted his hands, and unleashed more wytchfire. Then, Maddoc saw Crovis.

The Grand Marshal had fought his way onto the flatboat. Blood dripped from his armor and adamune. His dark braid trailed behind him as he blurred past enemy after enemy. Bodies fell to the deck or tumbled into the water. Moments later, Crovis stood alone. Rather than returning to the longship, which was burning, Crovis gestured. His remaining Knights joined him on the flatboat. Algol came last, unfazed by his own wytchfire.

Maddoc was close. Smoke shielded him from the eyes of the Knights. He kept the oars in the water as he paddled, fearful that their splashing might be heard even over the din of battle. Wytchfire flickered to life, smoldering the oars as he rowed. Crovis was almost within range.

Then, Algol turned.

For a moment, the two Shel'ai regarded each other. Maddoc shuddered at the sight of violet flames burning in otherwise hollow eye sockets. A derisive smirk formed on Algol's lips. Despite the blood soaking his robes, he stood tall, as though unhurt. With taunting slowness, he lifted one hand.

Maddoc stood. The small fishing boat rocked, but he kept his footing. He held his hands in front of him, conjuring a protective shield of wytchfire, and braced himself for Algol's assault. But when it came, the sheer force of it nearly threw Maddoc from the boat. Dazed, he answered with wytchfire of his own.

Algol's laughter left no doubts that he'd survived. Maddoc struggled back to his feet. Algol stood on the flatboat, in front of Crovis. Maddoc wondered if Algol was deliberately shielding the Grand Marshal. He prepared to unleash a second blast of wytchfire.

Then, for the first time, he noticed the sword hanging at Algol's waist.

That moment's distraction was all Algol needed. A broad swath of wytchfire swept across the smoking sea. Maddoc bit back a scream and tumbled backward into the water.

Igrid abandoned her sword in a dying Dwarr's ribs, snatched up a spear from the battlefield, and threw it. The spear caught another Dwarr in the back a moment before he would have swung his long axe through the neck of a kneeling Knight. Though Igrid could not say for certain whether the embattled Knights before her were allied to Rowen or Crovis, she suspected the former. Then, she spotted Aeko Shingawa.

The swordswoman fought on foot. Blood splattered her armor, and her dark braid had come undone. She limped and held one hand to her side as though sorely wounded. A few Knights stood with her, but a greater number of Dwarrs pressed them on all sides, led by the largest Dwarr she had ever seen. Somehow, he still fought from horseback.

"Help her," Igrid cried. Breaksteel grunted his answer and heaved forward, his great mace cleaving a path through muscle and bone. Zeia followed, a shortsword blurring in each blazing hand. Igrid could not see Keswen but heard the sound of her unerring bowstring.

Dwarrs turned, stunned to see such unusual opponents tearing through their ranks. Igrid snatched up a longsword and a hatchet and drove toward the Dwarr's leader, screaming her challenge. But more Dwarrs formed a protective wall between them. Igrid fought them a moment then was driven back. She looked to Breaksteel for help, but the great Olg had fallen to one knee, a great gash in his side. Zeia moved to protect him, slaying one Dwarr with some kind of mental attack, slashing another from eye to chin.

Then, Igrid heard the same Shao cry she'd heard uttered in the practice yard at Cadavash. She turned. Despite her injuries, Aeko led the Knights in a furious charge. The Dwarrs held a moment then broke. Their leader was forced to wheel his horse and retreat. However, he did not get far before a force of Red Watch and slum-dwellers charged out of the smoke. They formed a half circle, blocking his escape.

The mounted Dwarr wheeled his horse like a master rider and rode back the way he'd come. The Isle Knights fanned out to stop him, but at the last moment, the Dwarr wheeled left, toward a fresh opening, and galloped toward freedom. He almost made it.

However, Keswen appeared out of nowhere. She stepped past Igrid, lifted her bow with eerie calm, and fired. A single arrow carved through the smoke and caught the horse's flank.

Igrid lost sight of the Dwarr in a crash of limbs and dust, but men cheered and surged forward. The last of the Dwarrs tried to reach their leader, but a squad of men in the blue uniforms of New Atheion encircled them with a wall of spears. Igrid turned back to find Breaksteel.

Zeia stood protectively over the kneeling Olg. Knights had closed in, thinking him an enemy. Igrid ordered them to stand back. They glanced from Zeia to Igrid. They might have refused, but Aeko appeared a moment later and echoed the order.

Then, she faced Igrid. "Well met, Iron Sister. Your company is strange, but your timing is impeccable."

Igrid noted the paleness of Aeko's face. Igrid turned to Zeia, but the Shel'ai was already kneeling over Breaksteel, pressing her burning hands to his wounds. Igrid stepped closer to Aeko. "Where's Rowen?"

"On the water, fighting Crovis." Aeko looked past her, surveying the fallen tents and bodies of the battlefield, as well as the ongoing violence in the distance. "This isn't over yet." Using her bloodstained adamune as a crutch, she headed back toward the fighting.

Igrid grabbed her arm. "Algol has Knightswrath."

Aeko sighed. "I feared as much when I didn't see you wearing it." She winced suddenly and slumped, but Igrid caught her. "Jalist's here somewhere," Aeko said weakly. "Maddoc and Fen-Shea, too. If they're still alive—" She coughed blood into Igrid's face.

Igrid lowered the swordswoman to the ground. "Zeia," she called, "if you're done with the Olg, I need you!"

Rowen transferred command to Hráthbam's ship, the *Winter's Prayer*. By then, Crovis's remaining Knights were surrendering, and all three galleons blazed on the sea like discarded torches. Rowen seized a junior officer and asked where Koroquin was, intending to leave the one-armed Knight in command while Rowen pursued Crovis.

"Sir Koroquin is dead," the officer answered sullenly.

The Dragon's Veil had lifted. With the mist gone, Rowen stared out over the railing at the sea, choked with smoldering wreckage and floating bodies. All the dead were Knights and squires, but he could not tell from their repose which side they'd fought on.

Rowen felt a wave of nausea wash over him. He closed his eyes and resisted the urge to vomit, reminding himself that all eyes were on him. He remembered retching in the Sylvan capital of Shaffrilon, despite all those watching him. He gritted his teeth, desperately trying to clear the images of the dead from his mind.

Slowly, the nausea passed, replaced instead by a deep, maddening grief. He kept his eyes shut a moment longer, lest he weep, then opened them. Hráthbam squeezed his shoulder.

"I sent some ships to help your friends on the shore," the Soroccan said in a low voice. "Looks like the battle's about won, though." He offered Rowen a spyglass.

Rowen took it, but before he had a chance to use it, Maddoc's voice rang out in his mind.

Rowen tensed, momentarily unable to move. Then he turned to Hráthbam. "Maddoc's in the water. He's hurt. Help him." He pointed.

"You're in command while I'm gone. Send men to the temple to look for Father Matua. And tell Aeko and Jalist to follow me as soon as they can."

Hráthbam frowned. "What are you going to do?"

"I have to follow Crovis," Rowen said heavily.

"Fine, let's go kill the bastard. Leave someone else in charge."

"No, I need you here. I'll take one squad with me, though." Before Hráthbam could protest, Rowen waved over the railing at the closest boat: a longship crowded with young, cheering Knights. When they brought the longship alongside *Winter's Prayer,* he descended a rope ladder that led off the deck of Hráthbam's ship.

Hráthbam leaned over the railing after him, scowling. "No offense, my pale friend, but I hear this Knight is Fohl's own champion with a blade. Are you sure you don't want, say, five times as many men?"

He doesn't think I can beat Crovis—and he's probably right! Rowen shook his head and finished descending the ladder into the longship. The young Knights bowed and clapped him on the back. Rowen's face burned. *I hope I don't get them killed.* He ordered the Knights to start rowing.

Zeia stood wearily in a massive tent dedicated to treating the wounded. At sundown, the sky opened up, unleashing a torrent of rain. Dark clouds swept in from the sea, shrouding the horrors of the battlefield. She listened to the rain patter against the fabric of the tent, mingling with the moans and cries of the dying. By then, she felt as exhausted and naked as she had after she'd been attacked by Algol.

Igrid and Keswen had boarded Hráthbam's fastest schooner and taken off after Rowen, joined by a squad of loyal Knights. Meanwhile, Zeia had spent the last few hours using her abilities to treat the dying. After Maddoc was plucked from the water—injured, but alive—he'd gone to do the same at Saikaido.

However, the dying were simply too numerous to save. Zeia had seen countless men perish during the War of the Lotus and had watched plenty more die since in the war for Dhargoth, but as the hours wore on, she wept. She tried to help all those she could, but for every wound she healed, dozens more bled and festered. She thought her battle to help the wounded—the fiercest battle of her life—would never end. When it finally did, the reeling stillness was almost worse.

Despite Rowen's request that Jalist hurry after him, the captain had elected to remain in the camp. After all, Aeko had nearly died and remained in a deep and dangerous sleep. The gang leader called Fen-Shea had been killed, leaving no one else who could command.

Zeia glanced at the slumbering figure of the Olg that Igrid referred to as Breaksteel. She'd saved his life though she wondered if it had been worth it. The magic she'd employed to save him from his injuries might have saved two, even three others. Besides, he was an Olg, but something had compelled her to do it. Looking around, momentarily able to rest, she wondered if Maddoc was as tired as she was.

She looked down at her hands. They flickered and vanished. She smiled sardonically at her scarred wrists. She reflected on the one benefit of having hands of magic instead of flesh: she did not have to stop and wash the blood off.

Dagath took my hands. Now, he's out there, getting away. Zeia shook her head. Rowen and Igrid had history with the one-eyed sellsword, as well. As much as she enjoyed the thought of killing him herself, she trusted her friends to see it done. Besides, Dagath had simply been acting on the orders of General Brahasti, whom Keswen had slain, and Zeia had noted how little actual comfort Keswen seemed to derive from Brahasti's death.

Jalist entered the tent, eased past a line of clerics bandaging the less seriously wounded, and made his way toward her. The Dwarr's eyes were dark and heavy, and Zeia guessed why. "I trust you've taken care of the prisoners?"

Jalist's expression of exhaustion became a grimace of disgust. "What's left of the slum-dwellers wanted me to kill them, but the Knights said otherwise. They took that damn Scion back to Saikaido." He glanced at the sleeping figure of Breaksteel, shook his head, and turned back to Zeia. "It's been at least four hours since somebody called me a traitor."

Despite her exhaustion, Zeia reconjured her flaming hands. "Give me his name, and he'll never say it again."

"He'll never say it again anyway. He was the last Dwarr who died on my sword." He paused. "He shoved himself onto it rather than accept my mercy. He said it was because of… what I've done."

Zeia thought for a moment that Jalist was referring to his friendship with Rowen or his past alliance with Silwren. Then, she realized he was referring to something else. She started to reach out, intending to squeeze his arm, then thought better of it. "There are many acts that can constitute betrayal. Love is not one of them."

Jalist snickered. "You sound like you've been reading the Codex Lotius."

Zeia could not think of an appropriate reply. Finally, she asked, "What do you think will happen on the island?"

Jalist shrugged. "Either the world will end, or it won't." He rubbed his eyes. "Gods, I need a drink."

The statement reminded Zeia of Prince Saanji. Despite her weariness, she smiled. "Find a cask of wine, Dwarr. I'll share it with you."

Jalist shook his head. "I promised I'd stay sober until this was done. But if Rowen manages to keep Crovis from damning us all to an even worse war than the last one, I think that's a promise I'm willing to break."

Zeia knelt to inspect another sleeping, injured man. Then she stood. "If you do, invite Maddoc."

Jalist scowled. "Do I really look that lonesome, wytch?"

"No more so than the rest of us, I suspect."

Jalist looked away. "This is all a lot of nonsense if you ask me. If Rowen had stayed here, this would all be as good as done. Gaulgodd's in irons. Crovis's Knights are beaten. Crovis can't get into the tomb without Knightswrath—"

"Which he has," Zeia reminded him.

"Which he can't use," Jalist countered. "Neither can this Shel'ai, Algol. If they even try…"

Zeia nodded. "It'll burn them alive."

"We should be so lucky," Jalist snorted. "I don't get why Locke left. The only way Crovis can get into the tomb is if he tricks Rowen to open it for him—and even Locke's not that stupid."

Zeia thought of Igrid. If Crovis captured the Iron Sister somehow, she knew he would try to use Igrid as a bargaining chip to make Rowen open the tomb. That had been Algol's plan, after all. But as much as the Knight loved the Iron Sister, Zeia did not think even he would sacrifice the entire continent to save her.

Jalist's right. There was no reason for Rowen to hurry off like that. It's like he thought Crovis might be able to— Zeia froze. "Gods. ."

Jalist frowned. "What is it, wytch? You look like you just saw—"

Zeia grabbed Jalist's arm. "Go to the shore and find us a boat. We have to catch up with Rowen, or the world might just end after all!"

CHAPTER TWENTY-SEVEN

ROWEN BLINKED AWAY THE RAIN as his Knights rowed the sleek, quick craft across the dark sea. He looked up. So far, he had seen no lightning, despite the dark clouds obscuring the heavens. Nevertheless, he could still discern the hauntingly bright swirl of stars that made up Armahg's Eye.

If you really are watching over us, Goddess, this would be a good time to act.

Rowen turned northwest, trying to discern the outline of his destination on the dark horizon. So far, the small, unnamed island remained invisible. Something told him they were rowing in the right direction, though. He'd been there once before, shortly after Father Matua discovered the infamous Dragonward scroll, and he'd felt the same faint dread in the pit of his stomach.

Common sense had told him he should return to the mainland, make sure Igrid and the others were all right, and gather his strength. But Maddoc's warning had filled him with certainty that whatever was about to happen, he had to reach Shigella's Tomb as quickly as possible.

Luckily, upon rescuing Aeko from the temple, Rowen had asked her to send a dozen trusted Knights to guard the tomb, just in case Crovis broke through. Crovis would have to fight his way through those to even reach the tomb. With luck, they'd hold off the Grand Marshal long enough for Rowen's reinforcements to finish the job.

Rowen glanced down at his borrowed sword and mismatched armor. He wished he had Knightswrath with him. He wanted to draw some small comfort from the fact that Crovis could not actually use the sword, but he had a terrible feeling that he had underestimated his opponents.

For some reason, he thought of Silwren as he'd last seen her: blazing, soft eyed but terrible. He imagined her rising out of the sea, woman shaped despite the reflection of a six-winged dragon spreading across the water. He imagined her smiling, returning from the dead to guide him, protect him, tell him exactly what was expected of him.

Rowen wiped his eyes. "Silwren, I could use your help."

His young Knights glanced at him questioningly. Rowen waved them off. Then, he took the place of one tiring Knight and rowed, driving his oar again and again into the dark sea.

Rowen and his Knights reached the island just as the rains stopped and a faint smear of dawn illuminated a mass of armored corpses strewn along the shore. With a sickening feeling, Rowen eyed a tiny, decrepit harbor before them. Crovis's boat sat there, empty. Though he could not tell at that distance whether the dead Knights on the beach had been his or Crovis's, Rowen got his answer a moment later. A squad of Knights moved solemnly from the jungle and fanned out in a long row of torn azure and soot-darkened kingsteel. Instead of cheering Rowen's approach, they fixed him with a fierce, quiet stare.

"Bastards," one of Rowen's Knights muttered.

"Traitors," said another.

"They'd say the same about us," Rowen countered.

His men fell silent, and the only sound was the splash of oars in water as his Knights carried him closer and closer to the shore. Rowen stood tall in the boat, drew his sword, and saluted Crovis's Knights. To Rowen's surprise, they returned the gesture with grave dignity.

Even odds. He thought of the handful of longbows sitting in the boat, which his Knights could easily use to attack Crovis's men from afar. He guessed they also had bows, and like him, they seemed unwilling to use them.

Both forces quietly eyed each other as the distance between them shrank. Rowen could tell by then that Crovis and the Shel'ai were not with them. Despite his hurry, he resisted the urge to order a reckless charge. Instead, he climbed out of the boat first, ready to protect his Knights if needed. Crovis's men watched and waited, giving them plenty of time.

One of Crovis's Knights stepped ahead of the rest and sheathed his sword.

Rowen recognized him. "Sir Ulni." Rowen held up his hand, halting his Knights. He sheathed his own sword and started forward alone, keeping one hand on the hilt. As he drew closer, he saw splatters of blood on Sir Ulni's armor.

Rowen faced Sir Ulni for a moment, then the two men bowed. As Rowen straightened, he looked at the dead Knights lying around them. "This is what the Grand Marshal has in mind for all of us, you know."

"I know," Sir Ulni answered. His voice had an odd rasp to it.

Rowen stared at the Knight, surprised by his reply.

"The Grand Marshal has continued on to the tomb with Sir Kai and the sorcerer. Those Knights behind me are still determined to stop you. I, on the other hand, have changed my mind."

Sir Ulni drew his sword. Rowen drew back a step, but Sir Ulni sank slowly to his knees. He reversed his sword, holding it by the blade. He braced the pommel against the ground.

"Forgive me, Sword Marshal," he said, expressionless, and pushed his throat down onto the tip of his own sword.

Rowen stared a moment, then the sound of shifting metal caught his attention. He looked up in time to see Crovis's Knights lifting their own swords in salute. He wondered if they were saluting him or the fallen Sir Ulni. Before he could make up his mind, they charged.

Knight battled Knight, so indistinguishable that Rowen sometimes could not tell friend from foe and had to wait until the latter revealed himself by attacking. Moments later, though, the last of Crovis's Knights fell quietly onto the sand and moved no more.

Gasping for air, Rowen leaned on his own sword for a moment, then turned to count how many of his own Knights remained. Two struggled to rise. A quick check of their injuries confirmed that they would live but could go no farther.

That leaves me to handle Crovis, Wyn Kai, and the sorcerer alone—and I'm not sure I can handle even one of them by myself.

Rowen glanced southward. Though he wanted Igrid as far from the fight as possible, part of him hoped to see her bright-red hair trailing in the wind, over the railing of an approaching ship crowded with Isle Knights and Red Watch. Instead, he saw only empty, blue water. He sighed.

"Stay here," he told his wounded Knights. "Protect each other." Then, he turned toward the jungle and went on alone.

Trees rose from the island, twisted but impossibly high, so thick that they appeared from a distance as an impassible, dark-walled stronghold. Rowen suppressed a shudder. As he had the last time he'd been there, instead of peacefulness, he felt a vague, inexplicable dread. Shaking his head, he pushed on through the trees.

The heady brine of the sea gave way to the grassy smell of the forest. Not for the first time, he wondered if those tall, strange trees were related somehow to the wytchwoods of the Sylvan homeland. That would certainly explain not only their size, but also the king who had been buried here.

Rowen listened for sounds of life, but apart from the surf lapping the beach behind him, no sound echoed from the jungle trees. He did not hear so much as an insect, let alone birds. The tiny island appeared as abandoned as it had been years before. Still, his heart pounded in his throat. He loosened his sword, kicked the sand from his boots, and edged deeper into the gnarled jungle.

He had not gone far before he spotted a familiar statue. Tangled with vines and half smothered by moss, it showed a man with tapered ears, smiling down at a swaddled baby in his arms. However, the moss and vines lent an ominous aura to the statue, as did the surrounding silence. Rowen found himself reluctant to show the statue his back as he pressed on.

The trees thickened until daylight thinned to a trickle. Rowen had a harder and harder time finding his footing. When last he'd been there, Knights had gone ahead of him to hew a rough path through the forest. That path had long since been swallowed by the jungle. Rowen felt a rising sense of panic, as if the forest itself were closing on him like a fist.

Rowen closed his eyes for a moment, holding his sword hilt. He reminded himself that he was a Knight of the Lotus. This place had most likely been founded by the Knights, Shel'ai, and Dragonkin allied with Fâyu Jinn. He opened his eyes and pressed on.

He arrived next at a low, ruined wall. Four statues stood behind the wall—three of them Knights, the fourth a female Shel'ai with stone flames rising from both palms. Rowen stared at the wall and wondered, as he had the last time he'd been there, if it had indeed succumbed to time or had just been made to look broken, portraying the defense of some ailing city that time had forgotten.

As he continued toward the center of the island, the darkness deepened until Rowen feared he'd lose his way. However, he felt the ground slope downward, through a tangle of weeds and roots, toward what seemed to him a darkened crater overgrown with vegetation. He drew his sword, wincing as the scrape of steel on leather interrupted the thick pall of silence. Then, using his sword like a cane, he descended.

He had not gone far when a jolt of power drove him to his knees. He thought at first that he'd been struck by a mental attack—what Zeia called a mind-stab—but he knew somehow that Algol was still far away. He thought, strangely, of the time when El'rash'lin had imparted his memories to Rowen so that he might better understand the plight of the Shel'ai. This sensation was different, though: brutal, insistent, unfriendly.

Rowen struggled against it. The world began to blur. Then he was falling, rising, being pulled in every direction at once. His body ripped apart, then his mind.

Rowen awakened and found himself staring up into the azure eyes of a Sylv. He knew somehow that this man was his father—even as he knew that was impossible. He laughed, joyous but unable to speak, and held up his arms, wanting only to be held.

Instead, his father drew a knife.

Rowen heard himself scream as the cutting began. The world went dark. For years, he felt nothing but pain. He drowned in darkness. He still had a mother and father, he knew, but they never touched him, never cleaned him, barely even fed him. They wanted him to die. He could feel it. But they feared retribution from the gods.

However, they feared more than just the gods. Cutting out his eyes was not enough. What if, one day, the others learned what he was? Unloved, unnamed, trapped in darkness, he waited for death to come and release him. Then, one day, the darkness withered.

The change began with a faint smear of color, a vague impression of light in the untouchable distance. Slowly, the colors sharpened, taking on shape. He saw his parents again—horrified—then his own reflection, staring back at him from a wading pool: a little boy, filthy, with hollow eye sockets.

Repulsed, he looked away, and a strange heat filled his skull. For the first time, he knew anger. No longer did he see his parents as beings whose love he had to win. Instead, he saw them through and through: not just their bodies, but their thoughts, their memories, their desires, everything down to the most shameful shred.

Suddenly, he hated them. He saw his own hands, so much smaller than theirs, swirling with flames the color of a bruise. He saw them run—then fall, burning. The smell filled his nostrils, both intoxicating and sickening.

He faced his reflection again. His eye sockets remained empty, but instead of darkness, they blazed with purple flame.

The boy reeled. Breath escaped him like blood leaking from a wound. Dimly, he realized he was running through the forest—chased, hunted. Something told him that if he ran toward the rising sun, he might find others like him. He might be safe. But would they only be like him, scarred and ugly? If so, better that he die alone.

He turned instead to the west, toward night, and kept running.

Hours stretched into days. He could still see, though he knew somehow that his vision was unnatural, wrong. The world looked sick, the colors blurry, unless he concentrated. When he did so, he felt heat in the hollows of his eyes. But that wearied him, and already, he had not eaten for longer than he could remember.

A terrible pain filled his stomach, though he found that if he concentrated, he could replace the pain with heat—with fire, half soothing, half maddening. He ran and ran. Finally, the forest fell away, then the plains, and he stood on a shore of thorns and wasted rock. There, for the first time, he gazed upon the sea. Had he had eyes, he might have wept.

Then, hunger returned. He stumbled down to the water. He stripped off his soiled clothes, and for the first time, he washed himself. Then, he felt fish gliding past his legs. He tried to catch them, but they were too fast. He stretched out a hand, sending jolts of fire that burned despite the water around them. In his mind, he heard the fish scream.

He laughed. Then, he ate.

For days, he lingered on the rocky shores, sleeping and eating, regaining his strength. He knew that this place was called the Dead Shores, just as he knew the names of distant lands and cities his strange eyes had never seen, but that knowledge seemed distant and alien. Standing on the westernmost edge of the continent, he thought again about dying. He even tried it. He waded out into the water until it closed over his head. Then, he opened his mouth.

But the fire kept him alive.

Still, everything hurt. The fire burned him, as well as the world around him. He faced west. He wondered what, if anything, lay beyond this wretched, rocky place. He decided to find out. But how to begin?

Finally, one day, he got his chance.

A group of fishermen appeared on the shore. They looked different from his parents. They spoke words he did not understand. He approached them. He tried to ask them for help, but they greeted him with fear and revulsion. As he had with his parents, he saw their thoughts, their memories, their sins. He burned them and took their boat.

He had no idea how to navigate the sea. He simply pushed the boat out onto the water, fumbled with the oar, and gradually found himself drifting farther and farther from the familiar shore. The rocking of the boat made him sick. The vast openness of the sea frightened him, but the coming of night brought stars, and he lay on his back and stared up at the heavens, entranced.

For days, he drifted in his little boat. He tried drinking the water, but it made him gag. Thirst grew like a jagged stone in his throat. He briefly considered cutting himself, to see if blood could sate his thirst better than saltwater, but he had nothing sharp to use. He leaned over the side of the boat, staring into the water, watching it endlessly reshape and demolish his reflection. He thought he saw fish swimming beneath the surface, but he no longer had the strength to burn them. Besides, thirst was his main enemy now.

The sun burned his face, his bare arms—a different fire than he was accustomed to. Still, each day ended in darkness, and in darkness, the pain was not quite so bad. The stars soothed him, heartening in their cold beauty, their faraway indifference. He told himself that soon, very soon, death would set him free. Then, perhaps whatever he truly was—his breath, maybe, or a warm bit of fog in his chest—would lift away from his body and drift upward, possibly to the stars.

But as he grew weaker, something terrible happened. His vision blurred then vanished altogether, and he was in darkness again. He tried to imagine the stars. But his thoughts roiled, feverish, and he could not concentrate even on so simple an image.

He decided he could take it no longer. He would climb over the side of the boat and throw himself into the water. He sensed that if he was too weak to see, he might be too weak to survive like a fish, as well. Even if death was painful, it would be preferable to this.

He made up his mind then found, to his horror, he could not even summon enough strength to throw himself from the boat. He tried rocking from side to side, thinking he might capsize the boat and drown himself, but even this small effort exhausted him before reaching fruition.

Then, one day as the sun was raking the back of his neck, his little boat ran aground. He felt rocks scraping the wood, inches below his face. The boat went still. Darkness persisted. He wondered if somehow, this was death. A strange new strength filled him. Suddenly he could see again. Though his limbs remained weak, with great effort, he pushed himself up and looked around.

A shore of strange rock lay before him. The rocks looked like different-sized shards of black, broken glass. He tried to climb out and fell. The glass cut him. He lay there, bleeding, and wept. Then, he turned and saw a cloaked man.

The cloaked man stood on the shore, so close that the boy could not believe he'd failed to notice him earlier. He drew closer still: strong, handsome, so powerful that the air itself seemed to shimmer in his wake. His clothes gleamed like the sea, like the stars. The boy covered his eyes and wished he could weep. The cloaked man took his wrists and gently pulled away his hands. He stared into the boy's empty eye sockets. Instead of withdrawing in revulsion, he smiled.

"Welcome, my son. I dreamt of you," the cloaked man said.

The boy heard the words not just with his ears, but also in his mind.

"Hush, now. You are safe here."

As though from thin air, the cloaked man produced a smooth wooden bowl filled with cold water. He offered it to the boy. The boy drank. When the bowl emptied, the cloaked man touched it, and it filled again.

The boy drank and drank then doubled over in pain. He retched. The cloaked man watched in silence. Finally, the boy straightened, and the cloaked man offered him the bowl again. The boy drank more slowly this time.

"My name is Nekiel," the cloaked man said.

The boy stared, speechless. Finally, he found his voice. "Do I have a name?"

Nekiel's smile broadened. He brushed his hand against the boy's face. "Not yet, my little prophet. But one day, you shall earn one. And when you do, I'll send you home."

CHAPTER TWENTY-EIGHT

CROVIS SCOWLED AS THE SHEL'AI rose slowly from his meditative position. Faint tendrils of wytchfire clung to Algol's body. Though Algol still wore the robes of a cleric, those robes had become so soaked in blood that Crovis marveled that the Shel'ai was still alive. In fact, when Algol had abruptly stopped and knelt, closing his eyes, Crovis had assumed Algol was attempting to heal himself. Yet as Algol stood, Crovis saw fresh blood leaking from his wounds, and the paleness of his expression said he was even weaker than before.

"What were you doing?"

"Just... sending a message," Algol answered, his voice barely a whisper. "Rowen Locke is here. But I do not think... he and I will have a chance to face each other after all." Algol started to laugh then coughed up blood.

Crovis glanced over his shoulder. He'd left his last three Knights in the forest, along with Algol's sellsword bodyguard, to deal with any pursuit. Only Wyn Kai stood near. The white-haired Knight paced anxiously, a torch in hand. Crovis had anticipated that they would be followed, but he had not dared to hope Rowen himself would appear. His pulse quickened at the thought of facing Rowen in single combat, but he told himself that such an indulgence could wait.

Crovis turned, staring at the tomb.

Had the ancient carvings on the structure not told him otherwise, he never would have suspected that a king was buried there. The structure was only one story high, smaller than a stable, overgrown with vines.

The tomb had no windows. What seemed at first like a door was just a depression in the stone, covered with more runes.

He might have been tempted, too, to think the runes were lies and the structure itself was just some ancient builder's idea of a joke. But lying on the ground were the broken tools from countless vain attempts to break into the tomb.

Now we have Knightswrath but not Rowen. Crovis smiled. *But we won't need him.* He turned to Algol. "It's time, Shel'ai."

Algol gave Crovis a long, cold look. Then he stepped forward, holding Knightswrath by the scabbard. He faced the sealed tomb for a moment then turned to face Crovis. A cold smile formed on his lips. "Knight, you asked me once how much I hate this world." His smile disappeared. "This much, Knight. *This* much!"

With that, he drew Knightswrath.

Purple flames blossomed from Knightswrath's blade. The flames poured forth, bright and angry, racing down Algol's arm. The Shel'ai screamed. His clothes burned. His skin blackened. But he did not fall. Instead, he twisted toward the stone wall, holding the flaming sword over his head. His body shook, and his scream changed—no longer a pitched cry of panic but a bellow of triumph.

The sword swept down, parting the recessed stone wall like a torn curtain and revealing a darkened room beyond. Algol pitched forward, silent, his body stiff as charred lumber. Knightswrath tumbled from his grasp and clattered on the stone floor within the tomb. What remained of Algol's body followed. When it struck the floor, it scattered into a heap of cinders.

"Gods," Wyn Kai gasped.

Even Crovis stared, speechless. Then, drawing his sword, he used his free hand to take the torch from Wyn Kai's grasp. He paused a moment. Then he stepped forward into ancient and forbidden darkness.

Rowen awoke and found himself in a quiet glade, still bleary with sunrise. For one terrifying instant, both his body and his surroundings felt unfamiliar, as though he were waking from a nightmare. He blinked and breathed deeply, and the feeling subsided. Slowly, he rose to his feet, wondering as he did so how much time had passed. He knew Algol must be dead. He wiped his eyes, amazed at his own tears. Then, a terrible urgency filled him.

Algol just used Knightswrath to open the tomb!

That meant Crovis was probably already inside. Rowen was too late. Nekiel had won. "Maybe not. Not yet, anyway." Rowen took another moment to steady himself then shook off the jumble of horrifying memories and hurried on.

He had not gone far when he saw two interlocked statues depicting Fâyu Jinn in combat with Nekiel. Both wielded flaming swords. In front of the statues stood three Isle Knights, very much alive. The three spotted Rowen as soon as he spotted them. Without a word, they drew swords and started forward.

For a moment, Rowen hesitated, considering his options. He had not anticipated that Crovis would leave additional Knights in the jungle. Rowen could not possibly fend off three trained Knights at once, but they were already too close for him to run. He could return to the beach and hope that the two wounded men he'd left behind could find the strength to assist him, but that would surely get them killed.

Why didn't I bring a longbow with me? I'll need it when I face Crovis, anyway!

Rowen sighed and drew his sword. "Listen to me," he called to the Knights. "Too many of us have already died. We don't have to do this."

One of the approaching Knights removed his placid facemask and tossed it away, revealing a young face covered in scars. "How many of us did the Jolym kill, Sword Marshal?"

"All that death was *your* fault," another growled through a facemask that resembled a snarling wolf.

Rowen opened his mouth to argue then realized there was no point. He took a deep breath and let it go, trying to steady his nerves. He let his head droop and his sword arm sag, as though exhausted and demoralized. He waited until the Knights were almost upon him. One, clad in a facemask with a wide mocking grin, drew ahead of the rest

Rowen waited for an opening then leapt forward. His sword blurred, so fast that it split the air like a cracking whip. The closest Knight had no time to defend himself. Rowen's blade found the gap between cuirass and helmet. The Knight toppled, wide-eyed, clutching his throat. Rowen saluted the dying man then turned to face his other two opponents.

They exchanged angry glances and approached him cautiously, one from each side. Rowen saw at once that they would not be so easily fooled. A moment later, they attacked in concert. One swung high, the other low. Rowen blocked the first sword, but the second landed a jarring blow on his thigh. Rowen twisted clear of a lunge that would have opened his face, but a second lunge drove into his cuirass and nearly knocked him down.

The scarred Knight who had removed his facemask snarled, "Bastard," and drove at him. He feigned a high cut but twisted his sword midswing and angled for Rowen's kneecap.

Rowen could do no more than lift his leg and take it off his armored calf since he needed his sword to keep the other Knight from cutting off his head. He winced as the force of the swing passed through his armor, rattling his muscles and bones. As he backpedaled to avoid two more blurring swings, Rowen flashed back to his battle against the Dhargot, Jaanti, against whom Rowen had felt as if he were standing still.

A moment later, one of the Knights caught his foot on a tree root and stumbled. However, before Rowen could strike, the scarred Knight selflessly threw himself into Rowen's path, shrugging off three blows from Rowen's sword before the sheer fury of his counterattack forced Rowen to retreat.

He just risked his life to save his friend. That's something a true Knight would do. Yet, this man follows Crovis. Rowen cleared his thoughts and lifted his sword above his head. His opponents edged in, approaching him from different directions again. Rowen sidestepped to keep the scarred Knight from flanking him.

Then he shifted, feigning an overextended lunge at the scarred Knight's face. The latter moved to parry. As Rowen hoped, the other Knight took advantage of the opening and leapt forward. Rowen twisted about and drove his sword into the other Knight's wolfish facemask. The other Knight toppled backward, senseless.

But the blow was costly. Before Rowen could move to defend himself, the scarred Knight landed two ringing blows on Rowen's leg, then nearly split his head open. Rowen backpedaled, completely on the defensive. The scarred Knight followed, cursing. Another slash cut off Rowen's tabard. In the corner of his eye, the azure silk fell to the grass. He wondered how long it would be before he fell, too.

Wyn Kai drew his sword and followed Crovis into the tomb. The Grand Marshal had fearlessly stridden far ahead as though already familiar with the place, taking the torch with him. Wyn Kai hurried to catch up. The air smelled stale, and the darkness felt like branches scraping against his skin.

"Grand Marshal…"

Crovis did not answer or slow. Wyn Kai tumbled when he caught his foot on a step. The floor struck his cuirass so hard that it drove the breath from his lungs. Luckily, he managed to twist his sword away to avoid cutting himself. He rose as quickly as he could, feeling in the darkness. He realized three steps lay before him, yet the Grand Marshal had not bothered to warn him.

It seemed to him that the tomb was bigger on the inside than on the outside. Shaking his head, Wyn Kai hurried up the stairs, toward a faint orange glow in the distance. Crovis stood before a stone sarcophagus. As Wyn Kai drew closer, he realized the entire sarcophagus had been carved out of jade and covered in what looked like Sylvan glyphs.

Crovis had never told Wyn Kai the key to bringing down the Dragonward, but Wyn Kai had always assumed that whatever it was, it lay inside the sarcophagus, alongside the remains of King Shigella. However, Crovis stared at the sarcophagus for a moment, unimpressed, then circled around and continued on. Wyn Kai followed. Crovis held the torch high overhead, illuminating a circle of strange glyphs carved into the floor, near the far wall, beyond the sarcophagus. Then, Wyn Kai gasped.

Cloaked figures kneeled within the circle.

For a moment, Wyn Kai thought they must be statues. Then, he realized that all six were rocking gently, like half-conscious children trying to stave off a nightmare. "Grand Marshal, who are they? How did they get in here?" Wyn Kai's words echoed, and he immediately wished he had not spoken.

Crovis flung the torch into the circle, and it landed dead center, still burning. Slowly, the Grand Marshal approached. He circled around the group of kneeling figures. "They have *always* been here," he answered. He reached out, grasped one black silk hood, and tugged it back, revealing a gaunt face, pale as bone, so pinched that the gender was indeterminable. The eyes were closed, but Wyn Kai saw tapered ears.

Crovis looked up and smiled. "Do not fear, Sir Kai. They cannot hear you. They aren't even alive anymore. Not really."

Wyn Kai resisted the impulse to turn and flee. "Gods… are they…"

"Dragonkin," Crovis answered. "These six volunteered to stay here for all time, in a deep sleep plagued by nightmares, so that their full power could be redirected into the Dragonward." He spoke with what sounded like grudging admiration. Then, he drew his sword.

Wyn Kai took a step forward. "They've been here… all this time?" He looked at each of the Dragonkin in turn.

Their hoods kept their faces welled in shadow—except for the one whom Crovis had unhooded, who more closely resembled a corpse that still had flesh on its bones. Shock turned to revulsion—then, unexpectedly, to pity.

"By the Light, how much torment have they endured?"

"More than either of us can imagine, I should think." Crovis moved to the next kneeling Dragonkin and pulled back its hood as well. Then, he did the same to the third. "That does not change what they are, though." He tugged down the fourth and fifth Dragonkins' hoods. "Remember, Sir Kai, even evil men can be brave at times."

Crovis paused before pulling back the final Dragonkin's hood. Unlike the others, whose gender Wyn Kai could not discern, that one was distinctly female. A little color remained in her face. Her lips were red, her hair long and the color of melted platinum. Like the others, she was rocking herself. Then, she stopped. Her eyelids fluttered open.

Wyn Kai cried out a warning, but the kneeling Dragonkin simply stared forward, at the torch still burning at the center of the circle. Her violet eyes did not blink. Then, she started rocking herself again. Wyn Kai thought he heard a faint moan escape her lips.

"Curious," Crovis said, unafraid. "Each of these was like a god once. Imagine how much power they must have wielded. And now… " Crovis swung his sword. The woman's head separated from her neck and fell into the circle with a damp, sickening thud. The body slumped, gushing blood that spread across the tomb floor like a shadow. Crovis faced the corpse and bowed.

Wyn Kai felt cold—colder than he had ever felt in his life. "Grand Marshal, wait… "

Crovis moved to the next kneeling figure. This Dragonkin continued rocking slightly, oblivious to what Crovis had just done. The Grand Marshal faced the kneeling figure for a moment, then swung his sword again. Another corpse slumped to the floor.

Wyn Kai opened his mouth to speak, to scream, but no sound came out.

Crovis slew the third Dragonkin, then the fourth, bowing after each corpse fell. The fifth Dragonkin opened its eyes but made no attempt at self-defense. Instead of performing another beheading, Crovis thrust his blade between his enemy's shoulder and neck, guiding it deep down, into the ribcage. A giddy smile shone on the Grand Marshal's lips as he dragged the bloody blade back out.

Wyn Kai found his voice. "Wait. Grand Marshal, you have to stop this."

Instead of bowing, Crovis frowned. "Don't lose heart now, Sir Kai. These are bloody matters, I know, but necessary if we are to—"

Wyn Kai pushed himself onto his feet and lurched forward. Crovis tensed. With deft ease, he moved his sword to block Wyn Kai's swing. He twisted his blade and shoved, sending Wyn Kai back a step.

Wyn Kai stared at his own sword arm, amazed at what he had just done. Then, he looked down at the bloodstains spreading across the floor of the tomb, covering them in a strange darkness that reminded him of a starless sky. He considered apologizing or trying one last time to reason with the Grand Marshal.

Instead, he raised his sword and charged.

Rowen blinked the sweat from his eyes. He'd learned a moment before that taking the time to wipe his brow was a mistake since doing so had nearly given the scarred Knight adequate time to behead him. Rowen fought to regain his positioning in the fight, but the scarred Knight seemed inexhaustible. He drove at Rowen with renewed speed and ferocity that reminded Rowen of Sang Wei.

Rowen wanted to ask the Knight's name. Instead, he felt himself being driven farther and farther back until he bumped into the dueling statues of Fâyu Jinn and Nekiel. Somehow, the scarred Knight attacked even faster, trying to finish Rowen while his back was against a wall of sorts.

Rowen managed to get free and even landed two strong blows on the scarred Knight's cuirass, then he saw out of the corner of his eye that the Knight he'd stunned earlier had nearly recovered. Rowen's blow had dented the Knight's wolfish facemask, forcing him to remove it. Blood covered his face from where a bit of splintered metal had gouged the man's cheek and forehead, but otherwise, he'd regained his composure and was hurrying to help his comrade.

This is it. I'm too tired to fight one of them, let alone both.

Rowen backed up and lifted his sword over his head, despite his weariness. "Listen to me," he managed, facing the scarred Knight. "When the Dragonkin come, forget glory. Just do what you can to protect the people. Remember the Codex Lotius. Don't—"

The scarred Knight spat and charged. The two locked swords, struggling for a moment, then the scarred Knight drove one gauntleted fist into Rowen's cheek. Rowen reeled. The scarred Knight bellowed and came at him again. Rowen lunged, but the scarred Knight whirled and, with one brilliant swing, disarmed him.

"He's mine," the scarred Knight told his friend. Then he stepped forward and swung again.

Rowen took the blow on his arm. The scarred Knight pressed on with savage fury, battering and battering Rowen's arm with his sword. Sparks flew. The rough music of denting kingsteel sounded through the trees. Rowen sank to one knee. Then he twisted his arm, caught hold of the scarred Knight's blade, and pinned it.

Startled, the scarred Knight twisted mightily, trying to free his blade. Rowen simply let it go, and the scarred Knight lost his balance. Rowen was tempted to use the moment to rest. Instead, he shoved himself forward.

The two men grappled. Rowen drove his head into the scarred

Knight's nose then sank low, grabbed the man's thighs, and hoisted him off his feet. Rowen dropped him to the ground then dropped his knee into the scarred Knight's already bleeding nose. He managed to wrest the sword from the scarred Knight's hand before the second Knight could attack.

But the second Knight easily battered Rowen's sword out of the way, landed two more blows on his cuirass, then swept his legs out from under him. Rowen landed hard, and all the breath left his lungs. A thorn found the side of his head, sharp enough to draw blood. He willed himself to rise, but his body did not move. Instead, he stared up at the morning sky beyond the treetops, filled with pale wisps of clouds.

Something stepped forward and blocked the light. Rowen saw a flash of steel and found himself staring up the long, curved blade of an adamune. A face covered in dried blood regarded him with open derision. "Any last words, Sword Marshal?"

Rowen thought back to the Codex Lotius and wondered which passage was most appropriate for such a time. His thoughts gave way to an image of Sariel and Thessa, then Igrid, her red hair spread across the pillow as she slept.

He smiled faintly and said nothing.

The final Knight waited a moment longer, lifted his sword, and stiffened. Fresh blood poured from his throat and ran down his armor. One hand moved to his throat, gingerly touching the tip of an arrow. He started to turn. A second arrow struck his face. Rowen barely had time to roll out of the way before the Knight fell.

By the time he'd sat up, the scarred Knight had risen, too. Despite his broken nose and cracked skull, the man was still alive. Snarling with rage, he snatched a sword off the ground and turned to face the archer. Someone whistled to get Rowen's attention. He turned to see Igrid emerge from the trees, a shortsword of curved kingsteel gleaming in each hand.

Igrid glanced past the scarred Knight at Rowen. "On your feet, you dumb bastard. Unless I'm wrong, we still have a Grand Marshal to kill."

Speechless, Rowen found the strength to stand. He picked up a sword, tears welling in his eyes. A moment later, he spotted Keswen, approaching at the head of a fresh squad of Isle Knights and Red Watch.

An arrow sat ready on her bowstring. She looked at the last of Crovis's Knights, then at Rowen.

Rowen faced the final Knight. "Enough. You fought well, but it's over. Throw down your sword, and you'll live."

The scarred, bloody Knight faced Rowen for a moment then twisted about and charged Igrid. Rowen screamed a warning, but Igrid was already moving. She ducked beneath the Knight's whirling adamune, twisted to avoid the knee he tried to drive into her chest, and rained two blows on his cuirass. The Knight turned to resume his attack, but Igrid stabbed the Knight's armored back, ducked under his sword again, and jammed both swords into chinks in his armor—one at his knee, the other at his side. The Knight grunted but did not scream. Nevertheless, when Igrid jerked her blades free, he toppled onto the grass.

"He's not dead," Igrid said, breathing easily. "Want me to fix that?"

"No." Rowen hurried over as fast as his aching legs could carry him. He pulled Igrid into his arms and buried his face in her hair for a moment. He kissed her cheek then winced when he saw he'd left blood on her face. He started to wipe it away, but she stopped him.

Keswen joined them, still warily eyeing the fallen Knight. "The Grand Marshal?"

"He's up ahead," Rowen said. "Algol is dead. He killed himself using Knightswrath to open the tomb."

Keswen blanched.

Igrid said, "Then we're too late… "

"Probably." Rowen rubbed his eyes. "We'll try anyway."

"My fault," Igrid whispered.

"No," Rowen said, "it's mine. All of this—"

"Enough talk," Keswen said. "There might still be time!"

Rowen nodded. He waved Igrid's men closer and pointed at the fallen Knight. "Take him prisoner. And see to the wounded on the beach." He eyed Igrid and Keswen and added, "We'll finish this ourselves."

Igrid frowned. "I'm all for killing Crovis, but what if he tries to get off the island?"

"He won't," Rowen said heavily. "I think he's waiting for me."

"He's waiting for a nice, honorable duel," Keswen said with a sneer.

"That's not going to happen," Igrid said sternly. "Keswen will fill the bastard with arrows. Either that, or we'll hack him up together. I've had it with honor. What matters is putting that crazy sonofabitch in the ground. Agreed?"

Instead of answering, Rowen stooped to pick up a sword, sheathed it, and headed through the trees toward Shigella's Tomb.

Dagath had not needed long to realize that the three Knights left behind by Crovis did not want him around. Besides, with his master gone—probably dead—he had no reason to stay. He'd been about to make his way back to the beach to steal a boat when he spotted a red-haired Isle Knight pushing through the jungle.

Isn't that the Ivairian bastard who killed Sneed all those years ago? The squire who got kicked out of the Isles? Fuming, he nearly charged right then and there. Then, he saw the squire-turned-Knight fight the other Knights that Crovis had left behind. Even after the former squire cut down one Knight who came in too quickly, Dagath could tell how the battle would end. Crovis's Knights might permit Dagath to assist them in killing the man, but that was not what Dagath wanted.

Dagath watched a moment longer then made up his mind. He decided he'd wait until the battle was almost over, assuming the former squire would kill at least one more of his enemies. Then, Dagath would intervene and kill whichever of Crovis's men remained. The former squire would be weak by then, and Dagath could give him the slow death he deserved.

Impatient, Dagath paced amid the trees, holding his drawn shortsword—the one he'd stolen from the former squire during their chance encounter years before. Barely able to contain his eagerness, he imagined the look on the former squire's face when he saw Dagath charging him. He forced himself to wait until one of Crovis's men was down. Then, he started forward.

Before he'd gotten close, though, he froze. In the distance, a new group was pushing through the trees, toward the fray. At first, he thought they were Crovis's men, coming to help. Then he realized they were coming from the direction of the harbor. Most were Isle Knights, but a few wore the scarlet uniforms of the Red Watch.

"Damn." Dagath backed up until he was concealed by the trees again. He decided to wait a moment and see what happened. He sheathed his sword, lest a glint of steel announce his presence. Then, his eyes widened.

Leading the Isle Knights and Red Watch were two women. He recognized them both. Though he was already hidden, he sank to his knees, further concealing himself in shadow. He wondered if he had the greatest or the worst luck in the world.

Dagath eyed the armed warriors before him and considered his options. He dared not get close, but some of the Red Watch had crossbows. If he could quietly kill one of them and take a crossbow, he might shoot one or two hated enemies from afar then run.

First things first.

Dagath straightened and edged through the trees, circling around behind the men. He hoped to find a Red Watch straggler, but a moment later, the entire squad—Isle Knights and Red Watch both—turned and pushed through the trees, back toward the shore, hauling a prisoner with them. Dagath hurried back into hiding, narrowly avoiding detection. He noted that none of the three he'd recognized were in that group.

They must be going on to face Crovis alone. He smiled. That changed things. He figured that Crovis and the other Knight, Wyn Kai, would kill at least one of the three, possibly two, meaning Dagath could easily creep up and finish off the third—even without a crossbow.

"Change of plans," Dagath muttered. He waited until the Isle Knights and the Red Watch were gone then turned back in the direction of the tomb.

CHAPTER TWENTY-NINE

"WE SHOULD HAVE SEEN THIS coming." Despite his weariness, Rowen waved off Igrid's assistance and pushed on through the trees as fast as he could go.

"We should have," Keswen agreed, "but we didn't." She moved ahead of them easily, scanning the shadows with sharp eyes, an arrow already fitted to her bowstring.

"Where are Jalist and Aeko?" Rowen asked.

"Alive," Igrid said. "Aeko's hurt, but Zeia's with her. Breaksteel's with her, too." She saw Rowen's expression and added, "Long story."

"And the Sons of Maelmohr?"

"Dead or driven off. The Scion's in chains—but it cost us."

Rowen shook his head. "I should have seen *that* coming, too. I should have known the Scion would ally himself with Crovis."

"Funny thing about madmen," Igrid muttered. "They're hard to predict because they're mad."

Keswen glanced back at them. Though she did not speak, Rowen read her impatience easily enough.

"I'll brood later," he said. "For now—"

"Crovis," Igrid finished. She squeezed Rowen's arm.

Moments later, Rowen froze in his tracks. The air had just gone cold—colder than the dead of night, colder than the Wintersea. Something drew his eyes to the eastern horizon. A moment later, through the trees, he saw a distant but impossibly massive wall of wytchfire leap toward the heavens. It spread to encompass the whole horizon, rising through the clouds—blinding but utterly silent—then vanished. The cold lasted a moment longer then faded.

Without realizing it, Rowen had fallen to his knees. Igrid helped him rise. For a moment, he was speechless.

Finally, he said, "It's over. Crovis killed the guardians. The Dragonward's been brought down."

Igrid and Keswen said nothing. Igrid clutched Rowen's arm through his armor. "Sariel... Thessa... "

"They're safe for now."

"Nobody will be safe for long," Keswen said. For the first time, Rowen heard fear in her voice.

Igrid said, "If we'd only been faster... "

Rowen swallowed the lump in his throat and shook his head. "I think Crovis was waiting, in case I fought my way through. I think he wanted to kill the last one in front of me. He just got impatient."

In a whisper, Keswen asked, "Where will the Dragonkin come from?"

Rowen flashed back to Algol's memories. "The west," he said.

"When they come, we'll fight them," Igrid said.

Rowen closed his eyes, willing away all the images of fire and blood, the horrors that awaited them. He opened his eyes. "Crovis first."

They had not gone far before the trees thinned and they found themselves before an ancient structure. Though it had no gate, a great, dark opening shone in one wall like a blackened wound.

Rowen slowed, spotting a heap of ashes and charred bone in front of the opening to the tomb. "Algol." He pointed. Then, he turned, scanning the trees for some sign of Crovis and Wyn Kai. "They must still be inside."

"There." Keswen nodded toward the gap in the tomb, where a dark shape was emerging.

Rowen almost did not recognize Crovis at first. The Grand Marshal's armor and tabard were splattered in unnaturally dark blood. Blood covered his face, too, obscuring his features—save for his eyes, which were wide and shining with strange giddiness. The Grand Marshal held a sword in one hand. In the other, he held the head of Wyn Kai.

"Hello, Sword Marshal."

Before Rowen could respond, the twang of a bowstring announced Keswen's answer. Unfazed, Crovis swung his sword and cleaved Keswen's arrow midair. Then he stepped away from the tomb, tossed Wyn Kai's head to the ground, and calmly awaited Keswen's next arrow.

This time, the huntress fit three arrows to her bowstring and drew them back. "Let's see you try that again," she muttered. But before she could release the bowstring, Rowen grabbed her arm.

"No, Keswen. Keep back. Stay out of this." Rowen started forward.

Igrid kicked the back of his thigh. "You're not fighting him alone."

Rowen switched his sword to his other hand. "Yes, I am." He reached out to touch Igrid's cheek, but she stepped out of range.

Igrid scowled. "We'll talk about it later." She faced Crovis. "After he's dead." She started forward.

Rowen pressed the flat of his blade to Igrid's breastplate and forced her back. "No," he repeated. He lowered his voice. "I need you to protect Sariel and Thessa. I need you to keep the children safe."

Keswen stepped forward, three arrows still fitted to her bowstring. "Don't be a fool, Knight. How many thousands, even millions are about to die because of him? Forget honor. The Knights will need you when the Dragonkin come."

"No, they won't," Crovis called. He took a step forward, resting his bloody adamune in the crook of his arm. He fixed his unblinking gaze on Rowen. "When Nekiel comes, I shall face him myself. He issued me a challenge, through Algol, and I accepted it. The Light wills it."

Rowen noted the pride in Crovis's voice. He wanted to argue with the Grand Marshal, at least to make him realize the true horror of what he and Algol had just done, but Rowen did not have the words.

Rowen started forward. To his surprise, Igrid did not follow. He glanced back at Keswen.

She stared at him in open disapproval then shrugged. "If you want to dance with him that bad, be my guest. I'm still going to put arrows in his face once you're dead." She relaxed her bowstring but kept her arrows ready.

Rowen turned back to Crovis. The Grand Marshal stared back, a derisive smirk on his face. The two Knights took another step toward each other. Rowen noted the exhaustion in his own muscles, the soreness in his bones. *I'm no match for Crovis on my best day. How am I supposed to beat him now?*

Crovis moved his bloody sword from the crook of his arm and swung it in a slow, lazy figure eight. "I've been waiting a long time for this," he confessed. "Well, Locke, are you finally ready to face the fires of judgment?"

No courage without fear... Rowen took another step forward.

Crovis's smirk broadened to a smug grin. "When the Dark One comes, he will bring unimaginable horrors with him. Many will die. But such suffering will help bring about a golden age of honor. I will be the Light's chosen emissary in this world. Through me—"

Crovis fell silent. Though his eyes remained just as wide, something in his posture spoke of sudden fear. He twisted sideways and stepped farther away from the wound-like entrance to the tomb. Rowen felt the air go cold again. Then the cold became heat, as though he were standing next to an invisible fire. He tried to keep his eyes on Crovis, but something drew his gaze back to the dark opening of the tomb.

Darkness faded, replaced by a faint, purple glow. Purple changed to white, and a moment later, Silwren stood in the opening—nude, with blazing violet eyes and hair like tendrils of platinum flame. She stared at Rowen for a moment, expressionless, then smiled. Her hands came up. In them, she held Knightswrath.

Instead of walking toward him, she glided, her bare feet hovering just over the dirt and tangled roots. Part of him wanted to look away, but he could not wrest his eyes from her. She shimmered, as did the world around her. Rowen realized he was crying, and he wiped his eyes.

Silwren stood before him, still smiling. She did not blink or speak. Then, she bowed. As she did so, she lifted Knightswrath. Her body shuddered like a flickering flame then began to fade. Rowen stared.

"Take the damn sword," Igrid called from behind him.

As though waking from a trance, Rowen dropped the adamune he'd claimed from the battlefield, and he reached out and grasped Knightswrath's dragonbone hilt instead. He held it where a carving showed a woman casting fire from her hands. The hilt felt like the handle of a torch. Violet flames appeared along the kingsteel blade. A moment later, they swept up his arm, accompanied by a terrible exhilaration.

Rowen wanted to cast the sword away almost as much as he wanted to hold it. Purple flames spread out before him, blinding him for a moment. Then, they receded into Knightswrath's blade like a withdrawing tide.

By then, Silwren was gone.

Fresh tears sprang to Rowen's eyes, but he willed them back. Instead, he faced Crovis. The Grand Marshal stared back, his expression fearful. The two Knights stared at each other for a moment, then Rowen started forward. Purple flames flickered along Knightswrath's blade.

Crovis tensed. "I was right about you, Locke. You have no honor."

Rowen answered with a fiery swing that shattered Crovis's sword and continued just as easily through Crovis' neck, though wytchfire instantaneously cauterized the wound. Crovis's body stood a moment, wobbling, then toppled backward, against the tomb.

For a long time, Rowen stood there, alternating his gaze from the headless Grand Marshal to the burning sword in his hands. He trembled. Gradually, the wytchfire faded, and Knightswrath was a simple adamune again. Rowen sheathed it and turned.

Igrid stood before him, pain in her eyes, as well as love and forgiveness, and shame filled him. Rather than speaking, he turned back to the opening in the wall of Shigella's Tomb. He wondered why it was still there.

"I should go inside," he said heavily.

Keswen came forward. "Why? There's nothing left to be done in there."

"I should go inside," Rowen repeated. He stared at the darkness, suddenly fearful, then stepped forward. As he entered, he had the odd feeling that he was entering the wounded body of the earth itself.

Dagath decided that his luck had soured after all. He'd been about to try and creep up behind the Sylvan woman, intending to cut her throat and steal her longbow, when the fiery sorceress appeared out of thin air. Moments later, Dagath had watched as the former squire—armed now with a sword that flashed with magical flame—had cut down the Grand Marshal with frightful ease.

Deciding enough was enough, Dagath ran back toward the harbor. He pushed through the jungle as fast as he could, no longer caring about revenge or honoring promises to the gods. If he didn't get off this island right away, he was a dead man.

Twice, he heard the metallic rattle that meant armored men were approaching and hid as Isle Knights hurried by. He guessed they were not loyal to Crovis when a handful of Red Watch followed a step behind. As he neared the shore, he asked himself what he would do if he reached the harbor and found it swarming with armed men.

He dared not surrender, knowing what would happen once that Iron Sister or the former squire returned to the harbor and found him in chains. But he doubted he could steal a boat with so many men watching. For one wild moment, he considered making for some other deserted corner of the island and attempting to fashion his own boat, but he had no knowledge or skill at such things.

"I guess I'll have to see how good a swimmer I am," he thought glumly.

He was still some distance from the harbor when he spotted a lone figure hurrying through the jungle. He squatted behind a tree and sized him up. Though the approaching figure wore the scarlet uniform of an officer of the Red Watch, he was unmistakably a Dwarr, with a strong build and massive arms. He was cursing and swinging a long axe, attempting to hack a clearer path through the undergrowth.

Dagath waited until the Dwarr had passed him by then quietly circled behind. The way the Dwarr carried himself hinted that he was an expert fighter. *Then again, I'm an expert, too.* Dagath timed each step to match the Dwarr's, so the latter would not notice the crunch of leaves and the shift of branches. Slowly, he edged closer. He drew his shortsword between his fingers to prevent the steel from scraping against leather. Only a few yards separated them. Dagath's pulse quickened. He braced himself, ready to leap forward and plunge his sword into the Dwarr's back.

"Turn around and face me."

Dagath was so startled by the voice piercing his mind that he nearly cried out. Instead, he froze. He considered hiding, but something told him that he had already been discovered. He straightened, watching as the Dwarr continued forward, oblivious. Slowly, Dagath turned.

A woman in plain, dark fighting clothes stood before him. She had short dark hair and tapered ears. Violet eyes regarded him with icy coldness. Despite the matching shortswords hanging at the woman's belt, she had no hands.

Dagath snickered. "I wondered if I'd ever see you again." He gave his sword a few practice swings. "Sorry, bitch. I can't remember your name."

The woman started toward him. Then, blazing gouts of wytchfire blossomed from her wrist stumps, forming fingers, with which she drew both her shortswords. The pommels smoked. Thin tendrils of wytchfire raced out from her new hands, darkening the steel blades.

Dagath said, "Neat trick," and raised his sword.

Then, she was upon him.

Rowen drew Knightswrath as soon as he entered the tomb. As though sensing his need for light, the sword produced tendrils of wytchfire that illuminated the stone sarcophagus, as well as the bloodstained floor behind. Rowen stared at the fallen Dragonkin, shaking his head. Though he'd never seen them, they looked exactly as he'd imagined: gaunt, shrunken, tortured.

Rowen reminded himself that no one—Fâyu Jinn included—had sacrificed more than those six to guard the people of Ruun from Nekiel. *And now, all that's over.* He forced himself to grasp each of the fallen heads and place it by its body. He composed the fallen Dragonkin as best he could then straightened and whispered a prayer in Shao.

Igrid came up beside him. "There has to be something we can do," she whispered.

Rowen swallowed a lump in his throat. "I don't think so. They made this place to be the source of the Dragonward's power. The guardians were what provided that power. Without them…"

"What about the Shel'ai? Can't *they* do something?"

Rowen thought about it for a moment then shook his head. "All the Shel'ai in Ruun couldn't do what those six Dragonkin did. Even if they were willing and we joined all of them together, they just aren't strong enough."

"Namundvar's Well, then?" Igrid shook her head. "Gods, I know Chorlga ruined it, but there has to be *something* we can do!"

Rowen thought of Nekiel as he'd seen him in Algol's memories:

merciless, calculating, even more powerful than Chorlga or Silwren. The cruel leader of the Dragonkin had been waiting over a thousand years for a chance at revenge. He would not let it pass him by.

"When Nekiel comes... I'll have to fight him." Rowen shuddered. He stared down at Knightswrath, hoping to draw comfort from its flaming blade, but even the powers of Knightswrath seemed paltry and inadequate.

"You won't be facing him alone. I'll be with you. I swear it." Igrid touched his arm again, but Rowen could not feel her hand through his armor.

He blinked back tears of shame at all the people who were about to die because of his failure. Then, bowing one last time to the fallen Dragonkin, he turned to go.

A flash of light stopped him. He faced the circle of runes amid the corpses of the guardians. As he watched, the runes began to glow, and a faint mist rose from the runes. Slowly, Silwren took shape amid the mist. As before, she did not speak but faced Rowen again. Her expression shone with deep sadness.

Rowen felt Igrid tense a moment before she backed away.

At the same time, Silwren came forward, holding out her hands. Rowen realized what she was asking for. Confused, he gave her Knightswrath. Silwren stood for a moment, holding the sword, facing him. Tears streamed from her eyes. Those tears turned into tiny tongues of fire that fell sputtering to the stone floor.

A moment later, Silwren turned and glided back into the circle of runes. Hugging Knightswrath to her body, she knelt on the floor. Purple flames blossomed from the sword and her body at the same time. The flames mingled, indistinguishable. The flames brightened and brightened until they became a blinding white light. Silwren shuddered as though in great pain. Then, she screamed.

Rowen reeled backward, horrified. The scream reminded him of how she'd sounded in Fâyu Jinn's tomb, when she'd thrown herself onto Knightswrath, giving her life to awaken its power. The scream grew louder and louder until it seemed to resonate from the air itself, from the world all around him, from everything at once.

Rowen realized what Silwren was about to do. He opened his mind to call out to her, to beg her to stop, but her scream drowned out his pleas.

He tried to crawl toward her, through the light, but something pushed him back. Then he felt Igrid's hands seizing him, dragging him away.

Somehow, Rowen broke free. He tried to crawl through the light again, but he had not gone far when Silwren's scream faded, replaced by an awful, unforgiving heat. Rowen collapsed, suddenly unable to move. Then, he was seized anew. Impressively strong hands swept him up and carried him away. The last thing Rowen saw was the light itself pouring into the floor, like water down an opened drain, revealing the circle of runes—empty.

Dagath realized with dull horror that he was about to lose the fight. The Shel'ai's blurring swords had already cut him in three places, and he had yet to answer with any damage of his own. Though he'd been a swordsman all his life, the woman was just too quick for him. Dagath wondered if she'd always been that fast or if her thirst for revenge had heightened her abilities somehow.

One of her shortswords nicked his thigh then blurred upward and cut his forearm before he could block. Dagath considered surrendering and begging for his life, but something told him the woman was unlikely to entertain such pleas. So he fought on.

Then, deciding he had nothing to lose, he risked everything on a daring feint. The two locked swords, and Dagath managed to drive his knee into the woman's stomach. She answered with astonishing quickness, countering with a parry that knocked the shortsword right out of his hands. Rather than retreating, Dagath leapt forward. They grappled, and he managed to wrest one of the shortswords from Zeia's grasp, slashing his own palm in the process. Ignoring the pain, he drove the pommel of his new sword into the sorceress's face, and she crumpled.

"Not so quick after all." Dagath lifted his new sword, but before he could strike, a flash of light blinded him. For the second time that morning, the entire eastern horizon seemed to have caught on fire. Purple flames leapt up to the heavens. The air tingled. For half a second, Dagath stared.

Half a second was all the sorceress needed.

She rolled toward him and sank her remaining sword into Dagath's leg. As he fell, she rose. She ducked beneath his return swing then grasped his sword blade with one flaming hand. Burning fingers squeezed, and the sword shattered.

Dagath flung the hilt at the Shel'ai's face. She took the blow off her cheek without flinching. Dagath fumbled at his belt, groping for his dagger. He had barely drawn it when the Shel'ai leaned closer.

"My name is Zeia," she whispered. She pressed one flaming hand to Dagath's face. He went rigid as a strange, terrible heat swept through him. Dagath screamed.

Rowen lay on the grass outside Shigella's Tomb. Whoever was carrying him laid him on the ground. Rowen closed his eyes for a moment, fighting back a surge of despair. When he opened them, he saw Jalist hovering over him, along with Igrid and Keswen.

Jalist stared at him then slowly sank to the ground. "Well," he said, "you want to tell me what in the gods' names *that* was all about?"

Rowen turned toward the opening in the wall of the tomb, only to find that it had sealed like a healing wound, leaving behind nothing but a long, scar-like crack. For a long time, Rowen stared at the crack. Finally, he said, "That was Silwren. She sacrificed herself again."

Jalist frowned. "I didn't know the dead could die twice."

"The sword was her link. When I held it, part of her could still reach across the… " Rowen trailed off, fighting back another surge of sadness. "She left the Light. Do you understand? She took the guardians' place. She damned herself and all the souls inside Knightswrath so that the Dragonward could be restored."

No one answered.

Rowen turned to Igrid, but she'd drawn away and stood apart from the others, facing the dark jungle. Keswen quietly removed the arrows she'd fit to her bowstring and slid them one by one into her quiver. Jalist picked up a long axe and used it to push himself back onto his feet. For the first time, Rowen noticed the age and weariness in his friend's expression.

Turning, Rowen saw Wyn Kai's head lying nearby, in the grass. Luckily, it was turned in such a way that Rowen could not see the dead man's expression. Next to it, though, lay the head of Crovis, the eyes still wide and terrible.

Rowen looked away. Then he looked down and saw ash on his clothes. He realized those ashes were all that remained of Algol. His gaze fell on the rest of Crovis's body, on a part of the Grand Marshal's cuirass that showed the engraving of a lotus flower. However, the armor had been so scorched by wytchfire that he could barely make out the engraving in the growing daylight.

EPILOGUE

ROWEN WATCHED THE SETTING SUN slide down the western walls of Cadavash and pour like molten gold into the darkened chasm. He sighed. For the moment, he was alone. Keswen was out on patrol. Sir Jontin and Sir Issa were drilling the newest squires—including a hulking, stoic Olg who towered over his instructors despite the constant deference he showed them.

Rowen glanced down at a scrap of parchment in his hands: a message from the new Grand Marshal, informing him that reconstruction efforts on the Lotus Isles were progressing well. The message also assured him that the Isle Knights had sent ships along all the coasts of Ruun. In that, they were being aided considerably by Noshan ships sent by Father Matua, as well as a small armada of Soroccan sailors—including Hráthbam. So far, no invading force had been detected. It appeared that, thanks to Silwren, the Dragonward had been repaired so quickly that no enemies had managed to get through.

The message bore the signature of Aeko Shingawa.

Rowen smiled, glad the Order was in good hands. Still, he could not shake off the feeling that something was terribly wrong. He told himself he was merely feeling guilt over all those who had died—including Sang Wei, Berric, and Fen-Shea—amplified a thousandfold by the knowledge that Silwren's spirit had spent the past month in torment, and so far, neither he nor Father Matua had conceived of a way to free her.

But it's more than that... Despite Aeko's reassurance, he still feared that somehow, Nekiel or some of his minions had managed to enter

Ruun during those few precious moments in which the Dragonward had been inactive. *But if Nekiel or another of his champions was here, wouldn't we know it by now?*

Rowen hoped that Nekiel was not simply hiding, biding his time—as Chorlga had done. If the sadistic Dragonkin ever did make an appearance, though, Rowen wondered what he and his companions could possibly do to stop him. After all, Knightswrath was sealed up inside Shigella's Tomb, all its power needed to hold up the Dragonward in the first place.

Rowen glanced down at the shortsword hanging from his belt—the waisted, Ivairian-style shortsword given to him years and years before, stolen by Dagath, then returned by Zeia after she killed the sellsword in battle. The shortsword was all he had by which to remember his brother, though he shuddered to think of what Dagath had done with the sword in the years he'd owned it.

Somehow, I'll have to find a way to make amends for that... and for everything else. He eyed his other weapon: a familiar adamune, its blade etched with chrysanthemums. The sword was a gift from Aeko, who had found a Shao smith able to mend the broken pieces of Sang Wei's blade. Aeko had first offered the sword to Maddoc, not just because of his relationship with Sang Wei but in recognition of all Maddoc had done recently to help the poor of New Atheion. But Maddoc had refused the sword, saying it should go to Rowen instead.

Rowen was considering the two different weapons, along with all they represented, when someone cleared his throat. He turned to see Jalist standing before him. "You always were good at sneaking up on me."

"Not really. It's just that you have the ears of a rock." Jalist looked around. "Where's Igrid?"

"Inside, with Thessa and Sariel."

"Still mad at you?"

Rowen hesitated. "I don't think *mad* is quite the word for it."

Jalist nodded. "You think Zeia's back with Saanji yet?"

"If not, she will be soon. I don't think anything could keep her away any longer."

Jalist scoffed. "Not that she'd ever admit it." He looked past Rowen, at the chasm. "Well, I guess it's goodbye again."

"You could stay longer," Rowen offered.

Jalist shook his head. "I have to try and fix things in Stillhammer if I can. Besides, I have to return this." He tapped the pommel of Forgefang, which hung heavily from his belt.

"I don't like the idea of you going back. You're not exactly loved down there."

"Most of Gaulgodd's men are long gone. Besides, I told you: King Typherius is donating supplies so he can try and butter them into opening trade. I imagine those wagons will come with a couple dozen Red Watch who can keep their beloved captain safe."

"Where are you meeting them?"

"At the Red Steppes, a few days from now."

"A lot can happen between here and the Red Steppes. Are you sure I can't send guards? You shouldn't be alone."

"I won't be alone. I'll have Maddoc with me."

Rowen smothered a grin. Though Maddoc was still mourning Sang Wei, often wandering outside of Cadavash to be alone in the wild, Rowen had noticed a growing closeness between the Shel'ai and Jalist. "Well, that's a start. I guess this is it, then... except for one thing." He pointed at a nearby stone bench, which held a long, narrow case made of polished wood.

Jalist scowled. "What, you need me to smash up some kindling before I go? Gods, Locke, get one of the squires to do it. That big Olg, maybe."

Rowen pressed his hand to Jalist's shoulder and half shoved him toward the bench. The Dwarr moved forward reluctantly, and Rowen followed.

"I don't like gifts," Jalist said. "Besides, Maddoc's waiting for me on the plains. Can't we just—"

"Open it, damn you. And be glad I'm letting you go without a ceremony."

Jalist sighed. He reached out, unlatched the case, and threw it open. His eyes widened. Then, they shimmered like wet stones.

Inside the case lay an elegant long axe with a blade wrought of gleaming, freshly forged kingsteel. The shaft was a graceful curve of polished wytchwood, wrapped in black leather. Inscribed onto the blade itself was the Dwarrish word for *friend*.

Jalist wiped his eyes. Then, he lifted out the long axe as though it were a swaddled baby. He stared at it, speechless.

"You're welcome." Rowen turned the axe-blade away, embraced his friend, then stepped back. "Take care of yourself."

Jalist cleared his throat. "Sure," he said gruffly. "You'll need me the next time you get in trouble."

"I'm sure I will." Rowen turned back to the chasm, pretending to study it, so that Jalist could leave without Rowen seeing him cry. Rowen waited until he was sure Jalist was gone. Then, wiping his own eyes, he turned from the chasm and headed toward the manse.

He glanced at the new squires as he passed by the practice yard. He noted that the other squires still seemed as reluctant to stand near Breaksteel as his instructors were to teach him. But Rowen had given strict orders that the Olg was to be given a chance. Though he had largely done so because the Olg deserved it, he admitted to himself that he'd also done it as a favor to Igrid, who had been increasingly distant since they'd returned from the Isles.

Rowen continued to think about Igrid as he saluted the guards outside his manse and headed inside. He could not blame her for being distant. She'd seen how he'd looked at Silwren—and how she had looked at him—not to mention how fiercely he'd tried to save her soul, risking his mortal life in the process.

Part of him wondered if Igrid would leave. The thought of remaining in Cadavash without her filled him with an aching sense of loneliness and dread, but the ache waned when he heard Sariel's laughter echoing down the hallway. He smiled, figuring the child must have finally recovered from Rowen's gift: the dragon ragdoll he'd brought back from the Lotus Isles, which had so frightened her that she'd promptly incinerated it. A moment later, Sariel sprinted from his study and raced into his bedroom, Thessa a step behind. The Hesodi girl saw Rowen and waved, a seashell necklace dangling around her throat, then glanced over her shoulder to find Igrid chasing her. Thessa squealed and sprinted after Sariel.

Igrid slowed. She faced Rowen. Her smile faded. "Did Jalist leave?"

Rowen nodded.

"Did you give him the axe?"

Rowen nodded again.

"Did he cry?"

"Not that he'd ever admit."

Igrid looked as though she was about to answer then changed her mind and raced after the children. Rowen stood where he was. A servant appeared, offering him a glass of wine. Rowen waved it off. Part of him wanted to leave the manse to go back to the practice yard while another part wanted to stay near the children. He chose the latter.

By the time he made his way down the hallway and into their bedroom, Sariel was crying. She lay on the floor, holding her face in her hands. Wytchfire crackled from her fingertips. Small tongues of flame burned the carpet beneath her. Thessa was stepping on them while Igrid knelt at Sariel's head and whispered soothingly to her.

Sariel cried a moment longer then removed her hands from her face. Violet eyes fixed on Rowen when he knelt beside her. Sariel sat up. Rowen held his arms open, and she ran into them, throwing her own smaller arms around his neck. He winced but held on.

"It's all right, little one," Rowen whispered in Sylvan.

Sariel clutched his neck for a moment then let go and ran to Igrid instead.

"She just got scared all of a sudden," Thessa said.

"Is she all right?" Rowen asked, drawing closer.

"She will be," Thessa said.

Igrid held Sariel but looked down at the singed carpet. Slowly, she lifted her gaze to Rowen's. She offered a slight, cockeyed smile. "She will be," she agreed at last and kissed Sariel's forehead.

MORE BY MICHAEL MEYERHOFER

The Dragonkin Trilogy
Wytchfire
Knightswrath
Kingsteel

ABOUT THE AUTHOR

Michael Meyerhofer grew up in Iowa where he learned to cope with the unbridled excitement of the Midwest by reading books and not getting his hopes up, Probably due to his father's influence, he developed a fondness for Star Trek, weight lifting, and collecting medieval weapons. He is also addicted to caffeine and the History Channel.

Michael Meyerhofer's third poetry book, *Damnatio Memoriae,* won the Brick Road Poetry Book Contest. His previous books of poetry are *Blue Collar Eulogies* (Steel Toe Books, finalist for the Grub Street Book Prize) and *Leaving Iowa* (winner of the Liam Rector First Book Award).

He has also published five chapbooks: *Pure Elysium* (winner of the Palettes and Quills Chapbook Contest*)*, *The Clay-Shaper's Husband* (winner of the Codhill Press Chapbook Award), *Real Courage* (winner of the Terminus Magazine and Jeanne Duval Editions Poetry Chapbook Prize), *The Right Madness of Beggars* (winner of the Uccelli Press 3rd Annual Chapbook Competition), *and Cardboard Urn* (winner of the Copperdome Chapbook Contest).

Individual poems won the Marjorie J. Wilson Best Poem Contest, the Laureate Prize for Poetry, the James Wright Poetry Award, and the Annie Finch Prize for Poetry. He is the Poetry Editor of *Atticus Review*. His work has appeared in a number of journals including *Ploughshares*, *Hayden's Ferry Review*, *North American Review*, *River Styx*, and *Asimov's Science Fiction Magazine*.